SLEIGHT

JENNIFER SOMMERSBY

Sky Pony Press
New York

To the humans and creatures in my house who sacrificed and put up with *so much* during the years it took this book to be born. Thank you.

Sky Pony Press books may be purchased in bulk at special discounts for sales promotion, corporate gifts, fund-raising, or educational purposes. Special editions can also be created to specifications. For details, contact the Special Sales Department, Sky Pony Press, 307 West 36th Street, 11th Floor, New York, NY 10018 or info@skyhorsepublishing.com.

Sky Pony® is a registered trademark of Skyhorse Publishing, Inc.®, a Delaware corporation.

10 9 8 7 6 5 4 3 2 1

Library of Congress Cataloging-in-Publication Data available on file.

Jacket illustration © Sarah J. Coleman
Jacket design by Kate Gartner

Hardcover ISBN: 978-1-5107-3208-7
EBook ISBN: 978-1-5107-3212-4

Printed in the United States of America

There are more things in heaven and earth, Horatio,
Than are dreamt of in your philosophy.

Hamlet to his best friend Horatio, *Hamlet*, Act I, Scene V

Our revels now are ended. These our actors,
As I foretold you, were all spirits, and
Are melted into air, into thin air:
. . . And, like this insubstantial pageant faded,
Leave not a rack behind. We are such stuff
As dreams are made on; and our little life
Is rounded with a sleep.

Prospero, *The Tempest*, Act IV, Scene I

"Vérité: The key to good is found in truth."
Delia Flannery

PROLOGUE

ONCE UPON A TIME, THERE LIVED A YOUNG GIRL WITH HAIR LIKE THE SUN'S fire, feet like the wind, and hands that enchanted even the lowliest sufferer.

Every morning, this young girl woke to her mother's singing and knew her day had begun. People came from far and wide, from the mountains and the sea, to her mother's apothecary shop tucked along the edge of a vast desert. There were whispers of witchcraft, but the girl knew no witch did what her mother could.

One morning, as her mother sang, a crash blasted through the front of the cottage, followed by her mother's command:

RUN.

The girl and her mother had discussed this: what would happen if someone came for their family's treasure. Passed down from one generation to the next, it had been hidden in a wooden box, a box with but a single key. That key was buried in a wall of rocks deep in the woods, covered in dirt filled with wriggling earthworms and fat beetles.

"But we could have a grand palace, and servants and maids, if only we used your grandfather's gold," the girl often reasoned.

"I only said it is a treasure. Who said anything about gold?" was all her mother would reply.

This day, the girl ran on her swift, bare feet, brambles snagging her nightgown, to the wall of rocks deep in the woods, her mother's instructions singing through her head: "Take the treasure. The horse will lead you across the desert. Follow the river to where the bones of kings lie."

The young girl hid herself high in the trees. She waited, hungry, cold, scared, until a stately owl took up residence on the branch above. Night had arrived. Only then did the girl sneak down to the frozen ground.

Silence.

The wall of rocks, where she'd find the key to their treasure, was buried in the mountainside before her. The girl counted as her mother had instructed: the fourth stone from the western edge. Eyes closed and with a deep breath in (for the girl had a healthy fear of bugs), she thrust her hand into the pocket carved into the rock's belly.

Once she touched the heavy iron key, a buzzing ignited in her ears. As she looked up at the rock wall, at its unremarkable face, a searing light exploded from the stony front.

The keyhole.

She pulled the key free from its hiding place and inserted it into the blazing stone; the flames licked her hand, yet her wrist was chillingly cold.

The key turned, and the stone door opened.

Ahead, a vault—and a new glowing. She stepped inside.

There it was: the wooden box—her family's treasure. Closer still, she saw the box—about the size of a house cat—resting on *its own stone pedestal, not covered in worms or beetles, just a thin coat of glowing moss.*

"Take the treasure. The horse will lead you across the desert. Follow the river to where the bones of kings lie."

The girl stepped forward, into the vault.

Pulling on the wooden box's rusted latch, she lifted the lid.

I

New Year's Eve Gala

HER FACE IS NOW THE LAST THING I SEE JUST BEFORE I FALL ASLEEP. SHE'S lying there in the powdery circus dirt, blood draining from her nose, a desperate look in her eyes. I can't not see it. The Cinzio Traveling Players, a well-oiled machine, has plans for all contingencies. Almost all. Delia falling three stories to her death was not among those plans.

I always inspect the equipment myself instead of leaving it to the crew—my mother's superstitions rubbing off on me. Check the knots, the rescue-8, my mother's lyra—a steel hoop through which she dances in midair. The tape isn't worn or sticky. Wire cables are solid. No tears, rips, signs of wear in the silks or the ankle noose.

We're clear for liftoff.

Performers move swiftly into line for the opening parade, sequined bodies and glittered faces reflecting the backstage light. Out in the ring, the orchestra kicks up, the xylophones tickling the air, that feeling you get just before the roller coaster plummets down the first hill. Stragglers hurry into the tent, arms encumbered by buttered popcorn or plumes of cotton candy. Every visit to the circus requires treats. My stomach growls at the savory butter and sugar that overrides even the aromas of animals and damp hay.

Though it's crowded backstage, Delia—or Mom (she answers to both, but prefers I call her Delia in public)—stretches into the splits, her storm of red hair knotted against her head. Her lips move as she chats quietly with her "friends," the ones none of us can see. She says they bring her luck. I've grown up with stories about these "friends"—Alicia and Great-grandfather Udish—though by now these tales feel like they were plucked from the Brothers Grimm rather than real life. But if Alicia and Udish keep her calm and able to perform? I'm all for it.

Circus folk are a superstitious lot, after all.

I touch her shoulder and she stops midsentence, looks up at me, smiles. Her eyes crinkle; the rhinestones glued to her cheekbones sparkle. She stands like a gazelle, one slender leg after another. Grace, thy name is Delia.

On a cargo box nearby, a congratulatory flower arrangement sits in its cellophane. I pluck a small, wilting blossom and present it to her: "Mom."

She pinches the flower's weeping stem, whispers to it, and it blossoms anew, the yellow petals stretching wide to a sun hiding ninety-three million miles away. There's more to Delia's magic than ghosts—my mother's fingers are like little supernatural botanists.

I have magic too. Ghosts and plants, not so much, but living creatures? Go ahead, break something. Nose, toe, finger, arm, whatever you prefer. I can fix it up for you in a jiffy. Just ask the red-breasted robin that crashed into the side of our Airstream when I was three. That was the first time. Mom said to touch the bird's wing. I did. The bright star burning in my head felt like it would explode, but my touch fixed the robin. She flew off, whole again.

"Keep it a secret, okay, Geni?" Delia said. And I did—at least, for a while.

Now she tucks the renewed blossom into the neckband of my costume. "A beauty for my beauty," she says.

Baby steps through the backstage entrance, his headset draped around his thick neck. His surrogate mother, an orphanage nun named Sister Margaret, gifted him with the ironic nickname because of his size. He kept it because the name given to him by the mother he never knew—Bamidele—often sprains a lazy English speaker's tongue. I always thought it was impressive, much like he is.

His job with Cinzio is crew boss and tentmaster—but his true calling . . . he's the other half of my mother's heart. When I was little, he told me his name means "follow me home" in the Yoruba language of Western Africa—and he promised that no matter how many times Delia went away, he would always be there to bring her back to us.

He's always kept his promise.

For Baby, the sun rises and sets on Delia's shoulders. He kisses the side of her head, now, as she stands next to our show's true matriarch, Gertrude. When Gert reaches her wrinkled trunk around to get her own kiss, Baby blows into its end.

He hoists Delia onto Gertrude's back, and Gert again throws her trunk back, seeking her own preshow ritual: a plump mango.

Baby waits to assist me, but the Secret Handshake with my best friend Violet has to come first: hand, hand, cross over, pull under, elbow, elbow, kiss, kiss. We've been doing it since I was added to the show the year I turned seven. Even though we're the same age, crazy Violet has been flying on the trapeze with her twin brother Ash, and their parents—the Jónás Family Flyers!—since she was four. She's a blond-braided, lipstick-loving maniac who laughs at danger and lives for the sequined glamour of the circus.

The last time we missed the handshake, Ash cracked his wrist. Logic would tell us it was due to Ash's hair—the dreamy, chocolaty "Locks of Love" coif—blocking his view of the trapeze, but Vi and I were sure we'd jinxed the show.

Now we never miss our handshake.

I steal one more nuzzle with Houdini, my face against the fuzzy, coarse hair on his baby elephant head. He loops his trunk around my hand—I'm his human pacifier—and I feed him a green apple. A gentle whisper into his broad, veiny ear and he seems ready to party. At thirteen months old, Houdini has only appeared in a few recent shows, and almost all have been perfect examples of toddler behavior.

"Genevieve, your turn," Baby says. He kisses my forehead and lifts a hand for a fist bump, and then up I go onto Gertrude, sliding in behind my mother, who smells of Baby's aftershave. "Have a good show, *a leannan*," he says, blowing me a fatherly kiss.

Two hundred thirty–odd shows a year, and I'm nervous every time.

Tonight is no ordinary show. This gala event is how we secure funding for our upcoming season. No one in the audience is wearing flannel or blue jeans. Even the children are gussied up, top hats and tiaras to match their tanned, Botoxed parents.

But Cinzio's operation is smooth, everyone's routines set after years of practice. Like clockwork, at least at first. Gert, all three and a half tons of her, takes her first lumbering steps into the spotlight. Houdini swings his tail behind her, puffing at the dirt, his glittery blanket fastened just tight enough around his belly to stay on. I hope he doesn't yank it off—again—and toss it at the horses lined up after him.

When the orchestra starts, heavy on the cymbals, the children in the audience jump to their feet. Gertrude plods forward, and I feel the warm spotlight hit us. Particles of circus dirt stir in the air like fireflies. Young and old, the audience cheers as we complete a full circle of the arena. The circus is the great equalizer. If you're not smiling, you're probably dead. Although if you ask my mother, the dead smile too.

Backstage, Delia and I are off-loaded, and Gert and Houdini follow their wrangler's bulging pockets of juicy snacks. The cogs whir forward: the music changes, the clowns tumble into the ring, and Vi waves as the Jónás Family Flyers climb up the support ladders, hand over hand, to the pinnacle of the big top. Trapeze to open the show, trapeze to close it.

"Geni, your momma," Baby whispers. In the far corner by the canvas doors, Delia stands with her head pitched toward the rafters, her face wrinkled.

Uh-oh.

I hop to her side and rub her frigid hands in mine. "Mom, what's up?"

"Spider. Big one." *Sight.* If it isn't one of her friendly ghosts, sight means spiders. Her fear manifests itself in huge, eight-legged nasties only she can see. And these spiders are always a warning, like an aura before a migraine.

I look up, knowing—hoping—I won't see an arachnid. "Well, he's gone now."

"Geni, it was huge." Her eyes dart around.

I know what comes next. I look across to Baby, but his back is to me as he helps the equestrian performers.

"Mom, any bad odors?"

Smell. When Delia sees spiders no one else can see, it's often followed by a smell she describes as a burp from the mouth of hell. Then—my mother raging at a threat only she's experiencing—screams of "Etemmu!" until Baby can get to her, whisper in her ear, and soothe her racing heart. If he's not nearby, the rest of us stand helplessly until she collapses with exhaustion.

Sight plus smell means Delia cannot go on.

"Mom?"

Delia's nostrils flare; she inhales deeply. Shakes her head. "No. Nothing." Her eyes soften. She pats my hand, which rests on her arm. "Maybe I didn't see that spider after all." She smiles.

Later, in the million times I replay the details of this night, I will remember—and hate myself for not noticing— how Delia's smile didn't reach her eyes. She was worried, and I missed it.

But in the moment, cues must be met.

The circus stops for no one.

My "adopted" uncle, Ted, the show's owner and ringmaster, calls our act "a showstopper." Few aerialists in traveling shows do what we do. I've trained as a dancer and acrobat using the silks, but in my primary role, I play the violin virtually upside down at twenty-five feet, suspended from my ankle in a padded noose while my mother—suspended in the lyra midair—performs an intricate gymnastics routine of spins, splits, and flips.

The music again shifts, and I know it's almost time.

I do my best to pull Delia's attention back to the show. "So I'll wait until you're in the first split . . ." She's not listening, her eyes far away. "Baby . . . ," I call.

The clowns skip through with their toy dogs, one stopping long enough to plant a brotherly kiss on Delia's cheek, leaving a red smudge. "Bump a nose, Lady Delia!" Clown-speak to wish her well.

"You girls all right?" Baby says, a thumb on Delia's chin to pull her gaze to his. She leans against him. "Love you," she says.

Out in the arena, the audience hollers, and I hold my breath. It means one of the flyers—likely Ash or Violet—has released the bar and is tumbling through space, awaiting recapture by the partner on the other side. I know the trapezists have a net, but still. They *throw* one another.

Though I'm backstage, I can picture the four members of the Jónás Family Flyers sailing from the heavens and plopping into the net below. Once Ash, Violet, and their parents take their bows, the equestrian team gallops out—the cue for Delia and me to move.

Violet smiles at me as she bounces through. From Ash, I get the typical high five: "Go get 'em, Ruby Red." In my romantic fantasies, I'd get a swoony good-luck kiss or long hug. Unfortunately, Ash treats me like another sister. Which suits Baby and my mother just fine.

I peek between the curtains to watch: I love how smoothly the riders and horses absorb one another's movements, as if one body. And when they bow, the horses drop to their knees, eliciting *awwwww*s from kids and parents alike.

The horses exit stage left, and my inner butterflies flutter madly; Mom wraps her fingers through mine and smiles. She's hardly ever nervous about performing.

We jog to the center of the first ring. Hands linked as the

spotlight burns through us, we bow deeply, gracefully, to the applause.

Upon straightening, Delia freezes, her grip tightening on mine.

My eyes follow what she's staring at.

Uncle Ted stands in the shadows just left of our ring, talking to a tall, square-jawed man. The black tuxedo looks like money, tailored to his broad shoulders and long limbs (clearly not sewn by a ringmaster's wife—Uncle Ted almost looks shabby in comparison), the knife-edge of his nose bobbing slightly. His heavy eyebrows are a sharp contrast to the absolute lack of hair on his scalp. He bows his head, eyes fixed on us, his top hat pressed to his chest.

He looks as delicate as a tarantula.

"Baby . . . ," Delia whispers.

Backstage, Houdini trumpets twice—probably because he's been told no—and Delia and I both jump. The orchestra leader, who serves as emcee between acts, jokes about Houdini's mother taking away his iPad. Nervous laughs titter through the crowd.

"Mom?"

She looks back at me, then curtsies—I automatically return the favor—and she pulls me in for a hug. Unusual, given the spotlight is still on us.

Delia pulls her good-luck charm, an antique key on a thick silver chain—the walls of our trailer are decorated with framed keys she's picked up along our travels—from her costume and slides the necklace over my head. She kisses both my cheeks. "The key to good is found in truth." Her good-luck wish to remind me to be my best self. She says it before every performance.

But she's never given me her key before.

Before I have time to question her, I'm climbing up the narrow ladder into the darkness of the upper tent, and my mother is gracefully draped through the lyra hoop.

Delia will be fine. Everything will be fine.

On the platform above, a stagehand stands ready with my violin and bow. In fifteen minutes, Mom will let me sneak some champagne and we'll refresh our lipstick to get ready to schmooze with the well-heeled and I'll hope that Ash will finally realize I am the girl for him. The same unfulfilled wish I make at every New Year's Eve Gala.

Up here, perched on the steel platform, I can see the audience in all its glory—elaborate hairdos, sparkling gowns, men puffed up like emperor penguins. My insides twist. Despite the rules against flash photography, someone blasts a few. The clowns continue to horse around. The musicians' faces are lit by tiny music-stand lamps. Delia sits in her hoop, quietly swaying in shadow, waiting.

I see the bald man who was talking to Ted. His top hat is tucked under his crossed arms, his eyes on me now, as Ted runs into the ring to announce us.

My ankle secured in the leather-and-sheepskin noose, I ease my body over into nothingness. That first look down always makes my stomach tilt a little. The stagehand passes me my instrument and winks. I'm lowered, violin tight against my chest, bow arm outstretched.

A few steady breaths to acclimate to the position. Delia's

winch engages, pulling her to the thirty-foot mark, a few feet higher than me, her toes pointed daintily. No harnesses or safety lines support my mother—an aerialist's rapid choreography prevents the use of exterior devices.

She eases into the splits as the spotlights slowly come up, one on her, one on me, and I pull hard against the bow to summon the first notes. Soft and slow, just as she prefers, cueing my mother into an upside-down split.

It's as if she's hanging from a gossamer thread, the way she moves around that hoop. In, over, upside down, from one foot, by one hand, into the splits, twisting into a tight spin. Equal parts beauty and fright—watching from the ground, you want to hold your breath.

Three minutes into our medley, I open my eyes to make sure we're still in sync.

Instead of dancing, Delia is standing on the lyra, staring into nothingness. "No matter how hard you come at me, you will never find it," she says.

"Mom!" I yell.

Delia smiles at the shadow only she sees—

Something slams into her. The lyra whirls like a half-dollar spinning on its edge.

My mother is thrown backward.

And she falls.

I am the first to scream. And then the children in the audience join in, their wails commingling with their horrified parents'. My violin's neck snaps upon hitting the ground next to my mother.

Baby's size belies his speed. Within seconds, he's next to Delia, bellowing for an ambulance. The ring crew forms a protective barrier as Ted, his ringmaster's cape swirling behind him, signals to the control booth. *The* signal.

The lights drop. The orchestra restarts, John Philip Sousa's "Stars and Stripes Forever." Like the Wallace Hartley octet that played while the *Titanic* sank.

"I can't move! Help me down!" I scream. Where is the stagehand? I see Ash ascend the ladder multiple rungs at a time. He reaches the platform and pulls me to safety, trying to tuck me into his chest, but I yank my ankle out of the noose. Reaching for the blue silk, I Tarzan to the ground.

"Genevieve, get back! Get back!" Hands push and pull at me. I drop to the ground beside Delia, my cheek in the soft dirt. She tries to smile through the blood trickling from her nose, staining her lips and teeth.

I have to fix her.

I grip her left hand in both of mine. She yelps—her arm is broken. "It's okay, Mom, it's okay. I'm going to fix you. Stay with me . . ." I close my eyes and let the star in my head ignite. I just need a few moments . . .

"My little bird," she says. "I'm so sorry . . ."

"Hush," I say, forcing waves of blinding-hot energy into her hand, the overwhelming nausea telling me how vast her injuries truly are. My head feels like it will split in two. I see her there, behind my eyelids, the light around her, but she's moving away from me, her outstretched arm fading.

"Sweet Genevieve," she says. I open my eyes. "Who said anything about gold?" she asks, a line from my favorite childhood story. A sad smile fades as her face goes lax. Then her hand slackens in mine.

I feel Ash scoop me up. I'm too weak from trying to save Delia. A gurney rushes past us.

As Ash struggles to carry me out of the tent, the distinguished man in the tuxedo takes in the scene.

He replaces his top hat, turns, and disappears behind the curtain.

2

THREE WEEKS LATER

DEATH IS THE GREATEST THIEF OF ALL.

It steals our ability to feel, to think. It replaces love and safety and happiness with a black hole in our chests. And when that hole seems to have finally twisted closed, something—a smell, a memory, a token—breaks the seal and it gapes again.

It's such a waste. My mother and how she cradled life in the palm of her magical hands and said thank you for every day, even when those days had her writhing in madness.

In Cannon Beach, Oregon, I linger in the diminishing surf until the bones in my fingers feel as though they'll crumble. Farther out, the frothy waves curl and pummel the sand. By the time they reach me, they're barely tiptoeing. Though my teeth chatter, I want my body to leave its impression in the dark sand until the ocean forces me back.

The cold lets me feel something.

Baby hollers from the driftwood log a hundred feet behind me, higher up the beach where a berm protects from buffeting winds. I shake my head no. Not yet.

I fold my arms over bent knees, my tears dripping onto the white marble urn tucked between my legs. Just enough of my Delia left to take into the big top. When her bouts with madness were so strong that Baby couldn't pull her back and she'd have to go to the hospital, she'd tell me she wished she could be in two places at once—wherever the doctors made her go, and at home with me.

Oh, Mom, finally you'll get your wish.

This small coastal town, Delia's most favorite place on the planet—we've come to say goodbye.

I see her, in my mind, a hundred yards from where I'm sitting, along the periphery of Haystack Rock. Navigating in low tide around the huge outcropping, investigating what the ocean's retreat has revealed in the tide pools, Delia would call to me, and whisper to Alicia and Udish, claiming the jutted rock stained with bird poop as if nature made it just for her to conquer.

Baby and I climbed the lower part today, in violation of the keep-off rule. Figured it was worth the risk to give Delia a proper forever home. We whispered to the birds, the starfish, the anemones as we scattered small handfuls of her ashes. "She will watch over you until asteroids give us the same fiery end that the dinosaurs met," I said.

In her absence, I am not alone. I have Baby. And Aunt Cecelia—Cece for short—and Uncle Ted, family not by blood but by choice. And Violet and Ash and . . . the elephants.

15

I hope Gertrude's not worried. Elephants are smart—Gert smelled Delia's blood on my costume. When I returned home from the hospital—from the morgue—she smothered me with her trunk, inhaling and touching my hair and face. She wiped off the tears by default. Gertrude is a hugger.

In a weird way, I have Alicia and Udish too. My mother's ghostly confidantes were a family, of sorts; she had whispered to them for as long as I could remember. She insisted Udish was her fourth-great-grandfather, and Alicia, not a relative but my mother's closest friend, despite the fact that she's been dead for nearly two decades.

My sandy hands rest on the freezing marble. "I will never forgive myself, Mom," I say.

For three weeks I've felt nothing, and now, sitting here risking hypothermia along the edge of the Pacific Ocean, I am feeling too much all at once.

I wasn't strong enough to save my own mother.

Baby whistles from behind and I turn again.

He holds the thermos aloft. Cocoa, probably spiked with Irish whiskey. I'm seventeen. He lets me drink a little whiskey when Delia's not looking—says, chuckling, he did far worse as a kid. Baby's reticence to talk about his childhood is proof enough that his past is best left inside his head, though the scars on his body offer painful hints of his time spent as the Orphan King. The tattoo covering his left upper arm and chest is in homage to a people he never knew and a culture bestowed upon him by a loving nun; he calls himself a child of the world. His African mother died just after giving birth to him, and the only thing known about his father was his French blood. Despite his powerful African name, Baby is about as American as stars and stripes.

And who better to have at my side, now that I've joined his parentless ranks?

I hold up my hand—five more minutes. I'm not done talking to Delia.

Baby gives me the five minutes, but then I see the scuffed tops of his black work boots beside me. "Come on, Geni. If you go home with pneumonia, Cece will skin me alive." He pulls me out of the muck, wraps a plaid wool blanket over my shoulders, and hands me the thermos.

I open the cap: definitely spiked. I don't bother with a cup. It burns going down.

"See? You're too cold. Come on." Baby plucks the urn from the sand and cradles it like a newborn. Then he wraps his massive wool coat around me, atop the blanket, even though his own skin ripples with goosebumps.

There is much busyness when someone dies unexpectedly and violently, especially from an incident related to work, and most especially in front of a crowd. The Occupational Health and Safety people have become familiar to all of us.

The departure to our next venue was delayed while the busyness happened. Questions, answers, more questions. I missed most of it, hiding in the trailer. Picking at the food people insisted on dropping off once their interviews with the authorities were over and they left town for the brief vacation granted at the start of every new year. Waiting for Cece to force me into the shower to tease the knots out of my grief-matted hair. Watching Cece quietly move my empty violin case into the storage cupboard under the kitchenette bench. Watering Delia's lavender and sage and aloe and dill that will now wither without her. Reorganizing Delia's books—medicinal herbals and healing remedies—and dusting and alphabetizing her apothecary jars.

Many colds and flus have been treated by a visit to Delia's traveling garden. Dr. Delia, the performers would tease, passing around vials of restorative tinctures and herbal concoctions to ease everything from coughs to allergies to performance anxiety. When my own muscles were sore, she would pull out her medicine and say, "Hold still, little bird," squeezing and kneading as peppermint oil hung heavy in the air. Knuckles in, her strong fingers worked the long muscles' soreness.

"You want a story?" she'd ask. Delia's stories made everything better.

"'The Girl with the Gold.'"

Her laugh could fill the room. "Why do you always think it's gold?"

"What else would they bury in the mountainside?"

"Listen carefully." And then she'd tell me the story of the young girl with hair like the sun's fire, who fled her home to save her family's treasure.

"Why don't you ever tell me what's in the box?"

"Because that's part of the mystery, isn't it?"

Then it would be her turn. But she'd need neither oils nor compresses.

Delia would situate herself on the kitchenette-table-turned-bed.

"What hurts most?" I'd ask.

"My back again. Just don't let your hands get so hot that it's uncomfortable for you."

Eyes closed, regulated breaths, I'd concentrate on the white-hot star blazing in my head. It's not really a star, but it feels like a little nuclear reactor inside me, trickling out through my fingertips to fix the ills of the people I love most.

Within a minute, Delia would relax, her muscles repairing themselves under the energy coursing out of my hands. When I was done, I'd flop onto the bench, tired. It always took a couple moments for my hands to cool down and the woozy feeling to pass.

"I wish you'd tell me what's in the box," I'd whisper.

"It's your story," she'd say, kissing my temple. "The box holds whatever your heart says, my magic little bird."

Baby stands guard outside the beachside bathrooms, my own personal sentinel. Almost funny, considering how few people are here today. And it's early yet. Other than the few diehards, it seems most haven't ventured out of their nearby hotel cocoons.

As I tease my damp hair from under the collar of the dry sweatshirt, the chain of Delia's lucky key snags on a few straggly curls. I pull it free and cradle the tarnished iron, its shaft etched with the word *Vérité*—"truth." Never without it, my mother would tap the key under her shirt when she caught me lying about how long I'd practiced the violin or if Violet and I were responsible for gorging on Chef's brownies.

That tap—it's all she had to do.

I emerge, wet clothes tucked in a plastic bag. Baby walks alongside, massive biceps bulging from rolled-up sleeves, his jaw pulsing. The Orphan King and Haystack Rock were sculpted from the same comet, which is why it is so hard to see him look so sad.

He slides the lightened urn back into the cardboard box behind the driver's seat and rubs his hands together in front of the heat vent. "What kind of food, Geni?"

"Whatever you want."

Baby looks at me, eyes hooded with grief. Through everything, he never left her side, never judged her, a woman whose dearest friends were ghosts. Where others called her crazy, Baby knew she was a seer—she could commune with the dead, connect with all the energies of the universe. As such, Udish and Alicia became just another part of our every day. Delia would say that I needed to hear the histories to understand how the old healers worked so that I could make sense of why my own hands could seal skin and bone, why "our people" had gifts others didn't.

Baby offers me an upturned hand; I take it. He's so warm. I wrap myself around his arm like when I was little and he would lift me up to the moon.

"Pancakes?" he suggests.

Delia's favorite. "Pancakes, it is."

The waitress pushes out her boobs when she gives Baby a menu. She looks back and forth between us, as if assessing the relationship.

He orders for us—coffee, pancakes, hash browns—and asks the waitress for a third plate. "You expecting another person, handsome?"

"Yes," he says, looking away.

Her smile fades a little. I don't know why I find this funny.

She brings breakfast, and the third empty plate. He sets it before the seat next to him, as he has done at every meal since she left us. "It makes me feel like she might come back, like she might breeze through the door at any moment with an armful of flowers," he said that first day after.

After he's laid waste to the stack before him, he nods at me. "You should try eating your food instead of redecorating your plate with it."

I stab at the sliced fruit. "I wonder how the elephants are doing . . ."

"Probably missing you a little."

"Gert's gonna be confused. About where Delia is."

Baby reaches across the table. He nestles a hand against my cheek, a broad thumb absorbing a tear. My eyes do what they want these days.

"*A leannan*, don't do this to yourself." Though I am not

his true daughter, a Gaelic leftover from Sister Margaret—the Scottish nun who raised him—says that I am his little girl. "She had been so good for so long . . . I don't know why I let my guard down."

The waitress comes by with a fresh pot of coffee and leans closer than necessary to Baby to take Delia's plate. I slap my hand on top of it. She frowns, whirling on her heel to go refill the next table's cups.

Baby sits back hard against his seat, a sad but coy smile tugging at his lips. "You are your mother's daughter," he says, ripping into another greasy strip of bacon.

A scratch on his left middle finger catches my eye, so I grab his hand, first running my finger over the fading tattoo on his ring finger—"Delia," in romantic script, a match to the one she wore, "Bamidele." Their promise to each other was a forever thing.

I splay his finger sideways so I can better see the long scab.

I don't ask permission. I need to fix something.

My eyes glaze over; the warmth starts. Just a quick pull from the star in my head, not enough to throw my stomach off-balance, and the wound disappears. His light brown skin again pristine, I blink my vision clear. Baby cups my shaking fingers in his hands. "She was so proud of you," he whispers, and then sits back again. "I talked to Ted Monday night after we got here."

"How are they?" I ask.

"Sad. But also dealing with the circus business."

"Do we even have a circus to go back to?" I hadn't

thought about that—what Delia's accident would mean for the show as a whole. The New Year's Gala serves as our meal ticket for the coming year. Ted Cinzio pulls in another twelve months of assurances from investors, and we have a future for another year. It's probably not great that someone died in the middle of the fundraising show.

But even if the show continues . . . how will I ever get back up in the air without her?

"First of the week, things weren't sounding great. Investors pulled out. Traumatized by what they saw, too much bad publicity, pressure from outside groups about us still having the animals."

"So stupid. They can come see Gertrude or Houdini or Othello or the horses whenever they want, see how healthy and loved they are. We have nothing to hide!" Anger flushes my wind-burned cheeks. I'm so sick of clueless activists throwing Cinzio into the same sentence with other shithole circuses.

Baby pulls out his phone. "According to the email I got yesterday"—he scrolls through and hands it over—"we've got a backer." I can hear Ted's voice in my head as I read; it sounds relieved.

"Triad Partners Group?"

"An investment firm. Details are still in the works. But one thing's definitely changing—we're going to be stationary. For a year."

"A whole year?"

"Eaglefern, Oregon." Baby finishes the coffee in one long drink. "University town. Not far off 26, the highway we took to get here."

"I don't want to be off the road. No one else will either."

"Think about the elephants. And Othello. Poor cat isn't getting any younger. Maybe you can make some new friends if we're in one place for a bit."

"I have enough friends."

The waitress comes by with the check, slides it under Baby's elbow but doesn't linger. I guess she finally got the message.

"There's a small private university there. Instead of taking your courses online, you should do a few at a real school. With real people closer to your age."

I'd still be younger than everyone else. I've been taking college courses for two years. Biology mostly. I've been considering a future as a big-animal vet, something I can do to stay with the elephants. But I suppose it wouldn't be too terrible to sit in an actual lecture hall. And having access to a decent research library would be kind of cool.

"When?"

"When we leave here, that's where we're headed."

"Wow. Surprise!"

"Come on. We have one more thing to do before we get on the road."

With the check paid, Baby and I hunker against the harsh breeze that has picked up during breakfast. Once we're in the truck, he pops open the glove box and pulls out a business-sized envelope, the corners bent.

My mother's elegant script across the front—*To Be Read in Cannon Beach, Oregon*—tells me everything I need to know.

A heavy hand rests on my shoulder. "Genevieve, she

made me promise. I was supposed to give it to you. Here. At the beach."

I break the envelope's seal, and my mother's scent fills the cab. A simple line of Delia's meticulous handwriting jumps off the heavy linen paper—"Cannon Beach Post Office, North Hemlock Street"—and a tiny silver key falls into my lap, a hangtag the size of a nickel dangling from a string through its hole. "Happy birthday," it reads.

I hold up the key, the silver catching a glint from a break in the clouds outside the window. "Any idea what this is?"

Baby shakes his head no.

I sniff and pull my shoulders back. *Let's just get it over with.*

"I guess we need to go to the post office."

3

WHEN BABY TURNS OFF THE ENGINE, THE AIR ALL AT ONCE FEELS COLDER. "I'll be right outside the door. Yell if you need me." He pats the back of my head in reassurance before I climb out of the truck.

I clench the key in my palm.

It's just a post office box. What could be hiding in something so small? Why am I afraid?

I'm alone in the chilly lobby, not entirely unexpected for a rainy Sunday in a small coastal town during the off-season. The tang of salt water and fresh seafood spices the damp air; sandy shoeprints mar the beige industrial-tile floor. The walls above row after row of small, brass-front mailboxes are painted with red, white, and blue accents. Oversized stamps feature Elvis and Marilyn Monroe and Martin Luther King Jr. A framed American flag is bordered by bleached-white drift-wood screwed to the wall and draped with fake crabs and gray plastic fish and musty sea nets caked with dust and age.

I flip the hangtag on Delia's key—"Happy birthday"— and I realize she hasn't written the box number.

My birthday is May 30. Is that what she means?

I look for box 530. Bottom row.

I slide in the key. My stomach twists like I'm on the platform all over again.

The lock turns, and the door opens.

It's empty.

My shoulders drop, equal parts relief and disappointment.

A rush of cold air from the side blows my hair further askew. I turn and utter a quick, startled yelp. A few feet from me stands a woman dressed in white.

At least I think she's dressed in white—more accurately, she's translucent, the wall of boxes behind her visible through her form.

Long dark-blond hair floats around her shoulders, weightless, teased by an unfelt breeze, a halo of white-golden light shimmering from her. Her feet float inches above the ground. A staticky coldness emanates from her lack of solid form.

The door swooshes open behind me. "Genevieve?"

Baby. I whirl around to face him.

"You okay?"

I turn back to look at the floating woman—and then again at Baby.

He doesn't give her a second look.

He can't see her.

If he could, he would've reacted. Gossamer, translucent thing floating a few inches above the floor, a bright glow coming off her like that around a flickering candle? Yeah, a person would probably notice that.

I open my mouth to ask him if he can see her—

She's gone.

"Gen, you're white as a sheet." Baby closes the distance and puts a hand against my forehead. "I knew I shouldn't have let you sit in the surf."

Did I really just see that? When Baby didn't?

My imagination—it's overtired.

That was a ghost. I don't see ghosts. Delia sees ghosts.

Delia is dead.

"Did you find the P.O. box?"

"What . . . ? Yeah." I move back to the open box and drop to my knees to inspect the opening again. That's when I see it. Taped to the roof of the metal chamber.

I peel it free. My name is lettered across the front in Delia's hand again, the long, yellowed envelope heavy, backside sealed with thick tape.

"We can go," I say, relocking the box. I drop the key in the general mail slot. I won't need it again.

Baby moves ahead, quick to warm up the truck. He looks at the letter in my hands, but doesn't say anything. I turn the envelope over and over, talking to Delia in my head. *If I open this now, promise me that ghost won't reappear. Please, Mom, tell me I didn't really see her. Tell me I'm exhausted and it was just a momentary blip from stress.*

Baby points out the window at the general store next to the post office. "I'm gonna get us coffee. For the ride home."

He climbs out, shutting the door quietly behind him. The engine's rumble vibrates through the floor and leather seats, the warm air blasting through the vents almost too much, a mixture of Baby's woodsy aftershave, Delia's home-made lavender hand lotion, and circus life. My eyes sting in the contrast of cold to warm, life to death.

I pull my pocketknife from my bag, slice through the envelope's edges, and withdraw the contents. It's rough-textured, handmade parchment, the special kind Delia used for drawing or writing letters to friends. The fold along the backside is sealed with a blob of wax embossed with à symbol I've never seen before, an upside-down triangle overlying a circle.

I run my finger over the grooved wax, hesitant to break it. I've never seen her use a seal on anything.

A tiny crack and the red wax snaps in two.

The weighty paper resists but I pull against it to reveal the words in pristine script across the middle.

My darling Genevieve,
Grandfather Udish warned me this day might come,
that I should pen a note to prepare you. I reclaimed
what he had lost, and now that I am gone, it must
pass into your care. Once you find it, it will become
your greatest treasure, and your most dangerous bur-
den. You will have to fight to keep it safe. Forgive me.
In my own way, I've tried to plant seeds along
the way to share with you our proud history, where
our gifts come from—all those stories, about Udish
and Alicia, about the old healers? They were only the
beginning. And the Etemmu—you've heard me fight
this terrible demon throughout the years. I wish I

could've told you more while I was with you—you'll
soon understand why I didn't.

Now you must collect these seeds to understand
your future. You will need to rely on old friends—be
open to their help and embrace what's coming. Their
answers will make things clearer in the days ahead.
And trust me when I say there is strength in numbers.

Baby will be your Horatio—true to the end.
Remember that night, the play we watched from the
heavens? You will question yourself, but like the tor-
tured Prince of Denmark, you are not crazy.

Genevieve, the key to good is found in truth.

I love you in this life and the next,

Mom

"Mom, what are you talking about?" I whisper to the paper. Couldn't she just leave a will like a normal person? Leave me her Nirvana T-shirt or her key collection or a million bucks in a safe deposit box? I squish my fingertips into my eyeballs until I see stars.

I open the letter again and hold it to my face. It smells of the beach, but subtle hints of Delia remain in these page fibers. The wax seal is odd, but so is seeing a ghost.

A brief smile at the thought of Baby being my Horatio— it reminds me of the night Delia sneaked us into a production of *Hamlet* directed by a longtime friend, and we sat high above the audience on the drafty old catwalk, watching the Danish prince succumb to the madness around him. *Horatio is Hamlet's truest friend, Genevieve. He never turns on Hamlet.*

He knows Hamlet's secrets. He's got his back at every turn. Those kinds of friends are rare. When you find one, never let him or her go.

I flinch as a blast of cold air dances through, but it's just Baby opening the driver's side door, two coffees balanced in one hand. I blink to clear my vision.

He hands me one of the cups and slams the door on the elements.

"How long have you had the key to the P.O. box? She had to really plan this out—write this letter"—I hold the parchment aloft—"rent the box, give you the key."

"The hospital stay a few years back, right around your birthday. . . . When she came home, she gave me the envelope with the P.O. box key and said to give it to you in case she didn't come home the next time."

I hated that she went to the hospital, that the people who made these decisions didn't listen—or believe—that Delia's problems were very real for her. But when an attack would come on in public and Baby couldn't get through to her, Delia was difficult to control. This particular time, it was in a mall— we were eating in the bustling food court, people-watching and nibbling on french fries and sipping Frappuccinos while Baby was off getting the truck's oil changed. Out of nowhere, Delia smelled the telltale stench, and then she was on top of the table knocking over our drinks and screaming about the flood of spiders and yelling at the Etemmu that it didn't matter what it did to her, she would never stop fighting.

That sort of behavior tends to freak people out.

So it's easier for emergency services personnel to lock her

up for a seventy-two-hour psych hold than risk her hurting someone, or herself.

"This letter's filled with stuff I don't understand."

"If you want me to read it . . ."

"Maybe later," I say. I need to think first.

He sighs heavily. "I called Ted. Told him we were heading out. Whenever you're ready."

The coffee scalds the tip of my tongue. That's the funniest irony—I can fix other people's wounds, but not my own. Alas, my tongue will burn until it doesn't.

Cup in the holder, I trace Delia's intricate writing and think about her hand shaping these letters, knowing that she might leave me, knowing that I wouldn't read this until she was gone. I learned early that creatures die, including people—life isn't a forever thing. But moms aren't supposed to die.

I've replayed New Year's Eve in my head a thousand times:

Delia on the lyra, in the splits, ready to perform.

Delia stands on the lyra, not part of the choreography.

Delia screams at something.

Delia falls.

She had to have been yelling at the Etemmu—a creature she said came from her Mesopotamian ancestors. Winged souls of the unburied dead, they wander the earth and attach themselves to their living prey. Most of the time, Baby was the one who fought the demons away for her, whispering and assuring her she was safe. He could pull her out, and then we'd sit up with her until she'd fall asleep in his tree trunk arms, confident nothing else would come for her. She called him her talisman; she felt safest when he was near.

Her behavior the night of the gala was consistent with prior incidents—although she'd never been attacked on the lyra before.

If she had, she wouldn't have ever been allowed off the ground.

When I replay it—again—it looks like something hits her body, but that's impossible. If, for argument's sake, we presume the Etcmmu is real, it had never impacted her in a physical sense before—it never made actual contact with her body.

And yet, the words she yelled that night, just before she fell, before she was *pushed*—"No matter how hard you come at me, you will never find it"—those were new. In fact, so many things about this attack were different.

I read the lines again: *I reclaimed what he had lost, and now that I am gone, it must pass into your care. Once you find it, it will become your greatest treasure, and your most dangerous burden.*

The "it" Delia spoke of just before she fell. Is that what she's talking about in the letter? What the hell could be so important?

I know there are no fingers around my neck, but it still feels like I can't swallow.

"The tiny consolation I carry with me every day now? Your mom is at peace. The storm that raged within her has calmed," Baby says, his voice small, interrupting my thoughts. "There is no place for the Etemmu where she is."

He's right. The Etemmu, whether real or imagined, can't get her anymore.

As Baby rests his head on top of mine, I consider telling him about seeing the ghost in the post office.

Maybe she wasn't there . . .

She absolutely was.

I could've asked her if she'd seen my mom.

Stop, Genevieve. It's too soon to take Delia's place as the resident crazy lady. I need rest and routine. I need to get back to work, back to the elephants. Everything will be okay then, and the lovely post office ghost will find her way back to wherever she came from. She's probably someone's lost daughter or mother, looking for her way home. Delia said the spirits sometimes get stuck. That's all this is.

"Shall we, my girl?"

I nod.

With a final look at the post office as we pull out of the small lot, I send my ghostly friend a message. *If you are real, I hope you find your way home.*

Though even as I ball up on the seat, my jacket doubling as pillow against the center console, I squeeze my eyes and do my best to ignore the sudden chill that rests like a hand against my cheek.

4

JUST OVER AN HOUR LATER, THE PACIFIC OCEAN HIDDEN BEHIND A MOUNTAIN range cloaked in dense Oregon forest, we turn off Highway 26 and drive a few miles south. Baby nudges my shoulder.

I sit up, unrested and thirsty, a slight sheen coating my upper lip from the cab's warmth. Delia's letter feels damp from me clutching it so tightly, her words echoing in my ears as if she were here reading it to me.

Did she leave a will with Baby or Aunt Cece—something that'll explain what she meant? Then again, her letter warns that whatever this thing is that she left, it's now my greatest treasure, and most dangerous burden. I can hear the conversation now:

"Hey, Cece, my mom wrote me this nutty letter about something I have to fight to protect—any idea what that could be?"

Cece, plopping a garlicky spoonful of mashed potatoes onto my plate, says, "Why, yes, Genevieve, she left you the Ark of the Covenant. It's just back here under our new costumes. Let me give Uncle Ted a pork chop and I'll get it for you."

My adoptive family's patience is endless, but I don't want to scare them so soon after Delia's passing.

And today is already weird. Normally, a move to a new venue is a sprawling caravan of semis and half-ton pickups pulling trailers, snaking up interstates, the rigs stuffed with gear and steel support framework and the gallery seating and the elephants and the lion and the horses, the big top rolled into what look like giant burritos hiding under huge winched-down tarps, the ribs of our trucks painted with the Cinzio logo, guaranteed to bring smiles and waves.

During these days, I usually ride with Violet, a tradition that started in first grade. The Jónáses' huge brick-red-and-silver motor coach has a queen-sized bed in the back, perfect for tea parties with the tiny porcelain tea set Delia brought me after one of her long hospital stays. Those tiny cups and saucers became the center of our young lives. Violet would wear the gown and tiara the costume ladies made for her; I had a peasant girl's dress and a sword, so I could be Saint Geneviève and ride into battle alongside my imaginary best friend, Joan of Arc. Our job was to tame the dragon (because slaying him was too uncivilized and a tame dragon is very helpful around the queendom), after which we would have tea and cookies with the newly docile, fire-breathing beast.

This one trip, however, Ash wanted to play with us, which would've been fine if he hadn't demanded to be king and not the dragon. He got mad at Violet and threw one of the small plates, and its chipped edge sliced a nasty line into Vi's pristine cheek.

The look on Ash's face when he saw that much blood . . . I jumped up and clamped my hand over Violet's mouth, toppling the filled teapot. "Vi, don't scream. It's okay." I knew we'd get in trouble. We were always getting in trouble with the twins' mother, Katia. *Genevieve, she doesn't trust us. The less Katia knows, the better,* Mom would warn.

Ash handed me a wad of toilet paper to soak up the blood. I could see he was sorry—though if it was fear or genuine regret, only Ash could tell you.

"Oh man, it stings!" More tears. I pulled Vi to her feet and dragged her into the tiny bathroom.

"Zip your lips, Ash," I said, closing the door behind us.

I petted Vi's pretty white-blond hair, channeling the calm I'd seen my mother use on people she'd help with her remedies. "Let me fix you. No one will know, okay?"

"My mom doesn't like it when you heal stuff, Geni."

"Our little secret, right? And I promise it won't hurt."

Violet held up her pinky for me to lock it with my own.

"Close your eyes and hold your breath." Shutting my own eyes, I pulled from the star and dragged a finger across the line that just did not want to stop bleeding. He got her right on the bone, unzipped the skin beautifully.

Once it was done, my stomach topsy-turvy, Vi helped me with cold water on my face and rushed out to grab a cookie from our tea party. "Thanks," I said, sitting on the closed toilet lid. "The sugar helps."

She kissed my cheek. "We're best friends forever so we look out for each other," she said, her tears drying. The sole evidence of the injury was the blood staining her thin cape, so we hid it away and returned to the world of Lady Violet and Saint Geneviève, taking tea while Ash the Newly Tamed (and Penitent) Dragon cleaned up the queendom.

I so hope I get to see the twins today; I've missed them. To be honest, I don't even know where everyone else in the Cinzio Traveling Players is right now. In the wake of recent events, I sort of tuned out what was going on with the rest of the company.

And it's probably rude to admit out loud, but more than my human family, I've missed Gertrude and Houdini. My little sweeties are probably so confused.

"Hey, Geni . . ." Baby points to an immense carved sign just before we pass it: *Welcome to Eaglefern, Home of the Fighting Eagles and Pacific Coastal University! Population 31,580—and Maybe You!*

The main street of Eaglefern looks like any other: small shops in old brick buildings, a movie theater whose neon is quiet midday, each block capped with a coffee house or tiny eatery. We pass a bustling bookstore, the tables out front cluttered with people in scarves and down jackets, laughing and drinking from green-and-white coffee cups. Two- and three-story, old-style office buildings and storefronts line the streets that branch off the main thoroughfare, and then give way to narrower streets of quaint little boxes with white fences and small porches. "Downtown" lasts about eight, maybe nine blocks, its end marked with a big blue sign that reads FAIR-GROUNDS — 2 MI. Then fields.

And a giant red-and-yellow tent beckoning in the distance.

"Welcome home," I mumble.

5

THIS IS NO ORDINARY FAIRGROUNDS. A FENCE OF ROUGH-HEWN LUMBER painted white the half-full parking lot. Lines delineating parking spaces practically glow atop the fresh black asphalt in the filtered winter daylight. The Cinzio trucks rest quietly along the perimeter of the lot. Against the backside of a massive outdoor stadium, the big top has claimed her spot, center stage in a huge field flanked on the far side by a distant woods.

She looks beautiful. A spark of excitement pops briefly through the gloom draping my heart.

"New tent?" I ask Baby as we walk toward the fencing.

"Guess so."

The red-and-yellow panels are vibrant, free of scuffs and tears, the canvas off-gassing its straight-from-the-factory smell. The disappointing thing about a new tent, though— on our old big top, panels along the backside had been signed by every performer and crew member for each season, like a yearbook. If you looked closely enough, you'd find the inconspicuous corner where a thirteen-year-old me professed her undying love for all things Ash Jónás with a swirly GF + AJ = Tru Luv 4Ever. This new tent is fresh, clean. A blank slate.

It's sad that so much history has disappeared.

Outbuildings line the parking lot along the northern edge of the main stadium. Four sizable cinder block boxes topped with metal roofs and accented with rustic, raw-wood trim and extra-large, double-paned windows. The costume, makeup, and prop trailers are parked behind—they've clearly chosen their new homes already. The longer building on the end must be the cookhouse, judging by the lengthy white tent stretching from its front and the two delivery trucks idling alongside.

"Where is everyone?" I ask, hand tight around Delia's letter stuffed in my jacket pocket.

Baby shrugs as we walk through the open gate. A booming voice echoes from the direction of the open stadium. Sounds like someone on a microphone. "Probably orientation. Ted asked folks to come back early from furlough so we can get to work on the new show." Judging by the number of cars out front, everyone, and then some, must be here.

We move beyond the outbuildings, following the path that leads to our living quarters. The silver Airstream I shared with my mother is already nestled into the wooded area, the exterior awning unfurled. Beside the trailer, someone has set out two dark red Adirondack chairs around a fire pit. Baby's older faded white-and-green travel trailer sits next to ours, as per usual.

The Jónáses' coach is parked a few trees away, although that doesn't mean they're here yet. I didn't think to look in the lot for the silver sedan they tow behind their rig.

"Should we check out the barn?" Baby points back over his shoulder at the dark blue monster capped with a blood-red roof, occupying the majority of the northwest corner of the property.

"Wow, quite a step up from scrawny menagerie tents, huh?" I say.

Baby smiles and heads toward the southern doors, and before my hand is even on the metal handle, the growls and trumpets start. They know I'm home, and I cannot get to them fast enough.

Horse stalls line the eastern side of the barn—my nose immediately tickles at the smell of hay—though at the north-eastern end and along the northern wall, closed white doors lead to what might be offices or storage rooms, and one door clearly marked KITCHEN. The center corral is laid with freshly combed dirt, the edges bordered by portable metal, three-bar railings that reach to my chin, though the oval floor around it is rubbery and soft underfoot. Four huge ceiling-mounted heat pumps whir with a pleasant wash of warm air, and bars of LED lighting mounted on overhead joists bathe the fully enclosed interior in a homey glow.

But it's the barn's southwestern side that houses my heart.

"My babies!" I sing, allowing two very happy trunks to smother me through floor-to-ceiling bars. Strong, yes, but also confining and a little intimidating. I'm concerned for

Gertrude. She came from a dreadful zoo where they zapped her with cattle prods and deprived her of food. Guilt bites at me that I wasn't here to help get them settled.

Happy-sad tears burn my eyeballs. Home is where my elephants are, but every thought, every memory is weighted by the person who's missing.

"Hello . . . Yes, I know," I say to the end of Houdini's trunk. "I missed you too." I push away for a sec to wipe elephant slobber from my cheek with the back of my sleeve. "Baby, how do I get in here?"

"Heyyyyyy, welcome home!" We both turn upon hearing Ted's voice as he jogs from the other side of the barn, a smile stretched across his lined face. Despite the grime of his flannel shirt and heavy work pants, he looks good. His salt-and-pepper hair has missed a date or two with the black dye, and his scruffy face is proof enough that his grooming habits have been granted a reprieve from the impeccable ringmaster look he sports during performances. But his hooded gray eyes are bright, more relaxed than they were just a week ago.

He and Baby clasp hands and exchange a quick manly, shoulders-only hug, and then my adopted uncle swoops me off the ground. "We missed you, kid." I hug him back, inhaling the mix of sweat and tobacco and circus that reassures me I'm home.

Ted puts me back on the ground, though a whining Houdini, trunk stretched through the bars, yanks my wrist and pulls me off balance.

"Can you open this before he amputates my arm?"

Ted laughs. "Get back, buddy." He pushes Houdini's

trunk through so it doesn't get caught, then lifts the lid to a rectangular gray box on the wall housing one green and one red button. Green pressed, the bars slide right, leaving Gertrude a great berth to plod forward and wrap her wrinkled trunk around my head, pulling me into the enclosure with them. I laugh as little Houdini pulls and sniffs and grunts alongside his mother, a giant girl making her own host of happy noises, her flapping ears whipping up a soft breeze. I don't know how anyone could be happy with a dog or cat if they could have an elephant.

Although I do in fact believe that Gertrude and Houdini consider me *their* pet.

I giggle as Gert lifts me off the ground; Houdini yanks at my jacket, tearing the pocket in his search for treats. "Not yet, you bad boy. Gimme a second."

When Delia's letter tumbles to the floor, the happiness of the reunion dims. Baby doesn't miss a beat, scooping it up, folding it in half, and shoving it into my back jeans pocket before Houdini stuffs the paper into his slobbery mouth.

"Thanks," I say. Baby smiles wistfully.

Ted rubs Gertrude's freckled forehead as she sets me down. "They have been making such a fuss today. I swear this old girl can tell time."

"You're a smart cookie, aren't you?" I pat and kiss her wide, textured cheek, one hand on her dominant, and thus shorter, right tusk. "I told you I'd be back today." Gert's happy voice—a low growl—vibrates through my feet. Her trunk sniffs at me, ears waving as I push myself into her side. Gertrude is so big, hugging her happens in stages. And baby

Houdini doesn't understand his own strength. He scampers about the enclosure—which is much bigger than it feels from the outside—throwing hay and trumpeting and knocking into me. I grab a mango and apples from the silver basin against the northern barred wall and he slows to eat and allow me a quick smooch atop his fuzzy head.

Hay and fine dirt cover the spongy floor; the drainage grates run along the sides rather than underfoot where they can irritate the elephants' feet. Heat lamps overhead make it cozy, perfect for the little guy. A fresh bed of bamboo lines the southern cinder block wall. I hope there's a gardener on staff.

The barn's interior is the perfect temperature thanks to the heat pumps—such a contrast to the old menagerie tents that cost the gross domestic product of a small country to keep warm.

"Did you have a hard time getting her in here?" I ask Ted.

He answers by moving to another panel along the southwestern side of the enclosure, where two more buttons hide. The green button depressed, a huge door disguised as a wall engages, sliding open to reveal an expansive, rock-walled yard complete with a shallow pool, sand, and a swath of fresh turf stretching along one side. I hadn't even noticed this from outside the main building.

It's the nicest place our elephants have ever seen. My heart, for the first time in weeks, is happy.

I follow Gert and her son out into the light drizzle now sprinkling us with tiny diamonds. I stop just long enough to hug Ted.

"Thank you. For this." I nod at the elephants.

"Anything for my family," he says, kissing the top of my head. He explains that when the elephants were first brought in, Gertrude was nervous about the bars, but they did a few walkabouts and she settled with a little carrot-cake encouragement.

Watching her now, her trunk inspecting the rock wall, one eye on Houdini as he splashes into the pool, this feels right. Even if the circumstances that led us to this place are terrible, like Baby said, I need to think beyond myself—these animals deserve better than twenty-plus states a year.

Othello's low-octave snarl echoes from inside the barn. "Sounds like someone else knows you're home," Ted says, smiling. "Hey . . ." He chucks my chin gently with his rough finger, his eyes darkening slightly. "You'll let me or Cece or Baby know . . . if you want to talk? If we can do anything for you?"

My throat tightens, the emotion choking off words. I nod and look down at my tattered black Converse, the sand of the elephants' yard mixing with the hay stuck to the sides.

"Maybe, if you're feeling up to it in the next few days, you could distract yourself with some Loxodonta mail. That always cheers you up, right? Seeing what the little kids have sent in." His hand is solid and reassuring on my shoulder.

In tenth grade, I had a school project that required me to found a mock charitable organization. So I started the Loxodonta Project, devoted to educating people about the circus life with specific focus on animal care, and then expanded to include education about both wild and captive elephants (African and Asian), the terrible state of poaching, and how to support reputable sanctuaries globally. *Loxodonta* is the genus for African elephants in the taxonomic scientific classification system, and since my Gertrude is an African elephant and Baby has African roots, I felt this name was perfect.

Ted, Delia, and I decided to keep it going as it would be a positive way to show transparency to our critics about how we treat our elephants (and lion). We wrote a mission statement, started a Facebook page, had an awesome logo made, and built a website. We printed stickers, pencils, and T-shirts that we offer in exchange for donations, and every year, we send that collected money to an elephant charity that shares our mandate.

We get correspondence from all over the country, most accompanied by art from kids who have either seen our shows or who've heard of Loxodonta from the internet. Every letter gets a response, even if it's just a glossy "signed" headshot of Gert and Houdini, or Othello.

And given that it's been almost a month since I've done anything Loxo-related, I can only imagine the stack awaiting my attention.

I turn to exit the enclosure before Othello really gets wound up, but Ted stops me again. "After you see that troublemaker, go find Cece, yeah? She's been chomping at the bit for her Genevieve fix."

Without waiting for my answer, Ted and Baby disappear back into the main barn, heads bowed in conversation. I'm guessing Ted has a lot of catch-up info for Baby. The poor guy's been doubling as my babysitter for the last three weeks, leaving Ted without his crew chief, forced to deal with most of this transition business on his own.

Houdini, trunk coated in sand, buffets into me, raises his trunk, and trumpets.

I pet the long, coarse hairs on his head—when not wet, they stick straight up like a sparse red-black forest. Right now, he's soaked, though a few strands have caught the drizzle, like fairy-sized silver balloons decorating his scalp. His trunk is wrapped around my arm and I'm rubbing his lower lip and cheek and the nubs that will one day be his big-boy tusks.

Gert moves over to us and drapes her trunk along her son's back, sniffing my hair, my clothes, my face. It tickles. "I was at the beach. Gert, the ocean is so big and beautiful. I'll take you there one day."

"Genevieve! You're home!" Violet squeals my name as she prances along the front of the enclosure, but she won't come more than a few steps in. After a show in Florida the year we turned ten, Gertrude was agitated about something. (Fish & Wildlife later found a nine-foot alligator submerged in the swamp behind our encampment—smart Gert!) Vi was helping me change out the hay when Gertrude started and shrieked and accidentally stepped on Violet's left foot, breaking three of her toes. Katia freaked out and wouldn't let me fix them. (I waited a few days and Vi let me do it anyway.) Since then, though, Vi stays on the outside of the enclosure.

I jog to her at the gate opening and she throws herself into my arms, her lustrous blond ponytail tossing itself over my shoulder. Ash says that if he ever misses Violet on a catch, he can always grab her hair instead.

I hug her strong but sprightly, pink-tracksuit-adorned body. Neither Vi nor I will break any height records, but she has the perfect flyer's body—part gymnast, part bird.

Oh man, I've missed her.

She steps back, but hangs on to my hand, pulling me free of the elephants' quarters, her elfish face bright with a wide smile. She's the only person I know who can pull off purple eye shadow—it makes her honey-brown irises practically pop out of their sockets. When we go into the makeup department at the mall, the clerks fight over who gets to paint Vi's face. Like a doll.

"I just saw Baby's truck in the lot. I've been looking everywhere for you."

"Have you guys been here all this time?" I ask.

"No, we just got in, like, twenty minutes ago. This place—it's nuts, isn't it?" Long-lashed eyes alight with boy-crazed mischief, she leans in and purrs, "Who are all these studs?" Her glossed lips pucker and roll as she scopes out the new dudes working as little worker bees do. Violet steps aside as one pushes past with a handcart of boxed supplies. "Oooh, that one over there is cute."

"And thirty."

"What's wrong with older men?"

"We're jailbait, Vi."

"Only for a few more months . . ." She winks.

"Walk and talk. I gotta say hi to the cat."

On the northwest side of the barn, safely separated from the elephants, is a huge reinforced steel enclosure. Inside is a jungle gym of bolted timber and a wading pool; half of the enclosure is grass, natural light spilling from above via huge skylights. A knotted rope hangs from the ceiling, and an oversized, bark-covered scratching post extends from the side wall. Along the bars, the world's largest tawny house cat mewls and paces, all four hundred and fifty pounds of him. The black tassel at the end of his long tail salutes the sky, his strong leg muscles flexing as his seven-inch-wide paws plod atop the dirt, mahogany eyes already fixed on me.

"Hey, you big man," I say, kneeling next to the enclosure. Othello chuffs and flops onto his side, pushing his back against the bars so I can bury my hands and give him a good scrub. And just like any spoiled cat, Othello wants me to rub behind his ears—the fur there is black, the softest anywhere on his body—though his favorite is when someone burrows their fingers deep into his black-and-tan mane. Initiate the happiness that sounds like a purr when he exhales. (Lions don't officially purr.)

I look up at Vi. She's standing a few steps behind me. "One of these days, you should really pet the lion. He doesn't want to eat you."

"I'm good. I can see how ferocious he is from here, thanks."

"You're an enigma, Violet Jónás. You fly five stories in the air but you won't pet a giant house cat."

She snorts. "House cat, my ass."

I flatten my hand against the bars so Othello can sniff and lick. Need exfoliation? Let a lion lick you, but only once. More than that, you'll lose skin.

"Where'd you guys go on break?" I ask.

"Down to LA to see my dad's family. Disneyland, the beach—Ash wanted to go to Vegas but we didn't have time."

I put my other hand out; she pulls me to my feet and side-hugs me, the smell of her latest favorite fruity perfume tickling my nose. "I missed you so much . . ."

"You too, Vi." My hand moves to my back pocket, to double-check Delia's letter is still tucked away.

"Whatever you need . . ." She pauses. "Me and Ash will be there for you."

I know Vi will. Ash does what Ash wants.

"Did you guys . . . her ashes . . ." Blond strands loosed from her ponytail frame Violet's round face; her wide eyes are watery as she looks at me, her full lips pressed tight.

"Yeah. She wanted to be spread at Haystack Rock, so that's what we did." I stop short of telling her about Delia's letter or the ghost in the post office. I don't know how to talk about my mother's death yet, and there's no rational way to explain what I might have seen today. Besides, how will I ever share Delia's letter with anyone other than Baby? Violet is my dearest friend, but I worry that she'd only see the last words of a beloved, albeit mentally unstable, woman.

Violet's smile contradicts itself as the corners of her mouth tug downward. "Delia loved that beach," she whispers. Our shoulders touch, a moment of grief between lifelong friends. Although Delia was my mother, in the circus, we're all family. I'm not the only one suffering.

Across from the main corral, more crew forklift bales of

alfalfa and hay into the empty horse stalls. A few nod and offer a cursory wave, but I don't know who these men are—new crew members? Where are the old guys?

Baby's not going to like this, the formal uniforms and all. He's not the *yes, sir, whatever you say, sir, certainly I will wear this ugly shirt, sir* type. Pretty much the only beings Baby takes shit from are Delia and the gods.

"I'm starving," Violet says, picking hay off my sleeve. "Let's go eat. They've brought in a huge catering truck and we're having barbecue!"

"You go ahead. I want to find Cece."

"'K, but meet me at the mess tent in a half hour or I'll come looking for you again. And Gen . . . I'm glad you're home." She flashes the *I love you* sign and slides out the southern door.

The elephants have meandered back inside, their trunks at the open gate, waiting for me. My hello to Othello finished, I should close the outer yard wall before Houdini makes more of a mess.

I move past Gert and hit the button to close the wall; Houdini tugs at my jacket, eager to play. "I gotta eat too, buddy. Tug-of-war after dinner?" He snorts, suddenly distracted by whatever his mom has found in their food basin.

Once I'm able to sneak out, I close their main gate and quietly step away, careful to not let the exterior barn door slam. A disquieting fog rolls in from the adjoining field, makes it hard to take a deep breath.

It doesn't matter that the circus has moved to a new venue. It's not far enough away from anything to be different—which means she should still be here. We still have the same trailers. The same waft of dung and hay and truck exhaust mixed with the wet of trees that always feels like home, the air heavy with precipitation.

There is no escaping it. No escaping *her*.

Not that I want to escape her. But lessening the ache in my chest—that would be welcome. Just for a few minutes.

When I faced other heartbreaks—small things in comparison—Delia would do something fun. The year Ash ruined Christmas by telling me Santa wasn't real (he so is), Delia and Baby whisked me away to Mt. Hood's Timberline Lodge on Christmas Eve. As we headed in from the snow for the night, she plucked a small branch off a fir tree and brought it back to our room. It only took a few seconds in her magic hands for the tree to grow as tall as my eight-year-old self, lusciously green and fresh-smelling, its newly fattened base tucked in an ice bucket stuffed with warm, damp towels, our very own magical Christmas tree. We spent the evening cutting snowflakes out of hotel stationery, stringing white and red thread from the complimentary sewing kit through their delicate necks to hang on the tree.

Delia loved Christmas.

Delia made sure I loved Christmas too.

The Christmas just passed was the last one I will have spent with her. Forever.

The ache worsens.

I find the travel trailer that doubles as the circus's main office. The door is unlocked. Upon entering, the evidence of Ted's life spent in here—the scent of tobacco and old coffee and Cecelia's perfume and body sprays—envelops me like a welcome-home blanket. Cecelia, however, is not sitting at the makeshift desk, its surface buried under an open laptop and paperwork.

"Aunt Cece?" Maybe she's in the tiny bathroom. I rap against the door. No response.

As expected, the trays on the countertop near the sink are bursting with Loxodonta mail. Just as well. Quiet work leads to a quiet mind.

I lean against the countertop, and the corner of Delia's letter stabs my butt through the denim. I pull it out, the broken wax seal now in pieces at the bottom of the thick envelope. I stretch the letter on the smooth countertop.

It punches me just as hard reading it the second time.

I jump when a chilled breeze flutters the wispy curls around my face, as if someone has thrown open a nearby window to let in fresh air.

There, hovering just a few feet away near the narrow bathroom door, her own hair again aloft, the white dress wavering against her shape, stands the willowy figure from the post office.

6

"WHO ARE YOU?"

This close, her large, almond-shaped green eyes burn with a fearsome intensity. Her earlier smile returns, though my breath catches in my throat. I don't trust what I'm seeing. Did she follow me? Will she hurt me? Does this shape start out benevolent and then become that thing Delia feared most?

Is this the Etemmu?

I sniff the room. Smells normal. But would I be able to smell anything off?

"Are you going to hurt me?"

She shakes her head no, the movements slow and exaggerated, as if she's underwater, but the smile never fades, the eyes never darken.

Just as fast as she appeared, she blows through me, and it feels like I've been iced from head to toe, the wind knocked out of me as I whirl to see where she's gone.

She's still here, just on the other side of the trailer, nearer to the sink.

She moves to a clear-glass sugar dispenser and spills it into a dry puddle onto the stained countertop, a few wayward crystals bouncing off the old Formica and disappearing under the edge of the black microwave.

I fold closed my mother's letter and step closer.

There, in the spill, letters form under the influence of the woman's delicate luminescent finger.

A
L
I
C
I
A

I look up at her, stunned. "You—you're Alicia?"

She smiles and nods again. My thoughts trip over one another in their haste to get to my mouth. "You're my mother's Alicia? Her friend?" The ghost nods yes. "That was you at the post office. Can you speak to me? Why are you here—"

I startle as the main door behind me opens, Delia's letter falling to the floor.

"My Geni girl! You're home!" In bounds my darling aunt, her bleached-blond, hot-rolled hair wrapped tight in a floral head scarf to stave off frizz, a never-ending battle when we curly-haired types roost along the West Coast.

I scoop up the letter and shove it back into my rear pocket, away from prying eyes. "Hi, Cece," I say, tucking into her outstretched arms.

Cecelia gently shifts me away, hands cupping my face. She eases off a leather glove and presses the back of her warm fingers against my cheek. Cece would check me for fever if I came in and told her I accidentally chopped off my own head. "You're so pale. I'm so glad you're home." She hugs me again as she talks into my hair. I hear her sniff and clear her throat before she holds me at arm's length for further inspection.

"I told Baby to feed you."

"I had pancakes this morning."

I look over Cece's shoulder, scanning the area behind her. No ghost.

Cece laughs as she dabs at the corners of her heavily mascaraed eyes. "Of course you did. And there's barbecue out there now." She tucks her tissue into her sleeve and rubs her hands up and down my arms. "Have you had a chance to look around?"

"Sort of. As soon as the elephants smelled me on the lot . . ."

"Yes, they've missed you. Sit." She adjusts the wall thermostat and turns around to the tiny kitchenette. "I'll make cocoa—oh! What a mess! Thanks, Teddy," she says, scooping the spilled sugar into the garbage can. I don't fess up. Instead, I break out in a cold sweat. The idea that Alicia—my mother's companion for the whole of my life—is now presenting herself to me . . .

Why can I see her now when I've never seen her before? Will I see her again?

The reek of all-purpose cleanser stings my nose as Cece

mumbles something about tidying up after oneself. She tinkers with the electric kettle and spoons cocoa power into a cup, and then answers her cell phone. Flashing me one long-nailed finger and a whispered, "Just a sec," she moves into the space that now houses filing cabinets and storage bins.

I move through the trailer to see if Alicia is hiding somewhere, waiting. Open the bathroom door. The closet. Peek out through the rough curtains over the window on the door to see if she's waiting outside for me.

Is Alicia here now because she is to be my friend, in Delia's absence?

A surge of panic prickles my chilled skin: If Alicia is here, could that mean the Etemmu is coming as well?

I stare at my reflection in the dirty kitchen window.

Cece is off the phone and moving toward me, a tight smile on her lips.

"So this new place is something else." I raise my eyebrows hopefully.

"Yes . . . it sure is." She resumes the business of making hot chocolate. "Our new investor, Triad Partners Group—it's a global investment firm, but the entertainment companies in its portfolio are apparently the CEO's pet project. He has an impressive record of helping businesses grow." She hands me a steaming cup.

"Is that what you guys want? To get bigger?" I have little idea about Ted's plans for the Cinzio Traveling Players Company beyond the "evolve or die" mentality among smaller circuses. It's the twenty-first century. Cirque du Soleil is king. We want to at least be a jester.

"Teddy wants to make sure everyone has jobs to come back to. You know this circus is his life." I detect a hint of regret in her voice. So much his life that it's all they've ever had.

"Oh, hey . . ." Cece skitters to her supply cupboard from which she pulls out an apple-embossed white bag. "I got you a new phone."

I pull the sleek device out of its packaging. Power on. Nice. My old phone wasn't much better than two tin cans and a string stretched between. Delia wasn't a fan of technology, so I made do.

"Thanks, Cece. This is great."

"Now Vi can stop nagging you about her missed messages. And this one is supposed to have a top-notch camera. You can take pictures for the Loxo site."

"Yeah . . . thanks. Very cool."

The trailer door opens and Baby's frame fills the space. "Gen, mess tent. Violet is following me around like a lost dog asking where you are."

"Hi, Baby," Cecelia says. He climbs in and gives her a tight hug.

"Hello, beautiful. You miss me?" Shameless flirt. "Mmm, hot chocolate. I might come back for some later." He turns to me. "Nice phone. Can I borrow it?"

"Not if you value your life," I say, dumping the nearly untouched cocoa into the sink.

Cece pokes Baby's arm. "Save some vittles for everyone else," she teases. "And after chow's done, you come back so we can go over a few things with Ted, yes?"

Brilliant. I could use five minutes of no one micromanaging my every emotion. I want to spend time with Delia's letter, alone.

The drizzle has stopped, but thick gray clouds look like they're preparing for some real action in the brisk, waning afternoon. The orientation meeting in the stadium over, my fellow company members are now thick on the grounds. Laughter floats from trailer row. Company members making their way to the meal tent wave a polite hello or stop to give me a sympathetic pat on the arm. They mean well, but by the time we get to the dining tent, my face hurts from the pretend smile meant to reassure everyone else.

It's weird to have the company home so early. New investor, new show. And it dawns on me—what does this mean for me? Delia and I were a duo.

I rub my fingertips together, violin calluses softening from three weeks of no practice.

I don't even have a violin anymore. It died the same death as my mother.

One step at a time. One handshake, hug, and heartfelt condolence at a time.

Baby holds the flap aside for me as we enter the upgraded mess tent. This one's bigger, brighter, and whiter, with fancy plastic windows stitched into the sides and laminate flooring that amplifies the sounds of our shoes. No more warped plywood for us. The tables wear their finest skirts and floral arrangements like posh hats. Each place setting offers a shiny black folder with silver embossing of *Triad Partners Group* and a graphic representation of an iris flower.

Violet hops up as soon as she sees us, stopping alongside me every few seconds so I can say hello to more of my family—a grandmotherly hug from Beatrice, the head costume lady, and Nicola and Becca, her two wardrobe-assistant daughters, fresh tears washing tracks in their heavily made-up faces; hugs and cheek kisses from Toby and Dan, the clowns, and their newest puppy, a fluffy Pomeranian named Peaches; and then the horse people, and then Blake, the circus's lead carpenter, and his very pregnant wife, and on and on. So many faces that remind me, even without my mom, I'm never alone.

The remaining Jónáses stand to the side, waiting their turn to say hello. Katia's hug is quick—evidence of her continued distrust of me—but Aleksandar lingers, speaking into my ear that I will always be their family too, and "never worry we keep you safe, like our Violet." Aleks pushes back, hands on my shoulders, and hiccups against his grief. He always did have a soft spot for Delia, which probably adds further weight to Katia's discomfort.

Ash nudges his dad aside. It's the first time I've seen him since we all went our separate ways for furlough. Despite the chill in the air, Ash's bare, muscled arms in his tight-fitting, white ribbed tank top give full display to the tattoo of the flying man, a small bit of defiant artistry that almost cost him his life at his mother's hands.

"Ruby Red, glad to have you back," he says, hugging me hard. Ash pulls out a chair for his mother just as Baby joins us.

I stifle a laugh as he sits, the plastic fold-up chair groaning its discontent. A young, not-bad-looking server dressed in black pants and a white apron (we have servers now?) fills our water glasses and offers a choice of entrées: barbecued chicken or beef, or perhaps a plate of grilled vegetable kebabs.

Violet toys with the end of her long, flaxen ponytail. "We'll both have the chicken," she says with more breath than necessary. The server blushes—of course he does. Vi, fresh and adorable in a different pink tracksuit, never misses an opportunity to practice her feminine wiles on unwitting members of the opposite sex.

When she looks away, the server's presence forgotten, I almost feel bad for the guy who's moved on to the next table, cheeks still aglow.

"You shouldn't do that," I say.

"Do what?" She winks and opens her folder, shuffles through the papers like she's interested in what they say. "One of the wardrobe ladies said there's a coupon in here for the mall. And I have my eye on these incredible shoes I found online . . ."

I leaf through, for lack of anything better to do while we wait for people to get situated. Stuff about Triad, Eaglefern, our new insurance, something called WinterFest coming the first weekend in February—Cinzio is apparently to be the headline act.

Violet's elbow jams into my ribs. "Oww!"

"Gen."

I follow where she's looking. A young man has walked into the tent, wearing a well-fitted dark suit and black gloves. Unkempt, dishwater-blond curls look like someone has just given him an "attaboy" tousle. Shoulders back, he's got a cardboard file box in his gloved hands. A woman I assume is with Triad points to where he's to put it, but when he bends to do so, the black backpack over his shoulder, made colorful by iron-on patches, flings forward and sets him off-balance.

His lightly tanned face flushes (who has a tan in an Oregon winter?) as he rights himself and the backpack and tucks his mutinous red tie back under his jacket. He glances into the seating area, looking surprised to find people in here; the eyebrow he hitches is cut in two perfect halves, like the hair forgot to grow in that narrow slice.

As he moves past us toward the back, he looks up just once, eyes the color of fresh spring grass. The patches on the backpack boast soccer ball motifs. Makes sense. He looks like a soccer player. Maybe he spent Christmas break kicking a ball around on a tropical beach—that would explain the tan.

"What I would give for cheekbones like that," Violet moans. "So unfair." I can practically hear the cogs of her heart kicking into overdrive. Baby snorts as he scrolls through his phone.

Plates make their way to the tables via the quick work of the hired waitstaff, their pleasant manners reminding us all that they definitely are not circus folks. It's too weird to have someone serving me my dinner—makes me uncomfortable. It feels like I've stepped into an alternate universe, everything so clean and shiny. And more space with this bigger tent. Gone are the hay bales along the edges to catch drips and to prevent our boots from squishing into muddy patches. The white and black tablecloths—actual cloth instead of the cheesy plastic dollar-store covers with poorly drawn fruit that Cecelia buys in bulk—are soft to the touch but hold their starched shape draped around the table's circumference. And there is a lot of silverware. *Start from the outside and work your way in*, Delia would say.

It's a little weird that they've gone to such expense—it feels like we're being seduced. Like these are the pretty bits before they come in and tell us they're dismantling the whole thing. If Triad Partners Group is looking at Cinzio as their next multimillion-dollar operation, some tight-ass in a suit is gonna lose his or her job.

All this fancy is nice, but I hope we get back to normal with breakfast. Circus folks don't need formal. We just need food so we can get to work.

This catered meal is top-notch—I doubt Baby even tasted the two slabs of dead cow they served him. And whatever heavenly glaze they've bathed this chicken in—Baby pats me on the head in playful approval when I clean my plate.

The tent flap opens again, and a new group enters, three men and one woman, her hair pulled back in a severe bun. All four are dressed in suits. Ted follows them along with another man, taller than the others, perfectly hair-free head, long, razor-sharp nose, a jaw that commands respect.

"Hey . . . that man. He was at the New Year's Eve Gala. Ted was talking to him while Delia and I were going on," I say. All at once, I'm in the dirt next to her, trying to bring her back to me, seeing her retreat behind my closed eyes and knowing in my roiling gut that no matter how hard I pull from the star in my head, there is nothing I can do to save her.

Baby doesn't answer. He sits ramrod straight, eyes fixed toward the front.

The bald man greets those around him with handshakes and a broad smile. When he scans the tent, I feel the weight of his stare like I did that night, just before he disappeared behind the curtain after Delia fell.

He must be the new owner.

The equestrian group sits at one of the front tables, an extended family that includes a few of the circus's youngest performers. The owner says hello to the adults and then kneels next to the chairs of two preschoolers. From nowhere, he pulls and presents them with big round purple lollipops. The girls dissolve into giggles.

When he stands again, his eyes find me.

And seeing him . . . I'm light-headed, my fingers tingly.

"I need some fresh air." I fold my napkin and push my chair out. Though I didn't ask for an escort, Baby is right behind me.

We're almost to the door when Ted turns and stops us. "Oh, great, I wanted to introduce you." The man responds to Ted's cue and squares his shoulders to us. Stubble darkens his cheeks and the sides of his otherwise hairless head.

He smiles sadly and offers a gloved hand to shake. "I'm Lucian Dmitri, the president and CEO of Triad Partners Group. You must be Genevieve Flannery."

"Yes, sir." He has that air of importance that makes you feel like you should be moving faster.

"Genevieve, though I am thrilled to be a part of the Cinzio family, it is with great sadness that we meet." His accent—British—softens the words, underscored by the melancholy in his hazel eyes. "I am so sorry for your loss. The evening of the New Year's Gala was a terrible tragedy, but for no one more than you. I wish I'd been given the pleasure of meeting your mother. Again, my deepest condolences."

"Thank you."

"If it's not too forward, I have left you a gift with your aunt. Ted told me you were without a violin after the accident. Your talents are such an integral part of this company. We do hope you'll accept it with our best wishes," he says, his palm brushing the small purple iris blooming from his buttonhole.

"Thank you very much." Frankly, playing the violin again has been the furthest thing from my mind.

He smiles gently, looks to Baby, and extends his hand. "Where are my manners? Lucian Dmitri."

Their hands clasp in greeting, though Baby's face remains stoic, his voice hard and flat. "Bamidele Duncan."

Baby never introduces himself by his real name.

"A pleasure to make your acquaintance. Ted has talked at length about your skills. I've been looking forward to finally putting a face to the legend." When the handshake finally finishes, Baby's fingers fist at his side, his body practically vibrating with tension. He doesn't take his eyes off Mr. Dmitri.

Dmitri crosses his arms over his chest, and a silvery glint catches my eye.

His tiepin—

Inverted triangle overlying a circle.

My brain cycles through where I've seen this image—the seal. Delia's letter!

Why does this guy have a tiepin in the same shape as my mother's mysterious wax seal?

"Father?" The backpack kid detours my train of thought.

"Mr. Duncan, Genevieve, this is my son, Henry," Lucian says, gesturing to the boy. I inspect the two faces side by side—same ears, square jawed. Daddy Dmitri doesn't have a bisected eyebrow, and the boy is more delicate—up close, his eyes, more of a blue-green, are devoid of the slight slant of his father's. Henry pulls at a stubborn curl at the part in his hair, as if he's trying to flatten it into submission.

I extend a hand and the boy meets it, leather-gloved fingers warm. "Nice to meet you."

"You as well," he says. He has his dad's accent.

"Nice gloves."

He smiles. "Cold tent."

Violet shoves past an aproned server and slides in next to me. "Am I interrupting?"

"No. Please," Lucian says.

She waits a beat before again jabbing her arm into my side. "Oh, right—Mr. Dmitri, Henry, this is Violet Jónás, one of the Jónás Family Flyers." Violet is radiant, her ponytail draped flirtatiously over one shoulder as she offers a bent-wrist hand first to Lucian, then to Henry. She lingers in the handshake, as if waiting for him to kiss it.

"You define grace in flight on your trapeze," Lucian says. "You have a twin?"

Violet grins. "Yes. I'm older, though. By four minutes."

"I'll bet you never let him forget it."

She giggles.

"Ladies, Mr. Duncan, it's been a pleasure to meet you, but duty beckons." Lucian nods, the business smile again in place, and steps back from our small gathering. "Henry?"

"See you again soon," Henry says. He looks at me over his shoulder as he follows his father, almost colliding with the tableclothed conference table now scattered with more glossy black Triad folders.

Violet barely waits until he's out of earshot before she pulls me toward the entrance and whisper-squeals in my ear. "He's so hot! And omiGOD, I love the accents!"

"Genevieve, you going to listen to their little speech?" Baby asks, hand reaching for the tent flap.

"Do I have to?"

"Yes, you're coming to sit with me! Are you kidding?" Vi says.

Baby lets go of the tent door, but I grab his wrist before he can leave. "Hey, you okay?"

He nods, but the set of his jaw tells me otherwise. "I'll come find you before lights-out," he says, patting my shoulder before setting out into the downpour toward the big top.

"Yeah, okay," I say to his shadow, my thoughts on that tiepin.

Why would Delia have a wax stamp with the same symbol? Maybe it has a common meaning? It's a simple design—inverted triangle overlying a circle, each point forming another small triangle at the three corners intersected by the circle's curve—but I've never seen it before. And now that's twice in one day.

I touch the letter in my back pocket and head through

the door, Vi right behind, still talking. Something about Henry Dmitri.

I stop under the awning that serves as amplifier for the deluge. "Vi. Vi. Violet."

"Yeah?"

"I need a nap."

"Wait, not yet! What about dessert?" She looks back into the tent. "They're talking about whatever's in the folders. We should probably hear this."

"If it's important, Ted will tell us."

"But . . . dessert. And Henry."

"You don't need a wingman, Vi. You got this." If Violet wants to chase the boss's son, I should warn her that that kind of money doesn't fall in love with our kind of people. As if she'd listen.

I pull her close and smooch the side of her head. "I'll catch you later, princess."

"Your loss. I'll give you a full report," she sings as she prances back into the tent.

7

I JOG TO THE AIRSTREAM, HEAD TUCKED UNDER MY JACKET'S FLIMSY COTTON hood, as rain pelts down.

I'm inside, door locked, wet jacket discarded, light on.

I slide onto the bench, pull the letter from the envelope, and carefully spill the broken wax onto the tabletop. Once fitted back together, it's the same symbol. Exactly.

I dig my new phone out of my pocket and search different descriptions of the shape, scrolling through options. Similar patterns pop up, ranging from Alcoholics Anonymous to the Deathly Hallows to the Illuminati, but nothing with this exact design.

Is there a connection between Delia and Lucian Dmitri somewhere, some shared interest?

That seems crazy.

Lucky for me, Mr. Dmitri of Triad Partners Group has left his fingerprints all over the internet—philanthropist; supporter of children's wards and medical fund-raisers from cancer to Lou Gehrig's disease; involvement with desalination technologies and water access for developing countries; Triad business dealings globally, including headquarters in Bucharest, Dubai, London, Paris, and Madrid; and an impressive portfolio of entertainment-related subsidiaries including a film production studio and a talent agency. I can't find anything that tells me who he is when he's not saving lives or donating money; every picture shows him with a professional smile plastered across his face, whether he's at a ribbon cutting, sitting in the cockpit of a shiny black helicopter, or crouched between two bald kids attached to IVs.

If he's ever stirred controversy, he's hired scrubbers to clean any smears off the web.

Delia has had nothing to do with any of these charities or causes, as far as I know, unless it maybe was something she did before I was born. Doubtful. But if it was something important to her, I probably would've at least heard of it. Delia kept her philanthropy closer to home, helping people with her healing plants.

I scoop the wax back into the envelope and refold the letter.

This has to be nothing more than a coincidence. Delia probably found an old wax press during her searches for antique keys at one of the zillion flea markets we've visited during our travels. Most of the available wall space in our tiny trailer is covered in small black gallery frames showcasing Mom's affection for strangely shaped, ancient keys.

Sadness paints itself black and heavy across my insides again.

I tend Delia's pots, cooing at the greenery as she would

(*Plants are conscious beings, Gen—always say nice things to them*), trying to remember the right amount of water so they don't drown or turn brown. "It's just us now, guys, so you gotta pull your weight and stay healthy and happy." The basil is doing well—Jean-Pierre, the circus's chef, has a lot of Delia's plants growing in his own motorhome. Says her sage, dill, and lavender are the best in the world.

Her coveted seeds, thousands of them catalogued in envelopes in repurposed wooden CD holders and stored in our mini fridge . . . *In my own way, I've tried to plant seeds along the way . . . Now you must collect these seeds to understand your future. You will need to rely on old friends—be open to their help and embrace what's coming.*

Old friends—as in Alicia? Will the ghost know something of my mother's "seeds"?

And embrace what is coming—what could that possibly be?

Seriously, Delia, it all sounds so apocalyptic.

This is too weird.

Just as quickly as it appeared in the work trailer earlier, the ghost's glowing form materializes in the corner near the bathroom door, feet hovering above the low-pile gray carpet, hair floating as if kept aloft by a spring breeze.

"Alicia?"

She smiles and nods. Does she know about this letter from my mom? What I'm supposed to do?

Has she seen Delia?

Before I can decide what to ask first, she's floating over to the door . . .

But she's not waiting.

She reaches a hand to the doorknob; the trailer's front door opens and her body fills the archway. She gestures for me to follow.

I pull on heavy boots and a raincoat and follow her out. Though I want whatever answers she has, I'm careful to not speak out loud, in case my fellow company members are heading back to work. Earlier at the post office, Baby couldn't see Alicia—which means no one else probably can either.

Talking to oneself in the rain—maybe best not to.

I follow Alicia away from trailer row, south along the property until the big top and stadium are to our left and a vast field sits ahead of me, the tall firs of a small woods far enough away to fit in the pinch space between my thumb and index finger.

And then she stops and turns around.

The silence between us continues. "Why are you here? Are you the old friend my mother spoke of in her letter? Do you know what she meant—" I reach around to my pocket for the letter—if I can just show it to her, maybe she can help me decipher its meaning—but in my haste to follow, I'd left it in the trailer.

Alicia's round, haunting eyes stare back, the kind curl of her pink lips, the floating hair a halo around her delicate features unperturbed by the light rain. For an instant, Alicia glows brighter, her benevolent face morphing from serene to serious as she sails toward me, repositioning so the big top is to our rear. She makes contact—startlingly cold and pin-prickly, a staticky chill rushing through her hand where it rests on top of mine. The buzzing travels up my arm, tickling to the point of discomfort, my wrist and elbow joints trembling with the pressure of her touch. A slight headache pings the back of my skull.

"Alicia . . . what's happening?"

No words. She floats forward, but I can't pull free of her grasp, my arm stretched between us as if our skin has melded. She motions with her free hand.

"I'm scared. Please . . ."

She tugs again. *You will need to rely on old friends . . . Their answers will make things clearer in the days ahead.*

Tentatively, I ease forward, hoping that whatever's coming next, those answers will be waiting for me on the other side.

8

THE FIELD BEFORE US SHIMMERS FROM A DULL GRAY WRAPPED IN RAIN AND low-hanging clouds to a vibrant sunset, the suddenly dry sky painted in a raving tapestry of oranges and reds and pinks. I blink hard, lingering with my eyes closed in the hope that I'll open them again and be back in our field, but the expanse ahead instead fills with bustling people. Three horses and a cow with huge horns munch on long grasses growing below a hitching post. No cars, and people are dressed weird. Like we've walked onto a movie set.

"Where are we . . . ?"

I try to stop again. Alicia doesn't, however, raising her opposite arm to point ahead at a picture that grows clearer by the second. Some sort of open-air market? The smell of burning lamp oil wafts toward us, the kind Delia would sometimes use in a hurricane lamp when telling her stories. Controlled fires burn in pits and on greasy torches perched along the market's edge.

One step farther, and we're in the mix. People with animated faces move between stalls where smiling merchants sell cucumbers and apples and carrots and leafy vegetables and a variety of breads in fat loaves and perfectly browned braids. Leather apron–clad men sweat over open grills where meats roast; white-haired women in half bonnets wrap twine around stems of herbs and flowers that are then hung upside down from thick, rusted nails. The men wear leather boots that reach up their calves, dirtied pants tucked under long tunics still ripe with the day's work, hair longish or longer, some loose, some pulled back in leather strapping that dangles down vest-covered backs. The women wear burdensome skirts, hems dirty from constant dragging across the earth, frayed braids roping down their backs or untidy buns showing wear in the hours since waking.

People bump into me, but they don't. I pass through them, like mist, their pixels scattering and then reforming. I reach out a hand to touch the arm of a woman stopped at a stall offering stacks of textiles. "Excuse me," I say, voice thick as molasses. She doesn't respond, and my finger slices through nothingness, the pop of static like socks on a cheap carpet.

Alicia pulls us forward again, the chilled connection between us seemingly unbreakable. Past more booths, more people talking, buying and trading wares, their voices faint as if the volume is turned down. It's progress—at least I can hear *something*.

And then she stops, eyes fixed straight ahead. The crowd has parted before a rickety wooden stage. At its center, a woman dressed in a head-to-toe green close-fitting outfit spins on a rope suspended from a crossbar, her body a blur in motion while a sloppily dressed violinist stage right scratches out a discordant tune.

At the melody's conclusion, the aerialist stops, jumps from the rope to applause, and takes a bow, her dark braid flipping in an arc before her. When she stands again, beaming, a few onlookers approach and drop coins in a black floppy felt hat along the stage's edge.

It's Delia.

"Mom?" At first, a whisper. "Mom!" I shout. The hair is the wrong color but it's her.

"Mom, please!" I rush toward the stage, Alicia moving alongside me, her hand still clamped on my wrist. But Delia doesn't see me, doesn't hear me as she separates the coins in the hat, the look on her face disappointed as she gives a few to the grubby violin man. I reach out to grab Delia's arm, but my attempt goes right through her. "Mom, it's me! It's Genevieve! Can you hear me?"

Hot tears burn my cheeks as the woman who must be Delia ties her performance rope to the side, slips her feet into tattered leather boots that reach nearly to her knees, and gathers her things—an old carpet bag, the remaining coins from the black hat tucked into the concealed pocket of a long forest-green cloak she pulls over the outfit that is so different from those on the other women moving about.

"Alicia, why can't she see me?" My throat hurts. "Why are you doing this? Where are we? Please . . ."

Delia's nimble feet bounce off tired wooden steps as she

exits the stage. Alicia tugs me forward again. We follow Delia through the crowd, her hood pulled low over her face so that her head is concealed from behind. The staticky interruption of other people's shapes snaps at my shoulders and elbows, even as I wipe tears off my cheeks because I don't understand what is happening. Is this some sort of afterlife? Is this Delia's version of heaven?

Why am I seeing it?

We walk another minute or so, past wooden cages of squawking chickens, the air pungent from blood congealed under dead, skinned farm animals hanging from hooks. The voices speak in unrecognizable tongues; the discomfort of contact with these people who cannot see or hear me adds to the throb at the back of my head. Sparkles shimmer in my peripheral vision, the early warning sign for the headaches I only ever get after healing someone's ills.

Finally, at the outer stretches of the market, Delia pushes the flap aside to a garishly decorated tent not much bigger than our Airstream. Alicia pulls me in after her, and the noise and smells from outside disappear behind the rough, weighty drape. The tent's interior is sparsely decorated with worldly possessions—a small wooden vanity and tattered-top bench, two cots with richly colored blankets, a straight-ish branch jammed into the tent's wooden framework where costumes hang, a worn but thick area rug underfoot. And plants—so many plants, the air in here fresher than outside thanks to their abundant greenery.

Delia pushes off her cloak and drapes it over one of the cots, pulling the long chestnut braid over her shoulder. As she sets to untwist it, her fingers come away darkly stained. She's hiding her hair's true color?

"Mom, can you hear me?" I say, approaching again. One look into Alicia's sympathetic eyes and I know that my voice is mute. "Why did you bring me to see her if she can't hear me?"

When Delia freezes and looks around the tent, my heart skips a beat—maybe she can hear me! "Mom! Mom, it's me! It's Genevieve! Mom, look at me!"

She rushes to the tent's backside, to a rear flap I didn't see upon first entering, and perks an ear close to the canvas. Are those . . . hoofbeats?

Delia throws open the flap, runs out, and Alicia thrusts us forward, in close step to wherever my mother is going. The tall grasses crunch underfoot, though Alicia floats effortlessly ahead, my arm again stretched uncomfortably between us. Low-lying piles of dirt kick into dusty plumes as Delia sprints toward an interruption in a hay-bale border along the backside of this encampment, the breach wide enough for a horse to fit through.

We stop alongside Delia, her hand over her eyes as she squints through the twilight. Ahead I make out a shape on the horse's back—a body hunched forward, the horse moving at a breakneck pace in this direction.

Delia runs out to meet the horse, into a field as empty as the moon, her arms waving to slow the frothing beast as he approaches. "Easy, boy, eaaaaaasy." The horse, gray and black like a wet river rock, slows to a trot and then stops, his sides under the saddle and blanket an accordion as he tries to catch his breath, teeth bared as he bites against the metal bit. "Ssssssshhhhh, you're a good lad, Bill, you're a good lad." Delia's voice sounds foreign, accented.

Reins in hand, she races to the slumped figure across Bill's back. "Udish, you're home now. Bill has brought you home to me. Open your eyes!"

"Udish?" I say to Alicia. "Her grandfather?"

Delia untethers the man's body and pulls him from the saddle, his limp form falling onto hers and pushing them both into the grass. She hurries from under him and shoves back the hood of his cloak.

The odor hits us at the same time, judging by how Delia jerks her head away. The man stinks, not just human odors from too long without a bath, but of rot and old blood. His cheeks, around his eyes, forehead, and chin are bloodied, bruised, cut. Deep cuts, oozing blood and whitish-green, malodorous fluid. One eye is swollen near shut, its bushy white eyebrow missing as if sliced from his head.

"Grandfather, open your eyes. It's Delia, you're home. I'm here. How can I fix you? Tell me what to do! Please!" Her hands move, search, pull a formidable pearl-handled knife from a sheath under her belt to cut through the thick muslin of his tunic to uncover even more injuries. She pauses when the fabric snags on a broken arrow shaft protruding out of his body just above his heart and below his shoulder. It oozes putrefaction.

My gag reflex tickles. I've never seen anything this bad on a human being.

"Dear gods, how can I fix this . . . ," Delia says.

I stand helpless, wishing I could do something. "Alicia, I

80

can fix him—I can fix him!" I drop next to the doomed man, pulling Alicia with me, the ground so solid under my legs and yet, when I touch the upper arm of Delia's beloved grandfather with my free hand, it slips right through.

"I want to help!" I scream at my ghostly companion.

Delia moves fast, slicing the tunic completely free from the ailing man's upper body.

The shock of the scene before us throws me back onto my butt.

Under infected scabs and the smear of rotten chewed plants from ineffectual attempts at a healing paste, someone has carved into the aged, olive-colored skin of his torso—an inverted triangle over a circle.

Like the seal on the letter.

Like Mr. Dmitri's tiepin.

"What the hell . . ." I clamber onto hands and knees to get a closer look, to be certain my eyes and the *pound-pound-pound* in my skull aren't playing with me.

"Who did this?" Delia growls.

The less swollen of the very old man's eyes flutters open and he smiles through cracked lips that bleed fresh against the strain, his teeth stained with grime. A single tear tracks a path down his dirty, weathered face. "Delia," he whispers.

"Yes, yes, Grandfather, it is Delia. Tell me who did this. Tell me how to fix you."

"He took it. They have it. My precious girl . . . It is lost." A shuddering breath ripples through his whole body, face grimacing and teeth gritting.

It is lost. In Delia's letter—*I reclaimed what he had lost, and now that I am gone, it must pass into your care.* Is this the "it" she spoke of?

I cannot peel my eyes from the shape gouged out of his skin.

"I don't care about that now—I'm going to get you into the tent. Tell me which plants—I must have what we need in the tent!" Delia scrambles for the saddle blanket. Udish groans with the back-and-forth as she positions him onto the thick woolen fabric. "I will pull you back inside, to the medicines—"

He grabs Delia's wrist, his knuckles whitening under the filth with the strength of his grip. "Go after it. You must . . . go after it. Or else he . . ." Another series of shudders, almost convulsive. When he coughs, blood bubbles against his flaking lips.

"Or else he what, Udish? Did Dagan do this to you? I will kill him!"

At once Delia jumps to her feet and throws back the flap of the saddlebag.

Her face falls and she leans her head against the horse, now grazing as if he didn't just deliver a dying man.

The immediate onset of a formidable dread—one I do not understand—tells me whatever was in that bag, and is now missing, was important.

But then the man's coughs pull Delia from the saddlebag. She drops to his side again and drags him onto her lap, whispering and rocking his body against her own.

"Help me fix you, Grandfather. Help me fix you," she sobs. But because I am powerless to help, and Delia seems so strangely unschooled in her plants' healing abilities, I know we will watch this man die. No one whose face and body leaks so much blood and rot can outrun Death when it is so near.

"It is yours now, my Delia. You . . . must find it. I will . . . come back to you."

"No. No. NO! Udish, don't you do this to me! Don't you leave me here alone without you!"

"You are never alone."

A final tremble and the man's chest eases, the air taking one final wheezy stroll out of his mouth.

"Great-grandfather Udish . . . ," I say, my own eyes clouded with tears as I look at Alicia. She nods, grief apparent in the slope of her luminescent shoulders, how her glow dims slightly.

Delia screams Udish's name as she rocks the dead man. "Please, no, come back to me. Please . . . let me fix you."

The electric waves of her sorrow buffet into me; I feel this death deeply, the scab ripped off my own recent loss.

Delia wails as blood and dirt leave woeful stains in her lovely green clothing.

And within a breath, the scene flickers and wavers as Alicia's familiar chill rushes through me, pulling me away from my mother and her dead grandfather. I'm on the ground, the sooty dirt and dry, sparse grasses of the vision replaced with the rain-soaked undergrowth of a typical Oregon January, my jeans wicking the cold and moisture, my head pounding ferociously, my rapid breath exiting in frenetic white plumes.

The big top and the red-capped barn that houses my elephants sit behind me.

Wherever I was, I'm back now.

The only thing that does not leave me is the feeling of endless sadness.

I look up when I see Alicia floating a few feet away, our connection now broken. Hiccups rock my throat and chest from crying so hard.

"Delia never told me that she knew Udish in real life. Was that real life? Not a vision of a heaven, but a real time and place, sometime in the past?"

Alicia bows her head; her silence is infuriating.

"But Delia . . . the same age as I knew her, and she and her fourth-great-grandfather. How could that be possible?" I stand and close the distance between us. If I could grab on to her arms and give her a solid shake, I would. "Alicia—was that real? Did those things really happen?"

The ghost nods slowly.

I clear my throat and wipe my tears on my damp sleeve. "That symbol . . . in his chest . . . it's the same as was on my mother's letter."

She closes her eyes and glows brighter for a long beat, as if her whole body answers me.

But what is it Udish lost? Delia's letter says she reclaimed it—and that once I find it, it will become my greatest treasure.

"She says I have to find whatever this thing is, but I don't have any idea *what* it could be. Can you not help me understand? Please? Showing me this vision, it's confused things even—"

Alicia jerks her head right, as if she's heard something. And then like a wisp of smoke, she's gone.

"Please . . . ," I whimper to nothing but the oppressive opaque clouds. And then, again sinking to my knees, I let the agony of my loss, of my mother's loss, of the confused questions this vision has brought carry me away, comforted only by the thought that wherever she is, if she is in the afterlife, I hope it is with her grandfather, and maybe that trusty horse Bill, tending the most magical greenhouse the heavens have ever seen.

9

I'VE BEEN OUT HERE FOR TOO LONG, JUDGING BY THE SUN'S FLIRTATION with the trees. The rain has stopped again but the pregnant clouds reflect an eerie orange glow. *Red sky at night, sailor's delight.* An owl hoots from its woodsy hiding place; a crow lands nearby in the grass, hopping in a safe circle around me, likely wondering why a fire-haired girl sits alone in his field.

It feels as if the bottom has dropped out of the world. The person I was when I woke up this morning—she's changed. This new version of me—she talks to ghosts? She has visions?

And how long was I "gone"? Did I really go somewhere else with Alicia? Was I catatonic, or did my body disappear? Is that why the crow watches me? Because I was here, then gone, then back again?

Most importantly, why did Alicia show me that scene? With only a nod, she confirmed it was real. But if it was indeed from my mother's past—even if it took place long before I was born—the vision looked so . . . medieval. Behind closed eyes, I comb through for details of modern day, a watch or a sneaker or a phone sticking out of someone's pocket. I'm no historian but the clothes on the commoners—those people were dressed far older than what one would find even a century ago—not to mention the glaring absence of what could be considered modern technology.

Delia was only thirty-seven when she died. That scene definitely wasn't from the last three decades, unless it was some elaborate medieval fair.

Old men don't die in empty fields at medieval fairs, though.

Udish said, "It is lost." Whatever he lost, it allegedly fit in a saddlebag, which means it might be an easy thing to hide in a trailer or safe. Delia wrote that she reclaimed whatever this mystery item is—suggesting it could be nearby.

And whatever "it" is, her letter says I'm to find it.

I don't know if I want anything to do with whatever "it" is.

I can't shake the images of Udish's chest . . . or my mother's face as she lay in the big top dying.

And why is Alicia here when I've never seen her before? Why did she show me that vision of Delia and Great-grandfather Udish?

I think of Delia's sad story about the little girl and the box of gold—or the box of whatever. That girl at least knew where to look for her mother's hidden prize. They'd talked about it. I doubt I'll find a cavern in a mountainside where Delia conveniently stashed her mythical box of mystery treasure.

Delia, why didn't you tell me everything when you were alive?

My head beats like a drummer has taken up residence, the swirling questions the cymbal crashes.

I hear a whistle—Baby stands outside the big top, at the edge of the field. I wave and pull my soaking wet self from the ground. As I trudge through the dead grass toward him, solar-powered lights around the walkways and outbuildings flicker on. I smell smoke from early campfires, likely stoked to fuel excited conversations to come once the sun pulls the covers over her head. I shiver harder thinking about the warmth of a crackling fire.

I'm surprised no one has come looking for me until now. Maybe they have. I forgot my phone in the trailer.

For whatever reason, I've been given a glimpse into my dead mother's life, and as uncomfortable as it was, I want to see more, especially if it's the only way silent Alicia can help me unravel the meaning in Delia's letter.

But why can I see Alicia? Where is Delia? Why hasn't she visited me? Will I see Udish? Has Delia sent Alicia in her stead? Is my mother suffering after death as she did during life?

My jaw aches from my chattering teeth. My hands are so frozen, my knuckles red and sore.

As I approach Baby, sleeves pushed high on his forearms, his face is preoccupied by the laundry list of worries he always carries with him. His eyes soften as he opens his arms and I walk into them. Without a word, he escorts me, protected and unseen, back to the Airstream that has been my home since birth.

Delia's letter and my phone are on the bench where I left them.

Baby clicks on the heater. I slide onto the kitchenette bench and clumsily tuck Delia's letter back into its envelope.

"I called you earlier—you didn't answer."

"Forgot my phone," I say.

"Try to remember to keep it on you." He opens Delia's cupboard, pulling out dry clothes. "You're soaked again. Throw on something warm and I'll send Cece over."

"Don't. Please. I have a raging headache. I want to . . . not think for a sec."

He pauses, then turns so he's resting against the countertop. "I saw you out in the field. You were there for a long time."

"I needed a few minutes."

"Figured as much."

"Did you happen to notice the shape on Mr. Dmitri's tiepin?"

"You were in the rain and muck for two hours thinking about a tiepin?"

"Just the shape of it . . . You seem like you don't like the guy."

Baby's jaw ticks, a brief flash of agreement in his eyes. "He's the boss. What's not to like."

"When I saw him, the New Year's Gala . . . it all came rushing back."

Baby sighs heavily and then moves to kneel in front of me. "The triggers will get fewer and further between—but don't fight it. Let the grief happen, okay? You're just one person, a kid, and you're not alone."

My hand against his cheek jolts him slightly. He takes them both and warms them between his palms.

"I have to tell you something."

He moves onto the bench across from me without releasing my hands.

"Her letter . . ." I give him the envelope, watching as he opens it and pulls free the parchment.

As he reads, his face loses color, the knob in his throat slowly shifting as he swallows. "No wonder you needed a minute."

"That's not all." I tell him about the ghost in the post office, how I now know that it's Alicia, about the vision in the field, how I saw Delia and watched her great-grandfather die in her arms even though it had to have been a *really* long time ago and I'm not sure how Delia knew her fourth-great-grandfather and she didn't even tell us that bit and this symbol has now shown up in three different places in the course of a single day.

I speak as fast as I can so he won't interrupt, careful to monitor his expression to make sure I'm not losing him, that my credibility isn't fading.

Pausing only to take a breath, I slide the letter from under his huge hands and reread certain lines out loud for his benefit. "'I reclaimed what he had lost, and now that I am gone, it must pass into your care.' Do you have any idea what 'it' is?"

Baby's lips thin into a stoic line.

"In the vision, whatever it was that Udish lost, it was a violent theft—you should've seen what was done to his chest. This symbol"—I slide the regrouped wax seal to the table's middle—"this shape was carved into his skin, Baby. It was horrible. But it's the same shape as on this wax seal *and* on Dmitri's tiepin. I asked Alicia if the symbol and my mom's letter were related, and she nodded *yes.*"

He remains quiet, eyes fixed on the letter, a deep V forming between his eyebrows.

"She says you're my Horatio. In the play, Horatio stands by Prince Hamlet, even when Hamlet seems to be losing his mind and everyone else turns on him. Hamlet and Horatio were best friends. Horatio was there for Hamlet, just like you were there for Delia," I say. "And Horatio knew Hamlet's secrets. You must know Delia's secrets."

I place my still-chilled fingers on his wrist. "She would want you to tell me."

"Are you okay? Did anything hurt you? In this—this vision?"

"No . . . wait, can shit hurt me in these visions? What if I have another one?"

"I only know what Delia went through when she had one of her episodes." He pulls a huge hand down his face, resting his chin against thumb and forefinger. "The letter— what she's talking about here—" He swallows hard. "I'm going to give you one piece of information, and that's all that's safe for now, until—I need to take care of something first. Now that I know . . ."

"Now that you know what?"

"That things are in motion. For you. To you. Alicia and the visions."

I feel like I'm waiting for the results of the most important test I've ever taken. Clammy hands, short of breath.

"Baby . . . please."

"She's talking about a book. An ancient, magical book. It's priceless, and dangerous. She's kept it hidden for years, but now that she's gone, it will pass on to you."

"Seriously? All of this cloak-and-dagger stuff for a book?"

He sighs and looks down. "I gave you one piece of information. That's all I'm sharing for now."

"No! I need more, Baby! Come on—ghosts and visions? Jesus, is the Etemmu next? You cannot leave me hanging like this. I have no idea what I'm dealing with!"

"Genevieve, I'm asking for your patience. I need to make one phone call. And then I will talk about this with you. Your safety, just like with your mom's, is my first priority."

But she died. You were supposed to keep her safe and she's dead. "Am I unsafe now?"

"No, no, everything will be fine, I promise," he says, resting his hand against my cheek. "But I want you to focus on the elephants, on Loxodonta, on looking into university classes—anything but this." He points at the letter. "And keep your head down. Stay out of trouble. No ripples in the pond, got it?"

"Until when? Can't you go make this call right now?"

He stands and zips up his jacket. "Keep the letter hidden. And don't talk to anyone else about this. Not Vi or Ash or anyone. Not a word."

And then he's out the door, moving up the pathway, his phone against his ear.

IO

DELIA'S STORY, ABOUT THE YOUNG GIRL—IS THIS WHAT SHE FOUND IN HER family's mountainside vault? An old book?

I'll bet she was disappointed. Gold seems far more useful.

As if more will be revealed by simply staring at the page, I flatten Delia's letter under my hands. What does a magical book even *do*?

The letter's conclusion—*the key to good is found in truth.* I pull her necklace from under my shirt and read the side of this old dumb key: *Vérité.*

Ha. "Like the truths you've told me here, Mom? How's that for irony." The heater clicks on and I jump, then chuckle at my skittish self.

Looking at the key in my palm, I remember that she has a locked wooden box hidden in a compartment in our shared clothing cupboard. It's worth a look. Otherwise, what am I supposed to do? Wait for another ghost to show up and drag me into some uncertain history? What if it hurts me next time?

My hands are sticky with nerves. It's a book. It cannot be *that* big—not if it fit in Udish's saddlebag. There are lots of places in here Delia may have been able to hide something that size—but will I know it when I see it?

Bookshelves first. Yeah, maybe too obvious for something "priceless and dangerous," but I can't not check. With every tome pulled off the shelf, I flip through the pages to see if anything unusual pops from the guts. Nothing. Books about plants, healing remedies, and Scottish Highlanders.

Next, I open the cupboard and toss Delia's clothes onto her bunk, trying to ignore the sweet, homey smell of my mother—lavender and her signature perfume and the rich, earthy scent of soil. With a hard swallow and a shake of my aching head, I ball my fist and give the paneling a solid bump. The edge pops up, revealing the rectangular cedar box that would nicely fit a pair of shoes. The key to it, ironically, is not hanging around my neck but rather nestled next to its imposter siblings on a fat key chain in the junk drawer. Dozens of tiny keys, and I have to try one after the other.

The lock clicks.

I hold my breath as I lift the lid, hoping that nothing flies out at me. Stranger things have happened today.

Inside, nothing but disappointment. Birth certificates, passports, a few rolled wads of money, a set of playing cards she drew and painted in arts and crafts during a prolonged hospital stay, one side featuring the faces of important people and places from her past, "some good, some bad," she'd said, the backsides decorated with renderings of the seeds of her favorite restorative plants.

But no book.

Though, if a man died over this magical treasure, Delia probably wouldn't hide it in a flimsy lockbox behind some eighth-inch paneling in a crappy mobile trailer.

Then where *would* she hide it?

I put the cards aside, shove the box back into the wall, and replace the wood and Delia's clothes. At least I know there's some cash in case I need it.

I look everywhere else a person could stash something: under our bunks, in all the cupboards, in the storage under the kitchenette benches, in the outside metal storage cabinet where we keep tire jacks, tarps, flares, and, apparently, a lot of rather large spider corpses.

No magical book hides in any of those spots.

I hop back inside, shivering in my still-wet clothes.

Head against the closed bathroom door, I feel like I could sleep for a month. But the elephants need dinner and I need a slobbery hug.

I stuff the letter back into its envelope again and stash it under my bunk's wooden support in an old shoebox full of memories of a childhood that feels foreign today. I pause and pull out a stack of photos from the box. Strangely enough, the one on top is of Delia and Baby standing solemnly next to a gravestone for some distant relative—Delia used to visit cemeteries whenever she could to pay her respects, even and especially to people she didn't know. An odd preoccupation, perhaps, to visit dead strangers, but she said it helped her appreciate what she had.

I laugh when I flip to the next photo. The Upside-Down

Clown Parade we did at a children's hospital in Los Angeles. Baby wasn't with us that day, instead working to set up the big top—but Delia had worn a full winged monarch butterfly costume as she floated around the wards. Ash and Violet and I—we were twelve that year—dressed up in head-to-toe clown garb, wowed the kids and staff with tumbling and acrobatics and silly pranks alongside our regular clowns, Toby and Dan. Ash tied balloon animals; Violet sang funny songs alongside my violin accompaniment; Delia made flowers grow before the kids' very eyes—a true magic trick.

We were all sore the next day from laughing so much.

Seeing the looks on those kids' faces? That was one of the best days ever. How lucky are we to live *this* life?

I kiss the photo and place the stack back into the box.

Clothes changed, I throw on boots and my warmest coat and head for the barn. I handled Alicia and the vision in the field okay, but I need normal and safe tonight. This whole day has greatly undermined my understanding of normal and safe. Within a breath, I'm awash with guilt for my occasional frustration regarding my mother's mental instabilities.

If today is even a taste of what she went through . . .

Seeing Alicia is one thing. She's friendly. After years of hearing my mother's stories, I feel like I know her. Sure, seeing a ghost is bizarre and unnerving, but so is stitching a broken femur back together with my hands.

Just please . . . tell me the Etemmu isn't going to pop up next.

As soon as I pull open the barn's exterior door and see the puff of hay falling over Houdini's back, the shadow of anxiety and fear dissolves. He trumpets once and spins around, charging the bars, his trunk reaching through for me.

"Hello, my little buddy . . ."

Gert growls and rumbles her greeting. If she could talk, I swear she'd beg me to take over Houdini duty. This kid has too much energy.

After the quota of hugs and tugs-o-war has been fulfilled, I excuse myself long enough to sneak into the cookhouse and grab food. Back in the barn, Houdini tries to steal my sandwich, but I have a pocketful of apples to keep him busy. My elephant plays fetch. Does yours?

I make the mistake of setting my paper plate down for two seconds, just enough time to pull my hammock from the tack box. "Houdini, no! That was mine!"

Good thing I was full.

Gert's trunk stretches toward her son. "Can I sleep in here with you tonight?" I ask. The meek breeze from a happily flapping ear and the weight of her trunk on my shoulder tells me I'm welcome, though Houdini ignores the dimming of lights and continues smacking me with a length of bamboo.

I settle into the hammock, pulling a heavy wool blanket over my fully clothed body. Houdini finally gives up pestering me, eats the bamboo, and snuffles under his mother, his trunk caressing the wrinkled skin of Gert's elbows like it's his built-in security blanket.

The scene of Udish lying in Delia's arms as he faded away plays again and again, the tragedy of his death made greater by the fact that it was evidently caused by a *thing*. He wasn't warring to save a village or the woman he loved—the evidence points to his murder resulting from paper and binding.

Yet he still had the strength to tell his granddaughter, *You are never alone.* Other people have said these very words to me in the last three weeks.

Despite the constant presence of my adopted family, human and beast alike, I've never felt more alone than I do right now.

II

BABY WAKES ME BY HOLDING A CUP OF STEAMING COFFEE UNDER MY NOSE.

"Rise and shine," he says.

I sip the brown nectar of awesome. "Thanks."

He leans against the bars. Houdini, not to be upstaged by coffee, throws hay at Baby's legs.

"Aahhh, you bad boy. Hang on." I toss aside the wool blanket and climb out of the hammock. "Houdini, scoot." I attempt to nudge him out of the way with my butt, but there is no nudging a five-hundred-pound baby elephant who is enamored with his own flailing trunk.

"What's on your agenda today?" Baby asks.

"Well, apparently I'm supposed to take care of elephants and Loxo business and not talk about hidden magical books."

"Genevieve, don't." He looks around nervously. "I gotta finish the big top. Start planting poles for the new midway. You got your phone?"

I pull it from my sweatshirt pocket. The pained look on his face makes me feel like a jerk.

"The new tent is nice," I offer.

"It's bigger."

"What about this crew?"

"They're all right. Robotic. But they listen."

"Makes it less stressful for you." I hug the coffee cup to my chest.

He pushes away from the enclosure bars. "I'll bring in hay. These bales are huge." He steps out of the enclosure without another word.

When he returns, a bale in gloved hands, he moves toward the tool closet just outside the pen. "You want help spreading?"

"I know how to use a rake."

He gives Gert a quick scratch. "I gotta go into town and get a load of concrete with a couple crew guys. I want you to look into university classes today, yeah? Take your mind off things. One of the guys said the new semester starts soon. I'll find you at lunch." Despite the grinding set of his jaw, he pats my head and steps out, disappearing through the barn's southern door.

Streams of early sunlight explode through the upper windows, dust motes dancing in celebration of a break in the gloom. Houdini trumpets.

"You want to go outside while I get breakfast?" I say.

I hit the green button, and like a puppy, he's at the sliding door, waiting to squeeze through. Gert sways, turning herself only to watch her son escape into the great outdoors.

"How's my Gertie?" I hug her, my head against her side. Stepping back, I see my reflection in her chestnut-brown eye. She bobs her head. "You sound hungry."

I step out to fetch their food but leave the enclosure bars open. Gert's a good girl. She might follow me to the kitchen, but new crew members drift through, and Gert won't tangle with strangers. At least they'd better *hope* she won't.

The farthest she'd go is to Othello's enclosure—when they were younger, she'd stand in front of his cage and I swear they were having a conversation none of us could hear. Othello came to us as a baby, so he's been hand-raised by humans. His parents, Andronicus and Hera, they were scary, despite the rescue by Cinzio and the loving care of Ted and his wranglers.

"Mornin', Othello," I say as I pass. He rubs against the bars long enough for me to give him a pet. He shakes his mane, dust scattering about his head in a halo. "Have you had breakfast? Are you hungry?" He bellows: *eeeeeeeeyouuuuuffffff.* "All right, hang on."

Our new kitchen's fancy. Stainless steel sinks and counters, a huge subzero jam-packed with the elephants' favorite eats—Chinese carrots, celery, sugar cane, cabbage and lettuce, mangoes, bananas, three varieties of apples, cobs of corn, industrial-sized tubs of herbivore pellets.

Through the swinging door, I run into a new face, sharp knife in hand, as he slices through very fresh meat. Dressed in the Triad getup, the white of his hair is pronounced against his black shirt.

"Good morning," he says. He washes his hand and offers a warm smile. "You must be Genevieve."

"The one and only."

"I'm Will Philips, the vet."

"Nice to meet you," I say, shaking his hand. I'm wearing old sweats, now dirtied with hay and elephant slobber, and I've got frizzed hair, fuzzy teeth. Quite the first impression.

"I've been hearing wonderful things about you. You're doing a remarkable job with your elephants."

"Thank you. That's high praise coming from a veterinarian."

He goes back to cutting Othello's breakfast. "Not sure if Ted mentioned it, but we did exams and blood work to check for parasites and other nasties—these things can be picked up along the road. Everything came back clear. It's very impressive."

"They're family," I say. I join him along the long counter-top to prepare the elephants' food.

"It's thrilling for me to be working with animals that have been so well cared for. It's obvious in how the elephants and the lion interact with people. Really something to witness."

"Have you always worked for Triad?"

"No, they recruited me. Spent the last few years down in Vegas, managing some of the big animals used in the shows, but the desert heat was too much for my West Coast blood. Plus the animals—let's just say not all of them get the same treatment as your beasts."

Over the next fifteen minutes, I learn that Dr. Philips has two sons, both of whom are in vet school—one at Washington State University, the other one at Purdue so he could follow his girlfriend who's in law school. Divorced, the good doctor loves his job. "Plus, what kid doesn't grow up wishing he could run away and join the circus?"

I laugh. "And now you have."

"And now I have." He washes the blood and meaty bits from his knives.

"It's so cool that both your kids are going to be veterinarians. Maybe I could pick your brain about vet school sometime."

"Absolutely. You thinking about applying?"

"Maybe. Pretty much would be my dream job."

"You'd get a glowing recommendation from me." His smile brightens his whole face. Best of all, he doesn't look at me with pitying eyes or say anything about my dead mother.

With Othello's breakfast finished, Dr. Philips pulls on a well-worn pair of leather work gloves.

"Oh, hey," I say, "in case Ted didn't warn you, when you or the other crew guys get near Gertrude, take off your gloves. She had mean handlers when she was young, and she frights when someone comes at her with work gloves on."

"Right-o. Ted filled us in the first night," he says. "These gloves are for Othello only. His food is bloodier."

With both our hands full, Dr. Philips elbows a half-dollar-sized button near the light switch. Poof! Magic! The kitchen door opens automatically. "Like John Hammond in *Jurassic Park*," Philips says, "they've spared no expense."

As we lug our bins out of the kitchen, a voice calls from our right, the bearer having just stepped through the barn's main entry doors. "Good morning." Lucian Dmitri waves, commanding in his black wool overcoat, his tall, lean body striding toward us. He's impeccably dressed—not a splatter of mud, not a wisp of hay. I feel even dowdier and dirtier as he approaches.

"Morning," Dr. Philips says, setting his bin down to offer his hand. Dmitri takes it and then leans over to peer into my bin.

"It is fascinating to me that animals as huge as your elephants subsist on a vegetarian diet," he says. "Pleasure to see you again, Genevieve."

"You too," I say. The bin is heavy against my legs, but I immediately look to his chest, to see if the overcoat is open to reveal his tie.

He's wearing the tiepin.

Across the barn, Othello paces back and forth along his enclosure, asking for his breakfast with a low-level roar.

Mr. Dmitri turns toward the lion. "I'm clearly interrupting the lad's meal," he says, his smile almost excited as he regards Othello, and then us. I suppose seeing such a fearsome beast up close might be exciting, even for a buttoned-up businessman.

"That's my cue," Dr. Philips says, excusing himself.

"Lions have been revered in many cultures throughout history," Lucian says. "The Mesopotamians regarded them as kings and used their image heavily in artwork and sculpture. The Romans used lions in gladiatorial matches and such, in the Colosseum. Seneca the Younger, a stoic, was one of the first detractors of using lions in sport. An activist before there were such things." He smirks. "I do love lions. Maybe don't tell the elephants." He winks at me.

I listen because my mother taught me to be polite, but I really want to know about the tiepin.

Just ask, Genevieve. Before he leaves. I might not see it again.

"If you don't mind, the symbol on your tiepin—does it mean something special?"

He looks down and nudges it with his knuckle. "It is allegedly an old magician's symbol, from back when magician meant 'healer.' A protection against evils."

Delia was a healer; she comes from a family of healers—and I am a healer. That could explain why she used the shape to seal her letter. Though it doesn't explain why it was carved in Udish's chest . . .

Or why it's securing Mr. Dmitri's eggplant-colored tie against errant breezes.

My mother's voice echoes in my head. *All those stories, about Udish and Alicia, about the old healers? They were only the beginning.*

But why would Lucian Dmitri, a businessman, have the same design? What does he know of healers? And what evils does he need protection from?

"It's superstition, really. It was given to me by a dear friend ages ago for luck. Why? Have you seen it before?" he asks, a pleasant smile on his lips.

I swallow. And lie. "No. No . . . it's just interesting."

His face grows serious. "Genevieve, pardon my intrusion, but—I felt lost when my parents passed. I was so young. I didn't know where to go, what to do." The sadness in his eyes is very real. I consider asking how they died, but it's none of my business.

"We want to do everything we can to make you feel welcome here. I'd be honored to help out in any way I can with your Loxodonta Project. And Cecelia tells me you're done with high school and two years of college already. Remarkable for someone your age."

"School's easier when there aren't twenty-five other kids to deal with."

"Certainly so. Eaglefern's private university is first-class, and Triad Partners has splendid scholarship programs you'd be more than qualified for. I'd be happy to talk to you about it more tonight at dinner."

"Dinner?"

"Perhaps Cecelia didn't tell you?" He smiles. "I'm hosting a get-acquainted dinner at our estate for your company of players, to properly introduce you to the Eaglefern community. Your aunt has all the details. It will be a privilege to welcome you into our home."

And then he reaches, as if to touch my face, and twists his hand next to my ear.

He presents me with a small purple iris, like he did yesterday in the mess tent with those two little girls and the lollipops.

"Ha! How'd you do that?"

He leans close enough to reveal he's wearing aftershave. "A magician never discloses the secret of the illusion. See you tonight, Genevieve." He winks and grins, moving past me toward Othello's enclosure.

Where did he get an iris, in January, in Oregon? And where did he hide it beforehand?

Cool trick. Ted has pulled quarters from behind my ear since I was old enough to walk, but a delicate purple flower?

And dinner—at their estate? Sounds fancier than

sweatpants and sneakers. Why hasn't anyone mentioned this yet?

I tuck the flower into my chest pocket—the baby will eat it otherwise—and return to the elephants, only to be greeted with a righteous mess. "Houdini, you turkey." He's back indoors and has pulled the folded hammock from the corner and tangled it in the bamboo. The floor's a muddle of hay and wilting veggies. I grab a couple of apples, and Houdini wraps his whiskered trunk around my head as he wrestles them free and bites down. Juice explodes under the crushing force of his teeth.

I wheel the dung cart and drag my rake and pitchfork into the enclosure. Elephant poop is heavy, and there's a lot of it. Within a half dozen scoops, I feel the burn. Spots that will become blisters sprout along my thumbs and palms. My calluses softened in the days off, and my muscles protest with even greater vigor when I drag the cart into the outer yard.

It's good to be doing something, although the vision from the field continues to run through my head—what exactly did Alicia want me to see? That my mother was a healer even back then? How old was the scene in the market-place? Two hundred years in the past? Three? Easily.

Which, in addition to the fact that Delia and her fourth-great-grandfather probably lived a hundred or more years apart, is impossible.

This makes exactly zero sense.

Raking dirty soil, that makes sense. It's tangible, stinky, and not three hundred years old.

With the yard clean, I turn to step back inside, but

Gertrude fills the doorway that separates the yard from the barn. She trumpets like she's been stung by a swarm of bees.

"Jesus, Gert!" With careful steps, I move toward her, then into the barn along the southern wall, hands in front of me so she can see I'm submitting. Something's spooked her.

She allows me entry past the open doorframe, but I stop a couple feet in and stuff my hands against my ears when she roars and trumpets with deafening force. "It's okay, you're okay, it's just me! Nothing's wrong . . ."

But she pivots quickly, in defensive position, ears wide, trunk raised and swinging. You wouldn't believe how fast a scared elephant can move.

The floor vibrates under my feet from her growls. I don't dare move. "Heyyyyyy . . . it's okay, Gertrude. Everything's all right."

She stomps, moving her bulk a quick half step forward, but her eyes are not on me, her head instead swinging toward the far northwest corner of the enclosure. She trumpets again, my ears ringing in the aftermath.

The light over the northwestern corner pops, light bulb shards raining into the hay. "Gert, you're a good girl—" But before the words are fully formed, the most god-awful smell hits me. I've experienced this nastiness once before—along a scorching Arizona highway while we fixed a flat tire next to a bloated coyote carcass still waiting for the maggots to slurp up its soupy insides. I throw my hand over my nose but the stench bleeds right through, filling my head.

Gertrude trumpets again, takes another charging step.

Moving my eyes from her is dangerous, but a bristled,

jointed, black-and-brown leg the length of my middle finger, followed by another and then six more, attached to a furry body the size of a respectable barn rat, pulls itself over the top of one of the silver food basins along the northern barred wall of the enclosure.

I clamp both hands over my mouth. If I scream—and I really want to fucking scream because oh my god that is the biggest spider I have ever seen outside a *National Geographic* documentary—Gertrude will lose her mind. I'm within strike range, and she's still multiple tons of wild animal.

I scoot as tight as I can against the wall, edging closer to the entrance, but the smell is making my eyes burn and Jesus, the first spider is not alone; two more, then three, smaller but still horrifying, clamber onto the food basin's edge, front legs raised like they're deciding where to land should they jump.

Oh. Oh no. This is not happening . . .

Alicia. The vision.

Stench. Spiders.

Etemmu.

I have to get out.

But before I can make my legs obey, Gert charges and there's no place to go and not enough time to think and her trunk grabs around my midsection and she slams me against the wall, pain exploding up my back, elbows, and head as I hit the painted cinder block wall. She quickly turns and positions herself in front of me as Othello looses his own series of hollers.

Gertrude's ears are fanned so wide I can't see around them, but my head is bursting with stars and I retch against the horrible reek and I have to get the hell out of this enclosure before Gert causes serious damage in her efforts to protect me.

As her ears flap back, forward, back again, I see it: a black shimmering in the far corner. Billowing, a nothingness that sucks all the light and air, like a thousand arms reaching out and then curling back into its core before reaching out again, over and over in a wildly grasping, gaping emptiness. I've never seen anything like it, not in the scariest movie or the darkest nightmare.

Gertrude trumpets again, another quick series of steps toward it, trunk swinging wildly.

The smell . . . *the smell* . . .

A huge hand grabs my sweatshirt, whips me out of the enclosure, and hits the red button that closes the main gate.

"No!" I yank away and press myself against the bars. Frantic, I scan the enclosure. All at once, it's gone. The stench, the spiders, the black maw in the corner. There is no evidence of anything unusual except me and a huge elephant flipping out.

Delia—is this what you saw? Is this your demon?

It has to be the Etemmu.

"Geni, what's going on?"

I push Baby away. I can't leave Gert and Houdini vulnerable to whatever's in there. She continues to posture, and when the baby tries to come into the building, she shoves him back out the door.

And I can't look away from the fresh layer of hay under the food basins, watching for the spiders.

I hold my breath, the taste of vomit fresh against the roof of my mouth.

The hay is still. No black-and-brown legs protruding from the straw. Nothing but shards from a broken light bulb.

Fear squeezes my chest. The back of my head feels super-heated where a goose egg rises under my hair.

"Baby . . . it's here."

12

"STAND RIGHT THERE. DON'T MOVE." BABY LOOKS AROUND THE BARN— seems the vet and the billionaire missed the action—but he waves off the few crew members who stand wide-eyed watching the elephant sway back and forth behind the bars.

Slowly, he steps into the enclosure, his hands and arms aloft so Gertrude can sniff him. When she calms enough to let him in, he makes quick work of sweeping up the broken glass and hosing down the floor.

With the elephants settled and the gate closed behind us, Baby cups the knot on my skull that *beat-beat-beats* like a tribal drum. "Well done. You need ice."

"It was here," I whisper, my eyes locked on the food basins. "The Etemmu. You should see this demon. No wonder Mom lost her shit."

When he nods, the gesture is like a mountain shrugging new-fallen snow off its rocky shoulders.

"Come on," he says, a heavy arm around my mid-back as he directs me out the southern door.

I feel sick, my steps heavy with foreboding.

First Alicia. Then the vision. Now this.

What does it want? *What does it want?*

I stop and bend over, hands on my knees. I can't catch my breath. And I can't get rid of the smell. *Delia, why didn't you tell me this could happen?*

"Gen . . ." Baby's hand weighs on my back. I stand and shrug him off.

"Is this about the book?" I stare hard at him, trying to read what secrets are hiding behind eyes the color of rich coffee. "Delia's words, just before she fell: 'No matter how hard you come at me, you will never find it.' The 'it' she yelled about—it's this book you won't tell me about? The Etemmu has something to do with it?"

Why won't he *answer* me?

If I just had this damn book, I could give it away or burn it, and the Etemmu could go haunt someone else. But where did she hide it? Would she have told Baby?

If I can find it, I can get rid of it.

Baby is silent as we stop at the work trailer for an ice pack. I wait outside; we both know, without saying it aloud, if Cecelia hears that I was injured in the barn, she'll make a federal case of it.

Through the open window, I hear her voice: "Why does she need an ice pack?" Baby reassures her everything is fine, that it's just a bump. A minute later, he's stepping down the creaky metal stairs, though he carries more than ice.

"What's this?" I ask. He hands me a clear plastic garment bag.

Cece is standing in the open doorway. "I was saving it for your birthday, but you should wear it tonight. I can't wait to see it on you. Green is so wonderful with your complexion."

I hold it up by the hanger. A lavish green cowl-neck dress with three-quarter sleeves. Looks vintage.

"Thanks, Cece. It's pretty," I say, my words lacking enthusiasm.

"Meet me in makeup at five, yeah? And I gave Baby your new contract—sign it and get it back to me ASAP." She blows me a kiss. "Oh—and there's a gift for you in your trailer. From Mr. Dmitri."

A gift. He mentioned at the barbeque he'd left a new violin with Cece. I'd forgotten about it.

"Come on," Baby says, turning me down the sawdust path.

As we head toward trailer row, a voice calls from behind us. "Hey, Ruby Red, those your new duds?" Ash says, pointing at the garment bag draped over my shoulder. Despite the rain, he's in his trademark sleeveless shirt, sculpted arms exposed.

Baby keeps walking, but Ash catches up. He flips away his too-long bangs and runs a hand over his tattoo, as if to remind himself that the Old World trapezist with the '20s-era moustache is still flying across his muscle toward the approaching bar.

"Green's good on you. Way better than Violet's dress. Seriously, it's like off one of those bad reality shows." She got a dress? Why didn't she tell me?

"What about you, Baby? Got a penguin suit?" Baby answers with a hiked eyebrow. "Some of the crew guys say

Dmitri's house makes the White House look like a shed." Ash's phone buzzes. "My fans await. See ya around, Red."

He turns to walk back toward the big top, but not before sharing one last gorgeous Ash smile. "Oh, and Genevieve—take a shower. You smell like elephant."

I flip him off—the only reason he doesn't smell like elephant is because his skin is suffocating under the layers of testosterone-laced body spray he rolls in every morning, like a dog rolling on a dead fish along the shoreline.

"I'll meet you inside," Baby says, handing me the ice pack and the file folder from Cece before disappearing into his own trailer.

Inside the Airstream, dress hung, folder tossed aside, I crack the pressure-activated ice pack and wince as it makes contact with the lump.

On the countertop next to Delia's plants sits a lustrous black violin-shaped case. An accompanying small card, the corner decorated with a purple iris, reads, "WISHING YOU ALL THE BEST. AFFECTIONATELY, LUCIAN AND HENRY DMITRI & THE TRIAD PARTNERS GROUP FAMILY."

With the hand not holding the ice, I snap the case locks. It's a gorgeous instrument. Maple body, a deep reddish brown. Brand-new, perfect, no scratches. Yeah, that won't last.

I won't admit it to anyone else, but not having a violin has been a good excuse to not face the reality of playing again—without Delia by my side.

The door opens, the entire silver bullet-shaped trailer shifting under Baby's weight. He's got something wrapped in a black plastic bag under his arm. "Nice violin. That from

Dmitri?" The tension in Baby's jaw when he mentions our new patron's name does not go unnoticed.

"What's your deal with him? Every time he's around, you look like you want to remove one of his kidneys."

"A human can survive with only one," he says. Then he points at the folder. "Sign that before Cece removes *my* kidneys. You were supposed to have signed it at the barbecue. Anyway, I've got something I want to show you."

I slide onto the bench and open the folder, pausing as I read: "Genevieve Jehanne Flannery, Aerialist, Violinist, Animal Caretaker, hereafter referred to as 'Performer.'"

Performer.

"We haven't really talked about what my role will be in the show."

"It will be whatever you feel comfortable and ready to do, bird," Baby says.

He points out where I'm supposed to sign—initial in two spots, a signature above the line where my name is printed in capital letters.

The Triad Partners Group line, the signature obviously printed by computer, has another name written under it: LUCIAN DAGAN DMITRI, President and CEO, Triad Partners Group Inc.

Dagan.

That name.

Why does that sound familiar?

I sign, my finger lingering over the auto-printed line.

Why do I know this name?

Dagan . . . Dagan . . .

Lucian Dagan Dmitri.

DAGAN snaps in my head like a rubber band against my forehead. "Holy shit." Dagan—the name Delia uttered in the vision yesterday, asking Udish, *Did Dagan do this to you?*

This is ridiculous. Impossible. The timing is impossible! No way. Dagan is just a name.

Except for that tiepin.

And the carving in Udish's chest.

If the man called Dagan was responsible for Udish's injuries and subsequent death, then he had to have been the one who took the book from the saddlebag.

But I don't even know when in history that event occurred. And how on earth could the circus's new investor be related to Delia and her strange past?

"Baby. Lucian Dmitri's middle name is Dagan." I point to where it's printed on the document. "In the vision yesterday, Delia asked Udish, 'Did Dagan do this to you?'"

Baby bites his lower lip but remains quiet.

Suddenly, everything becomes clearer. "Wait a second. Us landing in Eaglefern—this incredible venue, everything shiny and new for the failing circus—this is not a coincidence."

"I don't believe it is."

"You think Lucian Dmitri is involved?"

"I don't know. We need to be open to every possibility."

Reluctantly, I slide the document back into the folder, the name Dagan still on my lips. Baby pushes the folder aside and in its place, he sets the black plastic bag.

It's shaped like a book.

"Is this it?" I ask, scared he might say yes, and scared he might say no.

He shakes his head, and I realize I'm holding my breath. "It's where we're going to start." He nods toward the bag. Tentatively, I reach in and pull out a shoebox, decorated and colorful: Delia's.

I smile wide. "I remember making these." We spent a rainy afternoon in the trailer cutting out photos from old magazines and catalogs and then we glued our pictures onto shoeboxes. "Like the young girl in the woods, now you have a place for your treasures," Mom had said, her box plastered with plant life and her favorite quotes from literature and life written in her elegant calligraphy on slips of parchment.

I carried mine—decorated with elephants and violins—with me everywhere, tucking inside it trinkets and prizes that Violet and I collected during our travels, but after I left it on an uncovered picnic table overnight, the rain melted most of it, and my tears melted whatever soggy cardboard remained. I didn't bother to make another one. The "new" shoebox is decorated only with what its manufacturer left behind.

But Delia's box survived.

I'm so happy to see it again.

I open it. Slowly. Eyes wide. Knot in my throat. Unsure why I'm so nervous, especially because Baby said the magical book isn't in here.

Inside: remembrances of my childhood. Random coins from countries I've never been to. Keys that didn't make it onto the wall. A stack of unwritten postcards that look about a hundred years old. A baggie with a curl of my coppery hair, labeled, "Genevieve, 14 months." I laugh out loud when I pull out a tiny cotton bra with a wee little flower sewn to the front—Mom has labeled it with a hangtag, "G's first training bra." I can't believe she kept this.

As I pull out one item after another, a warmth of memory and happier times wraps around me.

The box holds a final piece along its bottom—looks like a magazine, facing down. I lift it, and nearly bite my tongue in surprise.

The cover photograph: a black-and-white shot of what looks like a very old, very thick book, its tired surface decorated with none other than the inverted triangle over the circle.

"This is where the symbol came from," I whisper, more to myself than Baby.

ANTIQUITY: Journal of Oddities and Ancient Times, First Edition, Quarter One, 1979. My heart pounds as I read the headline along the photo's bottom edge: *The AVRAKEDAVRA: Mesopotamian Fact or Fiction? Investigative Report by Andreas Schuyler, PhD.*

I crack the magazine open, the smell of dust and aged paper tickling my nose. Despite the publication's 1979 print date, a new-looking Post-it note hangs from the table of contents page: "Little bird . . . Collect the seeds. xoxo."

"Baby?" I look up at him, my eyes stinging as the last forty-eight hours rushes through my head.

He presses a finger against his lips and moves to a drawer under the counter's edge, drawing out a pad of paper and pencil, then scribbles something on the top piece and hands it to me: "Follow me."

13

I TUCK *ANTIQUITY* INTO MY SWEATSHIRT. BABY WAITS UNTIL I'VE STEPPED onto the concrete pad, locks the trailer, and gestures for me to follow him, away from trailer row and the big top.

We move out into the field, not far from where Alicia led me yesterday. It feels cold enough to snow, if not for the wind that has picked up, but that probably means another downpour is brewing. Oregon, you rain a lot.

When he sees me shiver, Baby removes his heavy work coat and drapes it around my shoulders. When he finally stops, he positions himself across from me, scanning the field as if he's expecting a predator to jump out of the distant thicket.

"Alicia, the vision, the incident in the barn today—the wheels have been set in motion. The book in that cover photograph, it's called the *AVRAKEDAVRA*. That particular one . . . belongs to your mother."

I pull out the magazine. "This is what she mentioned in the letter? The thing I'm supposed to find?"

"Yes."

"And you don't know where it is."

He pauses and runs a hand over his closely shaved head. "Delia never told me where she hid it. As much a part of this as I am, the book was always her responsibility, and hers alone.

"The talents you and your mother have—your mother's ability to see and talk to Alicia and Udish—everything stems from this book. Your mother's line, her family, have been custodians of this book since the days of Babylon— Mesopotamia—around a thousand years before Jesus."

I laugh, not because what he's saying is funny but because what he's saying sounds ridiculous.

"*A nighean,* please . . ."

He's pulling out the big guns. Calling me "daughter" in Gaelic. I drop the smirk and nod.

"Thank you." He continues. "So only three of these magical texts exist. Each book—*Life*, *Death*, and *Memory*—contains the unique spells that deal with that particular aspect of human existence. Udish, your fifth-great-grandfather, was one of the creators, alongside two contemporaries—men named Nutesh and Belshunu. They were something like doctors in their time, but their work was controversial because of the magical element—they kept what they did secret and filled the books with the spells they used to help people."

I open my mouth to ask the first of what will likely be a million questions but he puts a finger up, shakes his head slightly.

"As a descendant of Udish's line, Delia became one of

these 'doctors,' these secret practitioners. Which means you are too, based on heredity. The books give unique powers to the descendants—like your mom with her plants and you with your healing hands. Those gifts are apparently different for every individual family member—like how talents vary from one person to the next. One kid can draw, another kid can throw a football. Right?"

I nod again just as his phone buzzes in his pocket. He pulls it out and silences it without looking at the screen.

"There's a side effect of 'ownership'—in order to make sure the books are kept safe through the passage of time, the *AVRAKEDAVRA* grants the bearers long life."

I narrow my eyes, recalling the vision of Delia performing in the ages-old marketplace. "How long is long?"

He takes a beat before he answers, standing as tall as he can. "She lived six centuries, Genevieve."

I laugh, a burst from my mouth that echoes across the wide, empty field. "And here I was worried *I* was the crazy one."

Baby plants his hands, heavy on top of my shoulders. "You said you would listen."

I don't want to believe him, but Delia, her great-grandfather dying in her arms . . . "Fine." He releases me, and I take a step back, trying to maintain a straight face. "Delia was six hundred years old when she died."

"The *AVRAKEDAVRA* is very powerful."

"She looked pretty damn good for someone alive since—since when? The 1400s?" I laugh again. This is so bizarre. Seriously, if she was six hundred years old, I can't even do the math on how old Udish must've been if he was one of the original creators. My Babylonian history is a little rusty.

And what about her other family? Where are they if the descendants are granted long life? Delia never talked about her parents or any other relatives beyond occasional comments that the family suffered a lot of tragedy and she ended up on her own at a young age.

I shake my head. What does "young age" translate to in Delia years?

The only kin she ever really did talk about was Udish—and he was the sole dead family member she communed with, as far as I know.

"How did she blend in? Wouldn't people notice she wasn't aging?" I ask.

"The *AVRAKEDAVRA* families move around a lot. They change their identities, the histories they share with others," Baby says. He holds his arms up and looks around us. "*This* is the perfect life—the greatest thing about a circus is a person's ability to hide in plain sight."

"But *how*? How does a *book* allow human beings to live so long?"

His cheek tugs in a slight smile. "It's an ancient magic, Geni. I have no other explanation than that."

I cradle the scholarly journal on my outstretched palms, examining its cover. "It's sad, then, isn't it . . . a person living so long when no one else around you will. How much time did she spend alone, before you came along?"

He looks at me, square on, his brown eyes earnest. "We were together for a long while."

"Meaning . . ."

"I was born around the time Ben Franklin started playing with electricity."

"Baby, give me numbers. I suck at history."

He smiles softly. "Around 1750."

I do the math. "You're two hundred and sixty-seven years old?"

"Give or take."

"Then why weren't you in the vision?"

"I hadn't met her yet."

"But—your hands. You're not a healer."

"No. The *AVRAKEDAVRA*'s magic only gets passed on to direct descendants. When Delia reclaimed her family's book, she became a hunted woman. So she needed someone watching her back." He crosses his arms over his chest. "That was my job. Well . . . until I fell in love with her." He looks down at his feet. The pull of his lips is too sad to be a smile. "Then it became my whole life to make sure she was safe."

"But how did you come to be with her in the first place?" Baby has always been stoic and taciturn about his past. In fact, if what he's saying is true—if he is as old as he alleges, I know practically nothing about him. His mother died in childbirth; he had a rough childhood; he speaks fluent French but has no trace of an accent alluding to a life anywhere but on American soil, except when he's imitating Sister Margaret, that is.

Maybe Alicia showing up will finally get him to unpack some of his history.

"I've told you a little about life in the orphanage and

on the streets. Sister Margaret saw that I'd need a better life than what I was heading for. Being a huge half-black kid in a country that used African slaves as a cornerstone of their plantation empires? Dicey. Even with the Scottish surname from Sister Margaret—did you know Duncan means 'brown warrior'?"

I smile. "Fitting. I think I would've liked Sister Margaret."

"She was an amazing human. Strict as hell, though," he says, voice wistful.

"How did you end up in France?"

"I was born and raised in Paris. French slavers were responsible for the enslavement of more than a million Africans between the fifteenth and nineteenth centuries. My mother was among them. She was meant for Martinique but ended up in Nantes, and then Paris. She became pregnant with me under what were likely violent circumstances, and Sister Margaret cared for her until she died giving me life."

"Baby, I'm so sorry. You don't have to talk about this."

"Yeah, it's okay. Lotta years between there and here," he says. "Sister Margaret knew I'd be scooped up and sold, or worse, if she didn't find something better for me. I was street smart, and tough." He winks. "She taught me to read and write, and I had a head for numbers. I found myself in a little trouble—trouble that could've landed me in the hangman's noose—so Sister quickly and quietly arranged for me to work for a respected businessman named Nutesh. He'd provide the protection I needed, and I'd do whatever he needed doing."

"You were a hired thug?"

Baby chuckles. "Nutesh educated, clothed, and protected

me in a time when no one would. He trained me to be a warrior. He gave me a life I never would've seen on my own. I would've done anything for him. I still will do anything for him."

"Is he the phone call you had to make the other day." Baby nods. So someone more powerful is going to help us. That makes me feel a little better . . . "But how did Delia fit into this?" I ask.

"Nutesh—he's one of the book's original creators. Although Nutesh stood behind a French flag, it was for appearances only. He's Mesopotamian, and a very powerful magician. Udish's fourth-great-granddaughter required protection, so he offered the position to me. If I would agree to serve as her living talisman, I'd be granted long life. It wouldn't make much sense to swear a warrior who couldn't live as long as the person he was sworn to protect." His soft smile brightens an otherwise scary moment.

"Long life, in exchange for babysitting Delia."

He laughs lightly. "It seemed like a good trade."

"Any regrets?"

"Not a single one." The momentary brightness fades. "I've never loved another thing more than I loved her, and you. And I'll never forgive myself for letting her down." His eyes fog up and he looks away, hands on his hips like when he's trying to be manly.

"She loved you too, Baby. She died knowing she was loved."

He nods. Clears his throat.

"I did what I could to protect her. That goddamned

Etemmu; it was relentless. It was constant salt in a wound, terrorizing her like it was trying to wear her down enough that she'd break and give up where she'd hidden the book. I couldn't be with her all the time. We found a quiet rhythm together where we could still fulfill our sacred agreement but also have our own separate lives. A person needs that. But we were partners in everything," he says, sighing sadly.

"But . . . you're not my biological father. So you must've spent some time apart . . ."

His face darkens.

He turns and looks behind us, bypassing the question about my parentage, his boots squishing in the mud. "When the Etemmu got to her before I could intervene, that's when it was the worst. Because I'm just a sworn protector and not a blood relative, it can't hurt me—I'm not what it wants. It's only seen by people with your unique . . . skill set. Those of us on the outside can't see it. Same reason why I couldn't see your mother's friends."

I adjust Baby's coat on my shoulders, the wool growing heavy with the damp. As if the words coming out of his mouth weren't weight enough . . .

"As long as I could get to her in time, Nutesh's magic made it so I could shield her against the attack. If I could wrap myself around her, it would disappear. When I couldn't . . ." Baby shakes his head, and when a drop of rain hits my cheek, it feels like the clouds are mourning alongside him. "Every time she'd have to go to the hospital, a piece of me would die."

My heart flutters. "The people hunting Delia—the Etemmu is related to their hunt for her book?"

He nods.

"Nutesh isn't sure how the Etemmu was unleashed—this isn't magic only from the *AVRAKEDAVRA*. There are spells that deal with death and the spirits after death, but this demon is something darker. Nutesh thinks that whoever has summoned it may have somehow corrupted the magic of the usual spells, and he or she can't be working alone. It's beyond what even Nutesh knows how to deal with."

I shudder hard enough that Baby's coat slides from my shoulders. He shakes it off and repositions it over me. No matter. I can't stop shivering now.

It will come after me next.

"I think it killed her this time, Baby. That night—something slammed into her when she was on the lyra. It pushed her off. She didn't just fall."

His eyes harden as he stares at the ground. I know he's replaying the horror of the scene, again, just as I have a thousand times since. "It doesn't make sense—why would it change tactics now? After all these years? Why would it try to kill her when it's only terrorized her before?" he asks.

"You said three books, three families—so there are other descendants with the other two books?"

"Nutesh, he lives in France. He's got one. He's a close confidant of your mother's. Goes by the name Thibault Delacroix these days. He's a good man, a steadfast protector of the *AVRAKEDAVRA* and its followers. Your mother has another text, hidden somewhere. And the third belonged to Belshunu, the leader of the final family, but he's dead." Baby's jaw clenches like he's biting a boulder. "The location of Belshunu's text is, as yet, unconfirmed."

He positions himself so that I have no choice but to look up at his face. "Genevieve . . . it's a dangerous scenario if all three books fall into the hands of someone who doesn't respect their power. We can't let that happen, which is why finding your mother's book before someone else does is of utmost importance."

Magical books. Warring families. Mesopotamian demons out for blood.

I look at the journal again, rereading the word *AVRAKEDAVRA* and the article author's name: Andreas Schuyler, PhD. Some stranger who knows more about my secrets than I do.

I shove the magazine at Baby. "I don't want any part of this. There have to be other people who can fight over this and leave me the hell out of it." My eyes sting. Fear, frustration, anger. Delia should not have left me so unprepared. For all her harping about good and truth, she really dropped the ball.

He wraps his hands around my wrists, gently pushing the journal back toward me. "You have a responsibility to the book, and to your ancestors, to accept it now that Delia is gone." He looks to the sky for a second. "You can't not face this, Genevieve."

He puts an arm around my shaking shoulders. "Come on. Let's walk and talk. You're going to catch a cold."

I wish we could go inside. But given what Baby is sharing with me, I guess a small helping of paranoia isn't unexpected.

We move slowly eastward, in what will become a large circle of the field, the waterlogged ground slurping underfoot with each step. "What about other relatives?"

"You're the next in line. You are Delia's daughter." He looks around us again, lowering his voice. "When you were born, Nutesh—Thibault—he cloaked you in a magic that's protected you from the entities, human and otherwise, who meant your mother harm. You've been invisible to them. But the spell was anchored to Delia, so when she died, the spell died with her. That's why you're seeing Alicia now."

"And the Etemmu. In the barn today, everything she experienced—it was there. Why can't Nutesh redo the spell to keep me hidden?"

"If the Etemmu has made itself visible, it's too late. It knows you exist."

"Wonderful. That's just great." I wrap my arms tighter around myself, the magazine again tucked to my chest.

The carving in Udish's flesh—someone wanted his book badly enough that he or she tortured the old man—tortured him to death.

Did Dagan do this to you?

"The man, Dagan, who likely killed Udish—is he a descendant?"

"Yes. From Belshunu's line. One of his sons. He's been hunting these books for years."

Lucian Dagan Dmitri. No way. He can't be the same man.

He said he didn't know my mother. And as far as I know, he's a businessman, not a centuries-old healer.

Then again, almost everything I know of him comes from the internet. And just because he looks like a stately man in his fifties . . . if Delia was six centuries old, her grandfather older than that . . .

"Baby . . . could Dmitri be *the* Dagan?"

"I don't know yet. Nutesh lost track of Dagan a very long time ago—Nutesh himself would've been a fearsome adversary for Dagan or any of his followers. But Dagan is a gifted chameleon. Slippery, hard to track, countless aliases and disguised appearances over the centuries. This has made it next to impossible to figure out exactly who it is that's pursuing Delia's text so aggressively—if it's Dagan, one of his offspring, a zealous follower who's taken his name . . ." Baby kicks hard at a fist-sized rock, sending it flying.

"If Dmitri is *the* Dagan, he wants us to know. Why else drop that name on the legal paperwork? Why buy some tiny, obscure circus if not to get his hands on your mother?"

"But she's not even here now!" My throat tightens, equal parts anger and sorrow.

"No . . . but you are, Genevieve."

"What good am I? I don't know where the stupid thing is. And what does he want with it, anyway? Did he kill Udish to take it from my mother's family?" The world feels off-kilter. People don't commit murder over *books*.

"Geni—if we can prove who he is, we at least know where he is, and what we're up against. Nutesh has the resources to follow up on whatever questions we might uncover. Right

now, we need to focus—we have to find Delia's text and I gotta do whatever I can to keep you safe—"

I stop, surprised by an unexpected surge of anger. "Why are you mixed up in this? She's gone. You don't have to stay anymore. You can just go now and be free of all this insanity."

He cups my cheek with a warm, callused hand. "You are my daughter, even if not by blood, *a leannan*. There is no other choice for me. I will never abandon you."

I hug him as hard as I can with one arm holding the precious journal, relieved that he's not going to leave me to fend for myself.

Baby pushes me back, his hands like anchors. "I will help you find Delia's book. When we find it, you'll have to decide whether you want to continue to hide it and face what comes with that, or if you want to be rid of it."

Why didn't Delia get rid of it? "What happens if I keep it?"

"Long life, for one thing. But you'll be responsible for its protection until you have someone to pass it along to, or until you decide to destroy it."

"Responsible for its protection, as in, I have to keep it away from whoever else wants it."

"Yes." Baby stands taller and rolls his shoulders, like a thunderhead preparing to sucker punch the lightning.

This book has caused my mother so much pain—and we, as a consequence, suffered alongside her. And yet it's a part of who she was . . . it feels almost disrespectful to destroy something she spent so much of her very long life protecting.

But I don't want that life. I don't want to be on the run for centuries because of a magic I don't understand.

"If we find it—"

"When we find it," Baby corrects, a finger under my chin.

"*When* we find it, what if I decide I don't want the life Delia had—that maybe I just want a normal life like everyone else?"

"If you decide to destroy the book, Nutesh will help us."

"Will it make the Etemmu go away?"

"Nutesh thinks that it will." But Baby looks to the side as he answers. Is he telling me the truth? "First, though, we have to find it."

The rain picks up. Baby resumes our walk, moving us back toward the encampment.

"I don't have any idea where to start looking." And just like that, all the silly things I spend my time worrying about—if Ash will pay attention to me, what music I'll play when we start up again, if I even want to perform without Delia—it all fades to inconsequential white noise. "This is totally mental."

"Yeah"—he exhales loudly—"I've had that conversation with myself a time or two."

"So . . . Delia was a cradle-robber, huh?"

Baby laughs under his breath, but it's full of sorrow. "She never let me forget it either."

Growing up, how did I not notice that my mother and surrogate father never changed? How the twins' mother spends good money on antiaging creams, or how Ted dyes his gray hair black, the perfect ringmaster's coif, or how Aunt Cece takes tons of supplements to "keep away the arthritis" that runs in her family.

If the book guarantees long life, and if Lucian Dmitri is Dagan, why does he look older than Baby does? Is there a way to stop the aging at a certain point? Was Delia in her thirties forever? Is Baby in his forties forever? Great-grandfather Udish looked like an old man in that vision, even without the damage to his body.

So does the aging happen, just at a much, much slower pace?

Baby points at the journal still hugged against my chest. "We thought that would be a good place to start, to help you understand. The article was written by a Mesopotamian scholar, Dr. Schuyler."

I hold the magazine before us. The cover date says 1979—in a *real*, non-*AVRAKEDAVRA* life, Delia would've only been a year old then. But if the long-life component is true, Delia would've been long out of diapers by then, so she must've been the one who showed the *AVRAKEDAVRA* to Dr. Schuyler—which means he knew her in real life.

Maybe he'll know something that will help us find the book.

"Is this guy still alive?"

"Only one way to find out."

"She wanted me to find him . . ."

Baby nods.

I look down at my feet, one squishy step in front of the other. This is an impossible situation. I don't want it. *I don't want anything to do with it.*

"What if I can't find her book? How do I know the Etemmu won't destroy me first?"

He crosses his arms over his chest, a mountain of warrior. "Not gonna happen. You're strong. Like your mother."

"Like my mother . . . Look how well that turned out for her," I say, my heart squeezing.

"Geni, beyond whatever magic she had in her hands, beyond the fits that made other people call her crazy—she was tough as nails, and the fiercest, most loyal friend I've ever had. The truest. She just happened to have this set of gifts"—he cradles my chilled left hand in his—"like you, like what you can do to heal people. Like what you do with those elephants."

"The elephants . . . that's not magic."

"But it is. You're the same special she was, Genevieve. It's who you are, the people you come from. It's because of this book. Until my dying breath, I will see that nothing happens to you." His voice gets quiet. "I failed her. I won't fail you."

As we reach the end of our walk around the field, he pats my back with the "good talk" gesture he uses when he's trying to control his emotions. My pace is slowed by the weight of the world on my shoulders. But his thorough scan of our surroundings unnerves me. I'd do the same, if I weren't afraid of what I might see.

"Now, a few ground rules: under absolutely no circumstances are you to do an internet search from here, the fairgrounds—not on a laptop or phone—for more information about this book."

"Okay."

"Keep the magazine hidden. Like I said before, don't talk to anyone about this."

"No one would believe me anyway."

"I want to know where you are at all times. No sneaking away, no hiding from everyone. Text me and tell me where you are if you decide to go into town or whatever. For the foreseeable future, we are joined at the hip."

"What's the next step?"

"I'll be in touch with Nutesh again. We can trust his counsel," Baby says. "We search for any clues your mom may have left us. And . . . we're going into the lion's lair tonight, so it might be interesting to have a look around, yeah? See if Lucian Dagan Dmitri has any plausible connection to the Dagan from Delia's past. Keep your eyes open for hints—photographs, artifacts, anything that might give us a clearer picture of who this man is, for real."

What a terrifying thought. The devil could be right here on the doorstep, in literal control of our everyday lives. And I'm going to snoop around his house?

"Right. But if we *can* prove who he is? What if he *is* Dagan?"

"We need to prove who he is so Nutesh can work to keep you safe while we bust our arses to find your mother's book. Then Nutesh and I will coordinate an exit strategy."

"Wait—no—I can't just leave. What about the elephants? What about Ted and Cece and everyone else?"

Baby holds my eyes with his. "Genevieve . . . if this is Dagan, I can't risk anything happening to you. The look on your face—I know what you're thinking—so we're going to take this one step at a time. Okay? You follow up with this Schuyler. Tonight, we keep our eyes peeled, see what we can see, and then regroup."

I stare up at Baby, inspecting the lines around his eyes

that tell the story of what he's seen, of who he was before he agreed to take on the job of a lifetime.

Two-hundred-and-some-odd years old?

"What?"

"You don't look a day over forty-two," I say.

"Good moisturizer." He snorts and ruffles my hair.

We walk the rest of the way in silence, chunks of the field's limp, dead grass brushing off our boots as we move down the damp sawdust pathway along trailer row. The smell of lunch floats toward us. My stomach growls, but going to the mess tent means conversations and distractions and both of those things are not what I want right this second.

Baby unlocks and holds open the Airstream door for me, following me inside where he clicks on the heater. My care-takers, always worried I'm going to freeze to death.

"I'll find you before we leave for dinner," he says. "Oh— and take a shower. You smell like elephant."

I shrug out of his coat and hand it over. "Here. Now you smell like elephant."

"Like that's anything new." He looks at his watch. "I'll bring you some lunch. Give you a little time to think without Violet talking your ear off."

"Thanks." I could use the quiet to prepare myself for the evening ahead.

I watch Baby go, hanging on to his words: *I failed her. I won't fail you.*

Horatio didn't fail Hamlet, and yet . . . Hamlet still ended up dead.

14

than whether I smell less like elephant. Like, how can people live to be multiple centuries old? Do I really believe that? Revisiting the vision of Delia with Udish makes a pretty strong argument. But Baby, an orphan-turned-fighter plucked off the mean streets of Paris, sworn to protect my mother for all these years? And yet I know for a fact he's not my father. He said that he and Delia still lived separate lives—did they break up for a while? Where did he go, and how did she survive without him? Was he angry when they did get back together and he discovered she was pregnant with me?

Oh, Delia. So many secrets.

Right now, though, I'm more concerned about Baby's use of the words "exit strategy"—does he really think we'll have to run for our lives if Lucian Dmitri proves to be *the* Dagan? If Dagan is responsible for Udish's death, then certainly he's killed before in pursuit of this book.

The book is the one common factor in the deaths of Udish and Delia.

And if the Etemmu is some unfamiliar dark magic beyond the scope of the *AVRAKEDAVRA*, won't it find me anywhere, like it found Delia?

My mind is already tired. I have to tackle one demon at a time, or better yet, find this book before the demon tackles me.

When I emerge from the tiny steaming bathroom, a plate sits on the table. Peeling the foil back reveals a sandwich and a bruised banana—and a stack of oven-fresh oatmeal chocolate chip delights. *Good man, Baby.*

I open the journal and nibble on the cookies, though I soon realize that Andreas Schuyler, PhD, is way smarter than I am.

Thankfully, the bits I do understand correlate with what Baby told me. It seems all of this madness started in Nineveh, an ancient Mesopotamian city on the Tigris River. The spells in the *AVRAKEDAVRA* were used by a secret group of medical practitioners (so, Great-grandfather Udish and Nutesh and Belshunu) in at least the fourth century BCE, if not earlier, to help people across all aspects of our "very human existence."

Which meant Udish must've been about two thousand years old, plus or minus, when he died in that field.

This is insane.

Despite Baby's warning, I search "Andreas Schuyler," which brings up a surprising number of hits. One Schuyler invented a platform tennis paddle in 1981; two others were named in obituaries. And then I find him: former university professor of ancient religions and antiquities, specialty in ancient societies and theological literature. University of Groningen in the Netherlands, University of Paris, on to NYU, last at University of Washington.

Whatever he knows about the *AVRAKEDAVRA*—if he has information regarding the book's whereabouts—could save us time. We find the book, Baby calls Nutesh, and then we can leave. After that, Nutesh can do whatever has to be done with the book so the Etemmu can haunt someone else.

"So, University of Washington is where we start this adventure," I say to myself. I pull up the UW website, a blip of excitement surging through me when the faculty directory includes him, quickly followed by a deflated sigh when I see the letters "Ret." after his name and no office number listed.

Well, if he's retired, and he's not dead—I haven't come across an obituary that could be his—then maybe someone at the university will be able to help me track him down.

A quick knock sounds on the trailer door, followed by Cecelia bounding up the stairs and inside. I quickly stuff *ANTIQUITY* behind my back as she's turned away to click the door closed.

"I was coming to see if you needed help with your hair before we head to makeup." Cecelia lifts the foil haphazardly draped over my lunch plate. "You were supposed to eat that."

"I ate."

"I saw the stack of cookies he brought you. You could've at least eaten the banana." She rewraps the plate and moves to the green dress hanging on the back of the bathroom door. "Did you try it on?"

"No—sorry. I'm sure it'll be great, though. Thanks, Cece."

"Well, come on, then. Let's go get you ready for your close-up. Bring your outfit and anything you'll need to go with. Do you have Delia's pearls? Those always look so lovely . . ."

"It's not even five yet." Why do we have to get ready so early? I don't want to wear my mom's pearls. Her key necklace will be fine.

And I really want to call the university.

"Five minutes, yeah? I'm just looking online for music. I need some new stuff to play."

"Violin's nice, isn't it?" She nods at the case still sitting on the counter. "I sneaked a peek earlier before I brought it over."

"It's beautiful. Very generous of Mr. Dmitri." *Mr. Dmitri, who could be the same man who murdered my fifth-great-grandfather.*

"Five minutes, or I'm sending Othello in for you." She always says that, and it always makes me smile as I think of what a lion-sized house cat would look like curled up on my bunk.

As soon as Cece is gone, I dial the number for UW.

The woman who answers sounds frazzled.

"Yes, hello. Hi. I need an office number for Dr. Andreas Schuyler."

Keyboard strokes tick through the line. Then the other end goes quiet, leaving me with nothing but the echo of my rabbit's heart bounding in my eardrums. "Hello?" I say, hoping we haven't been disconnected.

"Please hold," she says, and the line clicks. I wait, the cheesy hold music playing some terrible cover of a recent pop song before it cuts off and she's back. "Thank you for waiting. I am unable to give out contact information for retired faculty."

"Is there any way you can get a message to him?"

"I can take your name and number and pass it along. However, I can't promise that he'll either receive the message or respond to it."

"Okay, thank you." I leave her with my name and cell phone number, fingers crossed that wherever Dr. Andreas Schuyler is, he will indeed collect his messages. *And* call me back.

"Oh, before you go, can you add a word to the bottom of the message for me?"

The woman exhales her frustration. "A word?"

"Yes. It's spelled E-T-E-M-M-U."

She spells it back to me. "Anything else?"

"No, that's it. Thank you. Have a nice—"

She hangs up.

All that anxiety, all to leave a message for a stranger who is probably too old to remember his own name.

For the hell of it, I look up "Dagan." I'm oddly relieved when Lucian's face doesn't come up. There's an entry for an Irish bishop, an Israeli military director, and a village in Iran.

As well as a Mesopotamian god.

This doesn't necessarily prove anything, though. Maybe the name *Dagan* really is nothing more than coincidence, simply an old name his parents gave him because they liked how it sounded. I'm named after two French saints, but not because they're long-dead family members.

From under my bunk, I pull out the letter from Delia's treasure box, wanting to read it with fresh eyes after what Baby's shared with me. The afternoon's revelations have given me a lot to think about—and a greater understanding of what my mother dealt with her whole life.

I'd put Delia's homemade playing cards in with this stuff—seemed more appropriate in this box than with the passports and money. I pick up the bundle and hold it against my face. I can still smell her. When I pull the band around the deck, the old rubber snaps and crumbles into a dusty pile.

Every card is different, except for the decorative English ivy twisting around each card's edges. The detail she's drawn onto the cards' backsides: the tiny lavender seeds that look like fleas, the BB-sized, brown-black sage seeds, the translucent, asymmetrical pouches of aloe seeds, the greenish dill seed with its lighter-colored edges, all drawn as if studied under a magnifying glass while her hand transcribed what her eyes saw.

I lay the cards out next to one another, hearing my mom in my head as she tells me the stories that go with the character images I've seen dozens of times—Delia's renderings of healers and friends and places allegedly from her past. One card I now recognize to be Alicia, her gauzy gown, the dark-blond, almost brown hair floating around her like a halo; Baby and his tattoos; a sturdy man, a mess of dark curls on his head, knife in one hand, a bloodied palm on the other; the nameless distant relations, men and women, who had healing gifts of every shape and size—one who could heal only animals, another who could find safe sources of water, yet another who could absorb a person's physical pain simply through a touch; the young girl and her mother the apothecary; a purplish-blue iris on a white background, the top framed by a blood-red banner that runs from corner to corner, unfamiliar golden script etched into the banner's fabric; the places Delia visited in her travels before I was born, castles and beautiful estates, dank dungeons, the Seine River in Paris, the field that looks so similar to where Udish died, mountain ranges as high as the heavens, a heavily forested graveyard, an ancient pyramid-like structure called a ziggurat, even Haystack Rock . . .

I hold my breath when my fingertip lands on the card of swarming blackness. She told me it was the Etemmu. Through a child's eyes, it looks like nothing more than an angry smear of black ink. Now I know better.

In the bottom row of cards sit the robed healers, the Keeper of Life, Keeper of Death, Keeper of Memory—

Wait.

Life. Death. Memory.

Of course! These are the men who created the *AVRAKEDAVRA*! One by one, I pick up the cards, study their roughly drawn faces. Great-grandfather Udish, Nutesh, Belshunu. All this time, they've been within my grasp.

As I stare at these cards, Delia's stories whisper in my head—the one thing many of these people had in common is that they lived and died under terrible circumstances, always in protection of their families.

145

I know now they were trying to protect a lot more than that.

I rebundle the cards and stash them and the letter away. Trailer locked up, dress and heels over my shoulder, I'm crunching along the sawdust path that snakes through trailer row when the afternoon's confessions settle heavily upon me. I check my surroundings, looking over my shoulder more than once as I near the parking lot's edge.

It's the creepiest feeling, that something is watching you, even creepier when you know exactly what that something could be, and what it could do to you.

And you're powerless to stop it.

15

IN FRONT OF A WIDE, WELL-LIT MAKEUP TRAILER MIRROR, CECE TSKS THE lump Gertrude's protective toss left on the back of my head. My adopted aunt tames my hair, and then we take turns playing makeup artist. The dress sleeves are a bit short given the season, so Cece brings me a brightly embroidered black silk opera jacket from her closet. She says I look straight out of an Audrey Hepburn movie.

As we descend the makeup trailer stairs, Baby is walking toward us from trailer row, looking more handsome than ever in a black tux and white tie.

"No. Way."

"What? Don't you like my penguin suit?"

I slow clap as he does a show-offy turn. "I didn't know they made tuxedos for mountains."

"And as for you, *ma petite oiseau*, good thing I'm going tonight. Might need to run back to the trailer and grab some heat." His eyebrow quirks playfully.

"Doesn't she look great?" Cecelia beams.

"The moon will implode with jealousy."

She turns to me. "You'll be okay while I get dressed?"

"We'll walk to the cars," Baby says.

"They're *here*? Already?" Cece hustles off toward her motorhome.

"Is all this really necessary?" I gesture to our fancy clothes.

His smile warms the chill of dusk. "Big fish, little pond, seeing who can swim fastest."

"What if they're barracudas?" I say.

Baby laughs. "I don't think these local fish will have much bite."

"That remains to be seen," I say quietly.

Raindrops ping off the barn's metal roof as we pass by, and Baby opens the black umbrella folded at his side. Looking up at him, I spy a cut under his chin. He's nicked himself shaving.

"Stop," I say, handing him the black beaded handbag Cecelia loaned me. I glance around to be sure we're alone. "Hold still." With something so small, it only takes a second: close my eyes, find the star, grab some light, rub a finger over the wound.

Poof. Sealed.

I blink away the twinklies in my peripheral vision, the job small enough to leave my stomach unaffected.

"You're handy to have around in a pinch," Baby says as he returns my bag.

"Couldn't have you bleeding on that fine, starched white

collar, now could we? What would the upper crust think of such brutishness?"

He chuckles, looking behind us as we move along the path at the barn's eastern side.

I stop him and he centers the umbrella over us. "I called the University of Washington. Dr. Schuyler—that's where he last taught. I'm hoping he knows more about the book than he wrote in the journal. More than anything, though, I want to know if it was Delia who brought it to him when he photographed it and if he has any idea where it is now."

"Did you talk to him?"

"I had to leave a message with the switchboard. He's retired. Gotta be older than dirt."

"Watch it—1979 wasn't *that* long ago."

At the far side of the barn, opposite where we're standing, the Jónás family moves up the pathway. Violet's dress—an explosion of pink so poufy her father has to walk a half step behind, her delicate hand cradled in his so she can keep her balance. Ash wasn't exaggerating.

"You know what dawned on me today? All those keys in our trailer. Each one was probably from some place or time in her life. I'll bet if she were here to tell us the whole story, every crappy key would have an amazing adventure behind it."

"Some of them do," he says quietly.

Baby runs the back of his fingers against his newly sealed cut, eyes distant. He offers his arm and I link mine through it again, my hand dwarfed atop his forearm as we walk toward the parking lot where waiting Town Cars are lined up behind the outbuildings.

"The *AVRAKEDAVRA*—these men who created it—they specialized in healing, but they also had magical abilities they had to keep absolutely secret. You know how the world treats people who are different . . ." Yes. Yes, I do know this. "They were well-versed in natural medicines and the healing properties of plants, trees, and animals. Followers would seek their help for everything from sick children to weak fishing to failing crops. The creators were trusted because they kept their people healthy and safe. They set out to make the world a better place, to heal and help. Like your mom. And you, if you decide that's what you want."

"And if I decide it's not?"

"You'll still do what's right. You have a good heart."

"Thanks, Baby."

He nudges against me.

"Genevieve!" Violet calls and waves. I offer her a thumbs-up about the dress.

"Geni, wait—" Baby stops me. He moves the umbrella so that it blocks the view of the people moving toward us. "The vision you had with Alicia—if you have another, you come find me. No matter what time of the day—find me."

"I'm not afraid. Not now. I want to see more. Maybe these visions will help us."

"Have you seen Alicia again? Since yesterday?"

I shake my head no. I wish she'd come back, though.

"Did you feel in danger during the vision in the field?"

"It was a little painful at first. Alicia basically pulled me through and her touch is so cold, it burns, but it's not the Etemmu. It's nothing like what I smelled or saw in the barn. I don't think Alicia would hurt—"

"What are you two Chatty Cathies doing over here? Sheesh!" Violet says, pushing Baby's umbrella out of the way. "Oh—I'm sorry. Did I interrupt?"

Baby holds the umbrella over Vi and me. "You look lovely tonight, Miss Jónás," he says, at once smooth as silk. She does, too—like a ball-bound Cinderella, blond hair stacked high, the pile studded with tiny white pearls.

She twirls. "I do, don't I? Look! Rhinestones on the tulle." She lifts the top layer of pink to expose the sparkling netted underskirt.

And just like that, Baby and I are done talking.

Violet pulls me toward the cars. "I love your dress, Gen. You look like an old-time movie star," she says, locking our arms tighter, a complicated maneuver considering the ratio of tulle to open space left on the planet.

Violet's lips don't stop moving as we walk closer to her waiting family. Aleksandar Jónás looks dashing in a black suit, Katia equally glamorous in an understated blue floor-length, mermaid-style satin dress. But when my eyes land on Ash, the butterflies that live under my sternum put on their dancing shoes and *tap tap tap* a new beat that somehow makes me forget how to form words.

"I knew the green would be good on you." Ash stands next to the shining ebony Town Cars, arms crossed against the gray pinstripe suit hugging all the right angles, white shirt with a dark blue tie, his usually mussed brown hair clean-cut and styled.

I like how it feels to have Ash see me dressed up. Baby's shoulders stiffen the longer Ash's eyes linger.

Drivers in all black wait to open doors. I can't believe they sent Town Cars.

"Holy smokers," Vi says, pointing. Cecelia hurries toward an open car, her crimson gown accentuating her curvy figure; Ted, handsome in a three-button tux, is shaved, his hair combed, and once again black. Too bad—he was sort of rockin' those gray roots.

I don't remember seeing everyone so dressed up in anything other than performance wear.

"You girls are a sight to behold," Cecelia says. Ash offers his hand to help me into our car after Cecelia, but Baby butts in.

"Find another car, son."

Ash pauses, and when he realizes Baby is serious, he stomps off to join his family in their car.

"Really?" I say.

"I was a teenage boy once," Baby says.

"Chasing milkmaids across France, were you?" I whisper. Baby snorts.

And I'm sure Ash is having impure thoughts about me right this second. As if. More likely, he's planning how to raid the open bar without his parents noticing.

I climb into the car after Cecelia; Ted and Baby slide in behind us. More than just Town Cars, these are proper limos.

Two soft, black leather bench seats, one facing the other, offer enough space for the four of us to fit comfortably. Tiny lights along the floor extinguish once the door closes, and a console slides out between Cecelia and me, complete with small bottles of frosty sparkling water and a stack of thin towels.

The pop of a foil wrapper is followed by aggressive chewing and the smell of peppermint Nicorette.

"Ted, you're not supposed to chew so many at once," Cecelia says. Ted's leg bounces on the ball of his foot. Why is he so nervous?

When Baby starts talking to Ted about the mix-up with the pole lengths for the midway canopies, I tune out. The frenetic energy coming off Ted enhances the jitters I'm already surfing on. We're going to Lucian Dagan Dmitri's house.

Did Dagan do this to you?

What if we find something in the house that proves Mr. Dmitri *is* the same Dagan? Will Baby excuse himself and call Nutesh the moment dessert is served? Then what? Will Nutesh or Thibault Delacroix or whatever his name is swoop in with the cavalry to save my future?

And what about Dmitri's handsome son? What might he know about any of this?

My underarms feel damp, though my hands are cold and clammy.

Treat tonight like a performance. That's all this is.

We head out of town, into a rural area edged with wide, sloping fields. Within twenty minutes, the car slows and turns into a drive, its opening flanked by massive stone pillars anchoring steel gates swung wide in anticipation of guests. Two huge letter *D*s twist in the elegant wrought iron at the gate tops.

D for Dmitri? Or for Dagan?

The cars move along a narrow lane, tires quiet on the smooth pavement. The largest house I've ever seen rises up before us, light spilling from the monster windows stretched across its expansive brick face.

Confirmed: the White House is now a shed.

One after another, the cars pull into place along a round-about; at its center is a fountain that could double as a pool, home to a collection of water-spouting sculptures. In front of the house, uniformed staff await our arrival. One man, his tuxedo immaculate, stands under a huge black umbrella being held by another's hand.

Lucian Dmitri.

My heart hiccups. *Are you the Dagan who tormented my mother and her grandfather?*

Violet pours out of the car ahead, her dress almost laughable in its circumference. Lucian's face is welcoming as he greets the Jónás family and kisses the gloved hands of Vi and Katia. Speaking of old movies . . .

We're next. Lucian stands outside the car, greeting Ted and Cece. Baby nods for me to go. "You first," I whisper. Then I can hide in his shadow. The bodice of my dress is suddenly too tight. I shouldn't have come. I should be with Gert and Houdini. This house is so big—I'm going to get lost if I go snooping around. This was a stupid idea.

But I'm here. Even if I don't yet know what I'm look-ing for. Anything to do with healers or the circle/inverted

triangle symbol or Mesopotamia or old books. Anything he might have had in common with Delia. As Baby said, artifacts, photos—one of Lucian Dmitri as a child in this century would be great as it could prove he's not the late Belshunu's centuries-old son. Or anything that might help Nutesh confirm that this *is* the slippery Dagan they've been looking for all these years.

My deep breath doesn't go deep enough—I feel corseted.

You hang three stories in the air, upside down, with a violin. You can do this, Genevieve.

Baby and Lucian shake hands, although I'm watching Baby and he definitely keeps his eyes on Lucian longer than maybe he otherwise would. When it's my turn, Baby doesn't budge, standing tall next to me. I'm grateful.

"Genevieve, good to see you again. What an enchanting gown," Mr. Dmitri says. When he offers a hand, I take it. "Thank you for joining us tonight." He leans close. "I trust you received the violin?" His eyes glint when he smiles.

I nod. "Thank you. It's beautiful."

"Excellent." Once the other cars are emptied, he takes a step back, inviting our party inside the towering carved doors. I survey his tuxedo quickly. No tiepin tonight, though a boutonniere—an iris, like the one he gave me earlier—adds a splash of tasteful color against the black.

We're greeted by dark-paneled walls adorned with art from every major period. Huge floral arrangements—more irises—decorate antique side tables in the expansive foyer and into the main hall. Music from a string quartet floats in from a softly lit sitting room to the left. Another room to the

right, lit by a roaring fireplace and a chandelier bigger than my trailer, is filled with new faces. The women sparkle, the firelight reflecting off gemstones around necks and wrists; the men look like advertisements for a clothier's catalog.

A handful of individuals stand apart from the rest. Their attire and glowing smiles tell me they're not Eaglefern elite. Ted and Cece introduce me to the handful of new performers I've yet to meet while Baby says hello to a few other folks he clearly already has been acquainted with. New people have been arriving every day, but not everyone is staying at the fairgrounds. I feel a little annoyed about being out of the loop, but if they're staying in town, we wouldn't have crossed paths yet anyway.

The stately rooms hold far more people—forty?—than I expected for an intimate, get-to-know-you dinner.

A girl with shimmering, straight black hair, heavy eye makeup, and wardrobe more appropriate to a depressed drama student than a formal dinner attendee stands at the edge of the group, a tight smile on her face as she makes acquaintances. Her sleeves are short; many woven bracelets running up both arms veil her skin. She turns her head and looks right at me, her eyes Arctic blue, like those belonging to a husky. She nods her head, though I'm not sure how to respond—do I know her?

"I was hoping you'd bring the elephants." I startle at the low voice so close to my ear. A quick whip around puts me face-to-face with Henry Dmitri, good-looking and tuxedoed and white-gloved, that stubborn curl at his part defying the

rest of his well-mannered hair. It makes him look younger than he probably is. My cheeks flush and a giddy fluttering ignites in my chest.

What a piece of work is man, Delia would say.

"Your pachyderms would be way more fun than this lot," Henry teases.

"They didn't fit in the limo."

"Pity. Though it's a wonder some of these blowhards fit in their limos." He grins and wiggles his eyebrows. "Can I get you a drink?"

I have to stay sharp tonight. "I don't really drink."

"Then you must be very thirsty." His eyes glint playfully. "We serve only a selection of nonalcoholic beverages in this establishment. My father is a stickler about liability."

Ha. Ash will be disappointed. "Then, yes, please."

As Henry strolls to the bar, situated against the wall adjacent to an ample doorway leading to yet another huge room, Violet, wide-eyed, stares at me from across the way. I gesture for her to come over but she appears stuck, smiling and bobbing her head, meeting people whose names she'll forget before their handshakes have finished.

I watch the girl in black, trying to place her. Have I seen her around the fairgrounds? Pretty sure I haven't. Is she a new performer?

I feel dumb standing there alone, staring at strangers and fidgeting with the beads on my purse. Just as I'm considering pulling out my phone to pretend to check for nonexistent messages or perhaps join Violet, Henry returns with bubbling drinks, a smile wide across his lips as he says hello to his father's VIP friends. This must be nothing more than a role for him. He seems so . . . practiced.

A tiny bell chimes. Servers in white shirts and black pants delicately herd us into the formal dining area, a seemingly endless, shining mahogany table adorned with more flower centerpieces and gleaming silverware reflecting like mirrors.

Lucian stands at the table head, smile fixed, the drapes on the towering windows behind him pulled aside to reveal the evening blackness. He waits as his guests find their spots, and I realize the seating is not random. Diners look for their calligraphed names on tiny place cards. The disdain on Violet's face is obvious when she realizes she's been placed between her brother and the depressed drama student.

As I watch, Violet navigates that bloated dress into a chair; Ash has to scoot over to make room. The girl in black stands and helps Vi, thrusting a tattooed hand as she introduces herself. She's striking, if not a little scary. Ash doesn't delay in sharing her greeting.

She must be a performer. A fortune-teller? Wire-walker? Maybe a trapezist. Would Aleks Jónás let Lucian add another to his Family Flyers?

And if I know Ash, that lingering handshake means he's thinking about more than what's for dinner.

I'm surprised when Henry swaps place cards with a gentleman a few chairs down. We'll now be table neighbors.

"You can thank me later." He pulls out my chair. "Mayor Gassy-Pants is a complete bore," he whispers close to my ear. It sends shivers down my arms.

Vi sees Henry sit, and her lips flatten into an annoyed pink line. Baby is seated to my left, three chairs from the table head. He leans behind and gives Henry the evil eye.

When Henry pulls his own chair forward, a subtle waft of cologne dances under my nose. He smells . . . delicious.

No. That's not what you're here for.

But sitting in this mansion with all these finely dressed people, I realize I am really in over my head. I don't reach for my water glass, afraid Henry will see my hand shake. There's no way I can sneak away to have a look around. This house is so damn big, I could wander for days and never find a single clue to Lucian's true identity. Anyone can be a collector of fine art or historical artifacts; it doesn't mean they're a thousand or more years old. Maybe the tiepin really was just a good-luck charm from a well-meaning friend, a fluke stemming from a shared interest in ancient history.

Lucian offers his welcome and explains the night's purpose—to introduce Eaglefern's latest attraction to the mayor and city council members, members of the Eaglefern Business Council, and the president of the local private university. Also at the table are two Triad executives from yesterday's lunch meeting. Baby was right: big fish, little pond.

Lucian then presents the guests of honor, performers from the Cinzio Traveling Players Company. When he gets to me, my cheeks ignite. Put me in front of a faceless circus audience, but don't call attention to me when I have no frilled costume to hide behind.

"Before I continue," he says, voice quieting reverently, "I'd like to toast a beautiful performer who could not be here tonight, an aerialist who sadly left us far too soon. To Delia: gone but not forgotten."

Crystal flutes hover in gloved and bejeweled hands.

My chest aches.

"To Delia," they repeat. I look up as Lucian gestures to me with his glass, his eyes lingering even as he takes a small sip. Baby squeezes my hand under the table.

And then Lucian moves on to the Jónáses, followed by the new performers who'll be joining the show: a husband-and-wife fire-eating, sword-swallowing duo; a former stock analyst turned herpetologist whose extensive menagerie will form a new sideshow; the Towering Turks, the team of tumblers from Istanbul who specialize in the Russian bar; and two contortionist/jugglers from China who are half of a troupe, their remaining partners awaiting work visas.

But the emo girl next to Vi—named Mara Dunn—she's not a fortune-teller or wire-walker or trapezist.

She's an aerialist specializing in *corde lisse* and silks. And she will be performing alongside me.

My pulse quickens. I eyeball Baby and lean forward to wordlessly question Cecelia and Ted—no one told me anything about a new girl taking my mother's place—but the look on their faces matches my surprise.

Baby leans over. "We just found out too. Take a deep breath."

I should get up. Storm out. No one even asked me what I wanted to do in the new incarnation of the show—they said there would be time to talk about it later—but it seems it's been decided for me.

Mara Dunn bobs her head and then looks right at me again, smiling politely—it feels like a challenge. Perfect teeth, button nose. I dare say if circus arts don't work out for her, she could head to the North Pole and audition to be an elf. Or maybe a sled dog.

When she breaks off and grins at Ash, I can almost see him sigh with lovesickness.

Barf.

I don't look away—she must feel it because she raises an eyebrow at me, followed by her glass, as if in a toast.

My water glass sits idle on the table.

I am not performing with her. She's not stepping into Delia's shoes already. "The body's not even cold," I mumble under my breath.

Soup bowls are delivered, followed soon after by the first course.

"One final note, and I promise to quiet down so you can enjoy your meal," Lucian says. "I'd like to make a special announcement. My son, Henry, will be part of our management team for this new venture in a work-study arrangement as he prepares for fall entry to Stanford. Triad is nothing if not concerned about the futures of our up-and-coming business minds."

The kid next to me is going to be my *boss*? No wonder he's so smiley.

While I've never been one to troll the circus crowds for romantic prospects, the twittery, nervous feeling I get when I look at Henry tells me that seeing him around the fairgrounds on a regular basis might be . . . nice. Which is terrible to admit. Because I'm not that girl who fawns over new people—especially new guys. In a year, I won't remember this kid's name. In a week, he'll only remember mine because he has to spell it right on my paycheck.

Although I'm pissed about Mara Dunn's slam-dance into my life, I smile into my napkin at the furrow in Ash's brow, the hints that having competition in the form of another handsome young man around displeases him, especially if said young man is acting in a supervisory role.

Aw, poor Ash.

This will be good for our flying Casanova.

The guests clap and return to their quiet chatter as Lucian sits.

I push the fresh spinach around my plate. Try to make it look as though I'm actually eating the tuna rather than maiming it. Watch the other diners so I can pick the right time to excuse myself.

Not yet. Not yet.

"What did that fish ever do to you?" Henry says, waving his hand over my plate. A twist of his wrist reveals a stem of small bluish-purple flowers between his fingers. Forget-me-nots. "For mademoiselle."

"Merci," I say. I don't see this variety in the flower arrangements. Irises. No forget-me-nots. His is a good trick.

I look across to Ash and am met with his glower.

I tuck the tiny flowers behind my ear and grin. Ash's eyes harden as he returns to his food.

"Does it match?" I ask Henry.

"Perfectly."

My eviscerated fish is removed as another course is passed around. Plates are cleared, more sparkling water offered. The string quartet's soft serenade is never too loud.

Everyone seems occupied in conversation.

I could maybe . . . have a look around.

No one would notice.

I'm afraid Henry will hear my thudding heart. I quietly wipe my hands on the cloth napkin and hope that I don't sweat enough to dampen the pits of my dress.

Now or never. I can hardly hear the din of conversation over the anxiety roar in my ears.

I crumple the napkin next to my plate. "Henry—where's the restroom?"

He twists in his chair and points. "Down the main hall. Past the piano room. Then first left. Third door on the right."

"Thanks. Be right back." I slip out, trying to remember the directions. *Past the piano room.* His piano has its own room?

I still have time to change my mind. I will just go the bathroom. And then back to the table. No harm done, right?

When I do find the bathroom, it's bigger than most apartments.

My nervous bladder insists that I test this very posh toilet while I'm here.

I wash up and check for accidental dress-tucked-in-panties action, and then lean against the counter and pull my phone out of my purse. As expected, no missed calls or texts. If it weren't so late, I'd call the switchboard again and leave another message for Schuyler.

You're delaying, Genevieve. Stop delaying.

A flash flickers in the corner of my eye, and her ethereal body appears in no more than a breath, floating near the door, brightening the bathroom as if a hundred candles were lit.

"Alicia!" I say. She smiles and stretches her hand to me. "Please. No vision. Not here, not tonight." I back away.

She nods her head yes, and gestures.

"Am I supposed to follow again?"

Another nod.

Tentatively, I move past her, the staticky chill tickling the already excited hairs on my half-bare arms. I turn the huge polished brass doorknob, opening the door carefully, not a hundred percent sure that the other side will still be the Dmitris' house.

It is. I thank her on an exhaled breath.

I look down the palatial hallway—left, right—no one's coming.

Alicia floats forward, to a door across the wide hallway, then points at another polished doorknob.

"Is there something in there you want me to see?"

Her head bobs yes.

I check the hall again. Still quiet. When I step closer, Alicia's hand hovers above the knob. Slowly, I move to it, her static electricity transferring to my wrist. I turn it.

"It's locked."

Like she did in the field, she grabs onto me; it's solid, as if a person were standing beside me, only a person with hands freshly carved from a block of dry ice. I try to flinch away from the biting cold but she holds on tight, and twists.

The knob gives, and the door clicks open.

"Useful trick," I say quietly. She releases me, and I step into an elaborate study, massive floor-to-ceiling bookshelves holding artifacts, vases, framed photographs. More like a museum. This is perfect. I try to move closer to the first set of packed shelves but Alicia floats ahead, beckoning me onward.

My heels sink into the plush, colorful Persian rug.

Alicia drifts into a smaller side room, and I follow. This space has no windows, again filled with bookshelves, though they're split in half by a mural—like a belt around the room's waist—comprised of painted panels. Each one portrays a different scene: a desert with hunched-over bodies looking lost under a relentless sun, writing that could be Hebrew scratched into the never-ending sandscape; a castle with flags on the keep, an angry sky in the background; a vast, churning ocean with tiny ships hurtled like toys among the waves; a portrait of a man in profile, his long, almost black hair tied with a ribbon and pulled to one side, draped over his purple-clad shoulder; a rider on horseback on one panel's left edge chasing after a woman in long dark skirts running across a wide field at twilight—

Her red hair like flames fanning behind her.

"*Delia?*" I whisper.

The final panel is a purplish-blue iris on a white background, a bloodred banner with gold lettering painted in the top third of the image.

I've seen this exact painting before.

In Delia's deck of playing cards.

I pull out my phone and take photos, as many as I can, of every panel of the mural, stopping only when Alicia inserts herself between my phone and the wall, reaching toward me again, the chill of her contact creating new shivers, her green eyes almost phosphorescent.

She encourages me to turn and then levitates in front of a glass case against the room's northernmost edge, lit overhead by a singular spot in the otherwise cave-like space. I was so taken by the mural, I didn't notice the case when we came in.

I step closer.

My breath freezes in my chest.

"Oh my god."

In the center of the glass case sits a chunky, very old book, its cover emblazoned with the inverted triangle overlying the circle.

It's an *AVRAKEDAVRA*.

I am instantly sick to my stomach, the revelations of the last few days whooshing past me so fast, I have to put a hand on the side of the glass case to keep my balance.

Only when I touch it, I snap my hand away. It's electrified.

"Alicia—is this Delia's book?"

Alicia shakes her head no. Even so, this book is a twin to the one on the front of *ANTIQUITY*. The one Schuyler wrote about so eloquently. Baby and Dr. Schuyler said there are three books.

Lucian Dmitri has one?

Maybe he's a collector of antique texts. Maybe? But combined with the tiepin and his name, the presence of another of the three *AVRAKEDAVRAs* in Lucian Dmitri's house seems clear proof that he's like Delia, like me, like Nutesh.

He must be Belshunu's son.

He must be the Dagan who stole Delia's book—and the man who killed Udish.

Oh shit, if that's true, it means he must also have gifts bestowed by the book—what the hell is Dagan capable of with his impeccably manicured hands?

I spin and look at the mural again, the panel with the fleeing woman.

It's no coincidence that Lucian has come into our lives now. Hundreds and hundreds of years ago, he killed to claim a second book.

Is that why Delia is dead? Has he killed again, trying to take back Delia's book?

No. Not Delia's book. *My* book.

But that doesn't make sense. Killing Delia didn't get him the text.

And Delia wasn't beaten or carved up—she fell.

Hands shaking, I take more photos, this time of the *AVRAKEDAVRA*, trying to get one where the tremor in my hand doesn't blur the picture.

I've got to get out of here. I have to show all of this to Baby so he can call Nutesh—

"Excuse me, what are you doing?"

16

HENRY DMITRI WATCHES ME FROM THE ANTEROOM'S DOORWAY. "YOU SERI-ously need to get out of here."

I shove past him, all at once realizing that Alicia is gone, but Henry grabs my arm before I can get all the way out of the study and I bump into a small side table next to a wing-back chair, toppling a stack of silver cups. A yellow ball rolls from one and bounces once on the lavish rug.

We both freeze at a voice in the hallway.

Henry beckons me forward. "Move!" He pushes me toward a louvered closet and *whoosh-clicks* the door behind us, his gloved finger pressed against his lips. As if he has to warn me to be quiet.

Through the door slats, we see Lucian stroll in, slowing at the open door, his expression darkening upon spying the tiny yellow ball on the floor. He drops to one knee, picks it up, and scans the room.

The closet smells of old books and dust. My nose tickles. *Please don't sneeze.*

The space is *very* small. My tightly crossed arms brush the navy-blue handkerchief in Henry's tuxedo jacket with every terrified breath.

Lucian pockets the ball plus several others taken from a crystal bowl on the desk, grabs the cups, and then disappears into the room that houses the encased book. Upon exiting, he triggers a hidden switch in the bookshelf next to the doorframe, and a pocket door slides solidly closed, blocking access to the anteroom. Lucian then strides toward the office's main door. It beeps as soon as it's closed.

Henry and I do not move for at least a million seconds. He scoots closer, his scent a mixture of cologne and young man, and angles his head to see as much of the room as possible through the louvered slats. It's uncomfortable, and exhilarating.

"Let's go." He unclicks the closet door. The room is indeed empty. Henry moves behind the imposing desk and points me toward the main door. "Grab the knob." I shuffle over and Henry counts down from three with his fingers, presses yet another concealed button. This room is full of secrets.

The door releases.

He joins me in the open frame and checks in both directions. "Come on." Door latched behind us, we take a few steps before he stops. "Wait. This is going to be too obvious. Come on, just in case."

He smiles conspiratorially and grabs my tingling, stress-chilled hand, his grip less demanding this time, and we sneak across the main foyer to the other side where the wide hall extends in the opposite direction.

Is he going to say anything about why I was in his father's office?

Surely Henry knows about the book in that electrified case—but does he *know* about it? The book's history and that it's connected to people who have incredible gifts? With all the signs pointing to Lucian being *the* Dagan, it's hard for me to not question young Henry's position in this—if his father truly is the bad guy in the narrative of my family's backstory, a man who has murdered before, how far does the apple fall from the tree?

The kid holding on to my hand doesn't look like he'd hurt a fly. But is he a friend? Enemy? Innocent bystander?

Blood is always thicker than water. Maybe Henry will wait until their fancy Town Cars have deposited us back at our humble trailers before telling Dear Daddy where he found me.

Maybe his job is to be nice to me so he can learn whatever he can about Delia and her book.

Just as my job is to learn whatever I can about Lucian Dagan Dmitri.

I cannot let on that I know more than what Henry sees on the surface. I'm nothing more than a dinner guest who took a wrong turn and ended up where she didn't belong.

I gotta play dumb and fish. See what the kid knows, what tidbits he's willing to part with, simply because he's unaware of what I know—that I'm ninety-nine percent sure his father is a butcher.

Henry stops in front of an expansive carved-stone mural that features two women, blank-eyed. Lucian Dmitri has a thing for murals. The first woman wears what could be a wreath of laurel, although close inspection might suggest it is her hair wrapped decoratively around her face and head; the second in profile, hair curled against the side of her head and framed with a crown-like band, a fierce-looking owl perched on her arm. Both women wear what can only be described as togas and overlying gowns—the sculptor's skill has given the stone cloth a graceful movement. Etchings in Latin script detail the background, shared with a sun and associated rays reaching toward the subjects.

My heart pounds so hard as I wait for him to speak first.

"Beautiful. Isn't it?" he says.

I stare at it. "Um, yes." I have no idea what I'm looking at.

Henry looks over the top of my head and then back at the art.

"This goddess is Roman—Minerva, goddess of wisdom, daughter of Jupiter. The Greeks called her Athena."

"I like her owl," I say, my voice weaker than I want it to be. *Wow. Super smart, Gen.* "Who's the other one?" Stronger this time.

"The Celtic goddess Sulis. She was worshipped at the hot springs in Roman England, in the city aptly named Bath. Actually, together, this whole piece is in worship to Sulis Minerva."

I step closer to it. "Is this a replica?"

"No. It's original. My father is an avid collector."

A collector. He collects antiquities.

Like the *AVRAKEDAVRA*? Maybe . . . maybe he's not anything more than a collector, then? Maybe his middle name is what piqued his interest in Mesopotamia?

No way. All evidence points to Lucian being Dagan—beyond just the name. The mural in his office, the *AVRAKEDAVRA* in the case, the fleeing red-haired woman . . .

He's after Delia. But she's gone. And now I'm seeing the Etemmu.

I could be in a hell of a lot of danger.

Genevieve, cast your line. I channel my inner performer to steady my voice. "Your father's collection is better than most museums I've visited."

"He says art is about the thrill of the chase."

"Then he must really love the chase," I say, looking directly at Henry.

"Have you visited a lot of museums? In your travels, I mean?" he asks. His smile widens, almost childlike. "I can't imagine how exciting it must be to stop at different cities every week."

"Don't you travel?"

"Sure. But it's by plane and always so proper and formal."

"Yeah. The circus isn't proper or formal." I give him a head-to-toe once-over. "You're going to fit right in."

"Are you teasing me?" He smirks.

I step closer to the wall, my nerves under control. "These drawings are amazing." Black-framed pen-and-inks hang around the mural's harsh-cut edges.

"Those are the surrounding structures. The hot springs and baths."

"The paper—it's in such good condition . . ."

"Oh, those aren't antiquities," he says. "I drew them."

"Wow . . ." I look closer at the drawings and back at Henry. "*You* drew those?"

"I can do more than smile and nod at my father's uppity friends."

The black-and-white scenes are etched with just enough interpretation that I know I'm looking at a drawing. Tall columns topped with ornate capitals, the stone stained by weather and the passing of centuries, perfectly symmetrical archways over worn pedestals of tired brick, the pool so real it looks like the picture is still wet.

"These are incredible."

"I needed something to do while my father was in meetings."

We move a few feet down the hall. Stop in front of a bronzed sculpture sitting on a polished tabletop. "I've seen this before. Rodin, right? I did a project on him for school one year."

"Yes. *The Kiss.* Well, my miniature version of it."

"This is the woman who had an affair with her husband's brother and then the husband caught them in the act and killed them?"

"Exactly. Francesca and Paolo. The story of this actual sculpture is pretty crazy—it was supposed to only be a relief done in bronze for doors on a French museum, but then the French government commissioned Rodin to do a larger-than-life piece in marble. I love his work, so I hope he doesn't mind that I copied it."

Henry moves closer to his sculpture. "The most tragic

part? Francesca's husband, Giovanni, discovered them at the moment of this kiss. He stabbed and killed them on the spot."

"Slightly morbid."

"But sadly romantic, wouldn't you say? It's powerful, what love will drive people to do." Henry blushes.

I lightly brush a fingertip over Paolo's bent knee as Henry steps ahead and gestures to one last piece, a huge book sitting open on a pedestal, a red silk bookmark dangling down the book's spine like a snake's tongue. "This, however—this is the *pièce de résistance.*"

I step closer. "Is that Latin? A bible?"

"My version of a Gutenberg Bible. Look closer. And then turn a page or two."

I do. Interspersed in Latin—a language I absolutely do not read—I find the words *Spider-Man, Batman, The Joker.* "Does that say . . . Superman?"

His eyes gleam. "Turn the page."

I do, and find the next two pages decorated with antiquity-quality drawings of childhood superheroes in full color and gold leaf, acting out scenes of biblical history.

"Who needs John the Baptist when you have Clark Kent?" Henry's devilish smile is contagious.

"Blasphemer," I tease.

"I'll take that as high praise. Just don't tell anyone I mixed up the comic worlds. DC Comics versus Marvel. There would be hell to pay from purists."

"The hell to pay from purists would probably come from remaking a *bible*," I say. "Why would you even think to make this? Did you handwrite all this text?"

"Nooooo. The Gutenberg Bible was the first movable type book printed in the West—you know, using individual blocks for each letter, which was actually invented in China in the eleventh century—but I didn't have years to get this done. It was an art project for school, so my pages were recreated in Photoshop and then printed via the wonder of the common laser printer."

"And the drawings?"

"Those are all mine. I made the cover from stiff paperboard, old leather, and some baubles from the craft shop, glued and stitched everything together, including my fingers—hot glue burns for a long time after it's peeled off flesh, I'll have you know—and *voilà*."

"Dude, I hope you got an A on this."

Henry grins and looks down at his feet for a beat. Humble—how refreshing.

"I can draw pretty much anything, but I like doing reproductions. It presents an interesting challenge. Copying someone else's work helps me understand my strengths and weaknesses, artistically speaking, as I develop my own style." He leans a little nearer, playfulness dancing off his face. "You should see what I can do with elbow macaroni."

The mural in his father's office—did he paint that? Does he know who the redheaded woman is? Does he know what the iris means? So many questions—but I don't want to reveal how much of that secret room I saw.

"Do you want to be an artist? As a profession?"

"Art is stuck in the hobby category for me, I'm afraid. Business school first. My father says I need to know how to sell what I make. I suppose he's right." Henry reaches into the inside pocket of his tux jacket and pulls out a small notepad and black pen. Turns to a new page. Scans my face. Flexes the bisected eyebrow and purses his lips together before uncapping the pen.

I watch his face as he draws, his lovely blue-green eyes seeing me but not seeing me as he scratches the pen tip across the paper. His tongue protrudes just slightly, boyishly, touching his top lip in concentration. A smudge of black ink mars his formal white gloves. Finally, the pen stops as Henry surveys his work. Appearing pleased, he tears out the page and offers it to me.

And there I am on the paper, as a wild-haired superhero, standing on top of an elephant, cape flapping behind me, violin in hand, a twinkle in heavily lashed eyes.

"Ha! How did you do this so fast?" I laugh. It's so great.

"When we have a bit of time"—his British accent strengthens and he stands tall and proper—"I'll make a spot of tea and give you the broad history of the world's greatest craft, the comic arts. It's my favorite medium, much to my father's chagrin."

I smile as the blush engulfs my face and neck. "I . . . will look very forward to that."

He takes the drawing back just long enough to sign his initials along the elephant's foot and then returns it.

"You're a leftie," I say.

"I am."

"Did you know that *left* is Latin for sinister?" I watch

his face carefully, as if something will be revealed by simply mentioning the word.

Nothing. He's adorable. And looks nothing like a keeper of nefarious secrets. Doesn't mean I'm going to pour my heart out just because a cute kid drew me a picture.

"Is that so?"

"Yes. So, FYI, when you're in the big top—because it sounds as though you might be spending a fair amount of time there—when you step into the ring, always go right foot first."

"Circus voodoo?"

"Something like that."

"Thank you, Miss Flannery, for preserving the safety of my circus mojo."

"I do what I can. Especially for left-handed newbies who make me into a superhero," I say.

He offers his arm and turns back toward the foyer, just in time for us to hear a sneeze moving down the western hallway where Lucian's office sits. Mara Dunn's ebony sheet of hair steers toward the bathroom. I snort.

"She does look rather scary. So much black around here . . ." Henry wiggles his fingers around his eyes.

"She's replacing my mother in the show."

Henry's quiet for a second. "They didn't tell you."

"First I heard was your father introducing her."

"Ouch."

"Whatever. I don't even know if I want to do the aerial act anymore."

We're back to the wide entrance of the dining room. He leans closer. "Remember, if anyone asks, you can comment on how lovely the *Sulis Minerva* is."

"Or I can tell them how you are a man of many talents," I say, flicking the cartoon between my fingers.

"No one would believe you."

As we stroll back to the table, I'm so relieved Henry didn't interrogate me about being in Lucian's private quarters. And his playfulness in the hallway—it's difficult to imagine him running to Lucian to tattle. Perhaps this architect of fake bibles is as naïve to the *AVRAKEDAVRA*'s hold on his father as I am.

Or perhaps he's not.

But if Henry Dmitri is interested in being friends, what reason do I have to say no?

Flies with honey, Delia would say. *Flies with honey.*

17

THE LOW HUM OF CONVERSATION AND THE *TINK* OF SILVERWARE ON FINE china greets us as we move back into the sprawling dining room. I concentrate on not looking guilty as I reach for my beaded handbag to tuck the drawing away, but Baby's eyebrow hikes up in a question as I sit.

"Hell of a bathroom break," he says quietly.

"Henry was showing me some fascinating artwork," I whisper back, staring at Baby intently. "Seems our hosts are *avid collectors* of rare antiquities. *Very* rare antiquities." I'm dying to show him the photos.

He holds my gaze for a moment and then looks away to lift the silver dome off the small plate sitting before him. A server places one in front of me, but I have no appetite for dessert, even chocolate mousse with whipped cream that looks more cloud than food. I'd like to press fast-forward on the evening and go home.

If Lucian is wise to the fact that Henry and I were where we shouldn't have been, he doesn't let on. Rather, he's standing at the head of the table, wowing everyone with the cups and balls from his study. Three silver cups, each the size of a shot glass, and the small colored balls tucked underneath slide around the flawless table under his agile hands. It's impossible to track the cup with the ball. Partygoers whoop every time he lifts the chosen cup and it's empty.

"In the days of my ancestors, as far back as Mesopotamia, magicians were regarded as healers. People sought their advice when illness struck. Kings and queens employed magicians in court; politicians relied on those in the magical realm before making decisions," he explains, pausing to present a red ball to his rapt audience.

The water I've sipped gets caught in my throat; I hold my breath, trying not to cough. *Ancestors. Mesopotamia.*

Lucian tucks the ball under the cup's edge. Such a simple game of chance might be played in a casino lounge or by a street busker. Until Lucian takes it to the next level by stacking the three cups, the red ball gone, and *tap, tap, tap,* it's replaced by two others—one blue, one yellow—when he lifts the bottom cup. His sleight of hand outclasses anything I've ever seen among circus magicians. I see no skip in his routine, no moment that would allow a quick slide down his sleeve or out of his pocket. He presents the cups to select guests to inspect for holes or hidden compartments. Every one comes up empty.

Applause partnered with *oohs* and *aahs* echo through the room.

Mesopotamia.

Did Dagan do this to you?

My fingernails bite into my palms. My eyes feel suddenly so scratchy, and I'm blinking too much. I sniff, my nose reacting to watering eyes, and the smell of food and flowers and perfumes is overridden by something unholy.

The reek of blood and putrefying flesh.

A deeper breath, and my nostrils fill with it. I put my napkin over my face so I don't throw up.

My heart races. I scan the room, desperate for the source of the smell. When this happened in the barn—spiders. *Where are the spiders?*

Out of the corner of my eye, I see the flowers in the lush center arrangement move and separate. I look just as a hairy, jointed leg the length of a pencil pushes past a fat, feathery white peony, followed immediately by more legs, the flowers bending to birth the spider's black-brown, kiwi fruit–sized abdomen.

I throw an elbow into Baby's upper arm but I don't dare turn away as the bristled arachnid ambles across the linen tablecloth toward the mayor and his guffawing wife.

"Baby . . ."

Where there is one spider, there are sure to be more.

I am so light-headed.

"Spider," I whisper when no other sound will come out because I can't breathe deeply enough to shove air through my vocal cords and it smells so bad and I am going to lose my dinner and then—

The blackness. In the corner, behind Lucian, the billowing swarm wraps around itself, throwing out those unending limbs that stretch toward me and then fold back in only to reform as it moves closer, now almost shoulder to shoulder with Lucian, who continues speaking in his soothing, hypnotic voice at the table head, a half smile on his face as he looks at his guests, and then directly at me.

I leap back from the table, Baby's firm grip catching my wrist and keeping me on my feet as the chair topples.

All eyes are on me, gleeful smiles melting in surprise.

The blackness, the stench, the spider . . . gone as quickly as they appeared.

"I'm sorry," I say, scanning the tabletop and the whole room. "I'm sorry . . ."

I pull away from Baby, grab my purse, and rush out. Baby is fast behind me, his tuxedo coat clenched in his opposite hand as we fly through the front door held open by stoic uniformed staff.

"Geni, what happened?" Baby stops me before I can climb into the car. Every raindrop is like an ice pick stabbing into my skin.

I grab his forearms—he's the lifeline keeping me from drowning.

"The Etemmu—it's here. And Lucian's got an *AVRAKEDAVRA* in his study," I say, probably louder than I should, that fact driven home when Baby checks over his shoulder to see if anyone's coming. Cecelia is moving toward us, her red gown bunched in her hand as the doorman holds an umbrella for her.

"Sweetie?" she asks as she catches up to us.

"I think I'm overtired. I'm just gonna go home, okay?"

"You go back inside, Cece. I'll make sure she gets home

safe," Baby says, opening the rear door of one of the Town Cars before the driver can. He nods to the open door, the rain dotting the black leather seats.

I climb in, my whole body shivering with terror. When I breathe, the stench lingers in my sinuses.

Baby leans down and kisses Aunt Cece's cheek. "We'll see you at breakfast." He's lowering himself into the car as another voice joins the conversation.

"Miss Genevieve, is there anything I can do?"

A fresh chill rockets through me. Lucian Dmitri, one hand on the open door, leans in, the rain bouncing off the shoulders of his midnight-black tux, the car's interior light reflecting softly off his hairless scalp. I want to believe the sincerity in his eyes is genuine—but how can I?

"I'm sorry for interrupting your party."

"You did no such thing," Lucian says. "I simply want to be sure you're not unwell."

"She's fine. Too much excitement," Baby says. "Thanks again for a swell dinner."

And then Baby slams the car door and gives me the look that we're not to speak because there is a driver who works for Dmitri. I slide as far over to my window as I can, stare into the inky night, and watch the rainwater tracking backward against the motion of the moving car. The shudders in my feet meet the ones cascading from my neck, worsening my nausea.

Etemmu. The *AVRAKEDAVRA*, in real life. Lucian Dagan Dmitri.

When the driver pulls into the fairground's lot, I hardly

let him stop before I'm out, sprinting, heels in hand, not caring that the sawdust hurts as it shreds my stockings. Baby hollers behind me to slow down, but I don't until I get to the trailer. Despite my freezing hands, I unlock the door and fly into the Airstream.

Purse tossed aside, from under my bunk I pull out Delia's box again. *The cards . . .*

"Gen, what are you doing?" Baby clicks the door closed behind him.

I kneel on the kitchenette bench and spread the playing cards out one by one on top of the table. The old healers. Alicia. The Etemmu. The mountains and fields and ocean.

The iris.

"Genevieve, explain." Baby towers over the table, the corners of his eyes creased with worry.

Phone pulled from my beaded purse, I open the photo gallery and pass it to him.

I watch as he scrolls through. At once, his finger stops, eyes widening.

He looks up at me, a flick of fear quickly replaced by something angrier. "Where did you find these paintings?"

"Lucian's office. In this anteroom—where he keeps the *AVRAKEDAVRA*. He has a mural— individual panels—painted around the room."

Baby stares at the photo in question, a deep exhale sneaking between pursed lips.

"This iris—why would Delia have the same iris that's hanging in Lucian's office?"

"It's him, Genevieve. It's Dagan." Baby's jaw pulsates; I swear I can hear his teeth crack. "The iris is Belshunu's family sigil. I've noticed the irises since we've been here, but—this is all the confirmation I need. God, I should've known." He scrolls back a few shots, and pauses. I know what photo he's on without even looking.

"My mother. He chased her. Didn't he . . . ?" Baby gives me back the phone. "This must've been the night she reclaimed the book." *Delia, why didn't you tell me* this *story?*

I scroll back to the flower portrait—no mistaking, it is exactly as Delia painted on her card.

"The Etemmu. It's why I ran out." I'm suddenly overcome by the terror of the experience. "Please, call Nutesh. Tell him everything we found out tonight. Tell him we need help."

Baby slides in next to me on the bench, his arm tight around my shoulders as he reassures me that it'll be okay and I'm not alone. That the Etemmu won't be able to haunt me as long as he's here. And I so want to believe him.

"I hate her for leaving me and not telling me the truth. I hate her for leaving me behind to deal with this." Trying not to cry is futile. I'm not brave. I'm terrified.

Baby pulls me into a hug, and I stain his white shirt with mascara. "She didn't want to leave you, little bird. It's all right," he says, a firm, soothing hand against my back.

He stands and pulls out his phone. "This is risky, calling from the fairgrounds . . ." He dials, rolls his shoulders, and stands tall. A beep sounds through the line, but instead of

Hi, yes, this is Baby, how are you, he waits. "A third text has been located. Haunting happened again. Will await further instructions."

And then he hangs up.

"That's it? You talked to an answering machine?" I sniff and reach for a paper napkin to dry my face.

The vein in his forehead throbs along with the increasing tension in his voice. "It's not an answering machine. Someone answers the line. They record everything I say. I tell Nutesh what I need him to know and he'll call me back with what we're supposed to do next." Phone again in his pocket, he sighs heavily. "You want cocoa or something?" He sets to making himself his nightly tea. No one would ever believe that a big, tough guy like Baby drinks a calming cup of chamomile every night. Another of Delia's everlasting fingerprints left behind.

Baby's spoon *tink-tink-tink*s against the mug as he stirs stevia into his tea.

"Could his *AVRAKEDAVRA* be a fake? Henry—he's really talented with reproductions. He showed me a copy of a Rodin and this amazing bible he made that's filled with superheroes."

"A bible with superheroes?" Baby lifts an eyebrow.

"Naturally. But it looks like a real bible. Well, except for Spider-Man and the Hulk sitting at the Last Supper. Maybe he made Dear Old Daddy an *AVRAKEDAVRA* too."

"Thing is, you'd have to have seen an original to make a fake. And why would Dmitri keep a forgery in an electrified case?" Baby's giant hand swallows the ceramic mug.

"Henry caught me. In his father's office. I want to know what he knows. I think I should talk to him. Poke around a little to see if he gives anything up."

Baby's already shaking his head no.

"He hid me in the closet so Lucian wouldn't find me."

"You were hiding in the closet? Together?"

"That's what you're focusing on?"

"Did he try anything?" Baby grips the mug a little tighter.

"Yes. We totally made out." I pick up a throw pillow from the bench seat and cock my arm. "Grow up."

"You were in a closet with a boy . . ."

"He saved my butt."

"Okay, points for the kid, then. But that doesn't mean we trust him. Not yet." Baby relaxes and sits back, thoughts drifting across his face. "You touched the case?" I nod. "Surprised it didn't set off an alarm."

Shit, I hadn't even thought about that.

The heater clicks off and we're left with only the *pitter-pat* of raindrops hitting the trailer's tinny exoskeleton.

"His *AVRAKEDAVRA* must be real," I say. "And the Etemmu certainly was real tonight. It was *right behind* Dmitri, but he was totally unfazed, so it can't be haunting him. In fact . . . Lucian looked at me when the demon was moving. Scary as shit—like he was watching my reaction. Like he knew it was there."

I tuck my cold feet under me. "Why would the Etemmu be bothering me if it's not bothering Lucian or even Henry? If that text is real, and Lucian is Dagan, a descendant like me—you said the Etemmu is only visible to people within these magical families, so why couldn't they see it? And if I *do* find Delia's text, how do we know the Etemmu won't keep haunting me like it did her? She had the book, and it just got worse." God, I cannot handle a lifetime of this.

"Baby, I think Lucian's got something to do with the Etemmu. It makes sense. Dagan wanted Delia's book; she was tortured for it for years; she lived through Udish's murder and had to steal the book back; and just before she fell that night, she yelled, 'No matter how hard you come at me, you will never find it.' She was yelling at the Etemmu. She was yelling at Dagan."

Baby nods. "That theory matches up," he says. "But this is where we need Nutesh. Like I said, the Etemmu is not *AVRAKEDAVRA*-level stuff. It's like *AVRAKEDAVRA Plus*. Which is why we haven't been able to make it disappear or tie it directly to Dagan. Nutesh needs to uncover the mechanism that's giving it energy, and he's been unsuccessful so far in doing anything other than creating the talisman spell for me."

Baby's phone chimes. He slides his finger across it and frowns. I'm off my seat, reading the text over his shoulder.

Find remaining property. Will coordinate rendezvous.

"That's it? That's all he said?"

Baby looks tired, maybe even a little scared. "Less is more. Less keeps you safe."

I close my burning eyes and lean my head against the trailer wall.

"Genevieve, our strategy is clear: we will find her book, deliver it to Nutesh to keep it from Dagan, and then you will be free. Of all of this."

When his phone rings again, I jump. He looks at the screen and answers.

"Hey, Cece . . . Yeah, she's fine. About to go to bed." He listens for a moment. "I'll keep an eye on her . . . Mm-hmm. Maybe . . . We can talk about it tomorrow . . . Good night."

He hangs up. Stands and moves to the sink to rinse out his mug.

"Talk about what tomorrow?"

He turns off the sink but doesn't face me. "She wants to know if we should call Dr. DeGrasse."

Delia's shrink with the wire-framed glasses and the alpaca sweaters drenched in patchouli oil. I shake my head no. I don't need a damn shrink.

"Cece is afraid you've got post-traumatic stress."

I laugh. "I do not have PTSD."

"She's just worried about you."

"Yeah, well, I'm worried about me too." It would be easier for them to have an explanation like PTSD. I don't know if Cece and Ted ever really believed my mother—despite what our magic hands can do. I overheard them talking once when their trailer window was open, something about Delia's fierce imagination but how they worried that I'd be deluded into thinking her stories were true or that her behavior was normal.

"I'll crash on Delia's bunk."

"You don't have to do that," I say, even though I really don't want to be alone.

"I hope you don't snore too loud." He musses my hair. "I have to get my beauty sleep." He flexes and kisses his biceps.

When Baby steps out, I stare at Delia's playing cards for another moment, taking them in with new eyes.

What clues did she leave me here that I don't yet understand?

The healers, Alicia, the Etemmu, the young girl and her mother, the curly-haired man, and now the iris—all of these beautiful, hand-painted cards mean something. The actual places she's painted, like Haystack Rock—her letter was waiting for me in Cannon Beach. But these other places . . .

"Where is it, Mom?" The mountains? A deserted field where her grandfather died?

Or in a vault in a cemetery.

Except there are an infinite number of cemeteries in the world, and Delia loved to visit as many as we could. Simple paintings on card stock do little to narrow it down, especially because there is nothing familiar about the images.

The cards gathered and again hidden back under my bed, I grab jammies and lock myself in the bathroom where I peel the dress's bodice over my waist and stand in my strapless bra and goosebumped flesh. Henry's wilted forget-me-nots fall into the sink. I pick up the stem and cradle it in a tissue, a momentary smile crossing my lips when I think what Delia would say: *Forget-me-nots, a true-blue flower . . . when someone wants you to remember them forever.*

These will find a home with my keepsakes. It's not every day a boy gives me flowers.

I lean against the vanity and stare at my pale, mascara-streaked cheeks in the mirror, but instead of my face, I see the Etemmu, writhing behind Lucian Dmitri, its unceasing arms and eternal blackness boiling, opening up like a putrid portal to some horrible underworld, coming for me—

And our well-mannered, debonair host, running his cups across the smooth mahogany, enchanting the room with his stories, voice fluid and soft, his old-soul eyes watching me panic.

Bastard knew it was there, and he watched me panic.

18

I PULL THE PRIVACY DRAPE AROUND MY BUNK, NESTLE DEEP UNDER MY STACK of blankets, and check my phone, just in case. A few texts from Violet about how hot Henry looked in his tux and where did I disappear to with him and Ash is already in love with Mara and she's moving into a new trailer tomorrow so we're all gonna hang out and help her get settled and OMG it's just going to be amazing.

How the twins love shiny new playthings.

No calls from Schuyler. I'll give it until lunch tomorrow, and then I'll try UW again and leave another message. If Schuyler still has a pulse, he needs to damn well call me back. The sooner I talk to him, the sooner we can either use whatever info he has to find Delia's book or rule him out as a possible help.

I am so, so tired. But when I close my eyes, I see that spider crawling out of the flower arrangement and that blackness that looked like it would swallow the whole room. I see the *AVRAKEDAVRA* sitting in the secure case and I know it's not because Lucian Dagan Dmitri is a fan of antiques.

But what is Dagan's special gift? Schuyler's article reiterated what Baby had said, that each of these books deals with a different aspect of human existence—*Life, Death, Memory*—where do Delia and I fit into this, and where does Lucian Dmitri? And what about his son? Are they healers too? How can that seemingly charming man who woos everyone with his money and fancy sleight of hand be a murderer?

The trailer creaks as Baby returns and tries to get comfortable in Delia's small bunk. I peek and see that he's got his curtain closed too.

If I weren't cold and scared, I'd go sleep in the barn. Hug the elephants. Play Houdini a lullaby on that beautiful new violin gifted to me by a man I don't trust. Instead, I bury myself under an extra blanket and check to make sure my phone alarm is off.

When someone wants me to wake up, they can come find me. I'll be here, hiding from the blackness that wants to eat my soul for breakfast.

19

I WAKE TO THE AIRSTREAM SHIFTING UNDER BABY'S WEIGHT. SQUINTING against the brightness of a day that started without me, I pull my drape back.

"Rise and shine, buttercup."

"Go away," I say.

He laughs. "Get up. Get food. Philips fed the elephants so just take care of yourself. There's a rehearsal meeting about the new show today."

I groan. "Why am I always the last one to know about this crap?"

"Cece reminded me last night when she checked in. They're going to start blocking and reordering the new acts. But you only have to go if you think you'll be okay to participate."

"Whatever."

I flop back on my bed, but as my brain wakes up—my phone! I scramble under my pillow for it.

Shit. No message yet.

"Breakfast. Come on, Geni. Don't fall asleep again. You should get Gert and Houdini out and walk them through the big top today. Let Gert get her nose on everything."

"How can the circus even matter right now? With everything else?"

"Because it's our job. And the elephants need you."

"Fine."

"Come check in with me as soon as you're up and at 'em."

When I finally feel presentable—a questionable state considering I'm waiting for either Alicia or the demon to show up and tap-dance on my frayed nerves again—I head out, moving beyond trailer row and into the heart of the Cinzio operations where it's just another day at the circus. Music streams from the big top. To the left of the second performance tent (dubbed "the mini"), a plume of orange fire explodes from the lips of a fire-eater. Beatrice and her daughter, Nicola, stop and ask me how I'm doing, taking turns holding the carafe and tray of coffee cups so they can hug me as they tell me that if I want to stop by the wardrobe building later, they'd love to talk about my new costume.

Not sure what the point of that is. I have little faith that I'll be performing anytime soon.

A few steps later, Toby the clown wheels by on a unicycle, tips his tweed paperboy hat, with Peaches, fluffy and freshly combed, yipping happily behind him. He hops off and presents me with a tiny yellow rose that he tucks in the buttonhole of my flannel jacket. "Your mom said that yellow roses mean friendship. This is from the miniature rose bush she gave us. She was always so good to Dan and me." He pats my cheek softly, his dark brown eyes sad yet kind, his wheat-colored hair closely cropped.

The Triad crew has been working long hours erecting canopies over walkways and our new side attractions for the coming WinterFest event. The souvenir kiosks are taking shape, though they're still empty of wares. Roy the herpetologist offers a wave as I pass, readying his own booth so patrons can sneak a peek at his spiders, scorpions, snakes, dragons, and geckos. No more bearded fat lady or alligator man. This is the twenty-first-century circus, folks. Step right up and learn about the family *Theraphosidea* and its harmless but frighteningly furry eight-legged members.

NO THANK YOU.

The mess tent is loaded to the seams. The new folks are all here, including Mara Dunn, holding court at a table in the corner. Vi, adorned in her usual pink-on-pink workout garb, sees me and waves excitedly.

I wave back, though I'm in no mood for small talk with the new girl who's taking my mother's place.

Once I've scooped eggs and toast onto my plate, I sit with Cece.

"Ah, my sweet girl." She gives me a side-hug from her squeaky fold-up seat. Leaning close, she lowers her voice. "You seemed spooked last night. At the party?"

I was spooked, Cece. Everything smelled like death, a giant spider crawled out of the centerpiece, and an ancient demon has decided he'd like to hug me with his bazillion swarming arms.

"Yeah. I was just tired." I'm a terrible liar, but as long as I don't make eye contact . . . I shovel in a bite of egg and flinch when the cheese burns the roof of my mouth.

Cecelia pulls her heavy wool sweater tight across her big boobs and tucks her hands in. It's cold in here, despite the upright propane heaters. "The new aerialist—she seems very sweet. I saw her audition tape this morning." Her face brightens, as if hopeful her enthusiasm will be contagious. It isn't. "Very talented. I think the two of you will really pull off something special, once you're ready to train again."

"I don't know if I want to do the silks. You know, for a while."

"Of course, of course. We can talk about that with Ted and the choreographer. Whatever you feel up to."

"I suppose they needed to pull someone in to replace Delia."

"Oh, honey, she's not replacing Delia."

Yeah, she is. It's not worth arguing. I can put two and two together.

I've had enough to eat. "I'll be in the barn," I say, standing. "What time is the meeting?"

"Eleven. If you're up for it . . ."

I give Cece a thumbs-up and walk away, plate in hand to dump in the dish bin.

Othello has a mouthful of cow femur when I walk in, but he perks up and drops the bone when he sees me. "Morning, handsome." He flops against the bars, asking for a back rub, and purr-growls when I dig deep into his coat. Houdini's having none of this and trumpets down the way, his baby trunk sticking through the bars.

"Sorry, big man. Gotta go see your little brother." Othello nudges my hand and returns to crunching into his morning treat.

The elephants' food basins are still half full. I check the clipboard hanging next to their enclosure—it holds a detailed checklist of what they were served, signed by Dr. Philips. It's reassuring to know that if Baby and I do have to bail suddenly, the streamlined machine I leave behind will keep the elephants safe and fed. Still, I feel a little defensive; these are my babies. I should be the one taking care of them.

The bars are open wide enough for me to slide through, just in time for Houdini to yank on my wrist and offer me whatever pulpy goo he's been chewing. "Hi, Houdini . . . yes, I love you, thank you for the slime." Gert, trunk aloft, sniffs me. "Good morning to you too, my girl." She snorts and offers me a chunk of sugar cane. "I ate, thanks."

I won't open the outer yard until they've finished breakfast. Otherwise slowpoke Houdini, like any little kid, will run away from the table before his belly is full.

"They're much bigger up close." I jump at the sound of Henry Dmitri's voice. "Sorry—did I scare you?" He smirks, his curls wilder this morning. Probably secondary to the drizzly weather still beaded and glistening on his black, waterproof Triad coat.

"Hey . . ." I straighten my well-loved quilted flannel jacket in a vain attempt to not look like I live and work in a circus. The tiny yellow flower fancies me up nicely, I think.

"I looked for you in the mess tent. Cecelia said I'd find you here."

He was looking for me?

"Why are you here so early?" I ask, hoping he doesn't notice my flaming cheeks.

"Apparently there's an important meeting in the big top, so I'm reporting for duty. It's all very exciting. My first official circus business." Now tuxedo-free, he doesn't look any less handsome in Levi's. I kind of hate myself for noticing. Aside from Violet's crush, it's too predictable to fall for the pretty boy.

"Do your elephants like new people?"

"Depends on the people," I say, picking clean Houdini's gift smeared across my front.

Henry leans against the open gate, finessing a coin between gloved fingers. Again with the gloves, this pair fitted, a tawny brown. The silver disc dances across Henry's digits between knuckles, a continuous motion, as if it were minted to do just that.

Watching him reminds me of his father's ease with the ball-and-cups game, how Lucian can pull lollipops and iris blossoms from midair. If the book in that locked case is a real AVRAKEDAVRA, my new friend probably inherited some special talents of his own. Why not?

I want to trust him.

I want to know what he knows, what he can do.

"Henry . . . ," I say, "last night—did you tell your father that I was in his study?"

He surprises me when he laughs. "That would make me a bit of a wanker, wouldn't it? Secrets are only secrets if they're kept locked away." He mimes locking his lips with an invisible key.

Henry then tosses the coin into the air and grabs it. He uncurls his fingers, one at a time.

The coin is gone.

"Did you see anything interesting in your brief expedition into the Land of Lucian?" he asks, his smile dimming but not disappearing as he looks right at me. Our eyes locked, I don't know how to answer. Do I tell him the truth? He has to know about his father's text. Maybe he knows what his father uses it for, why Lucian's after my mother's book . . .

But Baby's voice echoes in my head. *Not yet, Genevieve.*

"Just a lot of artwork," I squeak, looking away. I pull my collar higher to hide my neck, now also on fire.

"So," Henry says, breaking the awkward silence, "who are your very large friends?"

"This is Gertrude. The little one is her son, Houdini."

"Hello, Gertrude. I'm Henry." Gert eyes him cautiously, shuffling closer to me. "Gertrude . . . what a formal name."

"After Hamlet's mother. My uncle Ted names all of his creatures after Shakespearean characters."

"Right. The lion is Othello." Henry extends his hand, palm up. Gert continues to examine him. "But Houdini's not Shakespearean."

"I named him," I say, a small smile tugging at my lips.

"Ah. Good thing for the baby—Shakespeare was a fraud."

"Oh my god," I say, laughing, "doesn't that make you a traitor? Being British?"

"Perhaps—although I did become an American citizen when I was twelve, so I'm only half British these days." He runs a couple fingers through the front curls of his hair. I wonder if he even realizes he's doing it.

"Oh. Well, don't let Ted hear you bash the Bard."

"A big fan?"

"We also have a caretaker named Montague."

"You don't. For real? Where is he?"

"Ted and Cecelia have a permanent property down in Eugene. Montague is the caretaker."

"Did he rename himself after Romeo's family?"

I chuckle. "Nope. That's his real name. He's a master gardener, actually. Grows world-class roses year-round."

Montague used to travel with the show—until he had a run-in with Othello's father, Andronicus. It was one of the very few times that the rule about keeping my talents a secret was overruled. Montague was hurried, battered and bloodied, into the work trailer. Ted and Baby and my mother held him down while I knitted the broken bones of his lower arm back together. The severe gashes in his flesh, I could only partially heal. I wasn't strong enough yet—I was just a kid—and they needed to take him to the hospital for stitches so witnesses wouldn't become suspicious that the mauled man was miraculously not mauled anymore.

Montague the Mauled became his nickname; he used to thank me for leaving him with enough scars to prove how tough he was.

Houdini throws hay at me, interrupting my thoughts. Gert seems interested but won't come closer. I realize why.

"Take off your gloves. She needs to see your hands."

Henry pauses. "She doesn't like gloves?"

"It's her weird tic."

"Oh, that's okay, then. I can just put my hands behind my back. If it makes her uncomfortable."

"You're this close to our circus's matriarch, and you won't give her the courtesy of a pat?"

"I can't touch her with the gloves on?"

"Not if you don't want to get smacked by her trunk. She had some issues with handlers when she was younger. Now she hates gloves."

Henry licks his lips, his Adam's apple bobbing with a slow swallow.

"Are you nervous?"

He doesn't answer. His eyes widen, blinking rapidly.

"Not sure if you're gonna pass your circus work-study class if you can't even pet an elephant. It's good luck, you know."

His cheeks warm. "Right. Okay." Slowly, he pulls off one glove at a time and tucks them into his pocket. A slight tremor rocks his upturned hands, held out in front of him. *He's scared.*

"Don't worry. She won't hurt you."

Gert raises her trunk and sniffs, careful. I sneak past and toss Henry fruit from the basin. Houdini barrels toward Henry and steals the mangoes, shoving one, then the other, into his slobbering mouth.

"Told you. This one's easy," I say, rubbing Houdini's back. "Go ahead. Pet him."

Henry raises a tentative hand and then finally touches the baby's forehead. Houdini freezes. His trunk relaxes, his eyes soften.

"He's fuzzy," Henry says, his grin wide. "I never realized how much hair baby elephants have."

"Wow, he likes you. He never stands still for anyone, not even me."

"The mangoes give me an unfair advantage."

"Give me your hand," I say. Henry looks up at me, his boyish grin fading.

"Pardon me?"

"It's okay. If Gert sees me touching you, she knows it's safe for her to do the same."

"But I'm touching her son. Surely she can trust me."

"It's just her thing. Don't be afraid. She won't hurt you."

Henry again looks at his hands. He slowly steps toward Gert and me, brow creased, his eyes on me. It takes him another beat before he raises his hand, as if he really is afraid of the elephant and he's trying to find a way to back out.

But as soon as our fingers connect, my knees knock together. An overwhelming warmth flows from him to me—a low-level current, but calming and serene. The blue-green of his eyes, fixed on my face, are washed out as a vision pops into my head—dinner last night, the mural he showed me, him handing me the drawing.

He gently pulls his hand away. As soon as our connection is severed, the vision fades, like mist in front of a fan.

"What . . . how did you do that?"

His face flushes. Close up, with the smile gone, the purple under his eyes makes him look like he had a rough night's sleep. Or maybe he's just weirded out.

Like I am.

Excitement blooms in my chest. His hands have something special about them.

Just like mine.

I watch, amazed, as he hurriedly stuffs his fingers back into the gloves.

"Henry . . . what was that? What just happened?"

He's Dagan's son. Henry is a descendant, *like me.*

Do I show him what I can do so he knows he can trust me? Shit, does that mean he's aware or even a party to the hunt for Delia's book?

But then, if Henry is special like I am, why didn't he see the billowing blackness or the spider? Why didn't he smell the fetor of death in the grand dining room?

Henry's lips part, as if he's going to say something, but then he thinks better of it.

"Tell me what just happened."

"Please . . . I shouldn't have shown you that. Don't be afraid," Henry says.

"I'm not."

He swallows hard, the look on his face hinting that he has beans to spill. Has he had to keep his talents concealed his whole life, like I have? These odd gifts are what make us who we are, but they are not without disadvantage. Keeping such a huge secret is a constant reminder that we are different from everyone else.

If you can do that, what can Lucian do?

"Henry . . ." He looks down, as if something very interesting is going on in the hay under his feet. "Tell me I can trust you," I say.

His head pops up.

"Last night, you saved me from your father catching us." I lower my voice. "You also know that I saw more than artwork in his study. You didn't tell him, though. *Tell me* that means I can trust you." I could be risking everything here—even my own life—but I don't have an endless amount of time. The Etemmu could show itself again, at any moment. Even if Baby is reluctant to see what's hiding in this kid's head, I need to know.

I need to save myself and the people I love.

Henry spends an extra few seconds on my face, and then nods. "I don't have any cause to mislead you," he says. "Please, don't tell anyone about this. My father—" Henry's eyes are genuinely scared as he stretches his gloved hands before him.

"Your father what?"

"He—I'm not supposed to—this is meant to be a secret. Always a secret. It's best, for everyone, he not find out I've revealed this to you."

"I want to trust you. I have secrets of my own, secrets that could destroy me. *You* could destroy me with one word to your father."

Henry's brows crease. He looks confused. "I've just inadvertently disclosed something only a few people in my life know about. I think you're holding more cards here than I

am, Genevieve." He looks around us, outside the bars. He fidgets with the seams on his gloves. The rims of his eyes are pink and his face is paler than when he walked in a few minutes ago.

All or nothing, I say to myself. *If he tells his dad—if he's working me to get info to share with Lucian—then I'll run. I don't have time for games.*

I move to the tack box and pull out a utility knife. "Give me your hand."

"What?"

"Prove that you trust me," I say.

His slight grin seems sincere. Over his shoulder, Henry again inspects our surroundings. He follows me deeper into the paddock, moving slowly around Gert as she turns her head to watch him, until we're along the wall near the food basins, out of view of the rest of the barn.

"Take off your gloves."

He does, and I take one from him and line my palm with it.

"Give me your hand." He looks at me, unsure, but obliges. I'm careful to only touch him with fingertips at his wrist bone, cupping the back of his hand so it's splayed palm up atop the glove.

"This will sting. But only for a second," I say. Before he has a chance to pull away, I drag the opened blade along the meaty flesh where his thumb attaches to his hand, just deep enough to separate the skin and draw a healthy line of blood. He sucks in through his teeth but holds still.

"I hope you don't give me tetanus."

"Tetanus is my specialty." I wipe the bloodied blade off

on my jeans and quietly place it inside the silver basin next to us. "Watch."

I present my index finger and close my eyes. Find the star, dim in the back of my head until I visualize it growing bigger, brighter, like an Independence Day sparkler freshly ignited, throwing tiny, fiery bursts toward the ground as it illuminates everything around it. I pull, deep breaths, my heart rate slowing even as the pounding against my skull increases while I trace the new wound with my fingertip.

He gasps.

My eyes open slowly and I watch his smile broaden.

"You're—"

"A freak too? Yeah," I answer, wiping the fresh blood from his hand.

"I've never met anyone else . . ."

"Me neither. Except for my mother."

"She could heal like this?" Henry asks.

"Plants. She could touch a plant and make it grow hearty and strong. She used herbals in healing remedies."

Henry looks down at his splayed fingers and turns his hands over. He speaks slowly, as if considering every word. "When I touched you, I showed you last night. In the hallway . . . at the dinner party. I showed you a memory that we shared."

"Yes," I whisper.

"When I was younger, I didn't understand what it was— but as I got older, I figured out that if I touched another person, I would transmit a sort of energy. Though I eventually learned how to control what's transmitted, I can't turn it off."

"Every time you touch someone, you share a memory?"

"More or less."

"That's why you wear the gloves."

"That is why I wear the gloves." He toys with the untucked edge of his shirt and then looks around. "When my bare hands touch another person's bare skin, I can share a memory with them—one we've shared, one of my own; they can give me one of their memories . . ." He pauses. "Or I can select a memory without their direct consent."

"You can reach into someone else's head? Like, read their mind?"

"Sort of. It doesn't always work. It's much easier if the individual is willing to let me in. Sometimes I touch someone, and his or her memories will rush at me, whereas other times, nothing. It can be very overwhelming."

"How'd you get away with wearing gloves indoors for all these years?"

He laughs to himself. "A ghastly case of eczema? If people think you're at all contagious, they tend to back away. Although I do have remarkably soft skin now."

His hands *are* pretty. Not like mine, callouses from the violin, nails blunt and unpolished, palms rough from years of pitchfork duty. I hide my hands behind my back so he doesn't see my imperfections.

Beyond everything else, this is incredible. Finally—someone to talk to who understands how it feels to be so different!

"When I was in your father's study . . ."

He presses a finger against his lips, speaking just above a

whisper. "We shouldn't talk about this here." He looks over his shoulder again, shifting his weight.

"Henry—how old are you?"

He looks at me, confused. "I've just turned eighteen, on January 6th." Maybe he doesn't know.

"You swear? You're only eighteen?"

"Shall I produce my birth certificate?"

"How old is your father?"

"Early fifties. He's a bit vain about people knowing his age," Henry says.

Lucian is vain because he's centuries old—like Delia.

Your father, he's way older than his fifties. He's been lying to you, kid. Unless you're playing me right now.

"When did you figure it out—the trick with the memories?" I ask.

"I wasn't consciously aware until my first year of school. We had to join hands for a music exercise, and I saw into the life of the girl next to me—she had a new puppy, but her father kicked it. When the father came to pick her up after school, I ran out of the classroom and . . . Well, I sort of attacked him."

"A crusader for justice in the making?"

"I was only five. But I was suitably upset. And when I told the teacher and principal that the girl's father was a bad guy, they listened."

"Sorry for teasing. It's nice you saved the puppy."

"Nice, except my father pulled me out of that school and put me into another one. And then he made me start wearing the gloves."

"Who else knows you can do this?"

"My father. A few unfortunate nannies. No one else."

"None of your school friends?"

He laughs once, a doleful sound. "I keep my circle of familiars small. Side effect of being Lucian Dmitri's son."

He regards my hands, and then his own, eyeing the sealed cut where not even a scar remains. Something akin to happiness stretches across his face. "This is remarkable."

"Henry." I risk touching him, one hand on his bent arm. *Shit. Here goes nothing.* "That book in the electrified case in your father's office—how much do you know about it?"

"Just that my father values it greatly. It's some sort of old grimoire. Allegedly, there are others like it in the world that were stolen from him—and he wants to recover them. Says they're priceless."

I drop my hand and shake my head no.

"Did I say something wrong?" he asks.

"No. It's fine." I take a step back. *Your father is lying to you.* I stop before saying too much.

"I hope I haven't offended you somehow, Genevieve. Honestly, my father and I haven't spent much time talking about that old book. It's just another of his hundreds of prizes."

Which says a fair amount about Lucian Dagan Dmitri's plans for the future. If the books are to be passed on to the descendants of owners, it doesn't sound like Daddy is doing much to prime his son for taking over the family business.

Interesting.

"That book—it's more than an old grimoire. It's called

the *AVRAKEDAVRA*. There are three, belonging to three different families. *Our* families. It's why our hands can do what they do."

He squints at me, like I've just told him the sun rises in the west.

"Didn't you ever wonder why you have this gift no one else has?" I ask quietly.

Henry turns his hands over, palm down, palm up, in front of him, as if he's suddenly afraid of them.

"My father said it was hereditary. A genetic anomaly somewhere down the lineage. Which is why I'm blown away that you have the same 'anomaly.'"

"Lucian's hands—are they like yours?"

Henry's voice is quiet. "My father has other gifts." I give him a moment to continue, but he doesn't.

"Our gifts come from this magical book—our families' books. Each one deals with different parts of our existence— *Life, Death,* and *Memory.* I believe my mother's book was *Life,* given what she and I can do, so I'm thinking that the book your father has must be *Memory,* now that I know your ability."

I close the distance between us. "Henry . . . I think the circus is here, in Eaglefern, because your father wants my mother's book."

"I promise, Genevieve"—he raises his hand as if in oath—"I don't know anything more than what I've just shared. You saw our house. Lucian collects. He has some special fever for those grimoires—"

"The *AVRAKEDAVRA*."

"Whatever it's called. My knowledge is limited, mostly because I've had no reason to care."

You do now.

"To be completely honest, I'm just so thrilled to meet someone else like me." His seriousness fades, his cheeks pinking up and his eyes sparkling as he smiles—as if I didn't just give him information that has the power to change the course of both our lives. "Thank you for sharing your secret, Genevieve."

"Henry, why did you risk it? Showing me what your hands can do?"

"'*When you decide not to be afraid, you can find friends in super unexpected places,*'" he says.

"You're a philosopher too?"

"Ms. Marvel. The newer one, Kamala Khan. She said that."

"Wise girl."

"I'll loan you her comics. I think you'd like her. She's a bit like . . . us."

My phone sings from my pocket, startling Houdini who then grabs at my pant leg.

A text from Baby: *"Big top. Bring elephants in before the meeting starts."*

"I have to go," I say.

Henry checks his watch. "Right. Almost time for some of that work-study business, I suppose, now that I'm sure to pass," he says, nodding at Gertrude. "Would Baby allow you out for coffee? We could talk more. You could slice more holes in my flesh."

"Coffee could work. And I only slice between the hours of eight and ten every morning."

"Makes sense."

"Ask Baby yourself. About the coffee," I tease.

"What? I have to ask him?"

I laugh. "Are you chicken?"

"I'm not ashamed to admit that yes, I am chicken. Baby's rather frightening. All those muscles and tattoos . . ."

"Nah, he's harmless."

"I very much doubt that," Henry says.

He offers his gloved hand for a handshake. "I don't mean to belabor the point, but . . . I'm so pleased to know that I'm not alone."

The front curl of his hair curves against his forehead like a question mark. "Until our next covert operation, Miss Flannery." He half bows, turns, and exits the enclosure.

I'm almost giddy for a moment, the excitement of our shared secret bubbling over, even in the face of darker secrets ahead. I've put it out there—time will tell if Henry will turn on me.

But I want to trust him. I *need* to trust him. I need his help. And yeah, the part that he just happens to be handsome, polite, intelligent, and talented isn't lost on me. I know he's not perfect, but knowing, with little more than a shared look, Henry Dmitri understands even an iota of the impact this gift has had on my life—if what he's learned from living with Lucian Dagan Dmitri can shed light on what is happening to me now . . .

That's near enough to perfect for me.

20

I STUFF FRUIT INTO MY POCKETS AND LISTEN FOR RAIN ON THE SKYLIGHTS.
"Should we put your jacket on, squirt?"

Laughable. Houdini will have nothing to do with it. "You naughty baby. You're gonna get cold." As if he knows I've insulted him, he smacks my leg with his trunk and squeaks at me.

I grab the brightly painted wooden lead-stick, not because Gertrude needs it, but because I have to train Houdini that he has to follow the human when we go outside. The stick is only for him to wrap his trunk around, but that's enough of a game for a baby elephant. He can throw and chase it like a puppy when we're out in the open.

Thankfully, he isn't too adventurous when we're not in the barn. While he's been known to tear through the menagerie and yank a few horses' tails, he won't go far from his mom or me when we're in the big bad world.

Large overhead door opened, Gert plods forward into the chilly January morning, her trunk touching my shoulder and back every few steps when she's not wrangling her little man who keeps grabbing for her tail. I click my tongue and offer the lead-stick for Houdini to wrap his trunk. It works once I bribe him with the apples. "Good boy. Houdini's a good boy!" Just as quickly, he drops it and yanks the grass along the walkway's border. Grass is way more fun.

I take the long way to the big top to give Gertrude the lay of the land, stopping a few times so folks can offer pats and one of the apples or mangoes I've brought along. Gertrude is such a calm, pleasant girl. She loves being outdoors, trunk raised toward the trees to smell everything, to feel the free air around her. Her eyes shine, my face reflected in their depths, long, thick lashes blinking the slow cadence of a happy elephant.

I'm so grateful for these two—the one constant in this nomadic life. When Gertrude joined Cinzio, I was about three. She was skittish, having come from a bad situation. I would sit outside her enclosure in the great barn at the Cinzio property in Eugene, crisscross applesauce on an overturned milk crate, Ellie the raggedy stuffed elephant in hand, so I could watch Ted and Baby as they plied her with food and love, working for months to earn her trust.

One day, I stole into the barn alone. I didn't know to be afraid of her. Maybe she recognized in me a kindred spirit, considering my favorite toy was an elephant that smelled like cookies.

And I wanted to hug big Gertrude. She looked like she needed a hug.

I climbed through the bars and stood before her. She turned her head sideways, snorted, and then, with the care given to an egg, she wrapped her trunk around my four-year-old tummy and hoisted me over her head, onto her massive back.

When my mother and Baby and the Cinzios couldn't find me, a panic set loose on the farm. I heard them calling my name, but I just giggled and lay flat against Gert.

From then on, I was her girl, and she was mine.

I lean into her now as we walk, laughing as her trunk sniffs and tickles my face and hair.

When Henry touched Houdini, did the elephant relax because Henry showed him something, or does it only work with humans? Does it do that every time he touches someone?

What I saw in my head when Henry touched me was out of my control. It was like . . . energy, only it didn't hurt. It felt tranquil, and the images from last night played on the screen in my head but through his eyes, as he saw me. Me smiling at the artwork, laughing at his drawing of superhero Genevieve on Gertrude's back. Though the vision was only few seconds, it was friendly, not at all scary. Not like the Etemmu.

Houdini's squeaky trumpet snaps me back to the moment. Gert's trunk hovers in front of my face. I pluck the last of the treats from my sticky pockets—the short chunk of sugar cane she gave me earlier—and offer it to her. Walking back later will be tricky without bribery snacks for the little one.

Just as we approach the field edge south of the big top, Houdini attacks the dead grasses and runs about like a sug-ared-out kindergartner. It never stops being funny, watching a baby elephant go nuts in an open field. I hate that Houdini was born in captivity—his father, Nero, another of Ted's rescues, was only with us for a year, and Gert's pregnancy was *very* unexpected. But the circus life was definitely not for Nero anymore—he had a lot of issues from a difficult life, like so many circus animals do. So he went to a sanctuary in California to live out his old age, and regular updates assure us that he's a new man in retirement.

The day will come when Gert and Houdini will find their spot in a sanctuary, but until then, I'm doing everything I can to give Houdini his wildness back.

Fortunately, Baby sees that this naughty pachyderm, now halfway across the field, is not interested in behaving. He whistles and catches Houdini's attention—the baby loves our resident giant, so he takes off toward the big top, his mother standing like a lady alongside the red-and-yellow tent, trunk and ears swaying leisurely as she waits to be escorted indoors.

A couple crew guys hold the canvas flaps aside so Miss Gert can lumber through. Baby helps wrangle Houdini, cooing and chirping at him like you would a human infant, and we walk about the tent's interior so Gertrude can sniff everything, wrap her trunk around new bits of the setup. This big top is a whole ring bigger than the old one, so we don't want anything to spook her during the parade or performance. Gert loves her moment in the spotlight, as long as there are no surprises waiting in the wings.

The temptation of the freshly groomed dirt center ring is too much for Houdini—he rolls around like a freshly bathed puppy, quickly joined by two Pomeranians and a poodle.

"What did you feed him this morning?" Baby asks, nodding at Houdini. "I swear that elephant thinks he's a dog."

"His best friends are dogs. Makes sense." When the pups yap and bark, Houdini snorts back and throws trunkfuls of dirt.

After a quick look around to gauge proximity of other crew members, I'm confident no one will be able to hear me, especially with the racket the animals are making. I lower my voice anyway.

"Baby . . . you ever notice how Henry is always wearing gloves?"

He casually scans the area where we're standing. Only a few folks have come in for the meeting but his knuckles whiten around the lead-stick.

"When we were in the barn, Henry took his glove off to touch Gert, but he touched me first to show her it was okay. When our hands made contact, I saw something—images from last night, from the dinner party—*in my head.* He showed me a memory."

Baby's brow twitches but his unblinking eyes don't leave mine.

"He has the same weird hands that I do, Baby. If he touches someone with bare hands, he can transmit or pick up memories from that person's head." I'm whispering, but barely, my voice equal parts excitement and fear.

"Geni, you gotta be careful," he says as Gertrude, bored by her son's antics, moves closer to us. She drops her trunk over Baby's shoulder and sniffs at his face, as if she senses his change in mood. I'm not used to seeing him without a fresh shave; it accentuates the fatigue under his eyes.

"We don't know this kid from Adam, except that he's

Lucian's son. *Dagan's* son. We don't know where his loyalties lie."

"Doesn't it mean something that he trusted me enough to show me what his hands can do?" I ask. "I have to talk to him—see what he knows." I don't tell him about cutting and sealing Henry's flesh. That may have been a step too far. But I wanted Henry to trust me . . .

"Genevieve, bottom line: Dagan is looking for your mother's book—and we're not sure what angle he is going to take now that Delia isn't with us. We don't yet have a clear picture of whether he's connected to the Etemmu. You're the next to inherit the book. What if you strike up a great friendship with Henry, and then *bam*, he delivers all your secrets on a silver platter, right to his father?"

"Henry says he hardly knows anything about it. He called it a grimoire, for Pete's sake. Doesn't sound like Dad is spending a lot of time sharing family secrets," I say. "Besides, Dagan already knows everything about me he needs to know. I'm Delia's daughter. End of story. He and Henry can ask me where Delia's book is until they're blue in the face, and I still can't tell them a thing because *I don't know*."

"That situation is temporary."

"Baby, all I want to do is talk to this kid. Maybe go out for coffee."

"This has to be handled delicately."

"I can be delicate."

Baby turns to Gert, talking sweetly to the end of her trunk. "Gertie, if I give this kid a chance, can you make sure our girl keeps herself out of trouble? Can you do that?" Gert pushes her trunk against Baby's cheek.

The speakers crackle to life overhead as Ted taps on the mic. Company members, their voices a low hum from across the way, settle in to the gallery seating.

"Gert, let's go, girl." Baby clicks his tongue, his arm outstretched for her trunk, and we move toward the southern ring where Dr. Philips stands with a full food bin. Houdini skitters along after us, practically knocking the vet off his feet when he throws his trunk into the basin.

"Yes, he's starving because he had to go an entire half hour without food," I say.

As Ted starts in with his hellos, I consider taking the elephants back to the barn now that they've seen the big top.

Until I see Lucian Dmitri standing near the backstage area.

I probably need to at least pretend to pay attention.

Seeing him scares me.

Violet waves for me to join her. She's sitting next to Mara Dunn; Ash is on Mara's other side, hanging off every word coming out of her mouth. I point at Houdini, hoping Vi will get it. She gives me an exaggerated sad face and then bends over her phone.

Brat. Come sit with us. You're missing out on my new perfume. I smell GOOD, she says.

I stick my tongue out at her across the space; Vi laughs.

Ted launches into all the things bosses are supposed to say: it's gonna be a great year, team effort, energy, excitement, enthusiasm. Et cetera.

When Henry stands, I feel myself blush. *Way to be subtle, Gen.* He's handing out stapled packets; Philips has some for our small party over on this side of the tent. Ted goes over what's in the pages—rehearsal assignments, a list of absolute dos and don'ts not only in the big top but on the fairgrounds and around the animals, and the crowning piece, the preliminary schedule for the upcoming show, WinterFest.

I scroll through the acts, looking in the spot where Delia and I customarily resided. As expected, we've—I—have been moved. In fact, any place my name shows up, it's marked with an asterisk. What does this mean?

Houdini lets out a loud holler, interrupting Ted. "Thank you, Houdini, for your input." But the little guy won't stop making a fuss. Too much stimulation for one morning.

I try to act nonchalant as I look toward Henry, willing him to turn his head in my direction so maybe he'll follow, but he keeps his eyes on Ted.

Damn.

Lead-stick in hand, I direct my buddies to our exit stage right, through the field flanking the stadium and back into the barn. Houdini disappears under his mother—he just needed some quiet time.

I sit on the tack box and pull out my phone.

Still no missed calls from Schuyler.

I open the photo gallery and scroll through the shots I took last night, pausing on the painting of the iris—Dagan's family sigil—and then back to the painting where a woman, allegedly my mother, runs for her life across a field. The familiar lump strains my throat.

If she had just given Dagan the book, she could've stopped running.

And she would be here with me.

I scan the barn, listening to the snorts and sniffles and grunts of elephants and horses and a golden lion as they work on their respective lunches, wishing just for a moment I could be any one of them, wishing I could be sweet Violet with uncomplicated worries . . .

But I'm Genevieve, daughter of Delia, reluctant heir to a book that leads people to be murdered.

I don't want to add any more panels to the mural in Dagan's study.

If I don't find that book, we will never stop running.

And he will paint us yet again.

21

ROCK MUSIC PUMPS FROM THE STADIUM SPEAKERS. ASH FLIES OVERHEAD, lean body stretched long, then rolled into an airborne somersault as he soars from the released trapeze and grabs hold of the one swinging toward him.

Violet whoops from the platform high above as Ash swings back and does a double front somersault before catching the return bar. They switch out—Violet's turn. Easy swings first, transitioning without fanfare between bars to adjust her grip and get the cadence right. I don't know how she can think with Ash's music so loud.

Ash takes hold of the bar closest, waiting for the right time to jump so he syncs with his sister. This trick always scares me—Violet releases and does a double with a twist before flying into her brother's grip. I fight against squeezing my eyes shut.

And then she yelps as she mistimes the release and tumbles into the net, hollering at Ash about being the world's worst catcher.

"Dad! Did you see that? He flipped me off! God, you're such a child!" I smile as her voice echoes off the roof.

Aleksandar Jónás isn't listening to his warring offspring, instead preoccupied by his conference with Ted and the choreographer, Sarah. In addition to his lifelong training on the trapeze—fourth-generation trapezists from Hungary—Aleks was a competitive gymnast for his home country before he and Katia defected to the US in the '80s when Hungary was still under Soviet control. As such, he serves as our primary tumbling instructor. He eats blood, sweat, and tears for breakfast.

Today, though, the silks are up, and Sarah wants to see what the aerialists can do. Everyone else is excused for regular workouts—she'll make her way through the ranks.

My stomach knots.

I shoot Ted a pleading look. He nods and pulls Sarah aside. After a brief but quiet conversation, she gives me a sympathetic smile and detours to the small crowd of Russian bar performers, the equestriennes, and Mara Dunn.

Ted's arm wraps around my shoulders. "You're shaking."

I didn't even realize it. "If you don't get back on the horse, Geni . . ."

"This isn't a horse."

"You know what I mean."

"How can I go back up there without seeing her fall again?"

He hugs me tighter. "Don't let that fear keep you from doing what you love. Your momma wouldn't have wanted that. You can do this. One simple routine."

I try to insist that I have Loxodonta mail to tend to, but he asks me to just give it a try.

I'm not in proper workout gear—just a T-shirt and yoga pants under my very fashionable flannel—but maybe if Sarah thinks I'm terrible, I can avoid performing altogether for a while.

Every time I look at those silks, I see Delia . . .

This is going to hurt everything. I haven't worked out since the night of the New Year's Gala.

But that's the thing about a circus—if the bones aren't sticking out or your flesh isn't on fire, you're pretty much expected to work.

Aleksandar steps close and squeezes my shoulder. "Something easy today, yes? We show Sarah what you can do?"

I shed the flannel, my arms goosebumped with the tent's chill. Aleks helps me stretch—shoulders, hands, ankles, legs, feet. I'm tight and sore already.

When he starts toward the iPad sitting in its port, I stop him. "No music today." I can't hear the same melodies I rehearsed and performed alongside Delia. Not yet.

I've got the silks in hand, my palms damp with anxiety. The last time I touched this fabric, my mother died.

"Give me a second," I say. Aleks and Sarah exchange a look, but when I close my eyes, I see Delia fall. I see her hit. I feel myself tethered so far above the crowd and I cannot get down to help her.

Am I always going to feel this helpless?

"Just try. Little bit," Aleksandar whispers. I open my eyes again, the hint of his son's handsome but devilish face looking back at me. "You can do it."

Deep breath in.

Hand over hand, I pull myself up, arms shaking from so long away. Just like when climbing a rope, the feet act as anchor, pinched together to hold the body still; between legs and arms, the body is pulled higher and higher toward the sky. Watching from the ground, the climbing action looks almost froglike. Delia used to lean sideways and ribbit, to make me laugh.

I twist the fabric lengths around my leg and midsection and settle into a swing that supports my weight.

I can't stop seeing her fall.

It's making me so nervous. But I'm only fifteen feet up, and there is a mat below me.

I won't fall. If I do, I won't die.

Unless the Etemmu comes for me here.

Would it?

I scan the tent, spinning slowly, checking every corner and slope of the tent above me. Sniff for the telltale sign—it only smells like horse, sweat, and plastic from the off-gassing of the new tent and training mats. No ginormous spiders, no stench of death.

I wipe my sweaty hands on my yoga pants. I have to try, if for no other reason than to prove that I can do this. My hands, my muscles—they know what to do.

I stand against the tension in the fabric and ready myself for the first trick. My favorites are the ones where my hands are freed. The clothesline, where my legs hold me suspended, my body at a forty-five-degree angle. The candlestick hang, killer on the thighs, which are wrapped so that my body is completely inverted, arms wide. Regrasp the fabric and add centrifugal force, and it's like ice-skating in the air. The key to working above the ground is maintaining an understanding with the silk. If I respect the fabric, it will keep me safe. It won't burn against my skin as long as I twist the right way. When I wrap in preparation for a drop, it'll release and not steal my breath. It can hold me above an audience, nothing but the strength of my muscles and the integrity of silk to keep me from surrendering to gravity.

I don't get to do these tricks when I'm playing the violin for most of the act. I'll take advantage now, ignoring the protestations of weakened muscles, the tired ache in my fingers.

The show must go on.

And right now, I can't help but close my eyes and channel my mother, thinking of how beautiful she was every single time she climbed toward the sky.

I finish the split spin and pull myself upright, wrapping the silk tight around my waist. "I love you, Mom," I whisper.

I slide down, and Ted surprises me with a fatherly hug. "Proud of you, kid. That looked great." He smiles, his eyes a bit damp.

Sarah and Aleks offer a few notes, a few options for the next show, depending on what I'm ready for.

More than anything, I'm proud of myself. I don't need to decide about the next show right this second. I don't even know if I will be here for it.

As the adults excuse me to go about my day, the new aerialist approaches and offers a heavily tattooed right hand. "Mara Dunn. I am sorry we weren't introduced properly."

French accent? The ring through her bottom lip taps against white, even teeth. Not sure how she gets her bloodred lipstick on with that metal shoved through her flesh. And though this morning's eye makeup is less depressed drama student and more silent-film ingénue, the dark eyeliner makes her husky-blue eyes almost unsettling. Like her insides are made of ice.

"Genevieve Flannery," I say. Her fingers are clammy from her workout.

"You are named for a French saint."

I nod.

"That was very nice," she says, looking over at the dangling silks.

"I'm a bit rusty."

"I have seen your tapes, when you perform with the violin." I blush, and then I'm annoyed. I don't like that she knows who I am, who Delia is. Was. "And I saw you with your *éléphants*. They are beautiful. The little baby is so *malfaisant*. Mischievous!"

"Yes, thank you."

"I want to meet your big friends," she says. Her smile fades. "I am sorry about your mother, Genevieve. I lost my mother when I was very young. It is a hurt that stays with us, but you will learn to move on. Your mother would have wanted that. *Le temps guérit tout.* Time heals all."

Now I've had enough. "Thanks."

An uncomfortable silence stretches between us.

"Hey!" Ash hollers from overhead. Mara grins, her wave exaggerated, as if greeting a long-lost sailor.

"Welcome to our circus, Mara."

"*Merci.* Oh, I am moving in today, to a new *caravane.* You should come help us," she says.

Us?

She looks up at Ash, waves again, and lowers her voice as she returns her focus to me. Her smile changes, lips pursed as she gives me a once-over and finally rests her icy-blue eyes on my face. "I have good wine. Your friend, Ash, likes my wine."

"Yeah," I say, stuffing a folded call sheet into my back pocket, "Ash will drink just about anything. See you around." I'm not going to let this girl's encroachment on my life get into my head.

And I don't want to watch Ash's excited reaction to his new toy.

From overhead, Violet yells, swinging upside down from the trapeze bar. "Genevieve, check your phone! You suck at texting me back!"

That child is a maniac.

I oblige her request, waving my phone at her so she can see me. Flashing across the screen is a barrage of messages from Vi, who clearly wasn't paying attention at the earlier meeting.

Movie night tonight. You have to help me pick something adorbs. #Henry

Mara's moving in today. Come help us! You'll luv her. TEXT ME BACK YO.

Look at him in his little jeans. SO HOTTTT!!!!

Yes, I noticed the jeans, Vi. But his hands were what held my attention.

I text back, even though she won't get it until she's done defying gravity: *Movie night? What are we watching?*

Since I'm done in here, I hustle toward the mess tent before it gets too busy. My phone buzzes again—Cece this time. She's put the Loxodonta mail in my trailer since it was overflowing the bins and she needed the space.

Cool. At least doing mail duty this afternoon means a few minutes alone—I can call the university again.

The mess tent is back to buffet-style eating—good. No more fancy crap. I grab a premade sandwich and an apple. En route back to trailer row, the wind snaps my hair around so I run, slowing only when I find the main path blocked, the crew wedging a brand-new fifth-wheel into the blank pad across and up three spots from mine. I'm guessing that's for Mara Dunn.

Oh goody. We're going to be neighbors. I should bake her a cake. Maybe one of Delia's special recipes—with aloe vera and ginseng to "cleanse the intestines." Then she can share it with Ash over a nice bottle of her delicious wine.

Inside, I crank the heat, change out of my wet socks, and bite into my sandwich, thumbing through mail from Idaho, California, Georgia—even one from Toronto, Ontario, Canada. Everybody loves the elephants.

When the knock sounds on the door, I assume it's Baby.

"Come in," I holler.

"Gen, it's locked!" Violet. I look through the blinds as she pounds again. Shit. The twins and Mara Dunn.

While I know Delia's stuff is hidden under my bunk, I still scan the trailer—just to make sure.

Then I open the door.

"What are you doing in here, other than being antisocial?" Vi says, face sweaty and pink. She steps to the top of the three little stairs and leans against the doorframe.

"Loxodonta stuff," I say.

Ash and Mara help themselves to the Adirondack chairs, dry under the awning. Mara hoists a black, combat-style boot onto a fire pit rock. Violet stands so she's half in the trailer, half out. "Mara, you should see the cool stuff Genevieve does with her elephant charity."

"Charity? Wow," Mara says, "how . . . *philanthropique.*"

Does everything coming out of her mouth sound so snide?

"Do you need some help?" Violet asks. "It'll go faster if there are more of us to help put on stamps."

"I'm not licking stamps," Ash interjects.

"You don't have to lick 'em anymore, genius," Vi snaps at her twin. "If we get it done faster, you can come help us move Mara's stuff from her car into her new trailer. Did you see it? It's so nice!"

"Yeah. It's great," I say. "You guys go ahead. I'm gonna finish this up so Cece doesn't nag. She wants it done before dinner." She doesn't really, but I'm not spending the afternoon helping the new girl. Bigger fish to fry.

Violet blocks the doorway. "What Cece's gonna nag you about is spending too much time alone."

Ash throws a small pebble at his sister's head.

"Ow!"

"What's that supposed to mean?" Cecelia's sent them to babysit me?

Violet turns back around. "She just wants us to spend some time with you so you're not sad."

"Secret Sally spills secrets," Ash says to Mara. "If you have any nuclear launch codes, don't tell Violet or she'll trade them for a bottle of nail polish."

"Very funny, Ash-hole."

Mara snorts.

"Well, if you won't let us help with the mail," Vi says, "then you have to promise you'll come to movie night."

"In your trailer, or . . . ?"

"No! In the big top! It's going to be amazing. I just saw some of the Triad guys carrying in a ginormous screen—" Violet widens her arms. "And not some crappy old film, but a new release. Just for us!" She claps like one of those windup monkey toys. "Ooooh, and I saw Henry and he'll be there, which means I have to fix this hair." Violet shakes out her ponytail.

"You losers can stay here and talk about Prince Henry all you want," Ash says. "We're going to break into some fine wine Mara has cooling in her custom wine refrigerator." Ash waggles his eyebrows at me—like I'm supposed to be impressed that Mara has a stupid wine fridge in her stupid trailer. If she's dumb enough to not notice that her booze is probably the only thing Ash sees in her . . .

He stands and offers Mara a hand. Whatever. He doesn't belong to me. He's made that very clear on numerous occasions.

How can he be making eyes at her already?

Oh, right. Because she's female. And she has a pulse. And a wine fridge.

"Okay, loner. I'm coming back for you no later than five thirty," Vi says.

"Yes, boss." I kiss her cheek but she still pouts away in pursuit of her brother and their new cat toy.

I laugh to myself. Cat toy. *Yeah, Othello would love a go at the new girl.*

Meow.

As I'm pulling the door closed against a tantruming wind, my phone rings.

It's a 206 area code. Seattle.

I drag a nervous finger across the screen. "Hello?"

"Genevieve Flannery?"

"Speaking . . . who's this?"

"Dr. Andreas Schuyler. Returning your call."

22

THE TRAILER IS STONE QUIET, OTHER THAN THE *TICK-TICK-TICK* OF THE heater element. The silver bullet creaks when a strong wind knocks into the side, the decorative border of the unfurled awning outside dancing like a crowd doing the wave.

I had so much to say to this stranger, questions listed in my head—and now I can't remember a single one.

"Uhhh, hello. Thank you for calling me back."

"I saw the story in the newspaper, about your mother's accident. I've made several attempts to contact you. This proved more difficult than expected. Your caretakers—the owners of the circus—they're very protective."

He got in touch with Ted and Cece? And they didn't tell me? Then again, Delia has had a lot of weird friends over the years, and Cece has handled the flood of condolences since her accident. The Cinzios wouldn't have understood the importance of me making contact with Schuyler.

"Thank you very much for calling me back."

"I am so sorry that your mother has left us. She was a rare creature," he says. "How did you find me?"

"The article in *ANTIQUITY*—my mom left it for me. I think she wanted me to find you. To be honest, though, I don't even know where to start with my questions."

"Perhaps with explaining how you learned of the Etemmu."

I swallow hard, throat dry. "It's . . . I've seen it."

There's silence on the other end of the line. "Where are you located now?"

"We're in Eaglefern, Oregon. Just southeast of—"

"I know where it is." A vicious cough is followed by clicking on the other end, either from a lozenge against his teeth or loose dentures.

"Dr. Schuyler, please, if you knew Delia, I'd like to talk to you about her, about anything she may have shared with you regarding the *AVRAKEDAVRA*." I squeeze my eyes shut and count how many seconds he does nothing but breathe through the phone. *Eight . . . nine . . . ten . . . eleven . . .*

"I have something for you. She gave it to me years ago— told me if she ever had a son or daughter . . . If she died, I was to pass it along on her behalf."

She wouldn't have left the book with him, would she? "Can you tell me what it is?" My voice is smaller than I intend. If she left the book with Schuyler, then Baby and Nutesh can get us out of here right away so we can destroy the damn thing before Dagan has the slightest hint that we found it— and I hope, *I hope*, bring about the end of the Etemmu.

235

"Tomorrow, 10:00 a.m. I will grant you ten minutes. And then you will never seek my counsel again. I am an old man, and I wish to be left in peace."

"Where can I find you?"

"Outside the Suzzallo Library, University of Washington, at the Broken Obelisk. If you're late, I will leave."

I scramble through the junk drawer for a pen and pad to write down what he's just said. "Thank you so much, Dr. Schu—"

"Come alone."

The line goes dead.

I wipe my shaking hands on my pants and text Baby. *Professor called. Come see me ASAP.*

When the next knock sounds on the door, I know it's not Vi. Too loud, too insistent.

"That was fast," I say, stepping aside so Baby can enter. The trailer fills with the chilled aura of aftershave and the feisty weather.

"You said ASAP." Hands on hips, he looks like he's bracing for impact.

"Dr. Schuyler wants to meet. Tomorrow morning at ten, in Seattle. He has something for me, something she left with him that he was to give her son or daughter if she died. Baby . . . do you think it could be the book?"

He stares off for a beat, wheels turning, and then shakes his head. "No, I don't think she would leave it unprotected like that."

"He said to come alone."

"Ha!" Baby's smile brightens the space like a torch. "Yes,

236

Genevieve, here are the keys to my truck"—he digs in his pocket and pulls out his key ring, jingling it in my face— "so you can drive three hours north and meet with a total stranger. My arse, you're going alone."

"Fine. But you have to hang back."

The dark look on Baby's face stills the next question in my head before it tumbles from my lips. "We should leave here no later than five, six at the latest. Seattle rush hour is nightmarish," he says, looking at the watch whose face would consume my whole wrist. "You should get ready for movie night."

"Seriously?"

"Get out of your head for a while. There's not much else we can do tonight, not until we see what the nutty professor has in store for us."

"I guess."

"And Mr. Junior Management might be there." He waggles his eyebrows at me.

"What, now you like him?"

"I said I'd give him a chance."

My cheeks blaze. "If Henry's there, my primary objective will be to find out as much as I can about whatever he knows, and maybe what he doesn't even realize he knows. He's lived with the devil his whole life. *Something* must've rubbed off or sunk in. And if he happens to become so enchanted with my feminine wiles that he slips in some details about Daddy's magical secrets, I'd be okay with that."

"No feminine wiles. Forget it. I've changed my mind." Baby crosses his arms over his chest and shakes his head.

"It *is* sort of amazing to meet another freak of nature."

He snorts. "I know."

Of course he knows. "What's it like? Being alive for so long . . ."

"Fascinating. Terrifying. Lonely. It's hard to make friends because they will get old and die, and I will just be . . . this." He gestures at a body that clearly has no intention of getting old anytime soon.

"Take an hour off from thinking about all this. Have a relaxing night at the movie. Pretend you're a teenager for a little bit." He nudges the underside of my chin with a closed fist. "I have to go finish babysitting. Who knew bringing in a giant TV could cause so much fuss." Baby rezips his coat and nods at the Loxo mail spread all over the table. "Looks like you have something to keep you busy. I'll see you at dinner?"

He winks and plods out of the trailer.

At five thirty on the nose, Violet bursts in with an armload of fashion choices, her entire being crackling with an energy that would make Nikola Tesla envious. Her mouth moves nonstop as she buzzes about this evening's film—an action-with-romance thing with some Adonis in the lead role—and how I need to hurry up so we can eat and get beautiful before Henry arrives and *what should I wear pants or maybe this cute skirt and boots although it's sort of cold for a skirt so maybe I'll wear leggings and my new sweater what do you think Genevieve?*

"Jeans. Jeans are good."

"You have terrible fashion sense."

She's right. Great minds of modern society—Steve Jobs, Mark Zuckerberg—agree that there are far bigger decisions to be made every day than the perfect wardrobe. Henry David Thoreau believed that "our life is frittered away by detail. Simplify, simplify." Jeans are simple.

If we don't leave, I fear she'll catch fire, so we huddle together under a wide umbrella and jog to the mess tent. We snake through the buffet lineup, and then I follow her to the table where Ash is already situated—Mara tucked into his side, the two of them smiling and giggling at each other.

Yay. Dinner *and* a show.

When Baby and the head carpenter show up to occupy the remaining open chairs at our table, I assume Ash and Mara will tone it down a little. I assumed wrong. And judging by the glassy wash over Ash's eyes and the occasional slurred word, he and Mara must've opened the contents of the wine fridge.

"We got Mara all moved in," Vi tells the table.

"That didn't take long," I say.

"I do not have many belongings," Mara says, her voice sharp and clear. Must hold her booze better than our numb-skull trapezist. "I prefer to travel light."

"It's so nice," Vi says. "We're gonna have a sleepover!"

My fork clanks against my plate as I look up at Ash. "We?"

"No, not him," Violet says.

Ash mumbles under his likely flammable breath. "We'll see . . ."

"Me and Mara—and you, if you want. She has an awesome pullout couch. It could be like the old days!"

The old days in the Jónáses' coach when Violet and I would stay up all night playing with the tea set and braiding each other's hair and singing along to all the Disney movies that drove her brother crazy.

"You would be welcome to join our *soirée pyjama*, Genevieve. You, as well, Monsieur Baby. We wouldn't want you to feel left out."

Baby's hand stops halfway to his mouth. He looks up at Mara, and then finishes the bite.

"Well, that's super inappropriate," I mutter.

Violet moves right through it.

"It sounds so much fancier when you say it, Mara—*soirée pyjama*."

I've lost my appetite.

"Vi, should we go find seats?" I ask.

"Finally!" she squeals, her spaghetti only two bites lighter than when she sat down.

"What the hell was that all about? Mara asking Baby to come to her pajama party?" I ask Vi as we walk arm-in-arm to the big top.

"It's just how Mara is—always joking around. She's actually really funny."

She's creepy.

We see Henry at the northern entrance just ahead, wearing a pair of fitted black pants and dark army-green hooded jacket, folding his umbrella and smiling at whoever is greeting him. That hopeful flutter again kindles in my chest.

While Violet's excitement is about his pretty face and fancy accent, my motives are wholly different. Those hands. Those lovely, soft, magical hands.

"Henry!" Violet hollers, closing the distance between us in record time.

"Good evening, ladies," he says. "Excellent to see you again." He speaks to both of us but finishes with his eyes resting on me. Violet doesn't miss a beat, quick to corral the poor guy into our row. Cece and Beatrice hand out bags of popcorn as we await the opening credits, but Vi is working overtime to keep hold of Henry's attention.

When Ash and Mara amble in, they sit off to the side by themselves, a continuation of their invite-only party in the mess tent. And then I'm annoyed that I can't help the twinge of jealousy when Ash's arm drapes over the back of her seat, when she sits and feeds him a bite of popcorn. Ash and Violet are *my* friends. How has she moved in on my turf so quickly?

Violet waves a hand in front of my face. "Yoo-hoo . . ."

"Yeah. Sorry."

"Henry's asking how we do school," Violet says, gesturing with dancer's fingers as she turns in his direction. "When we're not on furlough, we have tutors and our own traveling schoolhouse."

"We even know how to read," I add.

"Remarkable." He laughs.

"Gen and Ash and I actually graduated two years ago, though. Genevieve does college courses, but I'm taking a break. Until I decide what I want to study."

"What interests you?" Henry asks. I snicker under my hand. Violet jabs me with her elbow.

"I'm not sure what I would study in college—I love the circus too much. But I'm only seventeen, so I still have time to decide. Right?"

"Absolutely." Henry looks past Violet to me. "It's impressive that you've already graduated high school. What are you studying now?"

"Biology. Thinking about vet school."

"So she can stay with the elephants," Violet finishes, wrestling hold of the conversation again. "Henry, have you ever tried the trapeze before?"

"Heavens, no. I'm terrified of heights."

"Oh, you don't even notice it once you're up there. It's like nothing else you'll ever experience. You have to try it," she says, draping a hand on his knee. "A total rush." She's positively luminous.

Henry is trying very hard to include me. It's funny to watch Vi's expression change. "What about you, Genevieve? Do you float through the air with the greatest of ease, the daring young girl on the flying trapeze?" He adjusts his leg away from Vi's contact.

Vi giggles. "Gen has only flown once. It was . . . awesome."

"And by awesome, she means terrible. Once was enough."

The lights dim. Shushes travel across the small crowd. I'm glad we're done talking. The sooner we get through this, the better.

Thirty minutes in, I'm bored. The film is predictable, and it kills me knowing that Henry is *right there* and we could be having such an important conversation, but instead Vi is leaning toward him, releasing a dreamy sigh every few minutes, her hand open and upward on their shared armrest. An invitation? He's not getting the point. Or if he is, he's ignoring it. She's probably scaring the poor guy.

Our on-screen hero loses the girl, for good this time it seems, just as something pings against the back of my head. I spin around to see if someone behind me is being clever, throwing popcorn kernels or candies. All faces are on the screen. I don't know where Baby is, but I don't see him in the seats above us, so I know it's not him being a smart-ass.

The smell of popcorn and body spray from so many humans is superseded by something else. Something foul.

Something dead.

Another ping against the back of my head. I swipe at it—it feels like something is stuck in my hair. I spin around again to see if someone really is being a jerk and throwing crap at me.

But then the smell intensifies. I bury my face into my sleeve, eyes wild as I whip around in my seat, looking for it, looking for what's coming for me.

"Gen?" Violet's voice is drowned out by a cacophonous roar in my ears.

It's so dark here in the seats, nothing but the glow of the hundred-inch screen when the movie has a well-lit moment.

The temperature plummets.

This is new.

I stand, popcorn bag tumbling to the ground. I have to get out of here. I cannot make a scene.

I clumsily excuse myself past the seated knees of fellow company members, moving to the aisle stairway. *Go down. Go toward the ground. Get to Baby.*

But two steps down, the acrid, rotten plume envelops me and actually pushes me backward into the aisle. I lose my footing and slam onto my back, painfully knocking my skull against the cold steel of the stairway. It feels like something has unzipped under my hair, but I can't move to touch it. I cough to catch my breath, which feels gone forever. It's as if someone's very cold hands are squeezing my windpipe.

Energy draining, I struggle to sit up. I can't grab onto anything to right myself—seats, another person, a safety rail. Another ping against my head, and then I feel it: tiny pointed legs against my cheek.

Something explodes on the screen and lights up the whole area around me: I am lying in an ocean of spiders, countless long-legged black-and-brown bodies fighting over one another to get to me.

I kick out, clawing at my face to loosen anything holding on, consumed in a fresh wave of horror, punching at everything and nothing, struggling to stand. My screams are a tsunami, one wave rolling atop the other as I gulp for air.

And then, levitating above me, forcing me back against the ground and the teeming legions of spiders, their bodies crunching under my flailing body, their guts dampening my clothes, the Etemmu in all its writhing, billowing blackness, wider and more sprawling than I have ever seen it.

My screams echo in my head, spider legs poking into my flesh. They're in my clothes. But it's almost inconsequential next to the Etemmu, now close enough to kiss me if it wants to, its countless arms and endless malignance thrashing close enough to steal my last breath, its expanding-and-contracting body alive with the movement of spiders, crawling over and hanging from the vaporous cloak wrapped around its undulating form.

I taste blood.

As the fingers of consciousness loosen, a cold wind engulfs me, and then strong arms scoop me off the ground, my body cushioned and safe as we run, run, run, the voice against my head familiar and yet a thousand miles away, whispering words only spoken by a talisman to his charge in a desperate attempt to keep her from falling into the abyss.

23

MY TONGUE TASTES METALLIC. AND HEAVY. I FEEL A STRONG HAND IN MY own. When my eyelids open a slit, I immediately regret it, light overhead burning my retinas. I groan and close them again. We're moving, and the motion is nauseating.

"Geni, look at me. Look at me. You're all right. You're safe now," Baby says. "Open your eyes so I can see you're okay."

I'm not okay.

I'm so far from okay.

I squint open again. Close again. "The light. Turn off the light." My throat—like pulling a steel rake across a concrete floor.

We're in Baby's truck. "Light's off," he says.

"Is it gone? Please tell me it's gone," I whisper.

"Ssshhhh," he coos, rocking me against him. The back of my head hurts so badly. I have to sit up. "Nope, hold still. You split the back of your head open. We're going to the ER." That explains why I feel like puking.

"No . . . no hospitals. Please, Baby," I say. Whenever this happened to Delia, they made her stay. Seventy-two-hour psych hold. But I don't have the strength to fight him.

"They won't hold you, *a leannan*. I won't let them keep you. We'll be there just long enough to get this stitched up." I close my eyes and relax against him. "You know, if you really wanted to get out of movie night, you could've held a thermometer over a match like a normal kid."

I try to smile, but really I just want to sleep. "It didn't get you? You're not hurt?" I ask.

Baby leans closer. "Nothing gets me."

And then it dawns on me. "Who's driving?" I crack open one eye and see the dark army-green coat and feisty curls of the person behind the wheel.

Henry Dmitri is driving us to the hospital? "Well, that's one way to make an impression," I say.

"I needed someone who knows the way to the ER," Baby says. "Henry offered first. You know Cece hates driving this truck. We wouldn't fit in her sedan, and there was no way I was letting go of you."

"Thanks, Henry." I can't make eye contact. I'm too embarrassed.

But the Etemmu. It was so big and so much scarier and—

"You're all right," Baby says. "Deep breaths. Everything's okay."

"Just up ahead," Henry says.

Within two minutes, I'm in the ER, Baby fumbling for his wallet for my insurance card because he refuses to let go of me. I won't lie: I'm grateful. Cece rushes through the whooshing entrance doors just as the desk nurse directs us to the triage room. Baby carries me in and the nurse there sees what must be an impressive wound, if the throb in my head is any indication, because she immediately ushers us into the back area where all the sick people are.

Two hours, one IV, three shots from impossibly long needles, and seventeen rather uncomfortable stitches later, I'm being admitted.

"What? Why? I'm fine! Let me go home, please!"

Cece pats my hand and says that because I lost consciousness, they want to do a CT scan, but the tech has gone home for the night so we have to wait until morning.

"So I'll come back then. Come on! Why do I have to stay?"

I look back and forth between Cece and Baby. They don't want to say it. "Is this a psych hold?" I squeak. "You said you wouldn't let them keep me, Baby."

"It's just for observation," he says.

But the look on Cece's face—she asked them to keep me. Goddammit, I know she means well, but if she had any idea what she's doing! I cannot stay here overnight! I throw a pleading look at Baby. When Cece turns away to fumble in her ginormous purse, I mouth the word *Seattle* at Baby.

He nods.

By the time an orderly arrives to escort us to a private room, I'm fuming, the pain medication failing to make me drowsy like the nurse promised it would.

I do not want to be here.

I need to be in Seattle in twelve hours.

At least the room we land in looks like it's part of a normal ward—no steel mesh on the windows, no harnesses on the bed, no exterior door locks.

Aunt Cece fusses with pillows and pesters the nurse as she hooks up a fresh IV bag. When she follows the poor nurse out the door, I know Cece's going to ask more irrelevant questions about my mental health. Because that's what she does, not knowing anything other than what is in front of her face at this very moment.

I can't be mad at her. She's only trying to protect me. But keeping me here? It's the opposite of protecting me.

Shit, what must the other company members think? *Oh no, here we go again,* or how about *Like mother, like daughter?*

And what about all the new people? They've probably heard the rumors and stories about Delia—and if they hadn't heard them before tonight, they will have by breakfast. God . . . even Mara Dunn was there.

This is so humiliating.

Baby pulls a chair beside the bed and sits.

"Did everyone see? Did they turn the movie off and bring the lights up to see me losing my shit?"

"Don't worry about anyone else, Geni."

"Easy for you to say. No wonder Cece wants to call the shrink."

"Yeah, a few people saw. We can pass it off as a seizure. Allergic reaction. Whatever. It's no one else's business," he says.

"Enough people knew Delia and her history. Fire up the rumor mill."

Cece reenters the room, confusion and worry etched all over her tired face. "Baby's going to sit with you tonight. I'll come back in the morning for the scan, okay? I'll bring you fresh clothes and some breakfast?" She leans over the bed, swallowing me with her hug.

"Thank you, Auntie." When she pulls back, I grab her upper arms so she can't look away. "I'm okay. I'm not Delia. Don't be scared. I promise I'll be all right."

Her eyes glisten. That's exactly what she's worried about. She watched Delia unravel, over all those years, and now she thinks I'm doing the same thing.

I wish I could tell her the truth. Even more, I wish she would *believe* the truth.

"You get some rest. I'll see you in the morning first thing," she says, patting my cheek before tiptoeing out the door, passing a nurse with an armload of extra blankets and pillows. She plops them on the room's other bed and proceeds to explain to Baby how to adjust the head and foot angles using the little buttons on the side panel.

"Uh, what are you doing?"

Baby smiles and thanks the nurse as she leaves.

"We're having a sleepover."

"No, we're not."

"Yeah, we are."

"This is taking this joined-at-the-hip thing to a weird extreme, don't you think?" If he stays in this room all night, there's no way I can leave without him knowing. And I *have* to meet Schuyler, even if I have to sell a kidney to pay for a cab.

Baby winks, but offers no further explanation. "You thirsty or hungry?" I stare at him. "I'm going to get coffee. I'll bring you some juice." His boots clomp down the hall away from me.

I don't want juice. I want to go home.

I lie back against the pillow and even though I command them otherwise, my eyes close despite the horror show replaying in the screen in my head.

The Etemmu—what can it hope to gain by tormenting me? Delia knew where she hid her book, but I don't. Does it plan on haunting me until I, too, fall to my death?

"Killing her didn't get you the book. Killing me won't either," I whisper to no one.

Baby says Nutesh doesn't fully understand the magic that drives the Etemmu. Not super reassuring. If Dagan is connected, maybe he's using it to drive me the same sort of crazy as Delia—maybe he's trying to isolate me from everyone. No one will believe what I say if they think I'm crazy—

Eyes open. I have to try to think about something else. Check clock. Three minutes have passed. Eyes closed. Open them again, four more minutes gone. Eyes closed, my lids covered in a wave of spiders. Open, six minutes later than the last time I watched the second hand in its slow twirl.

Morning is a million years away at this rate.

"Knock, knock?" Instantly, I'm upright, fussing with the sheet to remedy the unreliable coverage of hospital gowns. No need to flash handsome young Henry some boob from where he stands at the bed's end next to Baby, looking about as uncomfortable as I feel.

"He's been in the waiting room this whole time," Baby says. "I told the staff he's your brother, and that's why they let him come up. If a nurse asks, that's the story." Baby chucks Henry on the shoulder, shaking the poor kid's whole body. "I'll be in search of that coffee now. You have a half hour before they figure us out."

Baby gives me a meaningful glance, turns, and walks out.

"Why didn't you go home?"

"Well, I had asked you out for coffee, but this will do just as well." One gloved hand rests on the bed's footboard.

I gesture for Henry to sit in the bedside chair. As he moves, he pulls his other hand from behind his back. In it is a fluffy, stuffed blue elephant, a big plaid bow tied around its neck. Embroidered into the chest: "It's a boy!"

"It was either that or a pink giraffe that looked really . . . unfortunate. I bribed the security guard to open the gift shop for me—told him my wretched stepmum just had another baby so I should make a good show of things, you know, being a big brother for the eleventh time."

I laugh out loud. It hurts, but it's worth it. "He's perfect. Does he have a name?"

"Christopher Marlowe."

"Of course it is. What else would I expect from a Shakespeare hater?" It feels nice to smile, a real smile that isn't forced or polite to ease another person's awkwardness about my situation. "He's perfect. Thank you."

Henry's own grin lights up all one hundred watts of his face.

"Did they bring you anything to eat?" He looks to the

nightstand that holds nothing but a mustard-yellow plastic pitcher and a wrapped disposable cup.

"If I get hungry enough, I can gnaw on Christopher." I feign a bite to the elephant's plush ear.

His smile dims slightly. "How are you feeling?"

"Like I had my ass handed to me by a gorilla." I fuss with the sheet. Tug on the coarse white blanket haphazardly placed over my legs. Fidget with my phone. "I'm sorry you had to see that. All of that. It's embarrassing."

"Nonsense."

"You probably think I'm crazy now."

He shakes his head. "I think no such thing." He sits forward on his chair, eyes soft. "What happened?"

I search his face, looking for hints that he is someone other than a special boy with special hands. "Do you want the story everyone else is going to get?"

"I'd like the truth."

I take a deep breath to settle the nerves now pirouetting under the scratchy neck of my hospital gown. "There is a thing—a demon—called an Etemmu. Have you heard of it?"

He shakes his head no. Either he really is blind to its torment, or he's a convincing actor.

Then again, I wasn't subject to the Etemmu's wrath until Delia died. *You were cloaked in a magic given by a man far more powerful than Delia ever was* . . . Maybe Henry is protected by a similar magic?

I share what I've learned, the myth from prebiblical times about a demon connected to restless, angry spirits. "Except it's no myth. I've seen it. It tormented my mother for as long as I can remember. And now that she's dead, I've started to see it. That's what happened tonight." I take a deep breath against the nausea. "The Etemmu is after the *AVRAKEDAVRA*. We think it was trying to wear Delia down until she'd reveal where she hid it. But she fought . . . really hard." My throat is still raw from screaming. I sniff against the sting in my nose.

"And you believe this . . . entity might have had a hand in your mother's death?"

"I know it did."

Henry grabs the tissue box off the side table. I don't want to cry in front of him, but I'm exhausted. What's a few tears between mutants?

"I need to find Delia's text. Maybe if we can find it . . . maybe the Etemmu hauntings will stop. If I don't have what it wants, maybe it'll leave me alone."

"But you don't know where she hid her book?"

Gently, I shake my sore head no, watching his face carefully for any hint that he might know more than he's letting on. "There's an old friend of Delia's up in Seattle. I'm going to see him, to talk to him about her."

Henry bobs his head, eyes down on interlocked fingers. "Genevieve, I need to show you something." He slides to the chair's edge and slips off his gloves, placing an upturned hand on my bed.

I note the details in his face, the pale hair along his jaw and upper lip still too fair and youthful to be worthy of regular shaving. I want to ask what happened to the eyebrow to scare that thin stripe of hair from ever growing again. His blue-green eyes look solidly back at me, not a blink or flick to the side to suggest he is being less than honest.

He's one of the few humans alive who at least knows what an *AVRAKEDAVRA* is. So far, it doesn't seem like he's told his father what we shared in the barn.

But I can't ignore Baby's nervousness about me trusting Henry.

I'm in danger if I do, and I'm in danger if I don't.

God, it would be so much easier if I could just ask him outright. At least the suspense would be over—either Henry does know and is willing to share stuff about Lucian's possible connection to the Etemmu, or he goes to Daddy and spills all my secrets and I have to run like Delia did. At least I'd know for sure how to proceed.

My confusion is amplified by the throb in my injured head.

Slowly, I rest my right hand in his palm, and his fingers close gently around it. "Close your eyes," he whispers, his own lids dropping.

The warmth starts immediately as the scene plays out. The night of the dinner party, outside Lucian's office, only I'm looking at myself through another's eyes, a little higher in the air than what would be eye-to-eye with me. I see myself standing before the door in the green dress, in the moment when Alicia's hand reached down and grasped my wrist atop the doorknob. The outstretched hand, touching Genevieve's, is attached to me—I am Alicia.

I'm seeing myself through *Alicia's* eyes?

The door opens.

I—as Alicia—float ahead and turn to look behind to see Genevieve moving into the anteroom that houses the *AVRAKEDAVRA*, Genevieve pausing before the mural ribboning the room, taking photos of each panel. I move to get between her and the wall, redirecting her to the case. Genevieve moves toward it, fear overwhelming her features when she realizes what it is. She touches the glass, snaps back when it zaps her hand; Genevieve takes more photos of the book; she jumps when she hears a voice at the door.

It all plays in my head as if I were reliving it in real time, but through Alicia's point of view.

I yank my hand away from Henry, breath short. "Stop rooting around in my head," I growl. "You found the memory of that night—" But it can't be. I didn't watch myself do these things.

"Genevieve, the memory—it's not yours. It was given to me. It belongs to someone else." Henry reaches into his back pocket for his wallet and pulls out a tattered photograph. When he hands it to me, the shock translates through my shaking fingers.

It's a photo of a woman who looks remarkably like Alicia. Lustrous dark-blond hair teased by a breeze, wide smile, slight frame in a lovely blue cotton dress with a white belt, sandals clutched in one hand and her toes curled in the sand—and while the eye color is difficult to see clearly, the radiance glowing from them is unmistakable.

"I've seen her—but it can't be the same person. The woman I know . . ." How do I say this without sounding insane? "Who—how did you get this photo? I know her. She's . . ."

"She's a ghost."

I narrow my eyes and drop the photo onto the bed as if it were venomous. "Alicia . . ."

"Her proper name is Alicia Martine Delacroix. She's my mother."

24

ALICIA MARTINE *DELACROIX*.

Delacroix—I know that name . . . *Nutesh, he lives in France . . . Goes by the name Thibault Delacroix these days.*

That means the man Baby trusts to help us is Henry's *grandfather?*

"Genevieve, please—" Henry moves closer. "I know this is all very strange—it is for me too. My mother gave me the memory. She showed me what she saw."

"Your mother . . . if she can share memories and visions, then her book, the Delacroix book—it's *Memory*?"

"I honestly don't know—but I guess that seems logical?"

Which means the book in Lucian's office must be *Death*.

I feel sick: If Lucian Dagan Dmitri has the *Death* text, does he control what happens to spirits in the Afterlife?

Does he control the Etemmu?

But Baby also said the demon now haunting me is likely an enhanced dark magic, which suggests that Lucian isn't working alone. So does Lucian—Dagan—have an accomplice?

"Alicia showed me memories of your mother. They were friends once. But I didn't know who the flame-haired woman was, until I met you." His smile is sad. "Mom's been giving me memories all my life, as far back as I can remember. She died when I was a baby, so this is the only way I've ever known her. Sometimes the memories are just there when I wake up, as if they've come to me in a dream. And sometimes they don't make sense at all, like they were from an old movie or something, another era in history. So I wait until something happens in real life that'll help me understand what I'm seeing in my head."

From an old movie or something, another era in history.

He doesn't know about the long-life component. Damn. Poor Henry feels the same confusion all the time that I felt after just one vision in the field with Alicia. That sucks.

"Henry, these books—they do more than give us our weird hands," I say, lowering my voice. "The reason your mom's memories seem old—it's because they *are.* The *AVRAKEDAVRA*—it gives the families the ability to live very, very long lives."

"I'm sorry?"

I swallow hard, my throat tight. "Long lives. Like . . . they live for centuries."

Henry frowns at me for just a second before hunching forward, elbows resting on his knees. He rubs one thumb over the nail of the other, and I can see the wheels turning behind his unblinking eyes.

"Is that why you asked me how old I was when we were in the barn?" He straightens, his eyes still wide.

"Yes," I whisper.

"Well . . . that certainly does make some of what she's shown me clearer." He shakes his head, smile doleful.

"I'm sorry you didn't know your mother in real life, Henry."

"Thank you. And thank you—for telling me that. Really, it's, uh . . ." He stops, laughs sadly, and then continues, "illuminating."

"I'm so glad my mom and Alicia were friends at one point."

"Me too."

Maybe that means we can be friends?

"I see Alicia now, as a ghost," I say. "I couldn't before. Just since Delia died . . . Your mother is beautiful. I don't ever remember a time when Delia wasn't talking to her."

"Extraordinary," he says quietly. "Are you able to talk to her as well?"

"No. I mean, I can, but I can't hear her responses. She led me into the field the other day, at the fairgrounds, where she showed me a scene from my mother's life."

He laughs nervously but almost looks relieved. "She's given me memories of herself as a girl in France, a few of when I was a newborn baby, of when she and Lucian were happy. Sometimes I don't 'hear' from her for a long time. It's almost as if it's difficult for her to visit me, in my dreams. Like something is holding her back. Lately . . ."

He pauses and looks toward the room's half-open door, his face shadowed like he's short on restful sleep.

"It's like looking at someone through frosted glass," he

continues. "You can see their shape on the other side, but when you get closer, the shape fades and disappears. I get an odd feeling when she brings me memories, like a twinge in my head . . . That's how I know she's there. Well, that, and there's a new memory. It's all I have of Alicia—my father refuses to speak of her."

"He should tell you something about her. If he loved her enough at one time to make you . . ."

"I asked once about my grandparents, my mother's parents—he told me they were dead."

I shake my head no. "It's not true. Your mother's last name, Delacroix—do you know her father's name? Your grandfather?"

"Thibault Delacroix."

Nutesh.

"Henry . . . you're a descendant of two of the *AVRAKEDAVRA* families. Your grandfather, he is very much alive, and he's a very powerful man. He helped my mother, and Baby. He was—is—their *friend*. I can help you find him. I can get you in touch with—"

His face has lost all its color; he looks right through me.

"I think your grandfather would want to know you," I say. "It's not right that your father wasn't honest with you about your mother's family. You deserve the truth."

He blinks a few times as if to clear away something only he sees and looks down at the gloves in his hands. "Genevieve, forgive me. I'm feeling a little unsteady. So much I don't know."

I understand, Henry. God, do I understand.

A hulking form in the doorway blocks out the bright

hallway light. "Time's up, kids," Baby says, juice boxes stacked in one hand.

Henry immediately stands, his nervous face back in place. Baby has that effect on people, especially boys. Well, except Ash.

Before sliding his gloves on, Henry picks up my cell phone from the bed. "My number. In case you need feeding instructions for Christopher Marlowe."

"If he drinks apple juice, it looks like we have it covered," I say as Baby lines up four juice boxes on the nightstand. "Thanks again, Henry, for your help tonight."

"The pleasure was all mine. Get some rest, yes?" He smiles, though his eyes are troubled. He then stretches a hand toward Baby. "Mr. Baby, thank you for an eventful evening."

When their handshake has finished and Henry is out the door, Baby slides into the plastic bedside chair.

"Did you really just grunt at him? After everything he did tonight?" I ask.

Baby winks at me. "How'd your little talk go?"

"Your buddy Nutesh? Mr. Delacroix? Yeah. He's Henry's grandfather. Alicia is his mother."

Baby nods slowly.

"You knew?"

"We suspected. I told you—we weren't sure that Dmitri is who we thought. This man is a changeling. At the time of Alicia's death, she and her father weren't on speaking terms. Nutesh felt she'd turned her back on her family by consorting with people on the wrong side of history. And like you,

Henry has been invisible. But this—this news will be very well received in France."

"Lucian told him that his grandparents were dead."

"That's shitty," Baby says, his face drawn as he leans against the groaning chair.

I sit back against the pillows and close my eyes for a second. "My head hurts." *My everything hurts.*

"Juice?" He hands me a warm drink box. "The kid brought you an elephant?"

I smirk and lift the floppy-headed stuffed toy. "His name is Christopher Marlowe."

"Don't let Ted hear that," he says, winking at me.

"Well, now my new buddy Christopher can keep Ellie company when I'm out saving the world." Ellie, the ratty stuffed elephant I've had since forever.

Baby smiles, his eyes clearer for a moment. "Little Ellie—do you remember this?"

I do, but I want to hear the story again.

"We were in Vegas, and your mom and I took you into one of the hotels to eat. Mmmm, buffet," he says, grinning like a cheeseball. "There was one of those claw machines in the huge lobby, lights blinking and kiddie music blaring out of its speakers, surrounded by people throwing away their life savings on nickel slots. You wouldn't let us walk away from the claw machine. Damn, you couldn't have been more than two or three—you and your head of red curls bouncing to the music—we couldn't get you to leave. Even bribing you with ice cream didn't work."

"Hey, a girl's gotta dance."

"I finally scooped you up and you launched into one of your epic tantrums—you were so good at those—and then you just stopped. You froze, like you'd seen Jesus. But it wasn't Jesus—it was the little gray stuffed elephant in the claw machine."

I'm cracking up, even though my aching head doesn't like it.

"I spent an hour and eighty bucks trying to win that damn elephant."

"Aww, Ellie—a Vegas showgirl rescued into the loving arms of a girl with magic hands," I say. "You really are a warrior, Bamidele Duncan."

Baby smiles widely. It feels good to see him like that. And then we're quiet again, each of us lost in our own memories of that day, of the days around it. The beeping from the nurses' station, the rattle of metal carts in the outer hall, the click of shoes on the polished floor floats into the room and reminds me where we are right now.

It reminds me again that one important part of what defines "us" is now gone.

Baby sighs, the clouds back in his eyes, and then stands and empties his pockets of wallet and keys and phone on the empty chair. "Enough Memory Lane tonight. You. Sleep. We conquer the world tomorrow."

"What about Schuyler?" I ask.

"First thing in the morning, I'll call him. See if he'll meet us in a day or two, once we're sure you don't have a brain injury."

I do not have a brain injury.

"Don't look at me like that, Genevieve. It's almost 1:00 a.m. I'm not calling the guy now, and we're not going anywhere until you've had the CT scan."

A gentle kiss to the top of my head, and my surrogate father sprawls fully clothed on the spare bed, covering himself with a thin hospital blanket.

At least he's a man of his word. Keeping me safe and all that nonsense.

"G'night," I mumble.

"Good night, *a nighean*. Love you."

"Love you back." I can't get comfortable on the stiff mattress. Scant light hums from the narrow fixture behind me. Within a few moments, Baby's breathing slows. He doesn't snore—Delia used to tease that she kept him around because he was the quietest sleeper in the world—but I'm envious he fell under so fast. Then again, I suppose he has reason to be tired, running a circus and babysitting me.

I turn over and watch his hulking form cloaked in near dark. I concentrate on matching my breathing to his, trying to convince my head that it's okay to sleep, that a giant lies nearby to keep us from danger.

I curl up around Christopher Marlowe and pretend that it's not synthetic fiber I'm hugging, but a fuzzy wee lad who graces me with slobbery kisses in exchange for apples and kisses of my own.

I want everything back the way it was before. I want to be back on the road. I want to race Violet to the gas station bathrooms and see who can eat the most sour gummy worms in under a minute and try on stupid mini-mart ballcaps emblazoned with inappropriate sayings.

I want to see the silly things that make this country weird and awesome—the World's Largest Ball of Twine Rolled by One Man in Darwin, Minnesota, the leathery Merman in Hot Springs, Arkansas, the Very Large Array on the Plains of San Agustin in New Mexico.

To spend the day with Delia combing for seashells along the sands of Florence, Newport, and Cannon Beach.

Eaglefern, Oregon, was never on my list of Places to Go Before I Croak. There is no twine, no mermen, no giant galaxy-monitoring antennas.

No Delia.

I want to go back to the shitty diners where Ash and Violet and I would try to outdo one another's pranks. I can't count how many times I'd later open my bag to find a stolen coffee mug or plastic menu holder from Ash the klepto. Midnight stops on the road were part of the adventure, our traveling population stressing out exhausted waitresses but rewarding them with fat tips. And if the restaurant held families noshing on their own travel food, the clowns couldn't be reined in.

I want to see excited families stand around the periphery while we exercise the animals. I want to take Gert and Houdini to the fence so the townspeople can feed a real, live elephant. I want to watch the big top rise to grand queen of the landscape, her flags whipping against a setting sun, the cricket symphony serenading us as the wind dies down and the locals go home.

And most of all, I want the air to sail past my ears as I spin high above the applause, feel the silk in my palms, hear the beat of the bass where there is only me, my mother, and the music.

I want to go home.

This is not home. Oh, so far from it.

An hour or so in, I've done nothing but toss and turn, tangling this stupid IV tubing around my stuffed elephant's trunk. Baby is sound asleep, nothing but the soft exhaled *puhhhhh* whenever his chest falls.

The clock says 2:35 a.m.

Plenty of time to get to Seattle by ten.

Schuyler said he has something for me, from Delia. This book isn't going to find itself.

When I stand to test my legs, I know there's no way I can drive that far alone. Woozy.

Baby has made his sentiments regarding this whole business very clear.

I stare at my phone, willing it to give me the answer. Ash would do it. He likes playing the rebel. And this would certainly qualify as rebellion, sneaking out of the hospital to drive to Seattle a few hours before dawn.

But how do I even start to explain it—this, whatever *this* is—to Ash? And how would I keep Violet and their parents out of the loop?

Wheeled IV pole in hand, I sneak into the bathroom and

hope that once the thick wooden door closes, I'll still be able to get enough bars to connect to the outside world.

I scroll through my few contacts. My finger hovers over his name. Hit Call.

"Hello?" As expected, he was asleep.

"It's Genevieve. I'm sorry to wake you."

He clears his throat. "No. Not a problem. What can I do for you?" Henry says.

"How difficult would it be for you to maybe drive up to Seattle with me?"

"Uh, when?"

"Now."

25

THIS HAS GOT TO BE THE STUPIDEST THING I'VE EVER DONE.

And it's a good thing I'm from a family of magicians: the real trick here is going to be sneaking out of this room, past my sleeping guard.

My resolve wavers when I realize I'm going to have to remove the IV myself. I've seen the vet do it with the animals—I know what to expect—but it is super gross when you have to do it to yourself. I use a washcloth to stop the bleeding once the needle is out and grab gauze and tape from the shelf over the toilet to improvise a Band-Aid.

Being able to heal myself? That would come in super handy right now. Ridiculously unfair.

Even though my shirt and sweatshirt from earlier are stiff with dried blood, it's all I've got. I tie off a quick, loose braid with a rubber band stolen from around a wad of sterile-packaged swabs, shivering when my mother's lucky key slides under the neckline of my shirt, the metal cold against my skin.

After I say a quiet thank-you to whoever left me the travel-sized toothbrush, I take a final look in the mirror: "You're insane, girl," I whisper to my reflection.

The door creaks and I freeze, hoping it wasn't enough to wake Baby. I listen too for the nurse and say a silent prayer that she won't use this moment to come check my vitals.

Baby's truck keys are still on the chair next to my empty bed. Holding my breath, I tiptoe over and place a wide hand over the keys. Henry and I had a brief whispered discussion about whose car we should take; he has his own, a zippy BMW that would get us there in record time, but he's concerned that if it's missing in the morning, his father will be suspicious. "My father and I don't breakfast together. He won't notice my absence. But he will notice the car gone."

We agree that I'll pick him up at the far end of their property—he said, with a hint of troublemaker in his voice, that his first-floor bedroom makes a window escape "simple for even a daft lad"—where the wrought iron fence turns east.

With Christopher Marlowe under my arm, I edge to the main door, throwing another look over my shoulder at Baby. Still asleep. Oh man, he's gonna be pissed when he realizes I'm not only gone but that I've taken his beloved truck.

Given the ungodly hour, the floor is quiet. To the left, a nurse at the desk chomps into a sandwich the size of her head. If I go to the right, she won't see me. A red exit sign serves as a beacon in the low light.

I keep my sore head tucked as I beeline for the stairwell. Clicking the heavy steel door closed, I bolt down the stairs toward freedom.

The lot is surprisingly full, but I know Baby's habits—he would've parked along the far edge to avoid door dings. Sure enough, the big black Dodge sits quiet in the spill of a tall lamppost.

The drive to Henry is only fifteen minutes, but by the time I've arrived, I'm feeling jittery from the cocktail of left-over pain medication and adrenaline. He climbs in, hoisting his soccer-patch-covered backpack onto the floor between us.

"I should probably drive. You look . . . unwell."

"What, you don't like my new cadaver-colored foundation?"

He smiles and takes my place behind the wheel.

"FYI: if you wreck Baby's truck, he will kill you."

Henry laughs nervously. "Good to know."

I point at his pack. "Tell me there's food in there."

"Schoolwork only, I'm afraid. Later, when we're back in town, it would be best for you to drop me at the library. That way, if anyone asks, I was there studying."

"All day?"

"Unlike you, Madame Graduate, I still have studies to tend to." He checks the road and pulls out. "So, where are we going?"

"Get us to I-5. How familiar are you with the University of Washington campus?"

Thanks to how obscenely early it is—quarter to five as we near Portland—we fly to the interstate that'll take us north, about 180 miles to Seattle. The drive so far has been quiet, save Henry asking every few minutes if I'm feeling okay. Quite the little caretaker. I steal a few sidelong glances as he drives. Handsome in his black peacoat, with his curly hair in what must be its natural wild state.

Whatever we find out, it'll inevitably help him too, won't it? Am I putting Henry in danger?

Like the danger that awaits when my phone lights up at 5:12 a.m.?

"Shit. Here we go," I say.

"Are you going to answer it?"

"If I don't, he'll call out the entire US military. He probably will anyway."

I slide my finger across the phone's face. "Hi, Baby."

He seethes through the phone. "Where the hell are you?"

"Baby, it's okay. I'm safe. Everything's fine."

"You have exactly three seconds to tell me where the fuck you are and why you took my truck and why you are not here in this hospital bed. Do you have any idea how goddamned worried everyone is?"

"I know, but—" He's not going to let me talk so I put the phone on speaker for Henry to hear.

"The nurse came in to check your vitals and she woke me and they put the hospital on lockdown. They called Cecelia and Ted. Jesus, Genevieve, what the hell were you *thinking*? And you took my truck? Are you on your way to fucking Seattle? Are you? Answer me!"

"I will. If you'll stop yelling. Are you done yelling?"

"NO!" he says, sighing in frustration. "Yes."

"I'm fine. No pain in my head." *(Wee little white lie.)* "I'm going to see Schuyler. I'll be back before dinner. I promise I'm safe."

"Pull off immediately. I'm coming to get you. You shouldn't be driving."

I look at Henry. Before I can answer, he does for me. "Don't worry, Mr. Baby. She isn't driving."

"Who is that? Who's with you?"

"It's Henry. He's being very good with your truck, so don't worry."

"Genevieve, I don't care about the truck."

"Keep Cece and Ted occupied. Make something up. And if you can, don't tell anyone else that Henry is with me. I don't want his father to be angry with him."

Baby's voice lowers. "Well, Lucian's here at the hospital reading the nursing staff the riot act, so I'm not sure how you guys are going to skirt around that one."

Shit.

Henry's grip tightens on the steering wheel, but he smiles regardless. "It's okay. I'll handle my father. And I promise to keep Genevieve safe. On my own life, sir."

Baby snorts, the sound he makes on the rare occasion he concedes defeat. "You call me the second you arrive in Seattle, and the second you leave. And then you call me again when you hit Portland. If you aren't back here by dinner, I am calling every police agency between here and the Canadian border."

"I'll call. And then we'll come home and you can ground me for a century."

"More like a millennium. Fat good it'll do me," he says, voice quieter. "Be careful, Geni. I'm not there to pull you out of anything, ya know? Henry, if anything doesn't look right, call 911. Got it?"

"Yes, sir."

"You're in so much shit, kid. This better be worth it." Baby hangs up.

I watch Henry's profile for evidence that he's upset. "I'm sorry. That I roped you into this."

"What? No. Don't give it a second thought. It's been a long time since I've had a good adventure."

"Your father has to know we've made this connection."

Henry's lips press together, eyes forward on the road, and then he nods. "Considering I was a model student who never skipped school until this moment, I think that is a very likely possibility."

"But . . . if he's looking for Delia's book, it seems he wouldn't be mad that we're together but maybe pleased?"

"Genevieve, you're the first person I've ever met who is like me. Of course I'm going to be interested in befriending you. And you asked me for help, so here I am." He laughs under his breath. "Despite what my father leads everyone to believe, I do have a brain of my own." He looks over at me, smirking playfully.

"Well, I'm gonna guess he's not thinking you've done a good job using that brain of yours today."

"He's probably just upset that I won't get the Perfect Attendance Award this year," he teases, but then his face darkens slightly. "My father is a complex man." He takes his eyes off the road just long enough to look at me. "So, I take it we're going to see this 'friend' you mentioned."

"He's a professor, actually." Since I've involved Henry in this stunt—definitely a rash decision I hope I don't live to regret—it's all or nothing now. So I fill him on Dr. Schuyler's article about the *AVRAKEDAVRA*, and explain that I'm interested in whatever he can tell me about my mother—she trusted Schuyler enough to leave something behind for him to give to her child in the event of her death. But the part I keep to myself: I'm equally excited about meeting someone who knew my mother in a way I didn't, before I was born. It's almost like I'll get to spend another moment in her presence.

"Any idea what she might have left with him?" Henry asks.

It would be great if it was her text. I know it won't be. Too obvious, too dangerous for Schuyler.

"A clue of some sort? Probably just a letter or maybe a key. My mother had a thing for keys."

Caution nibbles at me. Split loyalties and all that. *Henry's a Dmitri, Genevieve.*

And yet, so far, he's given me no reason to distrust him. He said he wants us to be friends.

I'm not above admitting that such a confession makes me feel a little warmer inside.

"Tell me the first memory Alicia ever shared with you," I say.

He smiles. "Easy. Two little girls, playing in a huge field of wildflowers. I wasn't in the memory, of course, but it felt like I was. There was a boy—I don't know if he was a sibling or a friend. But they played all day, climbing trees and picking flowers." Henry's eyes are dreamy and distant for a moment.

"Anyway, I was preschool age with this first memory. It was confusing for the nannies because I kept asking where the little girl with the white hair was. I really wanted to play with her."

"That sounds amazing."

He beams. "It was."

"Then there were a few of my mother and Lucian when they were together, when she was pregnant with me . . ." His voice drifts off.

"If you don't want to talk about this, it's okay."

His lips press tightly together. "My father wasn't always kind to her. She's shown me one occasion where he was physically violent." His jaw clenches. "After you told me that our family members are older than they appear to be—older than they've confessed to—I wandered around the house when I arrived home from the hospital, looking at everything my father has collected over the years. It makes me wonder how much of that he might've been alive for, as a witness to history rather than a collector after the fact." His face has paled. "I just . . . my head feels like a storm is blowing through."

"It's a lot to take in," I say. "I've been sorta freaked for the past few days."

His head bobs as if answering a question I can't hear, his gloved fingers tapping an unknown beat on the steering wheel. "I'd tell you that such things are completely mental, but given what we can do with our hands—what my father

can do—and the memories my mother has shared . . . The clarity is almost blinding."

"The books are supposed to be passed along to us, the descendants. I don't want Delia's. I can't live through the Etemmu coming after me forever."

"But aren't your healing hands bound to your family's book?" Henry asks.

"Yeah, but I don't want them if it means enduring what she did."

"No, I should think not."

And witnessing what Dagan did to Udish, Dagan's suspected affiliation with the Etemmu—the world would be better off if we destroyed Dagan's book too.

A thought I keep to myself. Henry seems quite attached to the gift that allows his mother to deposit memories into his head—it's his only connection to her. But if we destroy Lucian's book, does that mean Henry will lose his gifts, his one link to Alicia?

No—his connection should remain intact because of the Delacroix book, *Memory*. Right?

Either way, it's a chance I have to take. Delia's life is not my life. No book, no Etemmu.

"Just so you know, when we get to Seattle—Dr. Schuyler told me to come alone. You can't go with me to meet him."

"Uhhhh, negative. Baby won't be pleased with me if I just let you wander off by yourself."

"We walk on to campus together, and then we split. We'll stay in view of each other."

"Genevieve, you've probably got a concussion, and I know there are enough stitches in the back of your head to sew up a rugby ball."

"Just bring your backpack and hang out on a bench. Act like you're on your phone or whatever," I say. "If I need you, I'll flap my arms and caw like a crow."

Henry chuckles. "I'd actually love to see that."

"Don't tempt me."

"Fine. I'll wait off to the side." He leans down and opens the front pouch of his backpack with the hand not on the steering wheel and extracts another pair of soft leather gloves. "Any trouble, slip these from your pocket and put them on slowly. That will be our sign. Agreed?"

"Agreed."

Now all I have to do is count mile markers and hope that whatever my mother left for Dr. Schuyler, it leads me straight to the *AVRAKEDAVRA* so I can work a little magic of my own and make it disappear.

26

BECAUSE OF TRAFFIC AND THE INCREASED RAIN THE FARTHER NORTH WE GET, the trip takes a little longer than expected. Still, we'll make it in time. Let's hope Schuyler does as well.

We choose a parking lot off University Way to give us some distance to approach Central Plaza and scope out where Schuyler might be coming from.

Henry throws his backpack over his shoulder—he looks every bit the college student—and when he offers his arm for support, I don't decline. I am seriously starting to feel the aftereffects of no pain medication.

"You ready?" he says as we step out on to the soaked, gray sidewalk.

"Mm-hmm." I can't admit that I feel light-headed and that my stomach is flipping over itself, or he'll turn around and go back to the truck, the mission thwarted.

"You're a terrible liar, Miss Flannery," he says, wrapping his arm tightly around my shoulders. It should feel awkward, given our only recent acquaintance, but it doesn't. And I'm grateful for the physical support. This really was a stupid idea.

But I'm here now, and I'm committed, and we're making our way across this incredible campus on a freezing cold morning where everyone is going about their lives of studying and working and teaching, the trees bare and dormant, tires on passing cars hissing on the wet streets, the steady thrum of my heartbeat rattling in my ears.

We stop in front of Meany Hall—Central Plaza, otherwise known as Red Square, home to our rendezvous point, the Broken Obelisk—sits directly behind. When Henry's arm releases and he turns to face me, I feel wobbly.

A few deep breaths. "Don't leave me behind."

Henry deposits Baby's truck keys into my hand. "Not a chance."

Ten minutes until ten.

I approach the pyramid-shaped base of the massive sculpture. A few glances back reveal Henry doing his best to look inconspicuous.

"Miss Flannery." I jump at the voice behind me. "I'd recognize that hair anywhere." I turn, met with a man nearly a foot shorter than I am who looks like he might have seen both world wars. Under the brim of his black woolen fedora, thick, round glasses are too large for his sagging face, his skin paper thin, white eyebrows comically bushy hovering over weepy eyes whose irises have been misshaped by cataracts. His smile is pleasant, the perfect alignment and whiteness of his teeth proof enough of dentures.

My hand automatically offers itself for a shake, and he meets it, hoisting his golf-sized umbrella higher to provide coverage for us both. A subtle smile lingers as he inspects my face. "It is unlikely you even have a father. I think Delia scraped off a piece of her own self and sculpted you from there."

"Thank you so much for agreeing to meet me, Dr. Schuyler."

He clears his throat in that old-man sort of way, half cough, half grumble. "Your ten minutes wither, my darling girl."

"Right. Of course." My thoughts race. "Okay. As you know, I found you when I read your article in *ANTIQUITY*."

"Thank you for reading it. Few youngsters are interested in my work anymore."

"For that piece, you photographed the magical book, the *AVRAKEDAVRA*—"

When I say the word out loud, he looks around us.

"It is the Holy Grail of magic books." It sounds almost romantic surfing atop his accent. German? Dutch?

"I need to find my mother's copy of this text. Do you have any idea where it might be, where she might have hidden it?"

Dr. Schuyler looks unsteady on his feet.

"Honestly, any information you might have that could lead me to find it."

He hands me the umbrella and pulls off his glasses, swabbing his lenses with an old, once-white handkerchief teased from his pocket. "Delia told me she lost the book once to someone who made her pay dearly for it. She showed me the text for this one meeting, and then I never saw it again."

"Doctor, I told you—the Etemmu. It's come for me. I think it wants the book. I need to find it so I can put this all to rest."

Schuyler's demeanor changes. He looks around us, over my shoulder, over his own.

He grips my quivering hands, his gnarled fingers surprisingly warm. "I am so sorry for your loss, young Genevieve. The world is a dimmer place in Delia's absence. But this book, it is perilous. In my experience, those books have led people to do horrible things to one another. No good can come from harnessing whatever power lies in those pages. Let it remain hidden."

He reaches a hand inside his coat. From it, he extracts a yellowed sealed envelope.

"What's this?" I say.

"What you came for." He hands it to me and takes back the umbrella. Carefully, I open the envelope, afraid of what's hiding inside, but it's only an old rectangular seed packet, for *Anethum graveolens*—dill.

"Dill seeds?" Why dill seeds? Delia mostly used dill to treat stomach pain and farts. I shake the seed packet—it's empty—but the glue holding the folded paper together is unsealed. I pluck at it, and the packet unfolds.

Someone has drawn on the unfolded packet paper—it looks like stonework? The corner of a building? The inky sketch is incomplete, as if there are other pieces to make it whole.

Collect the seeds.

A puzzle?

"Thank you. For this." I replace the seed packet in the envelope and slide it into my pocket. "Is there anything else about these books you can tell me, beyond what you wrote in *ANTIQUITY?*"

"I understand your mother was pursued for her book. But more vexing is the notion that one person would want all three texts at one time. He or she cannot be an expert practitioner in the three specialties covered by the individual tomes; the research suggests that if one person possesses all three books, the magic overall is weakened." He pauses to squeeze a lozenge into his mouth, the smell of wintergreen immediate. "The person or family with purview of the *Life* text promotes the well-being of crops, protections against illness, plant treatments like your mother offered. The keeper of the *Death* text might help ease someone into the Afterlife, influence the beings who inhabit that realm, as well as other aspects of the transition we all must eventually make."

"Dr. Schuyler . . . beings who inhabit the Afterlife—does that include the Etemmu?"

He looks over his shoulder again, as if expecting someone or something to come out of the huge, gothic-front arched doorways of the library. "In theory? Perhaps. The Etemmu was an important part of Mesopotamian culture, as nasty as it is—the unburied souls of the dead. But what is less clear is that the spells of the *Death* text, as I understood it, did not have the power to bring forth a demon such as the Etemmu. The fact that it haunted your mother, and is now haunting you, is worrisome indeed. It insinuates that there is some greater force at work, perhaps in addition to the magic in the *AVRAKEDAVRA*."

I hold my breath when he shuffles a few steps away to deposit his lozenge wrapper in a trash can. I'm so afraid he's going to leave before my time is up.

"With that said, again theoretically," he continues, "the person with ownership of the *Death* text could exert some sort of control over beings in the Afterlife, perhaps including the Etemmu. According to the rules of the *AVRAKEDAVRA* as I understand them." Upon repeated mention of the Etemmu, Dr. Schuyler pulls a big, lumpy gold cross from under his sweater. He kisses it, whispers a quiet prayer.

Nausea sweeps over me in a cold wave.

"Again, this is all conjecture. Most academics would argue that the notion of a magical book and demons haunting the living is pure mythology."

I can assure you, sir, it is very real.

Rain patters on the huge green-and-white umbrella stretched over us, and although Schuyler's eyes are weepy and tired, within lies a clearness. It's comforting, talking to someone else who knew my mother, who knew her secrets.

An angry reddened scab snakes across the knuckles on the back of Schuyler's hand that grips the umbrella. I hold out my own hand and wait for him to meet it. "May I?"

I check around us; the red-brick plaza is dotted with students hurrying to get out of the rain but no one pays a second glance to the old man or me.

Once Schuyler makes contact, I close my eyes and pull

from the star, instantly regretting it when the sear of pain threatens to buckle my knees. I trace the wound, and hear his gasp.

Eyes again opened, I see the top of Dr. Schuyler's wool-capped head jolt up from his inspection of the now-healed cut. "Dear God, you are your mother's daughter."

He pats my cheek with his warm hand. "I wish you all the best, young Genevieve, wherever your adventures take you." And just as quickly as our meeting began, it ends. A woman, skin the color of polished onyx, the dark pink pants of her medical scrubs rain-splattered under the edge of her raincoat, smiles as she takes Dr. Schuyler's arm.

"Could I maybe keep in touch with you? I'd love to hear more about my mother . . . anything you knew about her before I was born."

He shakes his head no and looks solemnly at me. "You have Delia's eyes. I'm confident you have her courageous heart too."

They move away from me, the care aid helping the doctor up the half dozen concrete steps next to the Obelisk, not a glance back or hesitation because maybe he forgot to tell me something that will turn confusion into logic.

I scan for Henry, an uncomfortable spasm of panic creeping in when I don't see him. At once, my feet feel like anvils. I'm cold and wet and my head aches so badly, twinkling lights dance in the corners of my vision.

As I survey the plaza, a new jolt blasts through me when Alicia appears at my side. "No—please, not here." I whirl away from her and despite my tight, sandpapery throat, I yell for Henry, attracting only the attention of students rushing past.

"Alicia, please . . . no. Find Henry. Find your son." She smiles briefly before touching my wrist as she's done on prior occasions, the fierce, pulsing cold fusing us together, my arm stretched taut despite efforts to pull away. The vision takes over like it did at the old marketplace; the brick plaza wavers, replaced by a suffocating dampness, the air heavy with moisture and the walls too close. A single waxy torch burns against a thick-mortared, rough-hewn stone wall on the opposite side of closely set, corroded bars.

Under my feet lies a filthy floor, the cold in this new space relentless.

A person dressed in what barely passes for a nightgown shifts on the floor, the slow, erratic movements underscored by the rustle of chains.

"Where are we? Alicia?" My voice again sounds like I'm speaking underwater.

The body on the floor scrapes at the wall for a stronghold. As the dirtied hand hikes the body straighter, it becomes clear it's a woman, dark hair matted into an impenetrable nest against the back of her head, appearance obscured by heavy grime.

But when she turns her head toward the flame, I suck in.

Those fierce green eyes—it's Delia.

Heavy irons are latched around her ankles, the skin raw and tender, the telltale odor of infected skin reaching my nose.

We're in some sort of jail. Other human-shaped lumps

lie on the uneven stone-and-soil ground under tattered strips of cloth around the disgusting periphery. Huge four-legged, long-tailed burglars scurry about like they own the place, their long-whiskered noses twitching in search of forgotten morsels. It's unlikely they'll find any, and I wouldn't doubt the rodents are waiting for the slumped bodies to stop breathing altogether. Then a feast they shall have, if they like skin and bones.

Delia's tearstained face lifts as a man's screams echo outside the cell, from down a long, stony hallway. A loud thunk overrides the agonizing bellows, the weighty clunk of a lock mechanism, followed by a scrape—the sound of a heavy wooden door opening?

Footfalls. Within a few seconds, three bodies stand outside the cell: a stout, bearded man, fat-faced, a stained gray tunic over long, bunched black sleeves and what might have once been wheat-colored pantaloons, also splattered with untold horrors—in his hands, a blackened iron ring dense with keys; a slightly built, gray-haired man with a closely trimmed beard in clothes and cloak much finer, and cleaner, than the jailer's garb; and a third face that steals the breath from my chest.

Baby.

But younger, still as huge as ever, towering over his companions, his head covered in a close cut of black curls, a lot more anger on his face.

"Delia," the gray-haired man's gentle voice says into the cell.

The jailer, accent what would be considered working-class

British in today's world, barks at him. "Your price is better than the fancy gent's? 'Cos he's gonna have me head when he finds this whore gone."

The gray-haired man nods and pulls a pouch from one pocket; he shakes it, clearly heavy with coin.

The jailer takes the pouch and uses a sausage-fat finger to separate the drawstring, peering inside. "Not enough here for her husband and brat too."

Her husband and brat?

Delia had a child before me?

The jailer snorts and unlocks the cell, moving inside, past where I stand watching in frozen amazement beside Alicia, his rank body odor overpowering in such a small enclosure. He fumbles with the keys again, this time to release the shackles on Delia's shivering, squalid legs.

The gray-haired gentleman nods, and Baby shoves past the jailer. In one swoop, Baby scoops Delia's frail form into his arms and stomps out of the rat-infested space, but not before Delia comes alive with shrieks and hollers, fighting against her new strange-faced captor, her frightfully skinny arms reaching down the hall toward the source of the anguished screams.

The gray-haired man leans in close to her head, a feat in itself given how dirty she is. He whispers in her ear, calming her wild rant, draping her eyes in a clarity not there just seconds before. He wraps her tiny, half-naked form in his cloak and fishes her right hand from under the fabric, placing it on top of Baby's outstretched palm.

The gray-haired man places his own hand over Delia's

and Baby's, closes his eyes, and utters words foreign to my ears. A glowing emanates from the conjoined hands, widening the jailer's eyes and moving him a few steps back until he meets the damp stony wall.

This man—it must be Nutesh. This is the moment when he sealed Baby and Delia.

"Your father?" I ask Alicia.

She nods.

Whatever happened to Delia to land her here, whatever has made Bamidele "Baby" Duncan a necessity, it must have been horrible.

"I hope he paid you a pretty price for that one." The jailer jumps about a foot and swivels sharply toward the voice hidden by the hallway's darkness. With little more than the sound of the new voice, Delia flies into a renewed rage.

Nutesh nudges Baby. "Go. Get her away," he says. In less than a breath, Baby turns, clutching the feral woman in his arms tight against his chest, and disappears from whatever direction they came.

The jailer fumbles for the torch above him on the wall. Once in hand, he stabs the darkness and illuminates the face that drops my stomach into my feet.

Despite the full head of dark hair, it's the thin, sharp nose, those hazel eyes that see everything that give him away. Lucian, or more appropriately, Dagan.

This is the face painted on one of the mural panels in Dmitri's anteroom. It's so obvious now, the nose, the square jaw.

"Nutesh, like a savior in the night, come to rescue the

distressed damsel. And you brought her a talisman? Clever. I should've thought of that."

"She will be beyond your reach," Nutesh says, his voice sharp with warning.

"For now. But it's no bother, really—Xavier Darrow shall bear the brunt of her stubbornness. Though you likely hear that already," Dagan says, gesturing behind him. "Fealty is such a cheap commodity these days."

"Why must you continue this pursuit? Where is the child? Where is Aveline?"

Aveline? A girl? I had a sister?

"The child is unharmed. You think me a monster, old friend? Come now. How long have we known each other?"

"Long enough to know that monster is too kind a word for you."

More wails fill our ears. It sounds like the man being tortured—Xavier?—won't last much longer.

"Delia is such a scheming girl, sneaking away like a thief in the night—"

"That text belongs to her, Dagan. It belongs to her family. You have no right to it." Nutesh straightens his shoulders, his face fierce as he stares down his foe. "She will never tell you where it is."

"An unfortunate decision for which someone else will suffer."

"Return the child to me," Nutesh says. "You were a father. How could you hurt a child?"

He was a father? As in, past tense?

Dagan's jaw tightens but something flashes in his eyes, a hint of remembrance of someone he once loved.

"You have fooled yourself for too long, Dagan. Your father would be saddened by the choices you have made." Nutesh stands tall, and yet he is still inches shorter than his adversary. His gray, well-groomed beard juts with purpose, his dark-amber eyes reflecting the flicker of the waning torch on the wall. His tailored dark pantaloons and overcoat suggest he is a man of means, a stark contrast to the detritus of the prison.

Dagan takes a step forward but Nutesh doesn't budge. "Don't you speak of my father. You lost that privilege when you let him die in the desert."

"You once knew love. What has gone so astray in your heart that you now dwell in such hate?" Nutesh says, his voice calm and measured.

"Yes, I did know love once, a boundless, great love. But your selfishness, your lack of solicitude for my family"—Dagan slams an open hand against his chest—"one after another, you let them waste away. You let them die. You who were sworn to save and protect—the pact that you swore with my father, and with Udish. You let my family languish, one after another." Dagan's eyes are wild with anger and sadness and regret. "I will undo what you have done. What you have allowed. I will restore the world to its rightful order."

He steps back from Nutesh, straightening the lapels of his heavy black overcoat and replacing the sneer on his lips. "When Delia's ready to make an appropriate exchange, she may have her sweet Aveline back."

"You know she cannot do this. None among us can do this."

"Every soul has a price," Dagan says. With little more than a whisper under his breath, Dagan shoots a look at the jailer, who until this moment has been standing transfixed against the dank jail wall. The corpulent man drops to his knees, hands grasping at his throat, his face bluing, tongue protruded, until he vomits up blood and drops flat onto his face, nose crunching against the stone floor.

Dagan reasserts his gaze at Nutesh. "Tell her to think on it."

And then he's gone, and the scene fades, wavering before my eyes, replaced by the shimmer of modern day, of twenty-first-century humans going about their lives.

I'm on my hands and knees, soaking wet, hands frozen, heart thundering.

Not enough air.

Head hurts so bad.

I blink the water out of my eyes to see that I'm back, back from wherever I was, Henry in front of me, his hands on my face, trying to pull me up, away from the stares of the gathering, gawking crowd.

"Genevieve, I'm here! You're okay—look at me!" Henry says, helping me to my feet. My pants are so heavy from the rain. "You have to sit. Catch your breath—"

"Dagan—your grandfather—the little girl—I had a sister . . ."

"Genevieve, you're scaring me. Please sit down and get a breath. You can hardly stand."

So many people watching. My head pounds so hard, I might vomit.

Henry throws one arm around my waist to hold me up, the other under my bent elbow for balance. "Everything's fine. Nothing to see here," he says, pushing through the crowd. I see only my mother's sickly form, the wild look of terror in her eyes upon hearing Dagan's voice, the calm calculation on his face as he coolly delivered his ultimatum and murdered the jailer *without touching him.*

Suddenly we're at the truck. "The keys. Genevieve, I need the keys." Henry's voice is outside my head and inside at the same time. I hear words, but I don't understand what he's asking me.

He grips my lower jaw in his fingers, snapping with the other hand so I will focus on his face. "The truck keys. Where are they?"

In slow motion, I reach into my coat pocket. Extract the key ring. Drop it in Henry's gloved hand. He unlocks the truck and hoists me inside like I'm a three-year-old. He rushes to get the truck out of the parking garage, out of the neighborhood.

"He tortured her. For the book. And he took her little girl. Dagan—he's a monster! He tortured them, her whole family, over this fucking book!" The panic in my voice must scare Henry because he just about takes down a mailbox when he yanks the truck into a grocery store lot and slams it into park.

"Genevieve, look at me. Look at me," he says, sliding across the seat, cupping my face. I can't stop shaking. Before I can protest, he forces my head between my knees. The twirling lights are back. "Breathe deeply," he says, rubbing my back. "You're all right. Everything will be all right."

It hurts too much to be bent over. Too much blood rushing to my head wound. I lean back against the seat, but Henry doesn't move his gloved hand from my shoulder.

"It was a vision. Your mother came. She showed me . . ."

How can I tell him what I saw? How can I make this boy believe the truth about his horrible, horrible father, his own flesh and blood?

I watch Henry's face for a second. How can he be related to such savagery?

My brain wants my lips to move but my whole head feels like I've got too much bubble gum in my mouth and I'm trying to talk through it.

I will restore the world to its rightful order. What rightful order? What does this mean?

Henry has to be prepared to protect himself from his own kin.

"I can tell you about the vision . . . or you can watch it unfold." I slide my hand, palm up, on top of the console between us. Henry's eyes widen as he looks from my face to my hand and back again.

"Are you sure?" he asks.

"It's probably best that you see it for yourself."

Henry seems nervous but pulls off his gloves anyway.

"You ready?" His hand hovers an inch above mine.

I nod. I want him to go. Do it. Before I change my mind.

When he makes contact, though, it's not terrible. That same warmth from last time flows between us and I feel myself relax into the truck's leather seat, settling the cold shivers from my soaked clothing.

"Concentrate on the vision, Genevieve," he says, his words singsongy in my ears. I focus on what Alicia showed me, just the opening scene, and then, out of my control, the vision unfolds exactly as it happened, Henry's warmth cascading through me while he navigates us through the memory: the jail, Delia in chains, Thibault/Nutesh entering with Baby, the quick rescue, Lucian/Dagan entering, their knife-edge conversation.

The screams of the dying man down the dank stone hallway and the dying jailer.

The ultimatum.

Henry gasps and yanks away, the warmth shut off so suddenly, it spikes the pain in my head.

"No, that is not possible. It cannot be," he says.

I rub my hands together and blow into my cold, cupped fingers. "Has Alicia never shown you anything like that?"

The look on his face is confused and scared. "Why would she show you, and not me?"

"Probably because these visions involve my mother. I need this information to understand the history of my mother's text. I have to understand what she went through—maybe to help me prepare to take over the *Life* book, but instead it's making me more certain than ever that it needs to burn."

He nods, but his eyes are far away.

I don't know what to say. He just saw sheer evil from the man who has raised him, fed and clothed and protected him—and as far as I can tell, loved him.

"The gray-haired man—that's Nutesh, Alicia's father. Your grandfather." I pause to let the information sink in. "Nutesh spoke of Dagan's family—and Dagan reacted. He's lost someone close to him before, at some time during his life. I saw it in his face. I saw his heartbreak." I rest my hand against Henry's forearm. "People change, Henry. Just because he may have been this man a very long time ago doesn't mean he's the same man now. He's raised you. He's loved you. Right?"

Which, of course, I only say to make Henry feel better. Dagan has proven himself a sick bastard through and through.

Henry's face darkens again. "But if that really is my father—if Dagan is my father—why would Alicia ever get involved with someone so cruel?"

It's a valid question. For which I have no valid answer.

"Nutesh . . . my grandfather. My mother looks like him," Henry says sadly, tracing the stitching along his glove's inner seam.

"He saved my mother."

Henry nods and looks out the side window. As exhausted and uncomfortable as I am, it's only fair that I give Henry a moment to adjust to seeing evidence that his father is not at all the man he presents himself to be.

My phone buzzes, breaking the tense silence in the purring truck's cab.

Baby. *Everything OK?*

I text back. *Everything is fine. Another vision. You used to have more hair.*

Seven seconds pass. *Can't wait to hear about this. Get home now.*

I dig through the console box. When I find a sample-size package of ibuprofen, my eyes sting with relief. I swallow the capsules dry.

Henry moves us back into traffic, inching toward the freeway, neither of us speaking.

Beyond this tragedy, I'm stuck on the fact that Delia never told me I had a sister. At one point in history. *Aveline.* Is she still alive? If so, where is she now? Or did Dagan kill her too? She would've been older than me. Does that mean the book would've passed to her?

What would Delia have done if she hadn't died on New Year's Eve, when she saw Lucian in modern day? What did Lucian think when he saw Delia, there making her introductory bow, after a pursuit that had gone on for lord knows how long, while he stood talking with Ted as though nothing in the world could be more interesting than this piddling little circus? The strangest bit of this scenario—it was the piddling little circus he bought so that he could again be in control of Delia's life.

I use Christopher Marlowe as a pillow and curl against the door, my legs pulled into my chest. Henry leans over, glove off, and touches my soaked pants; he cranks the heat higher.

The envelope from Schuyler pokes out from the inside pocket of my jacket. I pull it out and open the empty dill seed packet, studying the drawing. Seeds. Clever Delia—so literal. This drawing, it's obviously incomplete—it looks like she took a snapshot of the corner of a puzzle, a section of what could be a stone structure covered in ivy. But if it's a stone building, we've seen a million of those in our years on the road. And where is the rest of this puzzle?

"Your hands are shaking," Henry says.

My whole body is on low-level vibrate—I could sleep for a year. But before I'm allowed to close my eyes for even a moment, Henry and I must align our tales for the coming Inquisition. And we need gas.

We pull off to refuel. When Henry jumps back into the cab, he hands me a protein bar and energy drink from the gas station mini-mart. "Your color isn't great," he says, pulling the truck away from the pumps but stopping before he reenters the freeway.

His jaw clenches before he speaks. "Genevieve, I don't understand what's happening—all of this, everything you've told and shown me—but before we get back to Eaglefern, I want you to know: I am my father's son, but my loyalty lies with what is right, not a family name," he says. "I told you that Alicia's visions often didn't have context in real life. But my mind is whirling because upon seeing the woman chained in the chamber, upon seeing my father—Dagan—do what he did—"

"That woman was my mother." I feel defensive, as if he's questioning the validity of what we both saw.

He nods and looks away.

"Henry . . . what is it?"

He sniffs and stares ahead out the rain-battered windshield.

"Tell me."

"The night of the dinner party—she brought me a new memory. I didn't want to think it possible. I wanted to believe that perhaps I dreamt it. But now I know. After seeing your mother, after seeing his face," he whispers. He takes a deep breath and swipes a hand across his face, catching a tear before it reaches his jawline. Clears his throat. When he looks at me, his damp eyes are almost neon.

"The books, the memories, your visions—it's all coming together now," he says, looking out the windshield and then back at me again. Henry unbelts and scoots as close to me as he can, reaching across the console. His gloved hand is on my upper arm. I look down at it, up at his face. His eyes don't stray from mine, his lips sealed and trembling.

Faster than I can protest, Henry's glove is off, his hand against my cheek, warmth swarming through my face, rushing down my neck as our eyes lock. Henry forces the vision into the front of my head so that I see nothing else.

A beautiful woman, radiant with new motherhood—Alicia—cradling a tiny, sleeping newborn in her arms. She rubs a finger along the side of his face, over the suckling blister on his puckered upper lip. He smiles, a baby's smile, rare and special. She pulls him closer and kisses him between the almost invisible eyebrows. In the next frame, a nurse helps Alicia burp the baby who has finished at her breast and hands her a glass of liquid. Gestures for Alicia to drink. She does, only when she pulls the glass from her lips, her head wobbles drunkenly.

A trickle of blood snakes from her nostril, across her upper lip.

Her eyes widen, the whites consumed with fine veins that burst and release their crimson contents. The nurse takes the baby from Alicia's arms and places him in the bedside bassinet, but she doesn't move to help the woman who is in obvious distress.

My breath tightens, feels like it's pinched in my chest. I clench Henry's wrist, willing him to pull his hand away. He won't.

The glass smashes against the tile floor, bringing about a fit of wails from the awakened baby.

Within a heart's beat, Alicia's form, gauzy and glowing and weightless as she appears when she comes to me, hovers over the baby, her once-sentient physical body lifeless in the hospital bed, blood from eyes, ears, and mouth draining in nightmarish ribbons onto her nightgown.

She places a ghostly hand on the screaming baby's head. He quiets.

But then her ethereal head pops up and she disappears, just in time for a bald, long-limbed man in an expensive suit to stroll to the bassinet's side and touch the baby's cheek with the back of a long, manicured finger, the proud smile a chilling contrast to the dead woman in the bed just a few feet away.

More tears burn my face, run over Henry's thumb. He pulls away.

"I know that he has stolen from me too, Genevieve." Henry slides his glove back on, tears streaming down his cheek. I can't move my eyes from his. I pull him closer, our foreheads touching.

27

WE DON'T LET GO OF EACH OTHER'S HANDS THE ENTIRE WAY BACK, THOUGH he saves me from further trauma by keeping his gloves on.

When Henry pulls the truck into a spot in the circus lot, the engine isn't even off when my door is thrown open, ushering in that familiar smell of home.

Baby cups my face in his hands, inspecting without saying a word. I push him away, brushing a few of the raindrops that have pilled on his black canvas coat sleeves. I study him for a moment—he's hardly aged a day.

"Baby, I'm fine." Which of course isn't true. But I have the story that Henry and I scabbed together ready to cover our tracks: we went because it was an orientation and open house for the veterinary program at University of Washington, only I had the date wrong.

Just lame enough that it might work, *if* I can steady the tremor in my voice.

"Cece is out of her mind, Ted has smoked enough tobacco to kill a village—and Lucian Dmitri?" Baby looks at

"Why didn't you tell me?" I say.

"I'm telling you now."

I'm terrified, and if the urgency in his voice says any thing, he is too. What if we're making a huge mistake? Wha if we're wrong?

Even worse, what if we're right?

"Henry . . ."

"I trust you with my life, Genevieve," he whispers, and covers my hand with his own. "Now trust me with yours."

Henry and then back to me, brows lifting. "I just hope whatever story you've concocted, it's a good one."

Henry's eyes look scared. I'm worried for him.

"Baby, please—Henry was helping us. Run interference?"

"Let's get this over with," he says, helping me out of the cab. We snake through the cars toward the grounds. Nothing else is said as we sidestep shallow puddles in the asphalt, Henry and I walking in matched cadence behind Baby's heavy stomps. With the pound of my heartbeat at the back of my skull, I can feel every single stitch.

At the lot edge where the blacktop meets the sawdust path, Lucian Dmitri stands waiting, as impeccable as ever in a dark trench, matching wool scarf, and leather gloves, his wide black umbrella protecting him from the elements.

My pace slows. Seeing him again, in the flesh, in modern-day clothing—it takes my breath away. I catalog every detail, the shocking lack of hair that only sharpens his features, the ferocity in his eyes burning as hot here as it did in the musty prison hallway. He's beautiful in a way that only monsters can be.

I shudder from head to foot, knowing what he's capable of, what he's done.

What did you do with Delia's family? Did you kill her little girl? My sister?

Henry and I glance at each other, a quiet understanding passing between us. Whereas yesterday we felt drawn together by the shared secret of our magical hands, today the landscape has changed; we are two motherless children, caught up in something too wild for the imagination, both of us unsure of the futures our families have already chosen for us.

"Welcome home," Lucian says. His stare is unyielding. My legs wobble but I lock my knees, my face reflecting the disgust scorching my veins. *I know what you did to her.*

I watch Henry examine his father, wide-eyed, as if this is the first time he's ever seen him.

In a way, it is.

"Cecelia is beside herself with worry, Genevieve. I know she will be so relieved you're home."

"Then I should go see her," I say. Before I can step past, though, Lucian sidesteps—it's clear he's not ready to dismiss me yet.

From the buttonhole of the suit under his wool coat, he plucks yet another iris blossom, twirling it between his fingers.

"I understand your mother had a remarkable green thumb," he says. "As did mine. My mother's name was Inanna. She had a special affinity for the *Iris versicolor*. Sometimes called the poison flag, which I always found so ironic—how could something so beautiful be poisonous?" He pauses, twirling the blossom in his fingers. "The iris takes her name from a Greek goddess, the messenger to the gods, the link between heaven and earth. Irises were planted on graves to summon the goddess to guide the dead in their Afterlife journey. I always found that bit fascinating. To me, though, it is a long-lasting reminder of my mother. Our love for our mothers, for our families, it's like nothing else, wouldn't you agree?"

Anxiety creeps behind my eyes at the mention of Delia, recalling her reaction to his voice in the prison.

Beside me, Baby takes a step forward, his forehead near impacting the rim of Lucian's umbrella.

"Your adopted aunt and uncle have told me a fair bit about Delia, in the spirit of furthering your care in the aftermath of events. I think that with her affection for plants, she would have had much in common with my own mother. Like Delia, Inanna used the fruits of her botanical toils for good."

He offers me the flower; when I don't take it, he tucks it into an inner pocket.

Baby clears his throat, annoyed impatience written all over his face.

"During my formative years, my parents worked diligently to impart a great sense of responsibility on me and my brother—the treasure that is family, the importance of mutual respect and humility before our elders. By helping Inanna with her fields of flowers, we learned the value of hard work. I'd like to think that the circus has done the same for you.

"Genevieve, your injury, and the event that precipitated it, weighs heavily on your guardians. Our number one priority is your health, mental and physical. We all agree that there is nothing more important than family."

Is that why you murdered Udish? And Alicia? And countless untold others?

In the name of family?

"While we understand you are grieving, you cannot behave recklessly. And what I know of you—"

"You don't know anything about me," I interrupt, my boldness surprising me.

Lucian bobs his head once, his face less friendly. "It's wise to remember how important family is in times of hurt, how acting out against their wishes can only result in greater hurt. Your family, though not by blood"—this dig stings, as if I need him to remind me that I have no living blood relatives—"they choose to care for you. As such, they deserve your respect and humility. Your youth guarantees that you will need their guidance in the future."

Is that a threat?

"I've just spoken to Cecelia, and we believe it to be in your best interests to return to the hospital. Perhaps talk to a mental health professional about your . . . experiences."

I squint at him. What, so now everyone thinks I'm crazy?

"I'm not going." I move closer to Henry, as if he can provide protection. "No more hospitals. And no shrinks. I'll rest, take antibiotics, whatever, but I'm staying home."

"How can you be trusted?" Lucian asks.

I want to laugh in his face, this despicable man who questions *my* trustworthiness.

"My word is enough."

A patronizing smile stretches across his lips, accentuating the unevenness of his front teeth. His gaze shifts to Baby. "I do hope you'll be able to keep a better eye on her."

"Genevieve is a big girl. She can make her own decisions," Baby growls, "even if you don't like them." The look shared between Lucian and Baby—it's about much more than me and my questionable choices.

Despite the warning bells in my head, my gaze is fixed on Lucian, the horrifying memory of the jailer choking on his own tongue fresh. But Lucian Dagan Dmitri's good at this game, offering nothing more than an almost imperceptible smirk.

Almost imperceptible.

"I will send my personal physician first thing in the morning." He steps closer, the umbrella swallowing the light between us. "As with my family, the well-being of my employees is my greatest concern."

"It's a shame you didn't own us before Delia died, then."

"That's enough," Baby says, stepping around Henry, his hand gentle but firm around my upper arm. "Let's go."

I pull away long enough to face Henry, my back to Lucian. "Thank you again," I say, my voice lowered. "I'm so sorry."

He surprises me by giving me a hug in front of his father. "I'll call you later," Henry whispers against my head before turning to follow Lucian to the parking lot.

Alicia, keep him safe.

28

After the Cinzios deliver a tongue-lashing that would shame most self-respecting dictators, I'm excused for nothing but rest. Ted's bottom line—if I'm going to act like a fool, I have to rejoin life. I'd argue that I didn't act foolishly, but what's the point. I'm so weighed down by the day's events, by the pain I saw and felt in the vision from Alicia and the one Henry shared with me in the truck . . .

Baby knows why I went to Seattle, why I challenged Lucian. My debt to Bamidele Duncan feels heavier now, knowing that he stepped in and saved my mother from certain death in that jail. At the end of *Hamlet*, while the prince lies dying from the envenomed tip of Laertes's blade, Horatio offers to drink the poisoned wine intended for his dear friend, to commit suicide so he won't have to live in a world without Hamlet. Baby's decision to serve as Delia's talisman, against a foe such as Lucian Dagan Dmitri, was akin to offering to drink the last of the poisoned wine. Honor, duty, and loyalty to the end.

Like Delia said, he *is* Horatio.

How can I ever express my gratitude?

I'm not too proud to admit that Lucian's admonition left me feeling even worse—the Cinzios don't have to take care of me. And here I am, making it more difficult for them. The look on Cece's face—I've seen that look a hundred times before, usually just before Delia was admitted for another long inpatient stay. It breaks my heart to know I've hurt Cece.

That I'll hurt her again soon, when I have to leave here.

Baby steers me down trailer row, both of us silently huddled against the storm raging around us. I'm anxious to see if this dill packet with the drawing has siblings in Delia's things.

Before we reach shelter, the door to the Jónáses' coach slaps open and Violet launches her pink-adorned self up the path toward us. The rain makes quick work of her nylon tracksuit. "Omigod, you are in so much trouble but I'm so glad you're safe!" she says, hugging me, but then she pushes back, hands on my shoulders. "What happened? Did you really get stitches? Did you really go to Seattle? Why? And OMG, did you really go with Henry? What was he like? Did you guys talk? Did he ask about me?"

"Violet, you girls can catch up later."

"Right. Okay. Well, if she's allowed out later tonight," Vi says, "come over to Mara's trailer. We're baking—me, Mara, Ash—well, Ash will be eating, but Mara's gonna teach my mom how to make these French cookies from Quebec and—"

"We'll see how she's feeling." Baby's hand on the back of my neck tells me we're moving again. I blow Violet a kiss. She scurries back toward their motor coach, arms above her head in a futile attempt to stave off soakage.

But hanging out with Mara? A reason to be thankful for house arrest.

I'm so happy to see the inside of my trailer—it feels like forever since I was here. Now I have a tiny understanding of how Delia would feel upon returning from one of her hospital stays. She'd drain the trailer's hot water heater and then spend twenty-four hours cozied in her bunk, cuddling with me, reading me stories, brushing and braiding my hair, talking to her plants, and, of course, we'd have one of our famous tea parties . . . whatever we needed to reconnect and close off the outside world. Even though I hated when she'd go away, I loved it when she came home.

Baby clicks on the heater and the electric kettle but I push past him.

"You should change—you've got blood on your clothes from last night." I ignore him.

Collect the seeds.

This dill packet—it can't be alone.

I pull out Delia's flowered box. Empty the contents on my bed—as I sift through the upended stuff, my heart beats excitedly in my chest.

I drop everything onto the kitchenette table: Schuyler's envelope with the dill packet, and her playing cards. I again lay them out, side by side, only this time, I put them face down so that the sides painted with seeds are looking up at me.

Lavender, sage, aloe . . .

Dill.

Baby moves next to me. "What's all this?"

"Clues." I drop to my knees and open the mini fridge, pulling out the three rectangular wooden boxes packed tight with seeds in packets and envelopes for every plant imaginable. I hand one and then another to Baby.

"Look for lavender, sage, aloe—" I refer to the playing cards and list the remaining plants so he can help me find the corresponding seed packets.

Once we have all nine as represented on her cards, including the dill from Schuyler, I clear off the table. Baby has a basil packet in his hand. "It's empty."

"They all are. Watch."

I unfurl the dill packet from Schuyler on the tabletop. "This is what I drove to Seattle for. See? It's a corner. Part of a structure?"

The table groans when Baby leans on it. He traces a finger above the drawing without touching it. "This looks like an archway or a door—like stone."

We unfold the remaining eight packets, each one a smaller piece of its bigger black-and-white whole.

A drawing.

Baby helps me position the packets on the cleared tabletop, like one of those number slide puzzles we give away as midway prizes.

An archway and top part of a wrought iron gate—three pieces. The left corner arch is on the dill packet from Schuyler. Another two pieces together finish the arch and upper third of the gate, connected by three midsection pieces—more gate framed by thick stone. The bottom three drawings are the stone base of the structure, as well as three thick stone steps, grass tall and cluttered along the edges, a bundle of flowers resting on the bottom step.

We've been here before.

I grab tape out of the junk drawer and secure the open packets into a giant poster. Once complete, I affix it to the bathroom door and we step back for a more global view. The detail is insane, especially around the gate's lock.

And I'm sucked back to the last time we went to Portland's River View Cemetery—midsummer, the air moist from a recent rain. Muggy, like thunder was near, the sky charged with electricity just begging for a spark to set it off. Baby's dark T-shirt was damp from exertion—Delia smiled and sang to herself, in her own little world, the light sleeves under her armpits soaked. My mother and her weird affection for cemeteries. She would pick the most neglected headstones and leave flowers and quiet prayers, and she always stopped at those honoring babies and children. She said it was good for the soul to care for those passed on.

We pulled so many weeds that day. Our hands smelled of soil and grass, our fingernails dirtied by the earth blanketing the dead.

But there was a mausoleum, standing apart from the headstones, tucked into a grove of trees—that's where she just left flowers. No weed pulling. In fact, she wouldn't let me stand close to it for more than a few seconds.

I move closer to the reassembled puzzle, noting that in the tangles of greenery and vine artfully drawn along the stony archway, a single word emerges when you're positioned at just the right angle.

It reads, "*VÉRITÉ.*"

My hand goes to my chest, pulling the chain that holds Delia's dumb old lucky key from under the layers of my clothing, the iron warm from contact with my skin. For the thousandth time, I read the engraving in the curved surface: *Vérité.*

"I'll be damned," I whisper. *The key to good is found in truth.*

Truth. *Vérité.*

"Oh my god, Baby. I know where it is."

29

MY HEART THUDS WITH UNCOMFORTABLE REALIZATION.

"We have to go." I glance up at the white-and-red wall clock—just shy of three. "It's gotta only be an hour from here, yes?"

"I'd say that you've had enough excitement for one day and that you can go tomorrow morning—"

"But you know I'm going now, whether you help me or not." I know it's there. We've picked up her seed trail; we're Hansel and Gretel had the birds not eaten their path home. I just hope there's no witch waiting on the other side.

"If it's there, Baby? What then?"

He leans against the counter and runs a hand over his face. "Pack a bag."

I check online for the cemetery's hours, and we agree to meet at his truck in ten minutes. Even if Baby had opted to duct-tape me to the trailer wall to prevent me from leaving, I'd gnaw my way out.

Nothing is keeping me from that cemetery today.

I change into clean clothing and then take a photo of the seed-packet poster so I know exactly which mausoleum I'm looking for. Pull on a heavy coat and tuck my hair into a knitted cap so it's not such a beacon. I think of Delia in that marketplace, how she concealed the color of her hair.

Now I know why.

Once the drawing is carefully rolled up, I stash it with everything else. I wish I had somewhere better to hide all this stuff than under my bunk. It feels so obvious. I'm being paranoid, but even if someone trashed the trailer, they wouldn't find anything that made any sense to them. Would they?

Alicia . . . if you're there, can you give me a sign? Are we going in the right direction?

Breath tight in my chest, I wait for an answer, for a flicker of light or the telltale cold that tells me she's here.

Nothing.

I pause for a second. If we do this, if we go to the cemetery and my mother's text is there—the ripple effect of finding it isn't a ripple at all, but a tidal wave.

We leave. We get to Nutesh. He destroys the book. Dagan—and the Etemmu—have nothing left to chase after. I am free.

But if it were that easy, why didn't Delia do it ages ago?

And will I be free? What will happen when Dagan finds out what I've done? What's going to happen to Henry, to this new friendship we've created?

How much trouble is he in right now, for helping me?

My phone buzzes. *At the truck. Go the long way around, not past the work trailer.*

I kneel on Delia's bunk and peek through the window overlooking the main path. From this angle, it appears clear of any well-meaning but curious bodies who might stop and ask too many questions. Door locked behind me, I tiptoe-jog around the south end of trailer row and into the field, squeezing out between the stadium and the last of the four smaller outbuildings. I can already hear the low rumble of Baby's truck.

I hop in, shivering against the warmth of the cab, nauseated from the fatigue and anxiety layering the head injury.

"You ready?" he asks.

The truth? No. I feel like shit but there's no way to go but forward. "Tick tock, talisman. Make haste."

He winks and pulls away from the fairgrounds.

"Cece's gonna be pissed when she finds me not in bed," I say.

"You're with me. Cece will be fine."

"What did you tell her?"

"That we're going into town to fill the prescriptions from the ER. Then dinner."

"We should probably do those things. Eventually."

"We will," Baby says. He's obviously not interested in speed limits today. I'm grateful—the cemetery closes its gates at five. We've only got an hour and fifty minutes to get there, get in, and get out.

"In Seattle, Alicia brought me another vision while we were in the middle of this crowded plaza. I saw when you were sealed to Delia."

316

His eyes are momentarily remote with memory. "At the prison. Terrible is too gentle a word for that place."

"You saved her."

"Nutesh saved her." Baby saved her as well, but he's too humble to take credit.

"You were a giant, even then. And that hair! Who knew?"

"I was a much younger man then." His smile brightens the shadows under his eyes.

"Dagan killed the jailer. Without touching him. After you and Delia left."

"I told you, he's dangerous, little bird." Baby checks the mirrors way more often than usual, a slight sheen on his forehead despite the cool temperatures. Is he nervous?

"He's a murderer," I bite out. "On the way home, Henry showed me a memory his mother brought him—from just after Henry was born, still in the hospital. A nurse gives Alicia something to drink. Next minute, she's bleeding out. Bam, Lucian comes in, touches newborn Henry's head, as if there weren't a dead woman—the mother of his child!—lying in the bed behind him.

"And yet Lucian had the gall to lecture *me* about the importance of family? Look at what he's done. Murderous prick." My jaw hurts from clenching against my anger. "If family is so important to him, why is he so good at destroying them?"

"I didn't know that's how Alicia died."

"It was horrible, Baby." Poor Henry. What's he going through right now? Is his father punishing him for helping me? And what's he been going through since the night Alicia brought him this memory—suffering in silence, not sure if what he saw was real?

"In the jail, Nutesh mentioned . . . Delia had another daughter. Aveline. Why didn't she ever tell me? Why didn't you?"

"What was she supposed to say? 'I had a family a few hundred years ago'? And it wasn't my story to tell."

"Delia never saw her little girl again?"

Baby shakes his head no. "That's why she's always been so protective of you," he says quietly. "She never forgave herself for losing Aveline."

"Is she still alive? If she's a descendant of Delia's, then the long-life thing would apply to her too, right?"

"Is it possible? Maybe. But unlikely. I never saw the child—she was already gone when I came into Delia's life. But if Dagan had her, I can't imagine he'd keep her. If he didn't kill her, disease or neglect probably did."

So, so sad. My heart hurts for my mother's loss, for the loss of a sister I never knew.

"She never spoke of it because how can a person trade a child's life for a book?" Baby says. "It was an impossible situation." He turns the wipers on high as the rain picks up.

"She should've told me," I mutter, head turned toward the window. The evergreen trees flanking the highway blur into a slab of unending green. "She should've told me everything."

30

office just off Taylors Ferry Road. The parking lot only has a few cars in it—maybe people are waiting to die until it warms up a little. Delia apparently didn't get the memo.

We agree that I'll go into the office.

Inside, a pleasant woman named Bert is happy to provide a map. When she asks what name I'm looking for, I freeze.

"I can't remember the name. My mother gave me this drawing," I say, pulling out my phone to show her the photo. This is risky but the cemetery is huge and I have less than an hour before they close.

Bert points out on the map where I can find the place I need to go.

Baby follows a few steps behind me, both of us quiet, his fists clenching and unclenching as he does when he's on edge. The dense clouds snuff out the sun and hint at snow. Fitting, as I walk among the dead. Cemeteries scare me, but not because I'm afraid of dead things. Because I'm afraid of what comes after death.

My stomach cramps. I should be thinking happy thoughts. Positive thoughts.

But I can't.

Step after step, the tiny gravel crunches underfoot. I can't stop feeling like a thousand people are watching me move through their dormitory of death.

When the building emerges from the light fog wrapped around the nearby fir trees, my breath hitches. The seed-packet drawing—it's a real place, standing before me in rough-cut stone and mortar and iron.

"Baby . . ." I look up at him, his own eyes wide.

It's not as big as I remember it, but I was just a little kid the last time I was here. The double pillars and arched entry make it look regal and important. All that I have left is to go in.

Easy as pie.

Unlucky for me, I'm more of a cake person.

I pull out Delia's key, warm from my body heat, hanging from the chain around my neck.

"Now or never," I say.

He bobs his head once. "I'm right here. The whole time."

A thorough scan of the surroundings—we're alone. Three shallow steps up, and I'm at the gate.

Ivy has overgrown the pediment's gray stonework. I reach up on my toes, prodding to push the bushy greenery aside in search of the final clue that tells me I'm in the right place.

It's faded . . . but sure enough, carved into the stone: *VÉRITÉ.*

"The key to good is found in truth," I whisper.

I swallow hard. Close my eyes for a beat. Tell the voice in my head that I can't run.

Eyes open. Iron key in the lock. Turn.

Click.

Behind me, Baby stands with hands on his hips on the bottom step, fierce as ever. With a final look shared between us, I turn back to the gate.

The heavy wrought iron creaks apart, splitting itself down the middle to reveal a door. It groans open, old wood wearing a mossy coat, until the inside of the vault sits before me, dark except for a solitary human-shaped glow in the far corner.

"My little bird . . . how I've missed you."

31

"MOM?"

She's weightless, a translucent glow dressed in a sequined scarlet macaw-inspired circus costume—the outfit she died in—brightening the corner of the confining rectangular structure. Instead of her hair knotted in a tight show bun, it flares around her head in a halo of fire, the way it would look in those moments she'd relax in a swimming pool when the world was quiet. She looks as vibrant as she did New Year's night, minus the worried lines around her eyes, the permanent groove between her brows. She shines so brightly, just as Alicia does when she comes to me, and though the performance rhinestones and sequins along her cheekbones are missing, her wide green eyes seem lit from behind, her lipstick red like it was just applied.

I blink away tears made up of equal parts confusion, fear, and happiness, not wanting to blink at all because she could disappear in the millisecond my lids are shut.

She closes the distance between us, reaching for my

cheek with her hand that looks more hologram than human flesh, but instead of warmth and lavender-infused softness, it's a cold, prickly charge sparking between us. I don't care. I lean into it, the cold burning me like it does when Alicia pulls me into a vision.

The stone mausoleum is otherwise dark and bitterly chilled, the damp walls redolent with age and decay. I fear they will close in on me, if not for the light Delia radiates, like a feisty flame that flickers around the edges, stretching as far as it can go before sliding into shadow.

"I miss you so much," I say, unable to control the sob.

"Don't cry, my girl," she says. "There is much to be said and no time to say it. You're here for the book. Once it's in your care, the *AVRAKEDAVRA* will grant you new gifts, gifts special only to you."

"I don't want new gifts. I want you to come back to me." Everything inside me feels broken. I just want my mom to step into the dwindling daylight, sentient and whole, and take me home.

She beckons me closer but I can't hug her. There's nothing to hug but freezing, snapping mist shaped like Delia.

"Get the book to Nutesh. He'll teach you what I cannot. Baby will keep you safe."

I take a step back, unable to tolerate the cold even though I never want to let her go.

"Geni, listen to me. We're on sacred ground here"—she gestures to the surrounding structure—"which is why we can communicate—but it's only a matter of time before Dagan and his hounds sniff out this place." She dims slightly. "I am so, so sorry, Genevieve. I hoped I would've been able to deal with this without you ever knowing."

"Alicia showed me . . . She showed me how you suffered."

Delia's eyes close for a long beat, her hair aloft and dancing in its own breeze. "I gave her those memories so she could show you what I couldn't. I needed you to understand."

"I'll do whatever you ask—if that means taking the book to Nutesh, I'll do that. He can help me destroy it—whatever we can do to end this."

When Delia looks at me again, it's a face I've seen before, but only when the news involved hospital stays or the death of a beloved pet.

"Nutesh won't help you destroy it. Not yet. The three books must be brought together first. You can't destroy just one. All three must be present in order for the magic to be undone. It's not been undertaken before because three books in one place is very dangerous." She flickers but brightens again. "Genevieve, the practitioner who harnesses the power of these three books in one place has the ability to influence time."

I stare at her, not quite sure what I've just heard.

"Dagan wants the books so he can move backward in time and save the family he lost. But manipulating time, it affects everything. Us—you, me, Baby, everything—all gone. Unmade."

Lucian's words from earlier replay in my ear: *Our love for our mothers, for our families, it's like nothing else, wouldn't you agree?*

He wants to bring back his dead family?

"That's impossible." Even as I say the words, it flashes

in my head that if Dagan can manipulate time—if *I* could manipulate time—I could bring my mother back.

For a millisecond, I understand why he might want to possess these three books. My love for my own mother . . . it's like nothing else.

But then she floats before me, as a ghost and not a living, breathing person, and I remember why we're in this mausoleum in the first place.

Delia moves closer, static popping off her in tiny lightning bolts.

"Dagan's family died. An illness took his father, Belshunu, one of the books' three original creators. His mother, brother and sister-in-law, his wife and two very young children—they all died. Belshunu couldn't save them, not without Udish and Nutesh, but they couldn't get there to help. Dagan has never forgiven them, nor has he moved past his loss, for all his successes and centuries of living. Dagan was once a good man—he came from a family who pledged themselves to serve humankind. But his profound sadness twisted him, made him vengeful. He wants nothing more than to bring back his lost family, despite what it'll do to the rest of humanity, however warped that is."

"But he has a son now," I say quietly. "Henry. Isn't he enough of a family?"

"He should be, Genevieve," she says. "Nutesh and his family, they're good people. You, and Henry, can trust them. But the two of you are the books' rightful heirs."

Something rustles on the floor behind me. I spin toward it. The Etemmu won't find me here, will it?

I turn back to Delia, nervously, though—if that's a spider . . . "I don't want the book. And it seems as if Henry knows even less about it than I do. If what you say is true about Dagan's plans . . ."

The rustle moves into the spill of light from the door—just a tiny brown mouse squeaking to itself.

"We knew Dagan's bloodlust for the books was never going to end. As Baby probably mentioned, Dagan is a master of sleight of *being*. Nutesh has been tracking him for years. The plan was to get his text and deal with it once and for all, long before you were old enough to understand. But mistakes were made. And I had to be very careful—it became less about helping Nutesh, and more about protecting you."

"You lost Aveline, because of this book."

Delia's face is so forlorn. "Maybe now you understand. I tried to learn from my mistakes." She floats closer to me, crackling with cold.

"I wish you would've told me." I look down at my feet just in time to see the little mouse disappear into a crack in the stonework.

"Remember the story about the young girl and the treasure hidden in the woods?"

"You never told me what was in the box—I always thought it was gold," I say. "It was this book. All along, that was what you meant."

Her lips purse together in a small grin, her eyes crinkling at the corners. And just as quick, it disappears. "The *AVRAKEDAVRA* has run its course. It has lost its place in modern society, and the wrong people would seek to use it for the wrong reasons."

"How will we get all three books together?"

She nudges my chin with the energy sparking from her fingers. "You don't worry about that. Take our family's book and get it to Nutesh. He can protect you until the third text is secured."

"Okay. Okay, I can do whatever you need me to do."

She widens her arms and brings more light into the space, making it almost like the sun has burned through the roof. When she moves aside, behind her is a tall rectangular marble box embedded into the end wall.

I've seen this before—on the playing cards.

The clues have been there all along.

Before I step toward it, though . . . "Mom, you said I'll have new gifts once I have our book. Will you be there to help me figure it out? Will I be able to talk to you?"

"Our family's text grants a finite offering of individual gifts, all with the intended purpose that we use those gifts to help. It's different for every person, like eye or hair color. You might be given the gift of foresight or the ability to hear the dead, like I was able, or perhaps you'll inherit my green thumb," she says, a teasing smile dancing across her face.

"Your plants miss you. A green thumb would be helpful."

"The gifts manifest differently in every person, but once you have the book in your hands, it will know what you need," she says, dimming and drifting back a few steps. "But know once the books are destroyed, you'll lose these gifts.

Forever. It means a normal life. Well, as normal as you can get being my daughter." She winks.

My nose burns with imminent tears. "If it means getting rid of the Etemmu . . . I've been seeing it."

The mirth disappears from her expression. "Oh, Geni, that I can't be there to do anything about it—" She sparks wildly, floating between the confining side walls as if pacing, her fists tightly balled. "That magic, it's dark. But the *Death* text—Dagan's text—has a connection with all beings in the Afterlife, including those that make up the Etemmu. He's working in conjunction with something or someone else. I can't see it, though. I don't know what or who it is. Baby can pull you free of an attack, but they'll continue until Dagan gets what he wants."

"Mom, I'm scared." My bravery of just a few moments ago withers.

"You can do this, Genevieve. Dagan's energies will be focused on you now that I'm gone, but I raised you to be strong and fierce, didn't I?" Her eyes soften, her angry glow diminishing a little. "Retrieve the book. Keep it hidden. Take Henry, and run. Get to France. The saints you were named for were brave women—embody them, Genevieve. Start where their journeys ended. I promise Nutesh will not leave you to handle this alone." She fades again. Panic bites at me; seeing her again is wonderful and terrible at the same time, but what I would give for her to stay with me.

"Please, my sweet Genevieve, don't cry. I love you so, so much. I'm so sorry, for this, for everything." She approaches again, face sad, a cold finger pressed to the key I've replaced around my neck. "The key to good is found in truth, Genevieve. *Vérité*," she whispers.

Through the haze of tears warping my vision, I watch as she flickers and fades, leaving a dark emptiness behind.

"Wait—wait!" I plead, collapsing onto the floor, the centuries of cold seeping through my jeans into my shins and knees. "I can't do this without you."

I allow myself a few minutes to sob there in the unlit tomb, not caring about the renewed scuffle near the wall. Even if it's not the mouse this time, I don't care.

My mother's voice echoes in my ears. *"Retrieve the book. Keep it hidden. Take Henry, and run."*

I sniff and wipe my nose, digging into my bag to find my phone to use as a flashlight. Standing, I move to the mausoleum's end wall, to the tall, rectangular stone box. Light flashed onto its surface reveals that the lid is engraved with a foreign language—I've seen this on Delia's playing cards, on the mural in Lucian's study.

I place my hand flat on the bone-chilling stone, hoping that it'll recognize me, that my mere presence will move it aside. When it doesn't budge, I laugh to myself.

I use the *Vérité* key and my pocketknife for leverage—that's all I've got. And judging by the slowly dimming sky outside, daylight is making itself scarce.

The square slab gives, the lid separating just enough to wedge first the knife underneath, and then the key's bow end. With a particularly good shove, the marble top slides aside with a hearty exhale.

I shine the cell phone screen into the box's interior. An

ominous symbol smiles back at me: the circle overlaid with the inverted triangle.

I'm trembling so hard, the key slides from my hand and thuds against the stone floor.

The book's surface is caked in dust and yet the symbol radiates through, as if it has been waiting for this very minute for generations.

No turning back now.

I reach into the box and grasp the book with both hands, expecting it to be heavy. What I don't expect is the searing pain and wretched shrieks that tear out all other sensation and sound.

The book fuses itself to my hands and my knees give way. Images whoosh into my brain: people I don't recognize in clothing that spans history, of healthy crops and flushed, vigorous faces and new babies and squealing children and infant plants shooting through the soil as if on time lapse and families praying over supine bodies wrapped in shrouds and lovers kissing and broken limbs made whole by hands that look no different from mine.

So much life.

Slowly, the electric pain diminishes, and I'm back in the mausoleum, still kneeling, my hands pulsating with the energy transferring from the book's ancient leather cover. The space is much warmer and the intense sadness I felt at watching my mother leave, yet again, has eased.

I stand and turn toward the crypt's opening where it appears the sun has made a stunning comeback.

But it isn't the sun.

"Genevieve?" Baby says, immediately up the steps. I move around him, though.

Outside, floating above the cemetery lawns, are dozens of faces smiling back at me, so many faces that look familiar though I've never seen a single one of them before, all aglow with the same spectral brilliance I've seen with Alicia and now Delia.

The feeling of love and warmth and protection overwhelms me, and somehow, I know.

"My family," I whisper. Delia lost so much.

No more suffering, no more haunting, no more pain.

In the scared core of my battered heart, a spark ignites.

32

ONCE I STEP FOOT BACK IN EAGLEFERN, THE BOOK WILL BE RIGHT UNDER Lucian's nose.

So close, he could smell it if the wind were to blow in the right direction.

"When we get back to the fairgrounds, proceed directly to your trailer. Do not stop and chitchat with anyone. If Cece or Vi intercepts, act normal."

Tell that to my traitorous complexion.

"Although Lucian doesn't have any business reason to be here tonight, we don't know where he is right now. Go inside, hide that book, and wait for me."

That's the extent of our conversation on the return trip. Probably for the best; I'm speechless from what I've just experienced, and Baby can't stop stealing glances at the multimillennia-old text resting on my lap.

My phone buzzes in my pocket. I pull it out: *1st floor west side 6th window.*

Not a number I recognize, and no clue what that means. I text back: *Wrong number, sorry*, and replace my phone in my pocket. Too tired. Too freaked out to think about anything other than Delia, about this book.

Before we arrive, I stuff the *AVRAKEDAVRA* into my messenger bag, hoping if I do see someone between the lot and trailer row, they won't notice that my bag looks ready to explode.

Baby parks at the far edge of the lot, near the big top so I can sneak back the way I came earlier. We pause, scanning the cars to inventory who's here and who isn't. "No Dmitri-mobiles," he says. "Nice and quiet. Head down. Just like you're out for a stroll, yeah?"

As soon as the truck doors open, the smell of dinner floats toward us, followed closely by that of campfire—means there might be some people sitting outside enjoying the mild winter evening.

"Right to the trailer, Geni," he repeats. My heart thumps, reminder enough of my need for stealth, as I squeeze through between the stadium and big top, hoping Ash isn't hiding out back here with a stolen flask.

I wrap around the end of trailer row and sneak in unnoticed, although with the door locked behind me and a peek through the front window, I can see the lights are on in Mara Dunn's very fancy new rig. Judging by the low rumble of bass coming from that direction, I'm guessing she's home.

Delia spoke of new gifts granted by the book—when will those appear, and how will I know? If ours is the *Life* text, what does that mean for the new talents yet to develop? What does it mean to be in charge of the spells pertaining to the process of living?

I think of the drawing Henry did of me. Flying. Flying would definitely be cool. Not at all practical, but can't a girl dream?

With another quick peek through the blinds around the trailer to be sure no one's coming to talk to me, I sit on the floor. Slowly, I pull the book from my messenger bag, the musty smell lingering from the mausoleum, spiced by the tang of tanned leather. I run my finger over the symbol that has made me so nuts lately.

Inverted triangle overlying a circle. The symbol of healers.

The book feels alive in my hands, as if powered by its own energy source.

"So much trouble, all for you." I drape the limp bag over my legs and set the book down, careful to open it, terrified of what might fly out at me.

Inside, however, is page after page of script I can't read. Accompanying the words are drawings—of plants and bugs and relics and blades and unfamiliar tools and charms and what look like amulets, as well as renderings of so many different wound types and broken bones and blisters and animal bites, each ailment accompanied by detailed instructions that I presume direct the user how to heal these afflictions.

We are healers. We give and keep life.

I can only imagine what the inside of Dagan's book looks like.

Voices holler back and forth on the path outside, and my

heart skips. Gently, I close the book and wrap it in a towel to protect the cover. Once back in my bag, it goes under my bunk.

I'm frozen on the floor, under the edge of the table and out of view of the windows, waiting for the voices to pass, so grateful when they fade up the path instead of growing closer or, worse yet, stopping to knock on my door.

The sooner I get this thing out of here, the better.

I check my phone, hoping to find that Henry called after our earlier run-in with his father.

Nothing.

I text him. Looks like he and I have new trouble to cause: *So sorry about earlier. I hope you're not in trouble. Please call me.*

Arms wrapped around my bent legs, aching head down, eyes closed, the aftereffects of the day's stress marathon roll over me like the surf. I hope Henry's like Violet when it comes to returning text messages.

Evidently, he's not. After ten minutes, I have to move or I'll fall asleep here on the coarse gray carpet.

Earlier Baby told me to pack a bag. I'm not quite sure what to take, especially given that I don't know where I'm going. France, sure, but where in France? What's the weather like this time of year?

I stuff necessities into my backpack; at least I'll be ready to go the moment Baby pulls the trigger.

Now all I need to do is convince Henry that running away from home, to an unknown location on the other side of the planet, is a better idea than taking me for coffee. We can get coffee in France.

I hug the stuffed elephants cozied on my bunk, Ellie and Christopher Marlowe, burying my face in the soft synthetic fur. "Wish you could come with me," I say, rearranging them against the pillow.

For good luck, I wrap my two favorite plastic figurines—a mother and baby elephant—in a sock and stuff them in my coat pocket. Dr. DeGrasse used to encourage Delia to keep a token near to center her when she felt she was losing touch with reality. She wore the *Vérité* key, of course, which I'm wearing now. But the elephants—they are a reminder of home, of everything I have to fight for.

Delia said to embody the saints for whom I am named. Geneviève saved Paris in 451 CE from the attacking Huns; Jehanne saved France from the English in the Hundred Years' War but died a fiery heretic's death tied to a stake in Rouen. *"Start where their journeys ended"*—but there are two "hers" in this equation—am I to pick one? Paris or Rouen?

Either could be a starting place.

Maybe we just need to get there first and worry about logistics once we're on French soil.

Will Baby and Nutesh work this bit out?

When the knock sounds on the door, I about jump out of my skin. Baby stands under the awning, a wrapped plate in one hand, a small white pharmacy bag in the other.

"Hey," I say, opening the door.

"Hey yourself." He climbs inside and looks around the tiny trailer before handing me the plate. "It's secure?"

"As secure as it can be," I say. "Is this dinner?"

"Yeah, I figured you'd want some time to decompress. I told Cece you're in for the night."

"Thanks." From the small paper sack, he extracts two amber-colored pill bottles.

"An antibiotic to make sure the stitches don't get infected and Tylenol No. 3. Nothing too strong," he says. "Take both with food."

From another pocket in his black cargo pants, he pulls out a chilled water bottle.

"Thanks, doc."

"Nutesh needs forty-eight hours to get everything in place. In two days, we walk out of here like we're going for dinner."

"And that's it?"

"Depends on what happens next. It's up to Nutesh."

"France?"

He nods.

I want to be Brave Genevieve and not Chickenshit Genevieve, but right now, the idea of leaving behind everyone and everything that means so much to me . . . Wasn't it enough that I lost Delia? And now I have to leave Gertrude and Houdini and Othello and the Cinzios and the twins and my circus family?

Baby wraps his thick arms around me and squeezes me against his chest, patting my back like he's done every time I've scraped my knee or sprained an ankle or had my girlish heart broken by dumb old Ash. "It's okay, *a leannan*. You'll be back. And it'll be better for you because this mess will be behind us. No more Etemmu, no more uncertainty. You can move forward with your plans to become the world's greatest vet and everyone who loves you will be safe."

He makes it sound so easy.

Baby holds me at arm's length and plucks a leaf out of my hair. Probably from the mausoleum.

I slide onto the bench and peek at what's hiding under the foil. Fettuccine and chicken. I bite into the garlic bread and talk, mouth full. "I packed a bag."

"Good."

"What do I do for the next forty-eight hours?"

"Say your goodbyes in your own way. Go about your life. Don't call attention or raise suspicion. And whatever you do, steer clear of Lucian Dmitri."

"You mean Dagan."

Baby's jaw grinds.

"What about Henry? We can't leave without him. Delia said . . ."

"We won't leave without him. Just stay close. Check in with me regularly. We aren't out of the woods yet. For tonight, though, eat, take your medicine. Take a long shower and go to bed early. I need you to be ready for anything, at any time. I have to go deal with some outstanding issues with Ted—these things need to at least be manageable by the crew so we can leave and the whole operation won't fall apart."

"You're not telling the Cinzios anything, right?"

"Absolutely not."

Cece is going to be out of her mind with worry. Suddenly, I'm so tired that even the act of chewing feels like too much.

Eat. Shower. Sleep.

I can handle this.

"Lock up behind me." He offers his fist for a bump, and heads back into the dark.

I finish what my stomach will hold, but before I crawl into bed, I have to see the elephants. It's been nearly twenty-four hours without sleep—and twenty-four hours since I've seen my babies. In another two days, I'll leave them behind. Every second in their calming presence is a second well spent.

I pull on one of Delia's hoodies that she stole from Baby—extra big to cover my head and face—and sneak up to the barn. Houdini's trunk is already outside the bars reaching for me.

"Hello, my darlings. I missed you." Gert plods closer and sets to sniffing everything about my head. Foreign smells—blood, antiseptic rinse, whatever antibiotic cream they smeared along the suture line that has made my hair so greasy. She's as gentle as an elephant can be but my head is damn sore.

"Easy, Gert. I'm okay." She reaches over into the food basin and pulls out a mango, offering it to me. "You're the smartest one here, aren't you, girl . . ."

From the closet beside the enclosure, I pull out the long-handled bristle brush. Gert never says no to a good back scratch. Although Houdini will have none of it, trying to wrestle the brush from me. I trade him for a length of bamboo, a quick tug-of-war until he decides that eating it is more interesting.

Othello yelps down the way, obviously jealous that his siblings are getting all the attention. "Wait your turn, handsome."

When Gert shuffles to the side and nudges Houdini underneath her, I know she's had enough of a scratch. It's late for baby elephants. Nearly eight o'clock. I hope she's not mad at me for getting the little guy riled up before bed.

Othello sits alongside the bars, but as soon as he sees me walking toward him, he hops up and lowers onto his front legs, butt in the air. He wants to play.

I tiptoe-run up and down in front of his pen, every bounce sending new jabs of pain into my head, but how can I not play with him? When he flops down tired, I sit on the floor outside his enclosure and lean against the bars, scratching his ears and finger-combing his mane, braiding what I can reach as he naps under my hands.

My phone buzzes in the pocket up against the bar, the vibration opening Othello's sleep-drunk eyes.

Finally.

From Henry: *Big top. Tonight, 9 PM.*

33

IT TAKES FOREVER FOR THAT HOUR TO PASS.

I hustle toward the big top, my hand wrapped around Delia's *Vérité* key, head down to avoid eye contact with anyone out after hours.

Dormant light strings extend from the big top's twin flagpoles down the guy-wires. The half-moon overhead when given the opportunity to breathe through shifting clouds casts the yellow-and-red tent in dark, muted shades. The *CINZIO* spire flags droop and then rally, the structure creaking and whining as the slight wind licks the rain-shimmered sides. Cecelia's lucky wind chime hangs under one eave, the bars tinkling occasionally, a discordant echo across the still stretch of the cold, adjacent openness.

I sneak up next to the canvas doors on the south end, peek through the plastic windows. The safety lights are on inside, the clear-bulb strings like halos at the junction of the main tent and the cupolas.

I push the door open and step through, but as soon as I

come into the light, it's not Henry waiting in the front row for me.

It's Lucian Dmitri.

And Mara Dunn? With the twins?

Mara stands with her left foot balanced on the wooden curb around center ring. Violet and Ash, side by side, their faces blank, kneel in the center arena.

What is this?

"Thank you for joining us tonight," Lucian says, gesturing for me to sit.

"What's going on? Why are they in here?"

"Who, the twinsies?" Mara says, her French accent replaced by the Queen's English, her icy blue eyes cutting across the space like a glacial wind. Draped in her traditional head-to-toe black, combat boots ready for duty, she moves between Ash and Vi, her tattooed fingers curled tightly around their shoulders. "We're having a soiree!" She grabs Ash's wrists and flails his arms like a marionette. His eyes stare into nothingness.

"How . . ."

"Well, dear Mummy must have given you something special too—she didn't save it all for me. Of course, these hands were meant to find bits in a body that need fixing, you know, how you can feel extra heat where someone has a nasty eating their bones? No? You can't do that?" She sprawls the fingers of her tattooed hands, holding them in front of Ash, whose body reacts as if shocked. "But with a little practice, I can make a willing body do"—she yanks Ash's head back without touching it—"whatever"—throws his head forward, chin against his chest—"I want. Really. At a cellular level. It's fascinating what the human body is capable of, given the right set of circumstances."

Mummy?

"Oh! By the look on your face, I'm guessing you haven't heard the news." Mara ceases the animation of Ash's body and steps closer to me. "Let me tell you a little story. Stop me if you've heard it: *'Once upon a time, there lived a young girl with hair like the sun's fire, feet like the wind, and hands that enchanted even the lowliest sufferer . . .'*"

Wait.

Stop.

This is the story Delia told *me*. "The Girl with the Gold."

"Did you think it was gold too? Every time our mother told me that story, I surely thought the box in the woods would be filled with gold," Mara says. "Did you ever, in your wildest dreams, think it would be a *book*?"

"You . . . you're Aveline? But . . ."

"But I should be dead? Certainly I should be. She left me. Twice. Once in a horrid jail while my father was tortured to death down the hall. All to save her precious book. A book that should pass on to her descendants.

"And *quelle surprise*—that means you and me! We! Long-lost sisters, reunited at last!" She laughs once loudly; it echoes off the canvas ceiling, worsening the chills already racing through me.

This can't be true. Mara Dunn cannot be my sister.

"How?" I look between her and Lucian.

"I probably should be very angry at Dagan for what he

did to my father. Xavier didn't deserve to suffer because of our mother's stubbornness. But when two people have a common goal, it's truly remarkably what they can accomplish together," she says, nodding reverently toward Lucian.

Dagan.

His name is Dagan.

As elegant and well-appointed as ever—the trademark iris blossom tucked into the buttonhole of his suit—he takes several long strides toward me, his expensive shoes kicking up tiny plumes of the fine circus dirt. "Dagan is my birth name. Forgive me for the masquerade. I detest fakery, especially since I do think of us as family."

Family? Because of our affiliation via the *AVRAKEDAVRA*. So he must be aware that I at least have knowledge of the books' existence.

"Genevieve, you know why we're here. Although I must hand it to my son—Alicia chattering in his head all this time. She's visited you, no doubt?" He stares at me, and then smiles and nods. "It was only a matter of when. It was a risk for sure, introducing you and Henry, but I think it will pay off nicely. And I must say, it's noble, really, Henry's newfound devotion to you. I was noble once."

"Where is he? Is he okay?"

"He's not dead, if that's what you're asking," Mara chimes in, still center ring.

"Henry knows his place. He stepped out of it." Dagan dances Henry's cell phone in front of me, tsking his son. "Actually, I should thank rather than punish him. I didn't think you and I would be having this conversation quite

344

so soon. But when I spoke to my son after your little jaunt north, I knew time was of the essence."

"Please, don't hurt him. It was my fault. I just needed a friend. I didn't mean to drag him into anything."

"Henry brought this upon himself. His punishment will continue until he decides that his loyalties are best with his family—the blood of the people who raised him—and not with you. Not with *them*." He jabs at the air with the phone before throwing it into the dirt.

"But where are my manners? You might want to sit for this," he says, gesturing to the front row of gallery seats. I don't budge. "Suit yourself."

He positions himself in front of me, blocking my view of the twins. I step to the side—I need to see where Mara is, what she's doing to them.

"I presume Alicia has been the busy little beaver she usually is—rascally girl. I can only keep my leash on her when it comes to Henry. You, however, seem to have presented new challenges."

"I've only seen her a couple times. And we can't talk to each other. She's only shown me snapshots of my mother's past. I swear, it's nothing more."

"Well, I doubt it's nothing—Alicia is very handy with memories. Since I don't know how much she has truly shared with you, allow me to properly introduce you to your sister. Though she prefers to go by Mara these days, you might best know her as Miss Aveline Darrow."

He turns sideways and presents Mara, center ring. She curtseys, head down, her dancer's arm nearly brushing the ground.

I have very few options at this moment, and zero leverage. I can't run; I can't threaten them because I have no strength to do so, physical or otherwise, and certainly not in the face of the skills Mara is actively demonstrating on the twins and with Dagan's special abilities still a great big unknown.

Which means I have to play along. Play the bluff.

Convince them of my ignorance.

"Please, Mr. Dmitri, I hardly know anything about what's going on. I swear to you that Delia never shared any of this stuff with me, about any of it. All of this is new to me, and to be honest, it's terrifying."

"Aww, that's so cute!" Mara says.

Dagan's eyes sparkle as he reaches into his pocket. What he pulls from it makes my stomach drop into my feet.

Between us, he dangles a lumpy gold cross on a chain.

Dr. Schuyler's cross, the one he kissed when I mentioned the Etemmu.

"I think he'd want you to have this," he says quietly, reaching for my hand and dropping the cross into my shaking palm.

"Did you hurt him?"

"Just a little," Mara says from the center of the tent. "But what he knew about Mum's book, it was a real dead end." She jabs Ash in the shoulder, though he remains unresponsive. "Get it? Dead end?"

Please tell me they didn't kill him.

"Dr. Schuyler has been warned many times over the years, but he's like a bear to a beehive: they cannot be persuaded otherwise, no matter how brisk the sting. You have come to know about the *AVRAKEDAVRA*, I presume?"

He doesn't know I have it.

"Only the very basics."

"It's impolite to lie, Genevieve. Even if your mother failed to prepare you for what's coming—an egregious misstep on her part, if you ask me—I'm sure your talisman has told you a fair bit more than that," he says. I avert my eyes, my throat tightening at the mention of Baby.

Dagan moves before me again, tapping my shoulder. "Please. Sit."

This time, I do. Because I'm afraid not to. Ash is now heaped in a pile, his tiny sister still frozen in place. I look right, praying that someone will walk out from backstage and interrupt. *Please, Baby, come find me.*

The red canvas backstage curtain remains inert; the yellow big top overhead whistles quietly under a brisk wind.

Dagan clasps his hands before him. "The *AVRAKEDAVRA* is the answer to all that ails us, then, now, in days to come. And it has been the bane of my existence for two thousand years." A tired sigh underlines his words. "At one time, I had two. Your mother reclaimed hers before I had the third. But those Delacroix"—he gestures at the sky—"Nutesh and his family, they are very, very clever.

"And our dear Delia . . ." His eyes soften with remembrance. "With her, I let my guard down. Before I knew who she truly was. She whispered promises of working together to acquire the third book from Nutesh—you probably know him as Thibault?

"Ignoring the knowing voice up here"—*tap tap* against his temple—"sometimes it happens. You open the gates. You *feel* something. It happened first with Delia, and then a few centuries later with my darling Alicia. Maybe you are familiar with this feeling, this . . . weakness?" Dagan looks at the ground before looking back to me, a smirk painted across his lips. "I see how my son looks at you. The possibilities for future heartbreak are endless.

"But, I digress. So enchanted was I by your mother, Genevieve. So genuine and pure. Brilliant, conniving girl, keeping our dalliance a secret from even her devoted husband. Oh, Xavier"—Mara flinches ever so slightly at the mention of her father's name—"that's a story you're going to want to hear too. But not now."

Delia had a romantic relationship with Lucian Dagan Dmitri? Her sworn enemy?

"Your mother, she was a fun distraction—and when you've lived as long as I have, distractions can be very hard to come by. It was a calculated risk. I lost.

"I loved her, Genevieve. I did. And I thought she loved me back. But she was simply obeying an ancient instinct that became an obsession. That, I cannot begrudge her." He's quiet for a moment, his eyes reflective of something he can never have again, no matter how many lives he owns. Behind and above him, moths flit about the safety lights, their shadows menacing atop the light-colored circus dirt.

"And then she left her only child behind, not once but twice, like no more than rubbish to be thrown out with the evening scraps. Sad, really." Dagan lifts an arm in Mara's direction. "Despite the child's broken heart, I do believe it worked out quite serendipitously. Miss Mara is a remarkably gifted magician who has thrived under my tutelage. It has been astonishing to see what a younger mind can do, the daughter of one magical family, left to her own devices, shut out of her family's teachings but brought into the fold of another. It's been a pleasantly symbiotic relationship—she's taught me as much as I've taught her. Like a sponge, little Aveline took a rather mundane ability and turned it into something truly awe-inspiring."

"I can't imagine my mother would've left her child without a good reason," I say. I don't want him aware that I know anything about the events in that prison.

"We all make choices, Genevieve. And your mother had many years to undo the harm of hers. She chose otherwise." He glares at me. "You see, at first I did not know waifish Delia was the descendant of a very powerful family— the fourth-great-granddaughter of Udish, a contemporary of my father's." He grins, like a wolf before burying his canines into his nightly hare. "I did not know until the *Life* text had slipped out of my fingers. And for all my best efforts over these last years, she's kept the book's whereabouts—and your existence—secret. Delia was gifted with secrets." He examines my face. "I don't think I need to tell you that, though, do I."

"What do you want from me, then?" I say, careful to maintain a humble veneer.

"Why, the book, of course."

"Lucian—Dagan—all I know is that I grew up with a mother who was haunted by demons we couldn't see. She communed with ghosts and grew plants that she used to help people. She spent a lot of time in mental hospitals"—I swallow hard, almost choking on the words as the vision of Delia floating in the mausoleum pops into my head—"and I didn't know she left me anything other than a gaping hole in my chest when she died on New Year's Eve. I certainly didn't know I was supposed to be looking for anything more important than a future without her." Angry, scared tears burn my lower lids.

"No, no, don't cry, Genevieve. I know how fresh this loss is for you." Dagan reaches under his overcoat and hands me a purple silk handkerchief from his inner suit pocket. "With your help, we will find the *Life* text so we can put this whole fiasco to rest, once and for all."

"Please, I don't know how to help you," I say, forcing fresh tears.

Dagan grabs one of the clowns' brightly painted wooden chairs, leaned up against the gallery railing, and sets it before me. He sits, leans elbows on his knees, and pulls off his gloves. My chest tightens but I focus on his manicured hands as he holds them in front of him, as if cupping something small.

"Have you ever held a baby in your arms, Genevieve? They are so tiny, so precious. They rely on the kindness of their family for every little thing, for their very survival.

"And please, don't misunderstand. I do have much to be grateful for today. But at one time, I had it all. Doting parents, a brother who was my dearest friend, a beautiful wife I worshipped like the setting sun . . ." He pauses for a moment. "I had children. Two. A boy, Tammuz, named for his uncle.

And Ningal—a 'great lady, a queen'—named for her grand-mother. Tiny Ningal. She was so perfect. A true little queen and I her lowly subject. Her sweet fingers would wrap around the end of my own, and she would bite"—he laughs wist-fully—"she would bite so hard. Like she was trying to crack through the earth's surface, even though she hadn't yet a sin-gle tooth. And that smile. That smile shamed the stars with its radiance." He again laughs under his breath, wrapped in a faraway moment.

But only for a beat. "We had to flee. Our village was under attack. People looking for my father, for healers—magicians before there were such things. Our practice was still new. The magic of the *AVRAKEDAVRA* wasn't yet refined. Sometimes it didn't work the way people expected it to, and that branded us as purveyors of witchcraft. We could not stay.

"When we left, my father, Belshunu, was ill. It was beyond our abilities to remedy—my brother and I weren't strong enough. We needed Udish and Nutesh—their combined strength would have saved my father. We sent word, but they didn't come. They let him die, Genevieve. One by one, the illness took them all. My mother and brother, our wives . . . our children. Belshunu's possession of the *Death* text could do nothing except ease the sufferers into the next life. We needed *Life*, those who could reverse the effects of the ravaging dis-ease. We needed the strength of *Memory*, so the bodies could remember what it felt like to be healthy. But Nutesh and Udish let my whole family wither and die before my eyes."

When Nutesh came for Delia's broken body at the prison, he reminded Dagan that he once knew love.

This is what he meant.

"I don't know why I was spared, why the disease didn't take me too. I wish it had. Never again in my expansive life have I felt the pain that came from placing Ningal's tiny head in the unforgiving earth. How can I ever forgive myself for failing her?"

When he finally looks up at me, his sad eyes are rimmed with memory and regret.

"I came to learn the power I could wield, the good I could bring to the world. If I did enough good, then maybe I could right the wrongs of the people who betrayed me, who served their own ends without concern for others, for defying the very covenants they were sworn to uphold and protect." He again stands, clearing his vision of emotion. "The deaths of my own beloved kin were in vain. Those who could've helped chose not to, for reasons known only to the betrayers."

"I'm so sorry for your loss," I say. "I understand how hard it is."

"Do you?" He gestures at Mara. She pulls Violet and Ash to their feet, and while their eyes don't register that they know what's happening, the grimace of pain on their faces indicates their bodies do.

Dagan reaches for my hand, inviting me to stand. When I don't oblige—more from dread than defiance—he curls his fingers and clasps his hands behind his back. "The AVRAKEDAVRA was meant to help humanity. Alas, there is more at stake here than my damaged heart." He pauses again. "Millions of good people have died because history went off course. We could remake the world, in the spirit the book was intended. Yes, my family—*your* family, your mother—will come back, and we will heal this world. One century at a time.

"You can help us, Genevieve. Like the saint you were named after," he says, "Saint Geneviève, savior of Paris in 451, you can be a savior for a lost people."

For a split second, I consider his words, that perhaps he means well after all.

"If your purpose is born of a need to do good, why did the Etemmu haunt my mother for so long?" My voice is barely above a whisper. "Why is it haunting me now?"

"Now, I am sorry about that. That loathsome little thing is simply a persuasive tool to remind someone that they are not wholly in control."

A persuasive tool? Jesus, he's a psychopath.

"I didn't intend for it to get out of hand as it did. Your mother, she was noncompliant. When I learned of you, well, it was time to move on to a secondary plan."

"You mean murder."

"Such an ugly word," he says, eyes dark as he stares into me.

Rage boils within, my hands squeezing the hard plastic armrests so hard I'm afraid my fingers will break, an unfamiliar burn pulsing in the star in my head, coursing down my neck and shoulders and zapping through my arms to my clenched fingertips. I quickly scan the area around me, unsure of this new sensation. The darkened red-and-yellow gallery seating rising up behind me remains vacant—no one else is here. No ghosts, no Baby.

Perhaps more importantly, no spiders.

"Genevieve, it's been a long day." Dagan pulls back his sleeve to check his watch. "Did our dear Delia leave you no idea where she might have secreted the *Life* text? I find it hard to believe she hasn't left you a single clue."

I stand, weirdly short of breath as I stretch my tingling arms wide, my body exposed. A stress reaction?

Bluff, Genevieve. BLUFF.

"I'm an open book, Mr. Dmitri. Search me. Search where I live. No one here knows anything."

"Well, no one from the circus, perhaps, but Delia's talisman knows a thing or two about it." He straightens his sleeve.

Baby.

I squint at him.

"Nutesh was a smart man when he sealed Bamidele to your mother. I likely would have had this handled centuries ago had he not intervened," he says. "It would be a shame if something happened to him."

"Please . . ." My bravado slinks back into the shadows. *Not Baby too.*

"I believe you want to do the right thing, Genevieve," he says, pushing a wispy curl from my forehead. "You have until the preview performance to find Delia's book and deliver it to me. One week." He slides his leather gloves on.

"I need more time. It could be anywhere!"

Mara stands on tiptoes as she peeks over Dagan's shoulder. "Perhaps the Etemmu will help convince you to move faster," she says. A subtle breeze wafts by, carrying with it the fetid odor of rot. *"Ma soeur chérie,* my darling sister, I suppose how fast you look will be in direct relation to how quickly people in your family tree start to fall. Baby, the Cinzios, these lovely kids over here, a lonely kindhearted lion . . . maybe even a couple of *éléphants*."

I want to punch her in the throat. I don't dare move, though. Alone, I don't stand a chance.

"Dagan, please, don't let her hurt the animals. I'm begging you. Everyone here—they're innocents. *Please*."

I flinch as Dagan encloses my hand in his, shaking it slowly as if we're closing a sale on a used car. Thank the gods he has those gloves on—though if he could climb into my head like Henry can, he certainly would've done so already. None of the last hour would've happened because he'd have immediately seen what I know.

That I have the Life *text.*

"You have my word, if I can have yours," he says.

I nod, and then I yank out of his grip. I don't want him touching me.

Dagan turns and steps into the center ring, left foot first. Fitting.

Always right foot first in the ring, Dagan.

He jerks Ash and Violet to their feet. Mumbles a few words. The twins turn and walk toward the exit.

"They won't remember a thing." Dagan stops in front of me. "But you will." His hand against my cheek is surprisingly gentle. "Do the right thing, Genevieve. I look forward to talking with you again soon."

34

INSIDE THE IMPOSSIBLY COLD AIRSTREAM, I COLLAPSE, UNABLE TO WRAP MY head around what the hell I'm going to do.

I've made a deal with the devil.

I cannot give him this book.

How can we possibly wait forty-eight hours for Nutesh to swoop in for the rescue?

I have to go. Tonight. I can't wait for Baby and Nutesh to figure out their plans. If I tell Baby what just happened, he'll go into lockdown mode, which means Henry is left on his own.

Henry. *The punishment will continue until he decides that his loyalties are best with his family . . . and not with you.*

Delia said I had to take him with me—I don't even know where he is! Mara said he isn't dead, but he's, at the very least, hurt. How will I get in touch if his father has his phone?

Go to his house.

Sure, I'll just waltz up to the massive front door, ring the bell, and ask the butler if he can bring Henry to me so we can run away together.

If I give the *Life* text to Lucian, everything will be undone. He will have only Nutesh's text to secure, and then we're all ghosts. Less than ghosts because we will never have existed in the first place. Lucian said he'd bring my mother back, that we could remake history. I doubt that very much. I think he has about as much intention of following through on our handshake as I do.

I have to protect my family. I have to trust that getting the book to Nutesh is the right decision, that he can help me protect the humans and beasts who live in my heart.

I have to keep the book safe.

And run.

I'm stuffing the last of my things into my backpack—double-checking I have Delia's letter and her precious playing cards—when my phone goes mental. A string of messages, from that same wrong number:

1st floor west side 6th window.

1st floor west side 6th window.

1st floor west side 6th window.

I seriously don't have time for this.

I text back: *WRONG NUMBER.*

The immediate response: *Shakespeare is a fraud.*

Henry?

But this isn't his phone!

No. It's not. Because Lucian—Dagan—had his phone.

Oh my god, it's a burner. He has a backup cell phone.

First floor, west side, sixth window—it's where he is!

The most worrisome part about these cryptic texts, though—he's in trouble. Whatever his father, and possibly Mara, did to him, it can't be good.

I perch on Delia's bunk, tucked tight against the wall, and watch through the split in the blinds.

Waiting.

I'm so glad I didn't take that souped-up Tylenol, despite the unrelenting throb along the back of my skull.

Baby texts once, startling me when the phone chimes again in the dead-quiet trailer: *Still working with Ted. Will crash on Delia's bunk. See you soon.*

I respond: *Going to sleep. See you in the morning.*

He has no idea what's gone down in the last hour.

But I can't tell Baby what I'm doing. I can't risk him talking me out of it. Henry needs help *now*. And the AVRAKEDAVRA isn't safe here, not with Mara Dunn—*my sister*—having shown the extent of her abilities. I don't want to give her any opportunity to use those hands on me to reveal the location of our mother's book.

Jesus, what would Delia think if she knew Aveline was still alive . . . *How does she not know?*

Just before midnight, when my exhausted body almost falls under, Mara ambles down the pathway. She gives one look toward the Airstream but then disappears into her own trailer. I wait for her giant TV to click on before I move.

"Alicia, don't let her hurt the twins. Please, keep them safe," I whisper.

The plan is simple enough: Get Henry. Get to the airport. Get to France. Burn the books.

Save everyone I love.

I slink through the Airstream, careful of my every movement so as not to jostle the whole thing. I drop Dr. Schuyler's lumpy gold cross in Delia's flowered box under my bunk, whispering my apology to him. That guilt will have to be dealt with later.

Backpack on, followed by my messenger bag full of the most sacred cargo ever. From the junk drawer, I grab Delia's set of Cece's car keys. From the cabinet above Delia's bunk, I pull out a pair of old binoculars. I have no idea what the security around the exterior of the Dmitri estate is like.

Head to toe in black, hair braided and squeezed under one of Baby's dark stocking caps, I'll look like no more than a shadow in the dark woods.

I lock the door behind me and stand under the awning, listening to the night sounds, the distant laugh of one of my neighbors, the thump of bass coming from Mara Dunn's trailer.

My legs move as if powered by their own engine; I move north through the woods along the backside of trailer row, pausing long enough to emerge for one last stop. It's a ginormous risk but I have to do it.

One more goodbye must be tendered.

Sneaking behind the trailers so I'm not spotted, I move to the narrow steps extending from the side of the Jónáses' coach.

Until Vi and I can have tea again, the set needs a trustworthy caretaker in my absence.

On the middle step, I place the aging and cracked wicker basket along with a note: "Keep it safe. Princess Violet and Saint Geneviève have dragons yet to tame."

And then, with nothing but the hope of ghosts behind me, I do what must be done.

I leave.

35

IF I COULD APOLOGIZE TO CECE NOW ABOUT STEALING HER CAR, I WOULD.

One day she'll thank me.

The road alongside the Dmitri residence has the worst shoulders. When I park south of the same spot where I picked up Henry for our Seattle escapade, it's at such a pitch that I worry a decent wind will dump the car into the drainage ditch. Now I start praying that the fence is neither electrified nor under video surveillance this far from the stone pillars.

Planted on land that slopes down toward the road, the fence extends forever along the property. I flatten against the freezing ground whenever a car flies by on the two-lane country road. I need a place to squeeze through, under, or over.

At the farthest northwest corner where the fence turns east, the continued ironwork is protected by a line of trees, the grounds less manicured than the rest of the property you can see from the road. I pick up a broken branch and poke at the fence. When there's no buzz or snap, I carefully tap it with a fingertip.

Nothing.

I drop to the ground and cozy up to the fence, binoculars hoisted against my eyes. This house is epic.

I can see the whole west side of the mansion, the giant greenhouse in the back—is that where Dagan grows his precious iris plants?—and part of the front, including Dagan's car parked in the roundabout at the front.

Shit. He's home.

On the first floor, I count windows. Sixth window from the front, or the back? There are nine first-floor windows on this side of the house.

I'll count from the front forward. If that's not it, I'll try it in reverse.

Binoculars down, I follow the fence. About twenty feet along, I'm thrilled to discover that a few of these later posts don't have the terrible spikes extending from their tops. Up and over the fence is as easy as climbing the silks, thanks to the pure fear thrumming through me. Crouched, I wait for an alarm or spotlight. When neither goes off, I run hunched in half toward the house's west side, counting every step, ducking and hiding behind trees flanking the wide-open grassy area. Geez, they could have their own golf course out here.

I kneel in the shadow of the trees, watching, waiting to be discovered. I count the windows again now that I'm closer—binoculars up, I zoom in on the two possibilities.

In the sixth window from the front, a piece of paper has been set against the glass.

It's the same drawing from the night of the dinner party—Genevieve as a superhero, standing tall on an elephant's back.

Bingo.

A scan of the upper-floor windows shows them covered with draperies, and as far as my dark-adjusted eyes can tell with the help of the binocs, no one is watching.

And then I see it: the security camera, perched at the midpoint of the western side of the house, just under a decorative eave capping the second floor. Of course they would have cameras. I stare at it for a dozen heartbeats, frustrated because it would be so much easier if I could just text Henry and say *hey look out your window I'm here for our next big adventure.*

I'm afraid to risk it.

And then a break. The camera pointed north at the grassy swath whirs to scan the area, repositioning south—and away from the sixth window.

I wait and watch, counting between scans. I have until the count of a hundred and twenty—two minutes—to get to the window and make Henry aware that I'm here. Now I know how Frodo felt when the Eye of Sauron was stalking him across Mordor.

When the camera moves the other way, I run across the lawn, slide into the rosebush hedge whose biting thorns are definitely not winter-dormant, and flatten myself against the building. Quick peeks only—once, twice—the curtains are split just enough for me to see past the drawing and into the room.

Henry's there. On the bed, under a blanket. I hope he's not a heavy sleeper.

Hands cupped around my eyes, I look longer into the

room, for evidence of bodies other than Henry. He appears to be alone.

The camera is going to see me. I've lost count. I curl down, arms wrapped around bent knees, behind the rose-bushes, hoping the camera won't catch an irregularity in the hedge. When the whirring indicates the camera is again turning southerly, I stand straight, post-crouch pins and needles stabbing the back of my knees.

Fingertip against the glass. *Tap. Tap. Tap tap tap.*

Henry pushes himself to sitting, though not without wincing and grabbing his ribs—shit, he's hurt. Okay, I can fix that. I just need him to *move* first.

He stands, wobbly, and comes to the window. Drops to his knees on the other side, a huge smile on his face as he pulls the drawing away and presses his hand against the pane. I mirror him, wishing the glass would dissolve between us.

I pantomime opening the window. He shakes his head and drags a finger along the side where a thin wire dances down the edge, along the window bottom, and back up, outlining the entire frame. It ends at a small white box the size of an eraser at the top of the window.

The window is alarmed. Of course it would be.

I point upward at the camera and drop into a ball again. Counting. Counting. This is taking bloody forever.

When I'm upright, Henry is fiddling with the alarm box—a magnet?—he unlocks the window and freezes. Waits.

He finally slides the window open, and I stretch my arms through. He grabs hold, yanks my face close, and surprises me with an insistent kiss. "I am so happy to see you," he whispers against my lips. "We only have a couple minutes before this magnet gives way."

"You are no daft lad, you know. Even if you hate Shakespeare."

He winks.

I nod and gesture at the camera with two fingers held up. Again I duck, counting it out, waiting for the camera to cycle in the other direction.

"I'll need a little help," he says, clutching his side. He shoves his soccer-patch-covered backpack through and I dump it into the bushes, doing what I can to ease his lanky body through the window and onto solid ground.

I grab his elbow, and count: "One, two, three—RUN!" I lead him into the trees. Once we're away from the house, he hugs me tightly. When I hug him back, he grunts. "What happened? What did he do to you?"

"Let's call it a persuasive interrogation," Henry says. I'd say I'm appalled by Dagan's decision to hurt his own kid, but after today, after hearing from his own lips the lengths he's willing to go to find this text . . .

"I can fix you. We just have to get the hell out of here."

"Do you have a car?"

"On the road. Can you make it?"

He answers by breaking into a skip-run—clearly something is not right with his left side. I lead him to the breach in the spiked fence, so grateful that my bags are still where I left them.

"You found my lucky spot," he whispers, pointing to the fence tips missing their spikes.

"Can you climb?"

His face pales a bit, but he squishes his backpack through the bars; I give him my knee and shoulder to stand on. He grimaces, takes a deep breath, and climbs, making way too much noise when he hits the ground on the other side.

I'm up and over, pulling him to his feet, trying not to freak about the wheeze when he exhales or the color of his face.

His bag on my back and his arm thrown over my shoulders, I hobble-jog him back along the tree line and down the front of the property. When Cece's crooked sedan appears from the blackness, I almost yelp with happiness.

I've never been so happy for a car engine to turn over on the first try. The road is hardly wide enough for the U-turn but I keep us out of the ditch across the way.

"Seems Daddy is very upset with me. I guess he didn't want us to be mates after all," Henry says, his voice weak. "So much for the work-study."

"What hurts the worst?" I check the mirrors obsessively, almost blowing through a stop sign at the main intersection where the country becomes town.

Henry looks over at me, head lolling to the side, the smile on his beautiful, bruised face erased when he coughs.

"You're not going to die on me, are you?"

His eyes close, and then open a little. "That would be rude, wouldn't it?"

"How did you know I'd be coming for you?"

"Alicia," he wheezes. "She was in the big top tonight. Seems she fancies you."

"How? I didn't see her." I'd looked around, hoping against hope I wasn't alone in there—but of course I wouldn't have seen her. Because then Dagan and Mara could've too. "And a burner cell phone. Very enterprising."

He pats his pocket, where I assume the phone is stashed. "In the event of emergencies. This might qualify."

"I've got it . . . the *Life* text. I found it," I say quietly. "That's why we're leaving now. I couldn't wait a minute longer, not after what happened in the big top. Nutesh—your grandfather—he's coming for you. In the next forty hours or so. We had it all set up."

"I like your plan better. I'm a fan of spontaneity. And fewer boots to the ribs." He smiles, but then trembles and winces when he coughs.

I can't heal him and drive at the same time. The process of fixing someone else's physical wounds requires my full attention. But when a passing streetlight hits his face, Henry's sunken eyes scare the shit out of me. One hand on the wheel, I reach over and grab him above the wrist. It would be easier if he didn't have gloves on.

"Henry, I need you to look at me."

I have to keep an eye on the road—but if I can channel even a little energy, maybe he'll come back from whatever precipice he's toeing.

Within less than a minute, my own vision begins to narrow, the drain as I draw from the star too much for me to continue. I release him, my pulse and breathing accelerated. I should pull over but I can't waste a single second of momentum out of Eaglefern, away from Dagan.

Henry's eyes pop open and he shudders, leaning forward, a hand against the dash as he catches his breath. "You are something else, woman."

"Are you . . . is that better?" It's everything I can do to keep the steering wheel steady.

"Yes. Yes. Thank you. My ribs—the pain is lessened. Thank you," he says. "Should I drive?"

"No. I just need a minute." I roll down the window, the cold air waking me up. By the time we're at the connector for Highway 26, other than the persistent pound at the wound site, I feel a little closer to normal.

"Where do we go now? SeaTac or PDX?" I ask.

"The farther, the better. Probably SeaTac," he says. "Except, dear Genevieve, I cannot let you suffer alone in your scheming." He pulls his backpack between his knees. Unzips it. Pulls something onto his lap. I don't have to wait for the overhead freeway lights to reflect on the circle and inverted triangle burned into its surface to confirm what I'm seeing.

"Oh my good god. *What did you do?*"

"You said you needed your mother's text to be rid of the Etemmu. I thought perhaps having a second one of these buggers might come in handy." His smile fades, the clouds moving back into his eyes. "And if my father doesn't have this book, maybe he won't be able to do to other people what he did to my mother."

The weight of his words—and his actions—settles between us. Learning that one's father is a murderer . . . I can't imagine the hurricane of emotion cycling in poor Henry's head, and heart.

"If Lucian finds us, he'll kill us," I say.

"Just in case, you should probably drive faster."

36

I DRIVE, AND HENRY USES MY PHONE TO CHECK FLIGHTS TO FRANCE—WE need at least an idea of when to show up at the airport so we're not sitting ducks wandering the terminal.

"Air France, 10:40 a.m., direct to Paris," he says. "Expensive. We may have to stage a quick bank heist."

I don't want to know how expensive. I have about five thousand dollars in my bag—Delia's emergency savings that I "borrowed" from the lockbox hidden in our trailer wall. That damn well better be enough.

"How long before you think we're discovered missing?" I say. It could be any moment for me—Baby will probably come looking as soon as he realizes I'm not tucked under my blankets. I'm surprised my phone hasn't blown up already.

"That magnet has probably fallen but the window just slams shut. Unless it remains open, and then the alarm might go off, but usually when I sneak out—"

"You sneak out often?"

"I went through a phase grade eleven year. People at

school tended to be much friendlier if you brought alcohol to their parties. My father has an impressive wine collection, so for a brief period, I was the sommelier for a bunch of delinquent sixteen-year-olds."

I giggle.

"Our house is alarmed but it's not Fort Knox." Henry's voice quiets. "If Lucian catches someone inside, he . . . deals with it."

I don't think I want to know what that means. I saw what he did to the jailer.

"I think as long as I wasn't impregnating the young women of Eaglefern, my father didn't much care that I was sneaking out. Until I stole the wrong bottle of wine," he says, hiking that bisected eyebrow. "I had no idea that a 1985 Romanée-Conti was worth twenty thousand dollars."

"I hope your friends appreciated it."

"They added it to one of those huge garbage-can punches they make with the dredges of whatever alcohol everyone's brought, so my fine aged French wine was woefully underappreciated."

I love how, even under these dire circumstances, Henry can find humor.

"What'll your father do when he realizes you're gone this time, other than feel glad you haven't taken more wine?"

Henry smirks. "This time, it's what he will do when he realizes *this* is gone." The cheer melts off his face as he nudges the backpack.

"Has he hurt you before? Like he did this time?"

"Only the occasional wallop upside the head when I've

done something idiotic. He was in rare form this afternoon," Henry says, blanching as he sits straighter. "Once he gave me a black eye, but it was explained away as an accident from an unruly horse."

"So he can't heal you?"

"My father's talents don't lie in healing directly, not like what your miraculous hands can do. He can expedite the body's natural healing process, but he can't heal someone completely."

Is this something Mara taught him in their time together? As he developed her skills, might she have offered insight into her own natural abilities? And what *are* his talents if he controls the *Death* text, other than manipulating the Etemmu?

Both Baby and Delia said that the Etemmu was beyond the scope of the *AVRAKEDAVRA*, and in the barn, when Mara mentioned it, the smell of death wafted past. Is she the one he's working with to harness this demon? Is she the master of this dark magic?

"Where do your father's real talents lie?" I ask quietly.

Henry's face is straight ahead, the lights of approaching cars reflecting in the lightness of his eyes. "Punishment," he says, voice low, turning his head away from me for a beat.

I've seen what Dagan is capable of via the visions, even without Mara's malicious aid.

The traffic at just before three o'clock in the morning is surprisingly heavy as the exits for SeaTac rise along the freeway. "We should ditch this car as soon as possible," Henry says. "We can leave it at one motel and book into another."

We agree on a busy run-down chain motel in SeaTac,

hoping that because there are so many to choose from, if—when—we have pursuers, they'll get lost in the maze of lodgings so close to the airport. The desk clerk raises an eyebrow when Henry pulls several hundred-dollar bills out of his wallet in lieu of a credit card.

We park in a rear lot, three motels away from where we're staying, and walk along the heavily trafficked street, heads down, hugging our sacred cargo close. Once we've raided the vending machines, we lock ourselves into the shabby, second-floor room.

With a single queen bed.

"I thought she said the room had two beds," I say.

"I thought so too." Henry's cheeks flush. "At least there's a nice view of the industrial area," he teases, walking to the murky sliding glass door that looks out onto a small, questionable balcony. "I can go back down and request a change, if you like."

"Nah. It's fine. I don't bite."

"I don't mind biting. It's the snoring that might be problematic," he says.

"You snore?"

"Heavens, no."

I throw a pillow at him. He winces when it hits the side of his head. "Oh god, I'm sorry. Are you all right?"

"Genevieve, relax a little."

"I should probably have a look at whatever is going on, though. I didn't do enough in the car." I point at the bed. "Take your shirt off."

"You're not going to buy me dinner first?"

"Hey, I bought you Cheetos," I say, throwing a thumb over my shoulder at the bounty on the crappy dresser.

When Henry's shirt is off, I have to hold in my gasp. His torso is a patchwork of bruises in different stages of healing. Like Joseph's Technicolor dreamcoat, minus Joseph and the dreamcoat.

"Lucian is not himself right now. Something's off—this kind of viciousness is out of character, even for him," he says, sitting along the bed's edge. He traces a finger along the tacky pattern in the duvet fabric. "I'm quite glad we don't have a black light with us."

"Henry—be serious."

His playful smile melts a little and he looks down at his gloved hands.

"I wouldn't tell him what Alicia has been showing me or what you told me about everything you've learned recently." He nods toward our backpacks and the messenger bag huddled in the corner. "Although this"—he points to a bruise on his ribs—"Mara's boot got the bit about Schuyler out of me. I am so, so sorry about that."

"You did what you had to do. I shouldn't have put you in this position in the first place."

"It was destined to come to this, Genevieve. I'm glad you turned to me," he says. "I take it you've learned about Mara being your sister."

"Yeah. I talked to my mom—well, to her ghost—at the mausoleum where she had the book. I honestly don't think she knew Aveline is still alive." A thought occurs to me. "Did you know Mara? Had you ever seen her before?"

"The night of the dinner party was the first time. She does seem to have some deep-seated anger issues, however."

I snort. "If anyone has an ax to grind, it's going to be Mara—Aveline—whatever her name is. My—our—mother basically abandoned Aveline twice in protection of this book. If she's really a descendant of Udish, of Delia, she's an heir. She wants it."

"But I can't imagine, if Lucian had in fact secured the *Life* text, that he would then give it to her. Is that what she thinks is going to happen?" he says.

"No idea. I just know I don't want it. The sooner we burn it, the better."

I sink onto the too-squishy bed next to Henry. He grunts slightly as he wraps an arm around my shoulders, pulls off my black knitted cap, static electricity popping between fabric and my frizzed hair, and kisses the side of my head.

"Lie flat. Let me fix you up," I say. "You ready?"

He nods, eyes wide with apprehension. "Will this hurt?"

"Shouldn't. But when it's done, I might need you to hand me that." I nod at the soda can on the nightstand. "Sugar helps."

Eyes closed, I hover my hands over the bruises painting his chest and upper arms. His ribs on the left side are particularly problematic, and I hear him grunt as my hands linger. Pulling from the snapping, popping star at the rear of my skull, I survey his body, feeling his flinch when my hot hands make contact.

"Big weenie," I whisper, eyes still sealed.

When my knees threaten to fold, I know I have to take a

break. I sink to the floor, head buried in my stinging, vibrating hands. The intense woozy feeling is a strong indicator as to the level of injury in Henry's body. Good for him—he should feel almost normal again—not so good for me, who feels anything but.

And I don't understand why my hands are so sore. They've never done this before when I've healed someone.

His voice comes to me from far away. He wraps my hand around the soda can, tips my head back so I can sip. So light-headed.

"Genevieve . . . open your eyes. Come on, open up."

After another hefty sip, the sugar hits. "Hey," I say, lips heavy like I'm drunk.

"Does it always do that to you? Because that is scary as hell." Henry hoists me off the floor, onto the room's singular chair. Nestled against the suspiciously stained vinyl back, I focus on regulating my breaths. Henry moves into the bathroom and returns with a cool cloth. He rubs the hair back from my forehead, pausing briefly, and then resuming. So soft. That feels nice . . .

When I open my eyes, I see he's removed his gloves.

"No peeking," I say.

"Scout's honor."

I sit forward and guzzle the soda. With a flick of my finger, I motion for Henry to stand for inspection.

He obliges, spinning slowly, arms raised. "It feels much better. Thank you," he says, pushing against his ribs.

"I'm out of practice. I don't do it that often, except for Delia and Baby."

Henry kneels before me, replacing the cloth against my forehead.

"So I'm curious, Sir Henry—how did you get Lucian's book?"

He rocks back on his heels, still crouched on the floor. "The Gutenberg Bible."

"Excuse me?"

"The bible project. In the hallway. Remember?"

"No way."

"I told you, I'm good with reproductions."

The laugh, part amusement, part fear, bubbles in my throat. "You made another *AVRAKEDAVRA*?"

He stands and bows.

"Oh my god, you sneaky brat."

"Well, yes, and it looked pretty good, if I do say so myself. It was lucky, actually—I started it last year, without my father knowing, of course—when I thought it was still just some creepy old grimoire. I wanted another big project because the Gutenberg was so fun. I remade a whole bunch of books. Just to see if I could." Henry pulls his shirt back on, to my dismay. I might smile inside when he leaves it unbuttoned.

"Kid, you need to get out more often."

He laughs. "The outer covers are leather, and then custom-ordered papyrus pages inside—I've seen the real one plenty of times, there in the case. If only I'd known then how important it was."

A spark of excitement sputters to life. "Did you remake the inside? Did you see what the book contains? Spells or whatever?"

"No, I only did the outside. The forgery is blank inside. I didn't quite make it that far," he says, rubbing the area over his ribs where the bruising, so purple just a few minutes ago, has faded to pinkish hues. "At the time I created it, I didn't have the case's security code."

"How'd you get it this time, then?"

"Among the housekeepers, there's one my father trusts most—he changes the codes in his study often, and she's the only person in the house who has them because she cleans in there. It didn't take much—I touched her upper arm and . . ."

"Henry! I thought you said you never peek."

"Extenuating circumstances," he says, grinning mischievously. "At that point, it was a quick switch. Sort of like Indiana Jones when he replaces the golden idol with that bag of sand."

"Did you wear the hat, though? Or use a whip?"

"You know, I did not."

"It would've been better with the hat and whip."

"That is a shame, isn't it." He smirks.

"How long before Lucian figures it out?"

"I should think not long. He won't know it's not real until he opens it."

"Henry, when you grabbed it—the real one—were you wearing your gloves?"

"Yes."

"So you didn't feel anything . . . weird?"

"No. Did you, when you touched your mother's book?"

I tell him about how I felt like the book was alive, that it caused a painful physical reaction but then I saw all those ghosts standing in the cemetery and felt that overwhelming love. It made me realize that I have to do whatever I can to protect the family I still have.

"Maybe I should have a go with Lucian's," he says, nodding toward the backpack.

"No. Wait. Just in case."

"Right. Probably best."

Henry moves to stand over me. I look at his outstretched, gloveless hand, then to his face. "I don't want to see in your head. But I also want you to know that you're not alone, that we'll get to safety. Together."

He pulls me from the chair, tentative, his breath matching the staccato, nervous rhythm of my own. When he leans into me, moistens his lips, it is not a gentle peck but a full, powerful kiss, the kind that convinces me I would do anything for this boy, and he in turn would do anything for me.

His lips linger, but I don't want to move. It tastes of affection, but also of shared chaos.

When he smiles, it's so obvious now who his mother is. I have to believe the harder angles of his face, the square jaw and the sharp nose, are the sole evidence of his father, that Henry's heart is good, like Alicia's, not warped by time and old resentments. Like Lucian's. Like *Dagan's*.

Henry places one of his now very warm hands on my cheek, the flush of memory pushing through me as a scene unfolds in the forefront of my mind—that day at the circus when we first met in the mess tent as I stood between Baby and Lucian.

But new with this memory is the feeling that accompanies it. Warmth, a fluttering in my chest, a surge of—attraction?

When he drops his hand to my shoulder and we focus on one another's faces in the present, he smiles. "I wanted you to know. What it felt like to see you for the first time." A shy smile dances across his lips, the earlier trepidation in his eyes replaced by longing.

With the lightest fingertip, he traces the contours of my face, alternating between touching my hair and my face, kissing me again, gentle but passionate. I bury my fingers in his mussed curls, pull him into me by his open shirt, and walk him backward toward the bed.

When his legs hit, he sinks against the mattress, pulling me onto his lap. Beyond the shared heat between us, a firestorm of images spills from his hands into my head, fast-moving snapshots of the time we've spent in one another's company—the dinner party, the barn, the hospital, Seattle.

A subtle burning tingles in me, like a match has been lit at the junction where my ribs protect my heart.

My hands map his firm chest, smooth but for sparse hairs sprouting from his sternum, my conscious mind ignoring the alarm bells ringing in my ears.

I've never felt a boy's naked chest before.

The few times Ash kissed me were nothing more than answers to truth-or-dare, and they meant far more to me than they ever did to him.

This, however? Awesome. And scary. But mostly awesome.

When his hands untuck my shirt and slide under, nearer to the hook on my bra, goosebumps race up and down my aching arms. The heat intensifies, sparking in my head as if I were preparing to heal, a white-hot light flashing behind my eyes before it sizzles down both arms and into my fingers.

Henry jerks back.

"What?" I say, panting.

He stares at my hands. "You—you shocked me."

"I what?"

"Just then—you shocked me," he says, grabbing my wrists lightly. "With an electric current."

"What are you talking about?" I yank my hands free, twisting to inspect them. "It was probably static electricity."

"Kiss me again," he says, pulling me back. It only takes a few seconds to pick up where we left off, all hands, tongues, heavy breathing.

The furnace in my head ignites, followed by a burn racing down my arms, through my wrists, through the bones of my fingers until it feels as if my fingernails will pop out of their beds.

"Ouch!" Henry leans slightly away, his hands circling my wrists. "What's going on?"

"I have no idea, I swear." I splay my aching fingers between us.

"Has this ever happened before?"

I edge back from him. "Are you asking if I've ever sneaked off to a shitty motel and made out with some guy?"

He laughs. "No—but that's an interesting conversation, and I do hope I'm more than just 'some guy'—no, I mean, have you ever shocked anyone before? Like this?"

"No. On both counts."

"Stand up for a moment." I do but he doesn't let me move away. With an arm around my waist, he offers his open palm held up in front of him. "Hover your hand over mine. Don't touch, though."

I do as he says, not sure what I'm supposed to see.

Until the spark jumps out of my index finger and into his. "Whoa!" I jerk away. He's laughing.

"That is an amazing trick. Why didn't you tell me you were made of electricity? I suppose technically, we're all made of electricity but—"

"This isn't funny! Jesus, Henry, what's going on? Why is it doing that?"

Is this why my hands and arms have been aching so badly? As much as I don't want to hurt him with the current, the relief from the release of that energy—it's like someone's thrown ice cream on a sunburn.

He slinks closer but doesn't touch me, his face lingering just above mine, eyes heavy with desire. He licks his lips. "It must be my animal magnetism."

"I wanna see if I can do it again. Hold up your hand."

"No! It hurts!" He flexes and contracts his fingers. "And I thought my hands were odd."

I stare at my fingers, the heat of our encounter lessening, the chill of the room sneaking back in to remind me why we're here and what we're meant to be doing.

What the hell? Is this from the book?

"I may need to lend you some gloves," he says, eyes twinkling.

I tuck in my shirt and finger-comb my hair. "We should get some sleep."

The earlier lust-induced cheerfulness dissolves off his face as he buttons his own shirt. "Right, then."

The room is cold so I crank up what is supposed to be the heater. It fills the room with the reek of ashtrays and wet dog, so I shut it off. Just as well. We should sleep in our clothes, anyway. To be ready for anything.

We share the junk food, taking turns in the bathroom. I should be falling over dead with exhaustion. Funny how a healthy dose of terror feeds a person's muscles.

Leaning against the shabby bathroom vanity, I place a hand onto the mirror, trying to recreate the zap that jumped between Henry and me.

Nothing.

The heavy aching-burning sensation that has pestered me for the last day is almost completely gone. Maybe I'm too tired. Sleep first. Then try again. It was probably just static. Cold air, crappy carpets. Had to be static.

No way that was static.

"So, one bed," Henry says as I exit the bathroom. "Do you suppose you can keep your hands off me long enough to get a few hours' sleep?"

"It's your hands we should be worried about."

"I don't know, Flash."

"Really? Jokes already?" I ask.

He pulls me into a hug, a lingering, sweet kiss against my forehead. "Let's get some sleep. We've got five hours before we need to be at the airport."

When he climbs under the blankets fully clothed and offers me a spot next to him, I don't resist.

My face pressed against his chest, I inhale deeply. Henry Dmitri smells better than ashtrays and wet dog any day.

37

THE BED JERKS.

And then it jerks again. Like a buffalo knocking into it.
Which is ridiculous because we're in a motel and not in a
Montana field surrounded by buffalos. Although the proper
word for a North American beast of this type would be bison.

Speaking of bison, I'm freezing. I curl into Henry, tucking my hands against his chest to steal whatever body heat
he has to spare. He's not very hairy, though. Not at all like a
bison.

"Wake up," the bison says, the bed bouncing harder this
time, like an earthquake.

My eyes open slowly, the room lit only by the hint of
sunrise. But the figure at the end of the bed is neither a bison
nor seismic in nature.

"Baby!" I yell, and I'm out of bed, out of Henry's arms.

"Good morning to you too."

"I can explain . . ."

"Good answer." He pulls me close and hugs me so hard, I feel my spine groan. "Thank the gods you're safe. You scared the shit out of me. And it's a good damn thing there are clothes on *both* of your bodies."

"How did you find us?" I ask.

"Other than the LoJack on Cece's car?" He points at Henry. "Get up," Baby commands. Henry's hair is lopsided from sleep. He stands, unsteady from the abrupt awakening. Baby grabs his upper arm and drags him into the bathroom.

"Baby, what are you doing?" I ask, mildly alarmed.

"Take your shirt off and put your head down," Baby instructs. Henry, eyes wide and confused, obliges. "Gen, get me a towel. And be ready to step in."

"What are you doing?" I ask again.

Baby holds up what looks like a phone—although it's not—and runs it over Henry's sides, his forearms and biceps, along his shoulders and clavicle, and up the back of his neck. Right of his upper spine, left of the scapular edge, the device beeps. With vigor.

Without a word, Baby reaches into one of the pockets of his military-looking black cargo pants and extracts several sealed alcohol wipes—and a scalpel still in its sterile packaging.

"Hey, what are you doing?" Henry tries to yank away, struggling against Baby's viselike hold.

"Wait—wait, Baby, just explain what's going on. Henry, it's okay. He's not going to hurt you."

"I should hurt you," Baby says, nodding at me in the

mirror. "Young Henry has a rice-sized personal location device under his skin. I need to carve it out."

"Carve? Bloody hell, no thank you!" Henry says.

"It's either that, or you can figure out what to tell your father when he arrives in the next thirty minutes or so."

Henry pales. "He's coming? Here? He knows where we are?"

"When a car is reported stolen, and then statewide police agencies are alerted to two runaways who have robbed a very rich businessman, the cops pay attention. SeaTac PD found the car in the lot down the way. They're out there right now."

"They called Lucian? But it was Cece's car—and I just borrowed it," I say, trying to mask my panic.

"Papa Dmitri is very unhappy about the antique you took from the house," Baby says, bobbing his head at Henry in the mirrored reflection. "And now that the police have the car, monitoring the police scanner tells us that Lucian's arrival is imminent. I'm sure I'm not the only one ready to strong-arm a desk clerk for your room number. Although registering as Christopher Marlowe was clever." Baby shoves Henry to his knees. "Hold your breath. This might sting."

Henry sucks in through his teeth with the first slice but holds steady, albeit a bit paler, as Baby digs and then eases the little capsule of medical-grade silicone out of its snug pocket under skin and muscle. I didn't even know this technology existed, but the tiny, bloody device in Baby's palm is all the proof I need.

It barely splashes when it lands in the toilet. "Flush it,"

Baby directs me. "And then seal this up so we can get out of here."

I move into position behind Henry. Eyes closed, I seal the incision, my free hand against Baby so I don't fall over. It's a small bathroom—the only place to go will likely introduce my head to the side of the stained bathtub. And I've had enough stitches for one week, thanks.

"Get dressed, Henry," Baby says, pulling Henry to his feet as he steadies me. "You look tired." He kisses the top of my head and hugs me for the thirty or so seconds until I've recovered. "You're a terrible listener, *a leannan*."

"I had no choice. Lucian—Dagan—he and Mara Dunn tricked me into the big top last night. I only went because I thought it was Henry. They're threatening everyone—you, the Cinzios, the animals—and Henry was hurt. I didn't know what else to do."

"And you didn't think about coming and telling me? Shit, Genevieve, this could've gone very south—"

"I knew you'd want to wait for Nutesh. You said forty-eight hours."

"Gen, come on, if you'd told me, we would've left immediately, together, and I wouldn't have spent the last twelve hours thinking all manner of terrible thoughts about what could be happening to you."

"I had to help him, Baby. He wasn't safe," I say.

"We need to move now. Talk later."

"We?"

"I brought friends." He winks.

"Where are we going?"

"Out. And down. Get your stuff."

I pull my black knitted cap from last night's ensemble back over my head. From another pocket in his pants, just below a rather large holstered weapon, Baby pulls out a second cap and throws it at Henry. He then moves to the frame where the sliding glass door once resided. No wonder it's so cold in here. The glass, off its track, rests against the lopsided dresser.

"Wow. That's secure," I say, tucking my hair into the itchy hat.

"Lucky for you, it's not." After examining the ground below, Baby steps over the balcony railing.

"What are you doing?"

"We're certainly not going out the front. Move quick. Sun's coming up." Sure enough, the eastern sky is exploding in ominous reds and oranges. *Red sky in the morning, sailor take warning.*

Baby muscles down from our balcony to the dirty white cinder block half wall of the first-floor room below us. Henry allows me to go next; I toss the messenger bag and backpack down to Baby to better keep my balance.

In under a minute, we're out. Baby leads the way, along a foot-worn path in dead grass skirting the first-floor patios, around the shabby cyclone fence enclosing the near-black, algae-rank waters of a long-forgotten swimming pool. His finger against his lips, Baby stops and looks around the corner of the main motel building, into the front parking lot—where multiple police cruisers have assembled. I can hardly hear his whispered instructions over my pounding heart. Henry grabs my hand, his face confirming that he is just as afraid as I am.

Baby points to a parking structure in the adjoining property—belonging to a nicer facility than the one we chose—and motions with his fingers, indicating that we walk, not run, and no talking. "Genevieve first. I bring up the tail," he whispers.

As casually as we can, we move into line. That last ten feet before I reach the door on the parking structure feels like a mile.

Once inside, Baby again takes the lead up two flights of stairs, and we sprint after him to a small, older-model SUV.

I point to the cheesy stick-people on the back window. "You have three kids and a dog?"

"What? It's my favorite color. And Hondas are reliable." He smirks.

Clearly he scouted this car before he retrieved us—it's not only unlocked but wires protrude from the steering column.

"Circus freaks know lots of useful crap," I say to Henry as he slides into the back seat next to me.

Once behind the wheel, Baby turns to us.

"Heads down. Crouch into the floor wells. Do not move until I tell you to."

"Where are we going?" Henry asks.

"Boeing Field. Now get down."

It's disorienting to be scrunched near the floor, the only landmarks the top third of passing streetlights and telephone poles and buildings and the upper limits of vehicles taller than ours. While Baby doesn't quite pull a *Bourne Identity*, centrifugal force doesn't play nice with our balance.

The car's sudden acceleration scares me, but then I see

the signs pass overhead. We're on the freeway. Northbound. This is good.

My left hand is shoved into my pocket because there is little other space for it to be, my body squeezed between the driver's and back seats. My fingers find the little elephant figurines in the sock—for a moment, I close my eyes and think about Gert and Houdini, hoping they're okay, that they're safe.

What I would give to go home right now. Curl up in the hammock and listen to Houdini's baby sounds. Take him and Gert into the field for pictures and music. Answer more Loxodonta letters from little kids who dream of running away with the circus. Even practice the violin under my instructor's punishing drills.

The throb in my knees and feet brings me back to present. So far from home, from my elephants. "Can we sit on the seats yet?"

"Nope. Stay down."

A few minutes in, a severe bump from behind jolts the car, the rear end fishtailing before Baby regains control.

"Stay down. We've got company," he says.

I don't have to see out the windows to feel the force of being pushed and pulled as Baby weaves through traffic. Blaring horns serenade our evasive route, underscored by the tense rev of the car's engine.

With a sudden deceleration, the car skids and careens right, and then around a tight circle—an off-ramp?—and I swear we're up on two wheels. Henry and I grab hold of each other's arms across the space, trying to maintain our positions so our heads don't smack together.

"When this car stops, I want you out and running. Do you understand?"

"Where? Where do we run?"

"West. Across Perimeter Road. Get to the hangar."

"Which hangar?"

"Just follow me!" Another slam from behind; Baby cusses and fights to straighten the car's ass end. "Are the bags close to you?"

Henry and I answer in unison as the car yanks to the right again. We're moving as fast as the car will carry us, sporadic trees and telephone poles flying past as if winged themselves.

"Almost there," Baby announces.

And then another hit. Only this one is so hard, there's no way this car meant for grocery runs and soccer practice can stay straight. We're sideways, tumbling head over wheels, Henry and I painfully untethered as we are thrown around like blobs of clay.

The car slams to an abrupt, jerking halt at the top of its second somersault. I'm thankful the rolling stops, but I'm nauseated. Head hurts. I scream against the torturous pain of a left arm that won't move properly. That uncomfortable burn again starts in my head, and behind my sternum, like an explosion waiting to happen.

Steam hisses from the car's front end; we've landed on the roof. The interior immediately smells of fuel and scarred grass. We've come to rest on a green strip that divides the four-lane road from the two-lane road that runs along the various hangars and aviation businesses. We're slammed up against a medium-sized tree, explaining the sharp smell of freshly cut wood, though neither car nor tree will make it out of this alive.

A much bigger black SUV with darkened windows bounces onto the grass strip just down from us. Before the door even opens, I know we have to move.

"Baby!" I scream. His massive form, already tight in the car's compact interior, is slumped against the ceiling, his arms slack up by his head, a burnt smell from the exploded airbag stinging my nose. "Baby, wake up!" I shake him. He grunts so I shake again, as hard as I can with one hand. "Wake up! WAKE UP!"

Shit, where's Henry? "Henry!" He's been thrown into the back of the car, lying crumpled in a bed of glass from three shattered windows. His eyes blink open and he struggles to turn himself onto his belly. Safety glass embedded in his forehead and a scary bulge along his perfect cheekbone give him a demonic look as blood streams down the right side of his face, soiling his teeth when he smiles.

"I didn't see anything about car chases when I booked this trip," he says.

An arm clothed in all black punches away what remains of my window and I'm yanked by my feet through the opening, away from Henry, out onto the freezing ground, gravel digging into my back. I scream, but I can't grab onto anything because my left arm won't cooperate and Jesus, it hurts so much.

Concussive stars flit across my vision. Head throbs. My hat is gone—my right hand to my brow comes away bloody. I throw up in the grass and try to roll away from it.

"That arm doesn't look right," the voice above me says.

Dagan crouches next to me on the pavement, pushes my hair out of my face, his touch almost fatherly. "It would've been much easier if you'd just given me the book, don't you agree, Genevieve?"

Clumsy, I push away, trying to get closer to the car and farther from him. At the back of the trashed, upside-down SUV, Mara yanks Henry out from the cargo area onto the narrow road. It doesn't take much for her to get his backpack off.

Lucian reaches for the messenger bag still tethered to my body. He grabs the strap; I scream as the fierce tug explodes fireworks in my eyes, the pain in my left arm threatening to pull me under.

"Wait . . . please, wait . . ."

"For what?"

He doesn't bother with niceties, instead moving right to the business end of this deal. The smell of rotten flesh swirls in a tornado of blackness around me. My view of the asphalt roadway, the wrecked car, the scarred grass is blocked by whirling, vicious midnight, a thousand arms reaching for me, burning my exposed skin as they make contact—yet another new perk, it seems—squeezing my chest and constricting my throat so I cannot do anything except beg for breath. So nice of him to spare the spiders this time.

I can't see Dagan; I'm powerless against his whorl of death. My right hand and arm are clamped over the messenger bag containing Delia's text but he's tugging at it. I can't let him have it, not when Mara has recovered the backpack with the text Henry stole from his father.

Consciousness pinches tight, squeezing so hard the light from my eyes, and when he hits the side of my left arm, the pain is the last shove over the edge.

I'm sorry, Mom. I can't fight it. I'll see you soon.

And just as my eyes are about to close, a body slams through the blackness, scooping me from the pavement, tight against his mighty chest, the smell of sweat and airbag powder and blood and aftershave.

Baby. My talisman.

He sets me on my feet, his body wrapped around mine, protecting me from the endless stinging of the Etemmu's touch. When he stands as straight and unstoppable as a minotaur, the blackness fades as though it's been vacuumed away.

Dagan hasn't disappeared, however—like an arsonist who watches his handiwork burn, he stands fast, his sadistic grin less smug once he sees the Etemmu won't take my soul with it today.

To our left, Mara has dragged Henry to the side of the blown-out car. He's on his knees in all that glass, though he's imbalanced, swaying. She helps steady him by grabbing a fist full of his curled, blood-matted hair—and pulling from her boot a pearl-handled knife that she then holds against Henry's neck.

"Lucian—Dagan—please . . . we've all lost so much," I say, begging him with as much humility as I can find. If I can only appeal to his humanity. "What would Inanna think? Your iris—it's a reminder of her, right? She would want you to be happy. Delia would want me to be happy. What you're doing, it won't make things better. You can't fix the past."

He stares hard at me for a moment, his eyes elsewhere for a flash.

Henry groans as a thin line of blood blossoms against the taut skin of his neck.

"Henry is your *son*. HE is your family. Don't let her hurt him, Dagan. Let us go, please. This is no way to live."

As if I said nothing, Dagan snaps back to present, eyes with pinpoint focus. "Since Henry is as yet covered by misplaced protections I gave to him as my own flesh and blood," he says, his words hinting at a bite of betrayal, "let us see how Mara's special tricks work on orphaned warriors."

He nods, and in what seems like a single smooth motion, Mara throws Henry flat onto his face, the knife sheathed, one hand in the air flattened right at Baby.

His legs collapse and he is on all fours, choking, grabbing at his throat. Just like what happened with the jailer.

"When the alveoli in the lungs overfill, they burst," Mara taunts, "*pop, pop, pop,* one at a time, until there are no more little sacs to help a creature breathe. It must be very painful."

"No!" I plead, pulling the messenger bag over my head just as Baby flops onto his side, clawing at his throat, desperate for a breath. "Let him go. You can have it."

Mara looks to Dagan, and again with little more than a nod, she releases her hold. Dazed, Henry crawls to Baby, rolls him over onto his back, slapping his chest to get the huge man to open his eyes.

"Gen . . . no," Baby wheezes, his voice small and pained.

"Remove it from the bag. I need to see it's real and not a forgery," Dagan says, throwing a look at his battered son.

Compelled by pure fear, I kneel clumsily, my useless left arm cradled against my chest, and open the bag's leather flap. I fumble to free the *AVRAKEDAVRA* from the protective towel.

I slide my right arm under *Life*, the book again feeling alive as I hug it to my chest. The drone of electricity inside me feels like I'm full of a thousand bees, their agitation growing to furor, my teeth chattering against it, my hands broiling so hot, I can hardly keep my fingers bent around the book's front edge.

If I zapped Henry in the motel under that level of physical excitement—bundled nerves and anxiety and excitement and fear of the unknown—and this is a million times more extreme . . .

I have no idea if this will work. But the incendiary throb from the star in my head radiating into my hands has to mean something.

"I knew you wouldn't let me down, Genevieve," Dagan says, taking a step closer. Mara's eyes are on the book. She must resemble her father; the cold calculation of her face contradicts any relationship to Delia.

Dagan reaches for the text, but before he can touch it, I release my hold, allowing it to tumble to the ground at my feet, and thrust my right arm forward, grabbing his exposed wrist. A blistering exchange of energy freezes both of us in place, teeth clenched so hard I swear I'm going to bite clean through the enamel, Dagan's face stuck in a horrible grimace, eyes rigid and stretched so the whites are fully visible.

The burn in my head and chest radiates throughout my entire body, down to the curl of my toes.

The release in the motel room was nothing like this. The burning ache I've felt in my hands and arms, like a blast just begging to be freed, practically sings its way out of my skin.

The smell of seared flesh overrides the pungent tang of fuel, the sweet bite of antifreeze leaking onto grass and pavement.

In my peripheral vision, the scene plays out in slow motion: Mara again pulls the pearl-handled blade from its sheath on her belt; Henry scrambles to his feet and launches toward me, and from a great distance, I hear him scream for me to grab his hand.

But I can't. My left arm is broken. I can't stretch.

He falls onto the ground and grabs my ankle, the skin bare just above my rolled sock, my lost shoe, thereby locking himself into this most unnatural embrace.

His own mouth grimacing, Henry grabs Mara just as she reaches my side, her blade drawn.

It all happens so fast, and yet like it's a film on slow forward, one frame at a time.

The four of us flex and contract, a circuit of whatever electricity I'm producing thrusting itself through synapse and muscle, until I feel the blackness creeping in.

In my head, a voice: *"Let go. Run."*

The voice is soft, welcoming. I want to let go. I want to go to sleep, right here. Just put my head down . . .

My aching hand relaxes, releasing Dagan, my damaged left hand limp against my stomach as the world snaps back into place, my mouth gaping like a guppy.

Dagan and Mara lie sprawled on the pavement, bodies spasming.

I catch my breath and stumble forward, falling against Baby, astonishment bright on his face.

"That's new," he says, voice hoarse, his hand heavy against my cheek.

A moan uttered behind me, reality rushes back, the haze fully cleared. "Henry!" He's on the ground, his body twitching from the assault.

I rush to him, throw one hand against his chest, and with the remaining dredges of my strength, I pull from the star in my pulsating head, just enough to get his eyes to blink open so he's back in the present.

"Henry, the backpack," I wheeze, on my own hands and knees, breathless, like sucking air through a straw.

Move, Genevieve. Move now.

Henry stands and limps to where Mara dropped his pack. He scoops it up.

My chest is still tight but the dizziness is abating. Baby grabs the *Life* text, stuffs it into the messenger bag, and he throws it over his shoulder.

When he stands, though, it's clear from how he favors his left leg that something is no longer whole. Not at all surprising given the state of our getaway car.

Without a word, Henry moves into position under Baby's right side. I don't know how long the electric hangover will keep Dagan and Mara down, but we're not waiting to find out.

We skip-hop awkwardly across Perimeter Road, our assemblage of broken bodies, through a nearly empty parking lot toward an open gate in the cyclone fencing adjacent to the white-and-blue aviation building ahead. Parked planes rest quietly on the opposite side of the fence, the canvas tarps over their windows reminding me of the sleeping mask Cece wears.

"Baby, where to? Which hangar? Where's the plane?"

"Around the front. Get to the front of the building. Next to the hangar," he says, sounding a little stronger, despite the terrible limp.

Sirens sound in the distance.

My arm. It hurts. And the fingertips of my right hand feel like the skin has been held to a hot iron.

With every step forward, though, my feet grow heavier, merry-go-round dizziness lunging inside my head.

"Baby, I gotta stop." And my knees buckle. I can't go anymore. The twinkling lights and light-headedness swarm my vision.

"Hang on, little bird," he says, throwing an arm under my noodle legs.

Baby continues the sad half-hobble routine around the front of the building, Henry staggering alongside him. We almost collide with two military-attired bodies—one of whom has a shockingly familiar face.

"Geneviève . . ." My name, spoken by a French tongue, the face looking back at me wearing mottled scars of a long-healed fight.

"Montague?" I say, lids drooping. This cannot be right. Montague the Mauled—our caretaker of the Cinzios' property in Eugene during the traveling year.

This makes no sense. Am I hallucinating?

"I've got Gen. Get the kid on board—he's bleeding a lot," Baby says.

I struggle to open my eyes again to see where Henry is bleeding; his stained, lacerated face is frighteningly white, and jacket gone, the backside of his torn shirt is completely soaked with red.

And just as I see the amount of blood Baby's talking about, Henry's eyes roll back and his legs give out.

"Move!" Baby yells. Montague strips the backpack from Henry's shoulder and tosses it onto his own back. Montague and the unknown man then throw Henry into a fireman's carry and take off.

To a waiting plane, its stairs extended onto the tarmac, the sun reflecting off the aircraft's white tubular body.

I see two of everything.

"Stay with me, wee lass. We're almost there," Baby says, his words shoved through gritted teeth.

At the stair's base stands a gray-haired man, his beard closely trimmed, eyes crinkled at the corners under thick gray-white eyebrows, the sharp cut of the cheekbones evidence enough that Henry is of this man's bloodline. He wears an impeccable suit, though his handsome face is wrinkled with alarm. He beckons the trio ahead of us up the stairs.

I know this face. The man from that horrible prison who saved Delia.

Nutesh.

Or, by his modern name, Thibault Delacroix.

"Hurry!" he yells, voice scant over the high-pitched thrum of the jet's engines.

Baby hops up the stairs, holding me so close to his chest that I can smell every molecule of terror we've experienced in the last five minutes—sweat, blood, grass, airbag explosive, fear.

Nutesh is close behind as Baby eases my damaged body into a cushioned window seat, though my devoted protector needs just as much attention as I do. At my feet, Baby drops the messenger bag holding the *AVRAKEDAVRA.*

I push up, toward him, reaching for the torn fabric of his black coat, surfing above the nauseating pound coming from my head and my very fractured arm.

"Baby . . ." The muscles in my throat ache from the tears that, once they start, will not stop. I don't want him to let me go. "Please don't leave me."

"It's okay now, *a nighean.* We're safe." He leans over me, wincing, shushing against my ear, his hand cupped against the opposite side of my head.

The plane's side is sealed, and the subtle increasing hum underfoot suggests that we're about to move. Baby hobbles just across the aisle, grunting as his own tattered body lands hard against a seat.

And then, just as it happened on Perimeter Road, my blurred consciousness snaps back into agonizing focus, the brightness of the plane's interior lights stinging my eyes.

"Henry! Let me help him!" I yell, struggling to stand.

Montague, paused just outside a narrow door that must belong to a cabin, scurries to kneel before me. He shushes and pats my cheek, urging me back against the seat. I don't have any fight left. Everything hurts too much.

"Drink this," he says, pulling a small bottle of amber liquid from what looks like a medical bag.

"Why are you here? How did you know? Is this medicine?"

"Drink first," Montague urges. I do. It burns.

"Whiskey?"

"No, *ma fille*. A restorative. Your mother's recipe."

"Give some to Baby," I say, sitting forward to look at him. "He's hurt too." Baby shuffles back across the aisle, his hand clenched to the adjacent seat as the plane moves at a faster clip. He eases into the seat next to me, wincing as his left leg stretches before him. I have to fix him, but I'm useless.

I turn sideways, painfully, my scorched right hand pressed against the cool glass of the thick ovoid window. My eyes desperately search the tarmac and surrounding structures blurring into a streak of colors as the plane accelerates. "Where's Dagan? And Mara? Oh god, they'll come for us. They'll hurt the elephants and Ted and Cece and—"

"Geni, it's okay. You're safe now. Nothing is going to happen to our family," Baby says, pulling me back from the window as the acceleration advances into g-force pressure, the nose of the plane tipping toward the heavens.

Baby makes me look into his tired but bright eyes. "Nothing is going to happen to our family," he repeats.

I want to believe him. I really do. But I saw the malevolence in Mara's eyes in the big top when she threatened everyone and everything I love.

I throw my good arm around his neck and squeeze until he grunts. "Promise me," I whisper in his ear.

"I promise."

I flop back against the leather seat. I'm out of fight for the rest of the day. Maybe the rest of my life.

"You're hurt," I say, one eye opened and looking at my talisman.

He laughs, grimacing as he does. "So are you."

"My arm is fucking broken."

He laughs louder. "Yes. It does appear to be the wrong shape."

The pain in my arm, in my whole body, reignites the tiny twinkling lights along the edges of my vision and my head flops forward for a quick bounce. Baby calls Montague for more not-whiskey. He helps me drink it, again the burn singeing all the way down, but the numbing warmth that follows is so welcome.

"Kid, you saved the day, with whatever is going on with your hands." He points at my curled fingers. "This . . . this is a new trick." My throbbing hand is blackened and sooty, my fingertips thrashed and raw. As if electricity coursed through them.

"How is Montague involved? Does he know?"

Baby sighs and leans back. "He's a friend of Nutesh, part of your life since you were small to help keep you and your mother safe."

Did I hear that right?

"So he knows? About the *AVRAKEDAVRA*?"

"He knows enough to keep the bad guys from finding and getting you."

"But he worked for Ted. He worked for the circus . . . when Andronicus mauled him—"

Montague crouches in front of me again. "All in a day's work, Geneviève," he says, patting my knee. The long scars running down the left side of his face, while impressive, were lessened by my healing efforts that day.

All this time, he's been watching over Delia and me?

The plane tilts hard, ascending higher and higher, away from Dagan. Away from Mara.

"Montague," Nutesh calls out, reemerged from behind the closed cabin door, his voice gravelly and deep. He says something in French, Henry's name thrown into it.

I wish I'd taken French.

"Is he dead?" I yell across the cabin.

Nutesh shakes his head and smiles. "No, my brave, brave girl. *Il n'est pas mort.*"

He walks the short distance to my front-row seat and kneels. "*Merci tellement.* Thank you so much, for saving my grandson." Nutesh places his hand against his chest, flattened on his bloodred tie, and bows his head. "You have done what I could not."

"He saved me too," I say. "We have the books—Dagan's, my mother's. We have them." I push the messenger bag at my feet toward him, realizing that now, this obviously very old but not old-looking man before me has in his possession all three texts.

My earlier conviction that we were doing the right thing falters.

The most powerful healer/magician in the world now has within his grasp the tools to do what Lucian Dagan Dmitri has been trying to accomplish for centuries.

My breath feels short in my chest as Nutesh opens the messenger bag. From his pocket, he extracts leather gloves and slides them over his long fingers, like a surgeon preparing to excise a tumor. He reaches in and pulls out my mother's text. *Life.*

"It is like seeing an old friend again," he says, and when he looks at me, his amber-brown eyes shimmer with moisture. He flattens his hand on the cover of the *AVRAKEDAVRA*, utters a quiet something under his breath—a prayer?—and replaces the book into my messenger bag.

"It belongs to you, and you belong to it," he says, closing the bag.

I sit straighter against my seat back, a sense of unease spiking in my belly. "I don't want it. Delia said you will help me destroy it."

Nutesh stands. "If the book my grandson has brought is also authentic, then we will have three, reunited at last."

A dull roar in my ears. Renewed tingling in my hands.

"And then you can destroy them, right? We have to destroy them or the Etemmu will haunt me forever. Please, my mother said—"

"Do not fear, young Geneviève. While you are in my care, I will do my best to protect you from the Etemmu."

"But we have to destroy these books. *I don't want Delia's life,*" I beg.

"The books will be taken back to their home, and there, we can at last lay them to rest."

I look at Baby, waiting for someone to tell me what the hell is going on.

"So, France? We can lay them to rest in France? Where we're going right now?"

Nutesh and Baby share a glance. Nutesh again lowers himself so we're eye to eye. "The books' home is in Mesopotamia. It was from that fertile soil they were born, and now in the arid desert, in the heart of Babylon, they must be brought to their end."

"Mesopotamia doesn't exist anymore. Babylon is gone. That was thousands of years ago." My mouth feels so dry. The transient numbness from the restorative tincture has transformed into my heartbeat thumping behind my eyelids, and my ears beg to be popped secondary to the cottony pressure from our increasing altitude.

"Mesopotamia does exist, and I will lead you there," Nutesh says, nodding reverently.

I throw a hard look at Baby. "You said *France*. Mesopotamia is not France."

"Genevieve . . ." He reaches to touch my uninjured arm but I jerk away, pain spiking.

"NO! You said we'd be rid of it—get it to Nutesh, and that was it. Do any of you know how to tell the truth?" I yell at the lot of them, this bizarre collection of damaged humans.

I lean back, closing my eyes against the shock, the hurt, the fear. I am with Delia, listening to her story in our trailer as she teases the tightness from my muscles after rehearsal.

The healer woman's instructions to her young daughter sing through my head, in a voice as clear as glass:

"Take the treasure. The horse will lead you across the desert. Follow the river to where the bones of kings lie."

I should've figured it out.

I crack my eyes open a sliver, and look down at the messenger bag on the floor that holds my mother's legacy.

The higher we climb, the weight of the sky grows heavier, launching me toward a future I never imagined, not in my wildest, darkest dreams.

This treasure she died protecting, I hate it. Not only has it stolen my mother from me but it's stolen the life I loved. It's taken me away from my elephants, my family, my friends.

But I will take it across the desert.

I will follow the river to the place where the bones of kings lie.

And with these new magical hands, I will burn open the heart of Babylon, and shove this legacy back where it came from.

AUTHOR'S NOTE

With regard to hair, eye, and skin color for the characters in *Sleight*:

Humans from the region known as Mesopotamia were a mix of ethnicities from all over the Middle East, Africa, Asia, and Europe. Mesopotamia, so named by the ancient Greeks, means "between two rivers," as it's situated in the area between the Tigris and Euphrates. Present for millennia before the beginning of recorded history, Mesopotamia in 3500 BCE was home to Akkadians, Assyrians, Sumerians, and Babylonians and is often called the cradle of civilization—it was the birthplace of writing (although writing was independently developed elsewhere in the world around this time, including in Egypt and China), first with pictographs and later with a stylus-and-clay system called cuneiform. For the first time, business dealings, governmental proceedings, and property ownership were recorded. The people of this era ushered in the Age of Inventions—they literally invented the wheel (somewhere around 3500 to 3200 BCE)—made advances in mathematics and law, and were the first to manufacture bronze. In modern geographic times, the area encompassed by Mesopotamia includes Iraq, Kuwait, and parts of Syria, Turkey, and Iran.

For the purposes of this story, my characters are from Babylon (in what is now Iraq), which fell to the Achaemenid Empire (or the First Persian Empire), under Cyrus the Great, in 539 BCE and again to the Macedonian king, Alexander the Great, in 334 BCE. Even though history was never my strong suit in school (learn to love history, future writers!), I've herein constructed a fictional narrative based on extensive research of Mesopotamia and the people who lived there during the times relevant to my story—with lots and lots of creative license, obviously. (We all can agree that human beings can't survive for the exaggerated durations we see with Thibault, Lucian, Alicia, Delia, and even Baby.)

Nutesh (aka Thibault Delacroix, born approximately 430 BCE) and Lucian Dagan Dmitri (b. 240 BCE) would've fled Mesopotamia with their families by the time Alexander the Great stormed Babylon. The *AVRAKEDAVRA* would not have been widely accepted, even in pre-Christian polytheistic times—the Mesopotamians had over a thousand gods—and the easiest way to vilify something we don't understand is to label it witchcraft or demon work. So, they ran. For centuries.

Taking all of this into consideration, this is the most important thing to remember: Mesopotamia was a hub of commerce, trade, and immigration in its heyday, and therefore it wouldn't at all be unreasonable for our main characters to have biologically diverse skin, eye, and hair color. The Hittites of Anatolia (approximately 1700 BCE, now modern-day Turkey) were described as fair-haired and fair-skinned; it's also very common among Afghan and Kurdish populations to find blue or green eyes and blond or red hair. So, Delia and Genevieve as green-eyed redheads, Alicia and Henry as blue/green-eyed dark blonds, and Lucian with the (once) dark hair and hazel eyes—these people fit on the genetic spectrum of this region, especially when one considers their birthdates.

According to scientists and researchers much smarter than me, ten thousand years ago, all humans had brown eyes and hair, until a genetic mutation changed things up. Since the roots of our story with Nutesh/Thibault, Belshunu (Lucian's father), and Udish (Delia's fourth-great-grandfather) happen 9,500 years *after* the *OCA2* gene mutated, it wouldn't be unexpected to find eye and hair color variants in these fictional Mesopotamians, and in their offspring (Lucian, Alicia, Delia, Mara, Genevieve, and Henry). Genevieve is a first-generation American citizen but is still a Mesopotamian descendant; Henry is a first-generation British citizen and both of his parents are direct Mesopotamians; and Bamidele, or Baby, born in Nantes, France, around 1750, is the son of an enslaved African woman from Sierra Leone and a French nobleman. The expression of Baby's genetic combination is a little more straightforward. (And if you think he looks a little like Dwayne "The Rock" Johnson, you're probably right. Hey, I have my muses.)

It's important to not let cultural bias predetermine what you think a character should look like, just because he or she harkens from a specific spot on the globe. It's my hope that with this story, we will see that humans of all ethnicities are worthy of the harmonious protections and gifts offered by the very fictional *AVRAKEDAVRA*.

Be good to one another.

ACKNOWLEDGMENTS

SLEIGHT HAS BEEN A PART OF MY FAMILY FOR A LONG TIME, STARTING BACK in 2007 when she was born as a short story about a thirteen-year-old circus kid named Frankie, her pet frog Hamlet, and the tragic accident that changed Frankie's life forever. The story has clearly evolved over the years—starting with the first draft, handwritten in my car over 360 nights, parked outside a Tim Hortons coffee shop where I sipped vast amounts of peppermint tea—to this latest version we offer you today. If you take nothing else from this book, take one lesson: perseverance. Do. Not. Stop. Pushing. Yourself.

And now, my sincerest thanks, as a lot of people have worked very hard to make *Sleight* a real Velveteen Rabbit:

My tough-as-nails Writers House agent, Dan Lazar. The inimitable Dr. Genevieve Gagne-Hawes, whose guidance led to our sale to HarperCollins in 2012 (and who became the namesake for my heroine), and later, editor Jim Thomas, under whom I basically completed the toughest MFA program ever designed. And Torie Doherty-Munro—Torie, Dan should pay you in gold bullion.

Hadley Dyer, this book wouldn't be in our hands if you hadn't believed in the story I was trying to tell. I valued our working relationship, and now I treasure our friendship. Thanks go to Jennifer Lambert, Suzanne Sutherland, Stephanie Nuñez, and copyeditor Linda Pruessen, whose cumulative efforts cannot be overstated or repaid.

Alison Weiss at Sky Pony, your boundless energy and enthusiasm for great books will take you far, and I'm so excited to be on your team.

My dear friend Jane Omelaniec for your unending generosity and use of your blissful cabin, where a lot of rewriting happened. When can we go to the lake again?

Thanks go to Yolander Prinzel for beta reading pretty much everything I write before I let anyone else see it, as well as to dear friends Kendall Grey, Adrienne Crezo, Amber Hart, Angeline Kace, Leslie Wibberley, and Bonnie Jacoby. I'd go on about you guys here, but be assured your contributions can only be measured in hugs.

Ira Bloom, Writers House brother and friend, for reading and blurbing. My Ira, sometimes when we talk, I have to google what the hell you've just said. For real.

Authors Michael Grant and Eileen Cook, you're both such incredible writers that I pretty much died when you agreed to read and then actually *liked* the book. Many, many thanks.

Sarah and Sir Toby Dessent and writer/comedienne Nicola Enright-Morin, my favorite Londoners, for ensuring that Henry sounded like he was supposed to. Special thanks to Sarah, who wrote me my very first fan letter back in 2011, which led to us becoming the best kind of sisters. And Nicola, darling, when are we having that gin?

Samantha Young, Toni Freitas, and Sarah Dessent for the Scottish help. (Also, the OutlanderWiki is pretty great. Thank you, Queen Diana Gabaldon!)

My awesome sisters-in-law Kim Bishop, Dale McManus, and Darlene Cruse, as well as my nieces Heather Bishop, Michelle McManus, and Stacey Alana, for reading the book years ago. Thanks go to my composer cousin Kevin Maxfield for help with musical info, all the way from the Land of the Rising Sun.

The character Baby was written in earlier drafts as a Māori warrior. Though we later changed this to preserve the cultural integrity of the Māori people, I must extend sincere thanks to librarian and academic Tamara Witika (*iwi* [tribe] affiliations Ngāti Whātua and Ngāti Tamaterā) for beta reading the manuscript with a careful eye on every detail, and to Matariki Williams at Australia's Allen & Unwin for the careful sensitivity read. *Tēnā rawa atu koe!*

Thanks to Bert at Portland's River View Cemetery and Carolyn at the Cannon Beach Post Office for taking my calls and answering my silly questions.

To the booksellers and store managers at the Coquitlam Chapters, especially Wedia Budiman, Victoria Harrison, and Yaunna Sommersby, thanks for listening to me talk about *Sleight* and for supporting all the books that come out of my brain.

Endless gratitude to the bloggers, fellow writers, and friends who've helped promote and cheerlead for *Sleight* since her earlier appearance (2011 onward): Sara Gundell Larson, Shana Benedict, Kara Malinczak, LJ Ducharme, Karly Kirkpatrick, Erin Entrada Kelly, Jackie Wheeler, Jennifer Messner, Jaime Arnold, Shannon Pearcy, Stacey Clifford, Caitlin Lomas, Alli Hope, Julie Morgan, Beth Elisa Harris, Missy Crossno, Ange Marrone, Patricia Mendoza, Jane Fielding, Chris Southern, Danielle and Elsa Sainas, Alysha VanDuynhoven, Emily Harden, Ayla Lukascik Sherman, Carmen Jones, Kyle Suenaga, Traci Lecheler, Estrella Perotti, Triva Solis, Bella Carillo Colella, Marsha McNeese, Lori Bulmer, Adina Weiss Ciment, Ann Moffitt Whitson, Loranne Brown, Rachel Krueger, Lisa Rutledge, Nichole Chase, Danny Meilinger, Rachel Scroggins, Andrea Pierce Thompson, Emma Jameson, Mandy Smith, and Jessica Estep. Oh man, I know I'm forgetting someone—I am so sorry.

Tracy Mueller and Sue Ho for helping with early editorial efforts way back in 2010/early 2011.

One of the coolest women I know, Amy Baldwin, for your quick research skills and for introducing me to some great comic book dudes, including Craig Nelson (thanks, Craig!); thanks to Dan Pagni and the members of the Marvel Comics Fans 1961-1986 Facebook group. (Superman FOREVER.)

To my movie star muses who made this book real in my head: Dwayne "The Rock" Johnson, Mark Strong, Jessica Chastain, and Saoirse Ronan.

And most importantly, thanks to GareBear and our awesome kids—Yaunna, Brennan, and Kendon—who have endured this alongside me, bought me elephants and Superman toys for inspiration, written me cards of encouragement, and made me so many pots of coffee and pans of brownies.

My parting note: If you're with people who don't believe in you or what you want to be doing, find new people. When my husband turned to me in 2006 and said, "You need to stop this nonsense and get busy writing," it was a turning point. If Gary hadn't said those words, my everyday uniform wouldn't be Levi's and Superman T-shirts—it would be a straitjacket.

Find your people. Push yourself. Work hard. Never give up. Save the elephants. Live with integrity.

And remember: the key to good is found in truth.